DRAGON'S FALL
Rise of the Scarlet Order Vampires

David Lee Summers

Hadrosaur Productions, Mesilla Park, NM

Dragon's Fall: Rise of the Scarlet Order Vampires
Hadrosaur Productions
Second Edition: June 2020
First date of publication: October 2012

ISBN-10: 1-885093-92-6
ISBN-13: 978-1-885093-92-9

This is a work of fiction. Names, characters, places, and incidents are either the product of the author's imagination or are used fictitiously, and any resemblance to any person or persons, living or dead, events or locales is entirely coincidental.

Praise for
DRAGON'S FALL
Rise of the Scarlet Order Vampires

"Parts of the book remind me of *The Robe*, other parts of *The Da Vinci Code* and some parts are pure David Lee Summers having fun with thoughts of an immortal life. The story runs parallel to many historical happenings and I enjoy the story line where vampires are seeking holy relics for their own enrichment instead of to destroy them." Melinda Moore, author of *A Sunset Finish*

"At the heart of this origin story is dark, descriptive writing that makes you believe that real vampires, not sparkly ones, do actually exist. An exciting novel that made me love a good vampire novel again." Stephen C. Ormsby, Author and Publisher.

"David Lee Summers has broken all molds of what vampires have come to mean to modern and past civilizations. His vampires in the Scarlet Order series will infect you with an incurable thirst. Once you begin the series, you will not want to let it go. Summers is a master of seduction, horror, and suspense, mixing history with fantasy. I strongly urge you to delve into the world of the Scarlet Order. I promise you, you are in for a ride you will never forget or want to end." Giovanna Lagana, author of *With Black & White Comes the Grey*

Books by David Lee Summers

The Solar Sea
The Astronomer's Crypt

The Space Pirates' Legacy Series
Firebrandt's Legacy
The Pirates of Sufiro
Children of the Old Stars
Heirs of the New Earth

The Clockwork Legion Series
Owl Dance
Lightning Wolves
The Brazen Shark
Owl Riders

The Scarlet Order Vampires Series
Dragon's Fall: Rise of the Scarlet Order Vampires
Vampires of the Scarlet Order

To my dear friends, C & B Badgett.
May your romance last through the ages.

DRAGON'S FALL
Rise of the Scarlet Order Vampires

Part I
Gorgon in Bondage

Chapter 1

From the Memoirs of Alexandra the Greek:

In my experience, there is nothing more terrifying than being sold.

My parents, brothers, and sisters were slaves to a landowner near Athens. His sons had pursued their own interests in the city and, when the landowner died, they decided to sell his farm along with all his possessions. The farmer treated us as well as any slave owner treated his chattel. Even so, I vividly remember the night he came and took my sickly baby brother away. Mother held me close and told me that it was for the best even as tears glistened on her own cheeks. Listening as my brother's pitiable cries receded into the distance, I knew the farmer was going to leave him on the hillside for the wolves.

I sobbed into my mother's breast and trembled. I was scared for my brother, but for the first time, I really understood what it meant to be the property of another. Laws in Greece governed the treatment of chattel, but as long as a slaveholder wasn't outwardly cruel, they could do as they pleased with their property. There were stories of slaves from neighboring farms who had been forced to work out in the wind and rain until they were so sick they had to be put out of their misery. There were also stories of willful slaves who were beaten so their spirits would be broken. How could the farmer's actions be deemed cruel when wealthy Athenians were encouraged to leave their own sickly children to the wolves just as the farmer had done with my brother?

I was named Alexandra in honor of the Macedonian who ruled our land at the time of my birth. There were slave owners who might have seen that as a presumptuous name for a slave to give his child – especially his female child. However, the farmer believed that my father was paying respect to the king and allowed his choice of my name to stand.

The farmer's youngest daughter taught me the basics of reading, writing, and music. Even though it was not uncommon for slave owners to allow their servants to be educated, there were plenty of slave owners that would not have bothered with more education than was necessary for a slave to perform their duties.

The landowner was good as slaveholders go. However, the cries of my brother have haunted me all my life and I never forgave the man for what he did to my brother. The problem of being sold was that I could be given over to a man I would hate even more. I had no more control of my destiny than my tiny brother did when he thrashed helplessly in the farmer's arms all those years before.

There was a flurry of activity over the next few days. The land was divided between the men that owned the adjoining farms. My older brother and sister were sold to one of the farmers while my mother and father went with the other. I wanted to stay and work the land, but neither of the neighboring farmers seemed to have interest in me or my skills. As I understood, each of the farmers had already purchased as much as they could afford. Instead, one morning an unsavory man who wore too many rings on his fingers and adorned himself in purple robes arrived at the farm and told me to pack my belongings.

"Who are you?" I asked. "What gives you the right to give me orders?"

The farmer's eldest son stepped up next to the man in the purple robes. "He is a trader from Athens. You will do what he says."

My heart sank. I was being given over to a slaver. Listlessly, I packed my few belongings, then sought out my mother and father and hugged them good-bye.

The slaver led me to his small horse-drawn cart. He told me to put my belongings in the back. The cart was only big enough for one rider. He climbed aboard and instructed me to walk alongside.

As we made our way along the gravel road toward Athens, I turned around and looked back at the farm with tears in my eyes. My father and mother waved at me. As I raised my arm to wave back, the slaver's whip cracked next to my ear. The slaver scowled at me and bellowed for me to keep up with the cart. Shoulders slumped, I turned around and followed him to the city.

The farm where I grew up was only eight miles outside of Athens. I had made the walk to the city many times with the farmer and either my brother or father. We used to go into the city to trade our best crops for items we'd need. I knew the road well, but it had never seemed so far to the city as the day I walked beside the slaver's cart. Usually when we would go to the city, the farmer would stop by one of the public cisterns just inside the city's walls and allow us to refresh ourselves with a drink and a little cooling water on our wrists and feet. The slaver rode right by the public cistern and barked an order for me to keep up as I looked longingly at the building. As though to taunt me, he lifted his water skin to his lips and drank greedily.

The slaver led me to a building not far from the city's walls. He climbed down from the cart and unhitched the horse, then led it to a stable where it had food and water. He then came back and told me to grab my things. Once I did, he led me through the gate into the building's courtyard. The building must once have been the residence of a wealthy man, but it had fallen into disrepair – probably during the years of the Macedonian's occupation. The slaver took out a key and opened a door. As the hinges creaked open, the odor of unwashed humanity assailed my nose. Self-consciously, I took a step backward.

"Your quarters are there," he said. "Some buyers are coming tomorrow. I think you'll fetch a pretty price."

When I didn't step forward, he gave me a rude shove from behind and I stumbled into the dark, smelly room, dropping my bundle of belongings at my feet. The door slammed shut behind me and the key rattled in the lock. I stood in one place, trembling even though the room was actually quite hot. Eventually my eyes adjusted to the darkness. Slivers of light entered from small windows set high in the walls of rooms surrounding the hallway I found myself in. I picked up my belongings and took a few tentative steps down the hallway.

Eventually, the hall ended in a large room. Eight pairs of eyes glared up at me from wool-covered straw mats that lay upon the hard floor. Most of the people just curled up again and one even snarled at me, clinging to his mat protectively. One man's gaze remained on me. He stood from his mat and stepped toward me. As he did, I could tell that he hadn't bathed in several days and I stepped away from him.

"I'm sorry." In spite of the way he smelled, his voice was surprisingly gentle. He was tall and well muscled. It was difficult to make out his face in the gloom and a week's worth of beard covered it, but I sensed he was about my age. "This is a terrible place, but hopefully someone will come soon who will buy us and give us new, respectable homes." He held out his hand. "I am Kallius. Come, let's find you a place to sleep and I'll get you something to eat and drink."

I followed him into the dank room where the mats covered the floor. He led me to one of them. I set down my belongings and then sat on the mat. He left, but returned a short time later with a bowl of water and some bread. "I'm sorry to say, this is all the slaver allows us."

"Thank you for your kindness." As I spoke, I heard the hoarseness of my voice. I took the bowl of water and drank greedily. He took it from me and refilled it, then brought it back. I drank the next bowl more slowly, then ate the hard bread thoughtfully. "How long have you been here?"

"About two weeks," he said. "The slaver says buyers are coming tomorrow. I hope that will be the end of my stay. I hope you won't have to stay longer than that either."

"Ha!" The derisive laugh came from one of the bodies huddled on the floor. "The slave trader is a poor one indeed. He hasn't made a sale in over a month! We'll be lucky if we end up shoveling out the city stables."

"Be quiet, you," called Kallius.

I looked down at the hard bread in my hands and tears began to flow. Kallius moved beside me and started to put his arm around me, but the smell of him caused me to flinch. I don't know whether he was offended by my flinch or thought I wanted to be alone, but he moved off to his own mat and stared up to the window. "If you need anything, please let me know," he said softly. I could hear the tension in his voice and I realized that I had hurt his feelings. Even so, I wasn't certain I wanted a stranger near me just then. I set the bread down, curled up into a ball and cried myself to sleep.

I awoke some time later when someone kicked me in the legs. I looked up bleary-eyed and saw it was the slaver. "There'll be buyers here soon," he barked. "There's water for cleaning in the courtyard. Make yourself presentable." With that, he turned and left.

Soon after, Kallius appeared with a chunk of bread and a bowl of water. Either I had grown used to the foul smells of the slave quarters overnight or Kallius had availed himself of the cleaning water. No matter the cause, his smell did not repulse me. "Thank you." I did my best to put on an apologetic smile.

"Don't mention it," he said. "You better eat quickly and wash up, before the buyers arrive."

"Truth be told, I would rather not be bought by anyone." I took a bite of the bread.

"You want to stay here?" His eyes widened.

I shook my head and washed down the bread with some water. "I would rather be free."

"Unfortunately, that is not an option. Better to be bought by a good house than remain in this hell hole."

I took another bite of bread and frowned while I chewed. Kallius was right, but I didn't like it at all. Even worse, I didn't like the fact that I had no say in who would buy me or what they might do with me. Hurriedly, I swallowed some water, stood and stepped quickly out to the courtyard. There, most of the slaves milled around. Two of them hovered over a trough filled with dirty water.

It was better than nothing. I stepped up and washed away the tears of frustration that threatened to burst to the surface. Returning to the slave quarters, I found my bag and retrieved the hairbrush my brother had made for me from the bristles of a boar he had killed. I did my best to tame my long curls, then tied my hair back with a leather strap.

As I put my brush away, I noticed Kallius smiling at me from his mat. "You look beautiful," he said.

I snorted. "I don't necessarily want to attract the kind of slave owner who buys me for my beauty."

"All the finest homes want beautiful slaves." He stood and indicated the door. "We should go and get ready. The buyers will be here soon."

As we stepped into the courtyard, the slaver was busy lining up all of the slaves, getting them ready for viewing. "There you are!" he barked. "Get over here!"

Kallius and I joined the others in the lineup. The slaver stood back and looked at us, shaking his head. "What a pitiful lot, but you'll have to do." With that, he went to the gate.

I don't know how long we stood out in the courtyard, but eventually the first buyers began to arrive. A dozen men in all, wearing colorful cloaks moved along the line, looking us up and down. Several of the buyers reached out and touched arms and thighs, evaluating the slaves' strength. Several of the men were happy to oblige by flexing their muscles. One old man who reeked of garlic grasped my arm and nodded approvingly – I had well developed muscles from my years in the field. A moment later, his hands drifted and he grabbed my breast. My breath caught and I resisted the urge to strike him. Much as I wanted to, I judged that the slaver would not hesitate to kill such an insolent slave. The old man winked at me and then joined the rest of the men.

There was some discussion among themselves and then the bidding began. They started at the far end of the line. Prices were shouted and soon the first slave in the line was ordered to stand apart. The next person in line was an older woman – about the age my grandmother would have been if she had still been alive.

No one seemed willing to start the bidding. The slaver tried to egg the men on, but there was a shuffling of feet and a shaking of heads. "Back to the quarters, grandma!" shouted the slaver. The old woman shuffled past us and through the door that led to the room with the foul-smelling mats.

The bidding process began again with the next slave in line. As the process continued, I saw that the old man who reeked of garlic kept eyeing me, while hefting the weight of his money pouch. About halfway down the line, they reached Kallius. The bidding was vigorous for him. I was not surprised. Out in the sunlight and cleaned up even slightly, it was clear that he would be a strong and worthy servant for whatever house succeeded in winning him.

Just as the bidding on Kallius reached a climax, a man in a simple white tunic embroidered with golden thread entered the slaver's courtyard. His eyes roved over all of the slaves, including those already purchased. When his eyes fell on me, I somehow felt that I was being examined far more intimately than I had been by the old man.

One of the buyers had succeeded in winning Kallius and was paying the slaver. The new man stepped up to the slaver and pointed to Kallius and then to me. The man who was in the process of purchasing Kallius protested, but the new buyer opened his purse and began counting out gold. Kallius's buyer looked only a little disappointed as he accepted the gold. The slaver did not look disappointed at all as he accepted his share. He pointed to Kallius then me and ordered us to stand apart from the others.

The new man approached us. "Please retrieve your belongings. We will leave presently," he said in a commanding voice. He looked over his shoulder. "I find these proceedings ... disquieting."

Kallius and I looked at each other and then stepped into the slave quarters where we quickly gathered up our bundles. We met the man in the courtyard and he led us out into the street.

"What shall we know you as, Master?" asked Kallius with humility.

The man smiled sardonically. "I am known as Democritus. I am the chief servant of the banker Theron."

"You're a slave?" I asked.

He simply inclined his head as he strode down the street. I noticed that Democritus led us into the heights of the city, closer to the temples, where the very finest houses were. He turned toward the largest house I had ever seen. My breath caught as I saw the gate. Hanging there was a bronze relief of a gorgon's face. I had seen bronze and stone reliefs of gorgons near doors and gateways before. They were believed to ward off evil spirits. However, this gorgon's eyes seemed to peer right into me. Its fangs looked all too ready to lock onto my throat. Democritus unlocked the gate and I stepped hastily past the grotesque relief and walked down the walled entryway toward the central courtyard.

In the courtyard was a statue of Medusa. Her countenance was at once terrifying and beautiful. Instead of giving this Medusa a head full of snakes as I had seen many times in the past, the sculptor had carefully woven the snakes through her hair as though they were faithful companions. The sculpture was painted so realistically that I half expected this statue of Medusa to step off her pedestal. "Our master seems to have a fascination for gorgons," I remarked.

"It is one of his eccentricities, yes." Democritus stepped up to me and indicated a lavishly appointed room to our left. "These are my quarters. Do not hesitate to see me if you need anything." He continued into the courtyard and took another left into rooms that were dimly lit. Unlike the slaver's quarters, my nose was not assailed by the smell of reeking humanity. Instead the aroma of baking bread and herbs greeted me. As my eyes adjusted to the dim light from the windows, I saw a kitchen where two women were working.

Democritus led us further down the hallway to a room with four beds. "These are the men's quarters," he explained. "They are out on errands for the master today." Leading us a little further on, Democritus indicated another room with four beds. "These are the women's quarters." He indicated which bed was mine and I set down my belongings.

As we continued down the hallway, I noticed storerooms and a workshop. Finally at the end of the hall was a small, tiled room. A woman heated water and filled the tub. "You should be presentable when you meet the master tonight," said Democritus. "Please bathe and rest. Take your time. We have several hours before the master will ... appear." With that, he turned and left.

Though I felt Kallius needed a bath worse than me, he allowed me the first use of the tub. The woman who was filling the tub invited me in and closed a curtain behind me. She placed laurel leaves and sweet-smelling herbs into the water. I pulled my dusty, sweaty chiton over my head and stepped into the bath, releasing a sigh as the water caressed my body.

The woman retrieved my chiton. "I shall bring you a new garment. The master likes his slaves well adorned." Although she wrinkled her nose as she picked up the tunic, I didn't care. The water felt divine and it was delightful to breathe in scents other than human sweat and waste. I was still frustrated at the idea of being owned, but Kallius was right. If one had to be owned, it was best to be owned by a good master.

Chapter 2

From the Memoirs of Alexandra the Greek:

Feeling refreshed after my bath, I dressed and sought out the woman who had prepared it for me. I found her in the women's quarters embroidering the hem of a tunic. She smiled and indicated my bed. "Rest and I'll draw a bath for Kallius."

I lay down on the bed and found it surprisingly soft, much nicer even than my bed on the farm. I found myself wondering about a master who would spend so much on slaves. Closing my eyes, I must have dozed off since when I opened them, the light had softened. The woman had returned to the room and resumed her needlework.

"How careless of me." I sat up and rubbed the sleep from my eyes. "The master must be very disappointed."

The woman's smile was hard to read. "Master Theron has yet to appear for the evening. All is well." She set down the tunic and I noticed her slender arms and fingers. I reasoned that she must have spent all of her time as a household servant in the city. "My name is Syntyche," she explained. "I only arrived a few days ago." When I introduced myself, her eyes widened. "Your father must have been quite bold to name you such."

"He was indeed." I looked around at the comfortable beds in the room and thought of the men's quarters. "Is Master Theron preparing for some task? Why does he need so many new slaves at once?"

Syntyche shrugged. "I do not know. Our duties are surprisingly light. I have been given little to do aside from tending the flowers in the courtyard and decorating this tunic. Through the day, the men are often sent on errands to the temple of Athena where the master conducts his trade."

I found it ironic that a man so entranced by Medusa should conduct his banking at the temple of Athena. Medusa and Athena were often said to be mortal enemies. However, my mother once told me a story about how Medusa was merely Athena's mirror aspect. "Tell me about the women I saw in the kitchen."

"They are Xenia and Pelagia and they do most of the cooking. They tell me their duties are rather light as well, since mostly they cook for the slaves. Master Theron is only home at night and consumes little."

I narrowed my gaze. "And what of Master Theron's wife?"

"He has no wife that I'm aware of."

Just then, Democritus appeared in the doorway. "Xenia has announced that dinner will be ready soon. Also, I suspect that near the end of the meal, the master will wish to view his new slaves."

Syntyche and I stood in unison. I followed her out into the courtyard. The table was set with an assortment of meats and fruit. There were even two jugs of wine. "Surely Master Theron is entertaining guests and we are meant to serve them," I said.

Syntyche shook her head. "No, this has been our standard fare since I have been here."

"It is truly delightful to be owned by a master who appreciates his slaves." I caught my breath at the sound of Kallius's voice. Turning, I saw him clean for the first time. His square jaw and upright stance exuded a confidence I hadn't noticed before. I also took time to appreciate his muscular arms and thighs.

There was a shuffling at the gate. Soon after, three men rounded the corner into the courtyard and sat on the stools surrounding the table as though they were nobles. Xenia and Pelagia appeared from the kitchen bearing bread and olives, then also sat at the table. Kallius held out his hand. I had only been under the care of the slaver for one night, but I found my mouth watering at the sight of so much food. I sat on one of the stools and began helping myself to meat and bread.

Conversation was sparse as the meal wore on and the light

began to wane. I realized the sun must have set and I began to wonder whether we needed to tend to our master. Just as that thought crossed my mind, I noticed a figure lurking in the shadows of the overhang opposite the slave's quarters.

"You have done well, Democritus." The voice held a peculiar accent that I did not recognize and I thought I detected a faint lisp. "I approve of the new slaves you purchased today."

Democritus stood and the other slaves quickly followed suit. "I am delighted, sir," said Theron's senior slave.

"Do you require food, my lord?" asked Xenia.

Our master released a faint chuckle. "No, I will tend to my own needs tonight. Thank you."

I peered into the shadows and tried to see our master better. As though obliging my curiosity, he took a step forward. My eyes widened as I noted his skin's extreme pallor – like the unpainted marble of a statue. The skin was further offset by the deep red of his cloak. His eyes seemed to glow as though a green fire raged behind them. Those eyes turned to me and then to Kallius. "Get some rest tonight. Democritus will assign you your tasks in the morning." Without another word, our master stepped backward into the shadows.

The next day, Democritus assigned me the task of cleaning and arranging Master Theron's living quarters. Facing the courtyard were two sparsely furnished rooms that appeared only lightly used. A little dusting and the two rooms were in order. Behind one of the rooms was a bath – much nicer of course than the one in the slave's quarters. The room was tiled in a lavish mosaic depicting a fierce battle. In the center of it all was a fierce gorgon – much like the one by the house gate – tearing soldiers limb from limb. Again, I wondered at our master's fascination for gorgons. Like the two rooms at the front of the house, the bathroom only appeared lightly used and needed little cleaning. I stood back and examined the room. Something was not quite right about some of the mosaic tiles. Bending down and examining them closer, I saw they were stained brown. The only thing I knew that would cause staining like that was blood.

I knelt down to take a closer look. I tried to scrape the blood with my thumbnail, but it appeared that the stains were rather old and dry. Standing, I crossed the courtyard to the kitchen where Pelagia politely acknowledged me. I borrowed a knife and returned to the bathroom. Setting to work on one of the blood spots, I was able to improve it somewhat, though I feared scraping too much and damaging the glaze on the tile's surface. I found another blood spot nearby and set to work on it. Looking closer, I realized there were more spots than I originally thought, but the brightly colored tiles disguised them. I began to wonder what had caused so many spots in the bathroom. The spots were sufficiently old that I speculated that the house had been owned by a high-ranking soldier – possibly a general given the size of the house – and that he had been wounded in some way.

As I set upon the third spot, I realized that cleaning them all was a job for more than one day. I did my best with the spot, then found some rags and a jar of water and washed away the dust I had made. I wondered if any of my predecessors had attempted to clean the spots.

After doing what I could with the bath, I paused and sat down to a lunch of cheese and olives with Syntyche. Kallius, who had been tending trees around the perimeter of the house, joined us. "You seem troubled," he said as he sat down.

"I find myself wondering about the history of this house." I took a sip of water. "I wonder if it is an older house that has seen owners before Theron."

Syntyche nodded and smiled. "That seems likely. We are in an older part of the city. Many of these houses have been owned by families for many generations."

Kallius's brow creased. "That is true, but the walls do not seem as weathered as many neighboring houses. Either this is a newer house built in this part of the city, or Theron has taken great pains to keep the house in the best possible condition."

I frowned, not liking either option. If it was a newer house, why were there old bloodstains on the mosaic tiles of the bath? If the house really was old, but Theron wanted it to appear brand new, the same question still plagued me.

My routine continued essentially unchanged during the following days. I would clean the four rooms of Theron's living quarters – all light work except for the bath where I would spend most of my time working to remove the old stains as best I could without damaging the tiles. If my efforts were appreciated or even noticed, no one said. Aside from our first night, I never saw our master. As best I could tell, he worked all day and slept all night. Democritus would take a small tray of food to the master's chambers after we finished our repast and then we would retire for the evening. It was hard to deny that life was good, but I did find myself missing life on the farm. I was used to working hard and then sleeping soundly at night. Even if life was easy as Theron's slave, sleep was not. The noises of the city were strange to me and I didn't feel as though I worked hard enough to truly become fatigued at the end of the day.

During my third day, I realized that there must be more to Theron's quarters than the four rooms I regularly cleaned. I walked the perimeter of the house with Kallius and saw that his side of the house was over twice as large on the outside as the area I cleaned on the inside. Oddly, there were no windows in the back half of his chambers. When I mentioned the strange dimensions to Kallius he laughed lightly. "He's a banker. That must be where he keeps his coins."

Despite Kallius's reassurances, I had my doubts. There was a simple bed in one of the four rooms I cleaned, but I never saw any evidence that anyone actually slept in it. It was always the same the next day as the day before.

About a week after Theron bought Kallius and me, we were finishing dinner as usual. As Democritus stood to retrieve the master's tray of food, he looked at Syntyche. "The master must work late tonight," he said. "He will need someone to attend to his needs. Please follow me."

Pelagia and Xenia exchanged knowing and somewhat frightened looks as Syntyche followed Democritus.

Syntyche had not returned to our quarters by the time we retired for the evening. Pelagia and Xenia both seemed nervous as we lay down. I thought of asking them what frightened them, but was afraid my perceptions were unfounded and my questions would seem impertinent.

Some time later, I fell into an uneasy sleep. For some reason, I awoke during the night and heard strange, distant keening sounds like the wailing of a bird or the cry of a cat on a rooftop. It struck me the sound could also be screams, muffled by thick walls. The hairs on my arms stood on end and I pulled my blanket close about me.

Syntyche was not back in her bed the next morning, or even the morning after. On the third day, I found Pelagia packing up Syntyche's belongings. I swallowed hard. "What has become of her?" I asked.

Pelagia shook her head. "I do not know." She licked her lips and took a deep breath. "All I know is that Democritus has told me that she will not be returning and I must clean out her things so there will be room for a new slave."

I felt Pelagia was holding something back. "Has this happened before?"

"Every week or two, a slave is called to serve Theron at night. Sometimes two slaves are called. Of the eight I have seen called, only two have returned the next morning. One of them was a man whose spirit was so badly broken, Democritus had to sell him to the slaver. Another was a woman who grew distant. Theron called her back a week later and she didn't return that time." Pelagia frowned deeply and a tear ran down her cheek. "It can only be a matter of time before Xenia or I are called."

My mouth fell open. "That's terrible. Is there anything we can do?"

Pelagia shook her head. "I do not know. I have spoken in private to Democritus. He says little, but he gave me the impression that there is some kind of trial for the slaves that Theron calls. If the slaves pass the trial, Theron sets them free."

My heart felt as though it skipped a beat. Freedom. Was it possible that we could be set free? Then I thought of what Pelagia said about those who returned changed. "What are these trials that Theron sets before us?"

"I do not know and from what I have seen, I wonder if freedom is worth the price."

I sensed Pelagia knew nothing more, so I gathered my resolve and set about my appointed tasks for the day. While sweeping the floor in one of the rooms furthest from the courtyard, I began to wonder again about what lay in the rest of the house. Laying down my broom, I examined the walls, wondering if there was a hidden door. A man cleared his throat and I jumped. Turning around, I saw Democritus.

"Sorry to startle you," he said. "Are you looking for something?"

I blinked a couple of times as I thought how best to answer. "I was just wondering if there are other chambers that I should be cleaning? I do not wish to be negligent in my duties."

Democritus smiled. "The master is most pleased with your work – especially in the bath. You have taken much initiative and he is impressed."

Thinking about my conversation with Pelagia, I wondered whether it was good to have impressed the master so. I swallowed hard. "I'm pleased."

"You only need concern yourself with the four rooms closest to the courtyard," said Democritus.

"There are other rooms, then?" I asked before I could stop myself.

He inclined his head. "You've been outside the house. Surely that must be obvious."

I simply nodded and retrieved my broom. "I apologize for being lax in my duties."

He waved off the apology. "I was seeking you for a special task. I was wondering if you would be so good as to help Kallius fetch the water for tonight's dinner."

"I would be happy to," I said.

I stepped from the room, feeling Democritus's eyes on my back as I left. Putting the broom away, I met Kallius in the courtyard. We each took up a pair of urns and left on our errand to fetch the water. It was a sunny day with a bright blue sky. I had not realized how much I had missed the sun, cooped up as we were in our dark rooms within Theron's home. Working the fields had been difficult, but it meant being outside where the sun warmed my hair and skin. I looked down at my arm and frowned. I wondered if I would become pale and thin like Syntyche if I continued to work indoors.

We made our way to the public cistern, passing several people. I found myself thinking how different life was on these city streets from the way it was out in the fields of the countryside. On the farm, you might not see another person besides your family for the entire day. There, the fields rolled away until they came to the mountains or a stream. In the city, people brushed by me and buildings obstructed my view on all sides.

I looked over at Kallius. He was tall and I couldn't help but notice his long, beautiful legs, bare under his chiton. I liked seeing how the light played across his muscles as he carried the water urns. He noticed me looking and my breath caught. For a moment, it felt as though a small fire had been kindled in my belly as I imagined those arms holding me instead of the urns. I smiled back. Just then, from one of the buildings, I heard a baby cry for its mother. Memories of my brother came rushing back to me and I found myself looking forward once more. I strode quickly to the cool shade beside the cistern and filled my urns.

Kallius came up beside me. He put his arm around my shoulder. "What's the matter?" he asked.

I shook my head. "Nothing."

"Then why did you suddenly rush ahead?" He reached out and gently touched my cheek and turned my head so that I found myself looking into his eyes.

"It was nothing." His gaze was so earnest that I wanted to laugh, but I also found myself wanting to trust him. "Just bad memories."

He pulled me into his arms and I was happy to let him do so. "I would like to help you chase away those memories, if they distress you so." He kissed me atop the head and then on the cheek. Then I felt his lips meet mine. My arms wrapped around him and I delighted in the sensation of the cloth of our tunics rubbing against my breasts. As our kiss deepened, his sex grew rigid against my belly. In spite of myself, the moisture of desire built between my own legs. For a moment, I wanted nothing more than to feel Kallius within me.

As that thought came to me, I also thought of what that could mean – of what a coupling could bring. Gently as I could, I backed away from beautiful Kallius. My breath was heavy and my lips still tingled.

He looked at me, his head cocked to the side. "Why do you retreat?" He took a step closer, but I stopped him with a hand on his chest. "I sense that you desire me as much as I want you."

I sighed and looked past him, toward Theron's house. "There are no children in our master's house." I turned away and retrieved the urns.

He smiled knowingly. "Ah, you're concerned about children." He went to the cistern and filled his urns with water. "I would be proud to be a father." He flashed a sincere smile as he continued his work.

"I know you would, but that raises another problem." I set down the urns and stepped up next to Kallius. "The slaves of Theron's house do not seem to stay long, do they?"

Kallius's smile melted into a frown. "No, they do not. Syntyche was called to serve the master but did not return."

"And what of the two who did not return shortly before we

were purchased? Do you suppose they were set free or sold over the course of the night?" I put my hand on his forearm.

He set the full urns next to mine, then turned toward me and took me into his arms again. He made a show of comforting me, but he was the one who trembled.

Chapter 3

From the Memoirs of Alexandra the Greek:

The next day, I resumed work on the tiles in the master's bath. Although I did not like what the blood spots might imply and was uncomfortable with the master's attention – even though it was apparently positive – I felt it would be far worse if I displeased him. After a while, my arms and knees grew weary and I realized that lunchtime must have been approaching. I stepped out to the courtyard where Democritus intercepted me.

"Xenia is not feeling well today," he explained. "I was wondering if you would be so good as to take lunch to the men working at the temple." Democritus indicated a basket on the table.

I nodded. "I would be happy to." I found myself curious about the work our master did at the temple and wanted to see it firsthand.

Democritus gave me directions. I retrieved the basket and set out. The day was pleasant and it was good to be out in the sunshine again. As I ascended the Acropolis, I found myself looking around at all the people going to and fro. Some of them were clearly slaves like myself. However, others were free citizens. The only free citizens I had really known before coming to Athens were farmers. I found myself wondering how all of these city dwellers occupied themselves. Perhaps I would have a better understanding when I saw Theron about his work at the temple.

The Temple of Athena was a large, gleaming structure at the top of the hill. Great marble pillars supported a beautiful arched roof. I gathered it had recently been rebuilt. The original was destroyed when Alexander invaded the city. Walking up the steps, I looked around in awe at the statues dedicated to Athena, along with statues of the other gods. The workmanship was superb and, if not for their great stillness, it would have been difficult to distinguish them from living people. I found myself thinking of Medusa's statue in the master's courtyard. These statues were like gods frozen in time by a gorgon.

I found Theron's servants near a statue of Athena. One of the men conducted business with a strange, dark-skinned man wearing brightly colored clothes. I waited for the man to depart before I approached.

Hermogenes saw me first. "Ah lunch, how wonderful," he declared.

"Thank you," said another of the men – Eusebios. He smiled charmingly.

I looked around and my brow furrowed.

"You seem troubled," said Hermogenes as he reached into the basket and retrieved a loaf of bread.

"I thought Master Theron would be here with you."

"Ah," said Eusebios. "Master Theron never conducts business at the temple in person. That is work for his slaves." He reached into the basket and took a handful of olives.

"Then how does the master occupy himself during the day?" I asked.

Hermogenes shrugged. "I have no idea. We see him only as often as you do. Democritus gives us our instructions in the morning and we return the ledgers and coins to him at night. I presume the master checks over our work, but it's Democritus who tells us whether we are doing well or not and how we might improve our work."

"Is that how most bankers conduct their business?"

Hermogenes indicated a few clusters of men around the temple. "A few, yes. However, most bankers oversee their slaves directly."

"Master Theron must be quite pleased with the work you do," I said.

Hermogenes smiled, but Eusebios chewed his lower lip and

shifted uncomfortably from one foot to the other. I sensed he had no more desire to attract our master's attention than I did. Hermogenes took up the food basket. "Thank you for the lovely lunch," he said. "We'll bring the basket back this afternoon."

I nodded. "May the rest of your day be a pleasant one." With that, I started back to Theron's house with even more questions about how free men – and particularly our master – spent their days.

"So, how do free people occupy themselves?"

Kallius and I were in the public market. Pelagia was a few steps ahead, examining vegetables in a farmer's cart. Kallius seemed withdrawn. He blinked a few times as though startled by my question.

"Free men have many pursuits," he said after giving it some thought. "Trading, farming, philosophy, the arts … there are many things that occupy their time."

"What about the women? If we had a mistress, how would she spend her days?"

"Women sew and supervise the house, take care of the children, supervise the slaves…."

"In other words, they would do the job that Democritus does in our house."

Kallius laughed at that observation. "I suppose that would be the case." His smile still brightened his features as he turned to look at me. "What makes you so inquisitive today?"

I shrugged. "What makes you so thoughtful?"

"I suppose I'm thinking about our conversation last week," he said. "I'm wondering what the future has in store for us."

I nodded and noticed that Pelagia had moved forward. I nudged Kallius and we followed. I looked around the market, trying to see if my father was there or perhaps my brother, but they were not. "Do you have dreams for the future?" I asked at last.

"I'm not sure I understand."

"If you could be anything you wanted to be, if you could live any kind of life you wanted, what would it be?"

Kallius thought about the question for a moment. "I suppose I would like to be a slave in a good house – one where I can have a wife and a family. I would like to live there until I grow old with my children about me." He pursed his lips. "I fear we are not in such a household, but I would like to be someday." He turned to look at me. "I would like it if you could join me in such a house."

My breath caught and I turned away, hoping he hadn't seen my reaction. I caught sight of a bird vendor across the way from the vegetable cart Pelagia examined. I stepped forward and looked at the multi-colored birds in their wooden cages, to avoid looking into Kallius's deep brown eyes for fear that I would drown in them.

"Why do you step away?" His voice was tense and I sensed that I hurt him without intending to. "Don't you find me to your taste?"

I turned and looked into his eyes. I set down the basket I was carrying and touched his strong hands. "I do find you attractive, but I find myself ... troubled by your dreams."

"Troubled?" His brow furrowed. He set down his basket and took my hands in his. "What do you dream of, Alexandra?" His lips curled upward. I found myself piqued by a sense that he merely indulged my fancies, but as he continued to gaze into my eyes his expression grew more serious. Deep down, he seemed truly concerned.

I turned my head and indicated the birds in their cages. "I dream of being a free woman. I dream of never having to answer to another person. I dream that if I have children, I will decide their destiny, not someone who owns me and them."

"Am I not part of your dreams?" Just a hint of sorrow tinged his words.

I sighed and gazed into his eyes. "You could be." I let him wrap his arms around me, let him press his lips to mine. His kiss was tender and giving, not full of need as it had been the last time he kissed me. I sensed his desire, but I also sensed he held it back. He wanted to win me over and that flattered me. I returned his kiss and allowed my hands to rove over his body.

After a moment, we parted. "What would you do if you were free?" he asked.

I shook my head and took up my basket. "I'm not certain. I suppose that is why I ask so many questions about what free women do."

"It is a good dream." Kallius retrieved his own basket. "Perhaps, one day, Master Theron will sell us to a home with a good mistress and your questions will be answered."

"Perhaps such an owner would help his servants achieve their freedom," I said wistfully.

"Perhaps…." Kallius's voice trailed off. We both turned and saw Pelagia with her arms folded, tapping her feet. We stepped up and she loaded our baskets with vegetables she had just purchased. Kallius remained quiet and thoughtful for the rest of the visit to the market. I wasn't certain whether he felt admonished by Pelagia's reproachful glare or whether he was uncomfortable with the prospect of being free and having to make decisions for himself.

The next day, Xenia felt better and I did not have to take lunch to the temple or accompany Pelagia to the market. Instead, I sat outside the walls of the house and ate lunch with Kallius under the trees. We spoke quietly of little things for over an hour. I told him about life on the farm and he told me of the homes he had served before. "Why were you given over to the slaver?" I asked at last.

"I'm afraid my previous owner liked to gamble his money away. I was sold so he could pay his debts," he said with a sigh. "For all of Master Theron's secretiveness, he does not seem to be a gambler."

I shrugged. "Perhaps he is…. Where does he spend his days?"

"If he is a gambler," said Kallius, "then he is a very good one. People were constantly visiting my previous owner's house, trying to collect debts. We have few visitors here."

I nodded in agreement and then noted how far the sun had

moved. "I had better get inside before Democritus misses me."
Kallius and I stood together. He took me in his arms and kissed
me. I picked up the food basket and carried it through the gate.
Looking over, I noticed Democritus standing in the doorway of
his chambers with his arms behind his back. I gasped in spite of
myself.

"Did you have a good lunch with Kallius?" There was no hint
of sarcasm in his question, but somehow his gaze made me feel as
though I had done something wrong.

I looked down at my sandals. "Yes sir, I did."

He reached out and led me gently to the courtyard by the
elbow. "Don't feel admonished, Alexandra. Our duties here are
light and you have performed them admirably. Master Theron is
most pleased." He sat down on one of the stools at the table under
the statue of Medusa and indicated that I should also sit. "However,
I must caution you about growing too attached to anyone in this
household."

"Why is that?" I looked up into Democritus's eyes. "As you
say, our duties are light. Why doesn't Theron retain slaves for very
long?"

"I have been Master Theron's servant for nearly twenty years,"
he said simply.

"But what about Syntyche? Where did she go so suddenly?" I
steeled my courage and leaned forward. "I have heard others have
also left very quickly."

I sat back, expecting Democritus to berate or punish me for
my words. Instead, he smiled kindly. "I don't think I have to tell
you that such questions have a certain danger. However, I am not
surprised to hear them from someone who has such a desire for
freedom."

"How...?"

He held up his hand. "It is no secret that you wish to be a free
woman – and there is no shame in such a desire."

"Do you wish to be free?"

"I did, once," he said. "However, I am old enough now that
I'm not sure what I would do if freedom were thrust upon me. I am

content to serve Master Theron's house."

"What did happen to Syntyche?" I asked quietly.

"I cannot answer that at this time," said Democritus. I opened my mouth to protest, but he shook his head. "Rest assured, your question will be answered eventually."

I considered what he said. "Will the same thing happen to me that happened to her?"

He pursed his lips as he stood up from the stool. He looked me up and down, then shook his head. "I'm not really certain." With that he returned to his quarters.

A sudden chill went up my spine despite the afternoon sun's warmth. I retrieved the lunch basket, took it to the kitchen and then returned to my duties in the master's quarters.

A few nights later, we sat down to dinner. A new slave named Myrrine joined us. She was quiet and reserved. I don't know if it was because of her manner or because the others sensed something, but there seemed less conversation than normal around the table. Hermogenes and Eusebios kept their eyes on their plates. Xenia, still seeming somewhat under the weather, ate modestly. As dinner drew to a close, Democritus cleared his throat. "The master must work late tonight. He will need someone to attend to his needs."

I caught my breath as Democritus's eyes fell on me briefly. "Kallius, please attend," he said after a moment.

I felt the blood drain from my face. Kallius reached out and touched my hand, then looked up at Democritus. "I am honored, sir." He stood and followed Democritus. I helped the others clear the table, but found myself stealing glances at the master's quarters. As the time neared to retire, Democritus emerged and stepped toward his own chambers.

I followed Xenia, Pelagia, and Myrrine to the women's quarters. There, I slipped off my sandals and lay down on my bed. Some time later, I heard the deep breathing of the other women, but I could not go to sleep. I crept out of the room and down the hall,

peering out into the courtyard to see if I could catch of glimpse
of Kallius or our master in the light of the full moon, just rising
above the courtyard wall. The wind blew and the trees rustled. The
shadows shifted and I thought I saw someone move out in the
courtyard. My heart skipped a beat and I quickly drew myself back
into the shadows. I sat with my back against the wall, next to the
door, waiting to see if I had been discovered. My breathing slowed
and my eyes fell closed even as I willed them to stay open.

A soft rustling from the courtyard attracted my attention. I must
have dozed off. My neck and back hurt from sleeping sitting up
against the wall. Quietly as I could, I drew myself to my feet and
peered out into the courtyard. The full moon hung low in the sky
and it cast long, deep shadows. It was almost morning. A slight
breeze blew causing the shadows of leaves to shift. The snakes on
the statue of Medusa's head in the courtyard appeared to writhe
with a life of their own.

I soft moan came from the columns to the left of the master's
chambers. Looking in that direction, I saw a mound. I crept toward
it. The dry grass crackled beneath my bare feet and I was certain
someone would hear and investigate. Still, I moved toward the
form.

I gasped as I drew into the shadows and my eyes adjusted.
It was Kallius. He lay on his side with his back to me, moaning
softly. His tunic had been ripped and blood congealed on his back.
Looking closer, I noticed the wounds were not deep. It was as
though someone had lashed him with a whip hard enough to hurt,
but not hard enough to do serious damage.

Moving around him, I discovered bruises on his wrists and
ankles, as though he had been bound. There was more blood on
his neck. Looking closer, I saw that he had been bitten. I ripped a
piece of my own chiton and pressed it to the wound. He reached
up, took the cloth and held it.

Perhaps most surprising of all, his tunic had ridden up,

revealing his erection. He was in pain and I wanted to help. Even so, I found myself fascinated by his member. Even in the wan light, I could discern that it was reddened and it looked like it hurt as I knew his back and neck did also.

"Release me." His voice was so quiet that I almost didn't hear him.

"Let me take you to your bed. You're hurt. You need help."

"I'm not hurt badly," he said. "Alexandra, please release me. The master refused."

I wasn't sure I understood what he meant when he said the master refused to release him, but looking at his cock, I was fairly certain I knew what kind of release he sought. I helped him into something of a sitting position. I still did not want to bring a child into this world, especially now that it had grown even stranger, but I knew that I could provide a certain release. I reached out and took his member in my hand and stroked it. He let out a soft moan and I felt my own belly grow hot. I was even more tempted to take him inside me to give him the release he wanted. His body fascinated me and it was difficult for me to take my eyes off his penis as I caressed it. I drew forward, brushed my hair behind my head and took him into my mouth.

The taste of him was heady and strong and I almost regretted what I had done, but hearing his moan of pleasure drove me to continue. I explored his balls with my hand while I suckled his manhood. It was not long before he reached climax and I nearly gagged as his seed spilled into my mouth. Even so, I found myself reaching down to stroke my own sex as he came. He was not the only one who sought release. However, once he was spent, the pain of his wounds began to argue with him. He would not be able to help me as I had helped him.

I stood, then crouched down beside him. Gingerly, so I wouldn't injure him further, I helped him to his feet and took him toward his bed in the slave's quarters. Just as we reached the doorway, I looked around and caught sight of a pair of eyes watching me from the shadows near the master's quarters and heard a soft, almost delighted laugh. I blinked and the eyes were gone.

I helped Kallius to his bed, then brought some water and cleaned his wounds. He groaned while I worked, but never cried out. At last, when I was finished, he was asleep. I retreated to the women's quarters and my own bed where I lay down and pulled the cover over my head, but did not sleep as I thought about eyes peering at me from the dark.

Chapter 4

From the Memoirs of Alexandra the Greek:

The next morning, I was startled awake by the sound of birds. I lay there in bed, simply looking up at the ceiling. Somehow, the sunshine streaming in through the window along with the cooking smells and shufflings from the kitchen had a surreal quality. It was as though darkness, silence and shadows were the natural order of things. Wan as the light was through the window, it felt as though it burned my eyes. I pulled my blanket over my head for a moment and took several deep breaths. Finally, I climbed out of bed and went to the kitchen to retrieve breakfast.

"You slept late enough." Pelagia's nose wrinkled. She turned her eyes back to the task at hand. "Democritus assigned your day's work to Myrrine. Xenia has gone to market."

I took some bread and poured a little olive oil into a dish. I dipped the bread into the oil, took a bite and chewed. Finally I looked up at Pelagia. "Where is Democritus now?" I took another bite and rubbed sleep from my eyes.

"Tending to Kallius." Her voice became a whisper. "I'm surprised to see that he returned. Perhaps he did not pass the master's trial."

I thought about that and I considered the nature of Kallius's wounds. He had said the master refused to give him release and I found him in the courtyard. Taken at face value, those facts seemed to match Pelagia's notion that Theron tested his slaves and released them if they passed. However, it looked to me like Kallius had been punished. Despite such punishment, it seemed he desired sexual release from the master. I shook my head, then drew some water from the urn and drank. My thoughts were too muddled. I needed to speak with Kallius to find out what really had happened.

I finished my bread and left the kitchen. Stepping down the hall, I came to the men's sleeping quarters. Democritus sat next to Kallius's bed and examined him. I cleared my throat and Democritus looked around. He stood and came to the doorway. "May I help you?"

"I'm sorry I overslept this morning," I said with a slight bow. "I was wondering if I might speak to Kallius."

"I'm afraid not," said Democritus. He took me by the elbow and led me back the way I came. "He is not feeling well and needs some time to rest and recover."

I nodded, understanding. "When do you think I might be able to speak to him?"

"Probably not long," he said. "Two or three days at most."

"Should I attend to my duties in the master's quarters?"

Democritus shook his head. "No. I have assigned Myrrine those duties for today. I suggest that you heat some bath water and clean up. When you have done so, come speak to me and I'll assign you duties for today."

I looked down at myself for the first time since climbing out of bed. My knees were dirty and there were bloodstains on my chiton from helping Kallius back to his chambers the night before. I reached up and felt my hair. It had become a snarled mass in the night. No wonder Pelagia had wrinkled her nose when I entered the kitchen earlier. "I apologize for my unkempt appearance," I said.

He waved my apology aside and stepped past me into the courtyard. I returned to the kitchen, drew some more water into an urn and placed it by the fire to heat. "What kind of trial do you think Theron puts us through?" I asked Pelagia.

"I gather you must have helped Kallius back to his bed last night," she said. "Perhaps you know more than I do."

"You say others have returned. Have they all been bloody and beaten as Kallius was?"

She nodded slowly. "They usually look as though some animal

has grabbed them by the neck, the arm, or the leg. I have wondered if the master keeps a wolf or a lynx in his chambers and the test is to get away from the animal."

"Perhaps...." Seeing a slight steam rising from the water in the urn, I took it with me to the bath chamber and poured it in the tub. I retrieved another urn of water and took it down the hall as well. With the tub sufficiently full, I removed my chiton and stepped into the bath water. My knees stung as the water washed over them, but the sensation gave way to a comforting warmth. I sat there for a moment and wondered what I would do if confronted by a large animal in the master's chambers.

Three days later, when I awoke, I discovered Kallius was no longer in his bed. I cleaned up, had breakfast and then looked for him. I found him outside the house, raking the leaves that were beginning to fall. His cheeks flushed when he saw me, and he looked away.

My eyebrows came together and I stepped closer. "I do not mean to embarrass you. I just wanted to see how you are."

He fell back against the trunk of a tree and sighed. "I'm better, but I still feel weak as a lamb." He licked his lips. "Democritus says you helped me to my bed the other night. Thank you."

"Do you remember what happened?"

He slid down the trunk of the tree until he sat on the ground. "It's all very hard to remember. Democritus led me into the master's inner chambers – the ones beyond those we normally see. It was dark – only a few candles relieved the gloom. Master Theron was there. He looked into my eyes." Kallius pinched the bridge of his nose with his fingers. "After that, it's very hard to remember."

"You said something about the master refusing to release you." I sat down on the ground next to Kallius. "Do you remember what that was about?"

His eyes pinched shut as though a great pain wracked him. I reached out to touch his shoulder, but he stopped me. "I have heard that Plato exalted the love of one man for another above the love of a man for a woman. I never understood how that could be. However, I now find myself desiring the master, much as I desire you." He looked up into my eyes and I saw a silent apology as though he had done something wrong.

I moved closer to him. "Do you remember what happened after you were with the master? Do you remember the courtyard?"

"I remember great pain and loneliness," he said. "I thought I would die. I remember you came and showed me kindness and love, but the details...." He shook his head again. "I wish I could remember the details."

I put my arms around Kallius and he rested his head on my shoulder. "What did he do to you in those chambers?" I mused aloud.

"I wish I could remember so I could answer your question." His voice was barely above a whisper. "However, I have a feeling that I'm better off not remembering just now."

I don't know how long I sat there and held him, but eventually I grew sore. I asked him if he felt able to go back to work. He nodded. "I think it's best if I don't dwell on what happened."

I stood and helped him to his feet. "Do you remember how you got into the master's inner chambers?"

He nodded. "That much I do remember. Democritus led me to the master's bath. There is a depiction of a gorgon in the mosaic. He pushed the tiles at the center of the gorgon's eyes, as though he was gouging them out. A door swung back and that is how we entered."

I ran my tongue along the inside of my teeth and watched as Kallius resumed raking the leaves. Slowly I walked back to the gate. While there, I lingered for a moment and considered the gorgon relief. Democritus passed me while I stood there. "I was wondering where you went. Did you speak to Kallius? He seems to be doing much better today."

"He does," I agreed. "He doesn't remember anything, though."

Democritus was silent. I turned to face him but his expression was unreadable. "I need to help at the temple today. Pelagia will be going to market. Would you like to accompany her?"

I considered the question carefully. The prospect of seeing my brother or father made it a tempting choice. However, I knew there was a real chance that I would be as disappointed as I was the other day. "I think I would rather resume my duties in the master's quarters, today. The bath still needs my attention."

He inclined his head. "Very good. Then I will send Myrrine with Pelagia." He stepped back into the courtyard and I followed close behind.

In the courtyard, I took a moment to look at the statue of Medusa once more. I had never thought that the entry to the rear half of the master's chambers would be through the bathroom. However, the mosaic tiles would conceal a door well and it's true that our master seemed to have a fascination for gorgons. Democritus, Pelagia, and Myrrine passed me as they left for their respective errands. I went to the kitchen and retrieved a knife, then collected a broom.

I set about my chores as usual and swept the small, unused bedroom, then straightened up the little sitting room. Finally, I moved on to the bathroom. The gorgon in the mosaic seemed to beckon me with her eyes. I wanted to see what was on the other side of the hidden door, but it seemed foolhardy to rush into the master's quarters alone. What if he really did have a wild animal in there? What if he was in there? He would be completely within his rights to punish or sell me. Strange as life was in this house of gorgons and shadows, it was not entirely unpleasant.

I knelt down and began scraping up another blood spot. This one did not seem as bad as others and I realized that it was fresher – perhaps only a few days old. It dawned on me at that moment that the blood was not ancient. Instead, I cleaned Kallius's blood from the tile. I looked up at the gorgon mosaic again and thought of Kallius's wounds. I thought of Syntyche who went through that door and never returned. It was likely I would be punished whether I was obedient or not. I stood, straightened my chiton and stepped up to the gorgon mosaic.

I pushed the gorgon's eyes and sure enough, they went into the wall. There was a snap and a click and the door fell open on smoothly oiled hinges. I peered around the corner and into an absolutely dark room. I could only see as far as the light from my side of the doorway penetrated. Quietly, I closed the door again and then went back to the slave's quarters where I retrieved an oil lamp. I filled and lit it. Xenia watched me, but did not ask any questions.

I returned to the mysterious door in the bath and opened it once again. Gingerly, I stepped through and paused, allowing my eyes to adjust to the limited light. The first room was apparently a small, empty foyer. Opposite the room was a door, blocked by a tapestry. I passed into the next room.

My little lamp illuminated a wooden table, not unlike the one out in the courtyard where we enjoyed our meals. Iron rings were mounted to the table at each of the four corners. The wood itself was dark and well polished. I couldn't tell with my faint light whether I was seeing wood grain or some kind of staining. Leather straps and coils of rope hung from spikes embedded in the walls. In addition to the table, there was a comfortable looking divan. Unlike the furniture in the other part of the house, this had seen use. A fireplace in one corner of the room looked and smelled as though it had been recently used. More iron stokers than seemed absolutely necessary stood next to the fireplace. A pair of whips and three swords also hung on the wall nearby.

Although the air was warm, the hairs on my arms stood on end and a shiver traveled up my spine. Two doors besides the one I had come through led away from the room I was in. I decided to look in the room to the right.

Whereas the room I had been in gave me chills, the new room was reassuringly familiar. In spite of being dark, it was clearly an ordinary sitting room. There were two tables and a variety of shelves cluttered with scrolls containing the scratchings and numbers I would expect to find in a banker's household. It was cluttered as I might expect for a room that no slave – except perhaps Democritus – visited.

I returned to the room with the large table and the weapons upon the wall. The last door out of this central room faced the entryway. I felt it must either lead into Theron's sleeping quarters or his vault. I checked the oil in my lamp and decided I had plenty to continue my explorations.

The final room appeared to be a well appointed bedchamber. Like the sitting room, it was reassuringly ordinary. There was a chair and a cabinet where the master undoubtedly kept his clothes. I moved my lamp around to the bed and my breath caught when I saw something on it, covered by a blanket.

A part of me said I should leave the room without exploring further. I had satisfied my curiosity enough. However, another part of me was curious about what lay under the blanket. *Theron is a bachelor,* I told myself. *He probably sleeps on the couch in the other room, or he sleeps in his sitting room. Those are probably just tunics, himations and chitons piled on his bed and covered over with a blanket.*

That answer would have been reassuringly normal and I suppose I wanted to convince myself that it was true. I crept up to the bed and pulled back the blanket. I immediately dropped it and stepped back several feet, bumping into the cabinet with a loud crash.

I had never seen him clearly, but it was apparent that Theron lay upon the bed. He was pale and appeared to be dead. I feared he would jump up and yell at me for waking him. Yet, in spite of the loud crash when I collided with the cabinet, he did not stir.

Gingerly, I stepped back up to him and held my hand over his nose and mouth. I could feel no breath. Theron was dead.

My mind immediately began to race and I wondered how long he had been lying there. I wondered if Democritus knew that the master had passed away. His body looked remarkably fresh, so I guessed that he must have died in the morning and I was the first to discover him. I reached down, took up the blanket and covered him again. As I did so, I wondered about the fact that I had found him covered in the first place. Perhaps Democritus already had found him, but if that was the case, why did he keep the master's death a secret?

As I turned toward the door to leave, I heard a shuffling from the other room. Someone was in the chambers with me, but that person had not called out. They were looking around quietly as I was. My first thought was that it might be Kallius, but I quickly dismissed that notion. Kallius was so honest and trustworthy, I would have expected him to call out from the door. He would not have entered his master's chambers without an explicit invitation. He either would have closed the door or left it just as he found it. Whoever had entered, kept quiet, seeking the person who had left the outer door open.

Quietly as I could manage, I stepped over to the bedchamber's entrance and waited. A moment later, the curtain was pulled back and a man stepped inside. I reached out and hooked the other's leg with my own, sending him tumbling to the ground. I lowered my lamp to the other's face and discovered that it was Democritus.

"Why am I not surprised to find you here?" he asked. "Your curiosity will be the end of you. We must leave at once."

"On the contrary," came a faintly lisping voice from the other end of the room.

I held my light up and sitting on the bed was a man that I would have sworn had been dead. He smiled, revealing fangs, much like the visage of the gorgon relief on the house's wall. He stood up and stepped over to us. The power of his gaze froze me to the spot and I could not will myself to stand or back away. For the first time, I really had a chance to look at my master and I found he was not grotesque like the gorgon relief, but beautiful like a masculine Medusa. His features were chiseled like those of an alabaster statue and even if I could, I did not want to look away. He reached down and retrieved the lamp from my fingers, then snuffed it out, plunging us into utter darkness.

Chapter 5

From the Memoirs of Alexandra the Greek:

When it went dark, I realized I was capable of movement. I tried to think where I had been in the room and where I would need to go to escape. However, before I could make a clear plan, a strong hand grasped my upper arm. It lifted me to my feet as though I was a petulant child and guided me forward a few steps. A curtain brushed past me and I realized we must have entered the room with the table, whips, and straps.

Somehow Master Theron could see in the room's complete darkness. He leaned away as though reaching for something with his free hand, and then led me to another location in the room. With pressure on my upper arm, he forced me to a kneeling position. I felt a rope being tied to my wrist and then being secured and cinched up to something – my guess was one of the iron rings of the table. Once he finished, I pulled against the rope, but found I was held quite securely.

"Your curiosity intrigues me," said Master Theron. I heard a shuffling from another part of the room. "Most slaves would not dare to violate their master's sanctuary."

"You are not at all like the farmer who owned me before," I said. "You are not like any other slave owner that I have heard of."

A spark flashed, followed by another. A moment later, I could see the silhouette of Master Theron's back in front of the fireplace's glowing embers.

Democritus appeared in the doorway, rubbing his arm, where he had fallen. "Sir, do you need anything further?"

Theron shook his head. "I sense the sun has not yet set." He cast a meaningful look in my direction, though I did not understand its purpose.

"No, sir." Democritus lowered his head.

"Please check with me after sunset."

"There is a certain danger…" began Democritus, but Master Theron silenced him with an angry glare.

Democritus nodded and then went to the curtain that led to the foyer. Theron moved back into the shadows as the curtain was lifted and a little sunlight filtered into the room. A moment later there was a bump and a click, and I was alone with the master. He turned his eyes fully upon me and again, I found myself captivated by his gaze. He was tall and thin and his features were surprisingly youthful. He appeared no older than Kallius or myself.

He stepped over to me and knelt down next to me. "What has led you to invade my quarters during the day?"

His gaze kindled a fire in my belly much like the one he had kindled in the fireplace. I reached out to touch the smooth lines of his face, but he swatted my hand away. "Answer the question," he said sternly.

"I was curious." I took a deep breath and let it out slowly. "I was curious about you and I was curious about what had happened to Kallius."

"You desire Kallius." It was not a question, but I nodded in response. "However, you have not decided whether you actually love him."

Even though the days were shortening, they were still warm. With the fire going, it grew hot in the room. I started to sweat from both the heat and the power of Theron's gaze. I took a moment to look him over completely. He was lean and graceful – his muscles were taut, like a wild animal, ready to spring on his prey. My sex was swollen and ready. I would have gladly allowed Theron to place me on the table and take me right then. I tried to communicate that with my eyes when I answered him. "I like him, but I don't think I love him. He does not desire freedom as much as I do."

"You seek release?" His eyes gleamed and his lip curled up, again revealing a hint of a fang.

"I do."

He stood and moved over to the wall. He retrieved one of the whips. Though my mind yelled at me to find a way to escape, I sat there fascinated as he slowly uncoiled it. Without a word, he cracked the whip in my direction. It nicked my naked arm and blood welled. There was hunger in the master's eyes. I turned as he raised the whip to strike again. This time it caught me across the back. Another lash followed in rapid succession.

"I have displeased you, my lord. I am sorry." I hated the fact that my voice trembled.

"You have not displeased me at all," he said. I heard him step closer. I turned as he reached out and grabbed hold of my chiton. He ripped it away, leaving me naked under his gaze. Again he knelt down beside me. This time he leaned forward and licked the wound on my arm. I closed my eyes, expecting it to sting, but his mouth on the wound was like a balm.

He helped me stand and then leaned me over the table. His tongue explored the wounds on my back. His member grew rigid against my hip. He wanted me as much as I wanted him. "Let me give you pleasure, my lord. Let me atone for the crime of invading your sanctuary."

He leaned close to my ear and stroked my hair. "Ah, but you have already given me pleasure," he said. "I shall do with you what I like."

He stood and I sensed he was going to leave me like I was, naked and sweating on the table, wanting him. He turned his head and as his gaze left me, I realized that he had only bound me by one hand. I kicked out and caught him in the back of the knees, causing him to drop in a heap. I reached up and untied my hand. Before he could turn, I pounced on him and pushed him to the floor. I sensed great strength as he struggled to free himself, but I was raised on a farm, used to coping with animals and an older brother. I held him pinned to the floor. I felt his rigid sex underneath me, protruding from under his chiton. I maneuvered myself over him. At that moment, I no longer cared whether I would get a child. I wanted relief and I slid onto him. We both moaned together as I rode him.

"I want my freedom," I said.

"And you shall have it." He reached down and ripped open the front of his chiton. He scratched himself deeply with his finger, then reached up and lowered my head to his wound. I lapped at the blood that rose to the surface much as he had lapped at my wounds. Several tremors went through my body as I reached climax. The grin that formed as he reached his own climax was wickedly boyish.

My belly suddenly cramped and I gasped. I rolled off of Theron, onto the floor, curling into a ball as I clutched my stomach. There was a rustling of curtains and I sensed Democritus had returned. "It is sunset, the slaves have gathered for supper."

Theron reached down and gathered me into his arms. I sensed his strength had increased. He lifted me as easily as a parent would lift a small child. "Ask Xenia to attend us tonight," he said.

"Very good, Master."

The pain increased as Theron carried me toward his sleeping quarters. I tried to speak but I could not. "The pain will be gone soon," he said.

He laid me gently on his bed. A few moments later, a sensation like sleep washed over me. I only had a moment to wonder if this was death before the darkness completely overtook me.

My eyes fluttered open. I felt very still and calm and then realized that I didn't breathe and my heart didn't beat. I panicked momentarily and suddenly I drew in breath and found that I could make my heart beat by willing it. It was a little like blinking – finding that you can control something that is normally a reflex.

There was no source of light that I could discern, but as I looked around, I could make out details that were previously hidden in the gloom. I stood and made my way around the room's perimeter, looking at objects that the master had acquired. I didn't recognize everything, but there were little dog-headed statues that I thought might be from Egypt and clay tablets with scratchings that I thought might be from another far off land.

A low moan sounded from the adjoining room. I made my way to the curtain and peered through. Xenia lay on the strange table. She was nude and both her ankles and feet were bound to the iron rings by leather straps. There were red streaks down her back where the master had lashed her. She was gagged and she writhed against the table as though she sought the release that I found with the master earlier. As I looked at her and the blood against her back, there was again a sensation in my belly. However, this time it was more hunger than arousal.

"Ah, Alexandra, you're awake. I am glad." I looked over and saw Theron reclined upon his couch. He wore a clean, red chiton and his smile was pleasant and inviting. My stomach lurched as hunger warred with desire. "You must be hungry." He pointed to Xenia lying on the table. "I have prepared your first meal."

I wondered what he meant by a meal, but some deep instinct told me that I desired the blood that I saw. I stepped over to the table, and bent over Xenia. The smell of her blood drove me on and I licked one of the wounds on her back. She moaned again and I clasped onto the wound with my mouth and began to suck. The blood helped to quiet my urgings, but it did not go silent. I could not get the blood fast enough.

I crawled onto the table with Xenia and pulled her hair back from her neck where her jugular vein pulsed. I pressed myself against her. As I felt her warm flesh against my own skin, I became aware that I was nude just as she was. However, I didn't really care about that fact. I was more concerned about the pulsing vein. Without conscious thought, I drove my teeth into the vein. At that moment, I realized that my teeth had changed and I now had fangs that drove into the blood vessel. Blood shot into my mouth and I nearly gagged as I had on Kallius's seed several nights before. However, as the blood moved down my throat, I felt compelled to drink more. I continued drinking until no more blood came.

I released Xenia and stood from the table, then grew faint and had to grab the table to steady myself. Xenia did not move or writhe as she had done before. She lay absolutely motionless. "I still hunger," I whispered. I tried to stand up straight and move toward

Theron, but my knees felt watery.

"It is best if you do not slake your thirst completely right now," explained Theron. "If you do, you will drink until you are sick – and I will have no more slaves."

"I feel strange." I put my hand to my forehead.

"Good Xenia was prone to taking Nepenthe to relieve herself of her ills. You are feeling the Nepenthe in your own system. It will help calm the hunger and allow you to rest until we can speak at length." He led me back to his sleeping chamber and I lay down on his bed. He covered me and soon my eyes fluttered closed.

A small oil lamp burned by my bedside the next time I awoke. This faint illumination was like a bright lantern to my enhanced vision and it was as though I woke to a day-lit world. A fresh peplos had been laid out for me along with a breast band. Unlike the chiton I wore as a slave, this dress was red and elaborately embroidered with gold thread. The smells of sweat, blood and my own feminine musk assaulted my nose and I hesitated to put on the fine, new clothes before I had a bath. However, I was uncertain how much freedom I truly had. Was I still a slave within Theron's home, or was I free to do what I wanted?

I slipped into the clean clothes and stepped from Theron's room into the central chamber. There was a faint glow from under the curtain of the sitting room. I entered and found Theron, reclining on a couch, reviewing a ledger. He looked up. "How good to see you awake."

"How long have I been asleep?" I asked.

"Almost twenty-four hours." He rolled up the ledger and set it aside, then indicated that I should sit. "Do not be alarmed, that is not unusual right after you have just been ... transformed."

"What exactly have I been transformed into?" Tentatively, I touched one of my new fangs with my tongue.

"I suspect most Greeks would call us lamias."

I tilted my head. "Lamias are women."

"As are gorgons." He held his arms wide, as though inviting

me to inspect whether he was male or female. "I believe you have deduced that I prefer to think of myself as a gorgon."

I nodded, acknowledging his assertion.

"The truth is far more complex than mere legend." He sat up and folded his hands in his lap. "Like lamias we subsist on blood. Like gorgons we bear a fanged countenance and our gaze can turn a victim to stone – after a fashion, anyway." He stood and picked up one of the little dog-headed statues that adorned his sitting room. "You and your fellow slaves speculated that I gave a test and if you passed, you would be given your freedom." He turned and looked me in the eye. "In a sense you were correct and I have given you the greatest freedom of all. You are free of death." He held up the little statue. "Anubis cannot claim your soul. Lachesis and her sisters cannot cut the thread of your life. You are like a god – immortal."

My eyes widened at the prospect. "Can this truly be?"

"It is." He set the statue down again. "However, immortality comes with a price. You may never walk in the sunlight again. We subsist on blood – but only blood." He waved his hand through the air. "Oh, you can ingest a few other liquids such as wine or water, but they are not nourishment by themselves."

"Xenia?" My eyebrows came together as I thought about what Theron told me. "Did I kill..." I couldn't complete the thought.

"I'm afraid you drained too much blood for Xenia to live." He sighed and looked to the floor. "When you are young and if you go too long between feedings, it is often difficult to avoid killing the ones you feed upon."

I put my face in my hands and wept quietly. I was not especially close to Xenia, but had shared quarters with her and I felt a terrible guilt at being the cause of her demise. He made no move to comfort me. He simply allowed me to regain control on my own. Finally, I looked up and wiped the tears away. "You say we can feed without killing?"

He nodded.

"What happened to Syntyche? Did you transform her as you did me?"

He stood and held out his hand. I hesitated a moment, but

finally took it. It was not warm as I might expect, but neutral as the air around me. He led me into the central chamber. "It is difficult not to frighten those we need to feed upon. Some – like Kallius – endure the experience and are merely disoriented afterward. Others – like Syntyche – become too frightened and do not survive."

"What about Democritus?" I asked. "Have you fed on him?"

"Many times." Theron's mouth turned upward in a grin. "He is quite strong."

"Yet you haven't transformed him...."

"I offered. He says he doesn't want to become one of our kind." He shook his head. "In a way, I don't blame him. He is wise beyond his years and knows me well. He knows that a certain boredom is one of the prices of immortality."

I looked around the room and my arm hairs stood on end. Realization began to sink in. I was immortal, but I would have to hurt and possibly kill others to preserve myself. The weight of that realization almost caused my knees to buckle. Theron noticed and caught me. He helped me lean against the table he had tied me to. I looked down at his strong, lithe hand around my arm and a question came to the forefront of my mind. "Am I truly free?"

He released my arm and bowed slightly. "You are." Then he held up his hand. "However, I would recommend that you stay with me – for a time, at least – and learn more about the ways of our kind."

I nodded, seeing the wisdom in that statement. "May I have a bath?"

He smiled. For the first time, Theron's face showed warmth. "Of course. Please allow me to draw it for you."

He stepped to the fireplace and built a fire. While waiting for the water to heat, I stepped through the foyer, into the bathroom and then out into the courtyard. I looked up at the stars above me in wonder. I listened to the sound of the wind blowing through the trees, the chirping of birds and even distant, quiet voices from nearby houses. I wrapped my arms around myself and wept, knowing that I was now free to choose my destiny.

Chapter 6

From the Memoirs of Alexandra the Greek:

I awoke the next day feeling hunger pangs. I was surprised to find the thought of bread, milk, or fresh fruit actually repulsed me. I craved blood as Master Theron – no, he was no longer my master – as Theron said I would.

Theron allowed me to sleep on his bed. He slept on the divan in the central chamber. As I lay there, waking up, surrounded by his scent and his possessions, I found myself wishing that he would share the bed with me. He explained that one of the prices of immortality was sterility. However, I did not feel that was a price, it was simply another dimension of the gift Theron had given me. The real price for me was this craving for blood. I feared what would be necessary to satisfy it.

I dressed and then stepped into the central chamber. Theron had already arisen and from the glow in the sitting room, I gathered he already immersed himself in his ledgers and numbers. I crept through the central chamber and opened the secret door to the master's bath. I covered my mouth when I saw Kallius gasp and jump back from the door. He started to speak, but I held up my hand to silence him. Quietly, I closed the door and led him into the outer sitting room.

"Thank Athena that you're all right," said Kallius. "When you vanished and then Xenia was ordered to attend the master that very night, we all feared the worst – especially when Myrrine was ordered to pack up both of your belongings.

"What were you doing in the master's bath?" I leaned forward.

"I was going to go in and ask the master what had happened to you."

I shook my head. "That would have been foolhardy. I'm glad I caught you before you entered." I took his hand. It felt almost hot to my touch, like Kallius was burning up with fever, but he did not appear flushed. He flinched and almost pulled his hand back.

"Your hand is like ice," he declared.

"The master has given me my freedom." I thought it best to change the subject.

He nodded. "Then why are you still here?" I thought I detected a glimmer of something in his gaze, perhaps it was hope.

"Theron has generously offered to give me ... instruction." I licked my lips, careful not to open my mouth too wide and reveal my new fangs. "As you know, I'm not familiar with the ways of free women."

He snorted and smiled at that. "Indeed you are not. I miss our talks and your questions."

"Hopefully we'll resume those talks one day." It had grown quite dark in the room and I was glad that Kallius could not see me well. No doubt he would remark at my pale skin. "It grows late," I said. "You should return to your quarters." I kissed him on the cheek.

He stood and pulled me to my feet, and took me in his arms. As he held me, I could sense the blood flowing through his jugular and instinct tried to grab hold. I was tempted to bite and drink – but I knew drinking my fill would be deadly and the master said it was possible to hunt without killing. I needed to learn before I harmed my friend. I pushed him away and ran back to the secret door.

He called after me. "Alexandra!" However, he was sensible enough not to pursue. I hoped he would be sensible enough to go to his room for sleep.

I stepped around the corner into Theron's sitting room. "I grow hungry and I fear I need you to show me how to hunt."

He set down his ledger and nodded. "I knew the time would be near. Did you have a good conversation with your friend, Kallius?"

My mouth fell open. "How did you...?"

"It is one of our gifts. We can sense the thoughts of others. It is likely what drew you to go outside upon waking."

"I didn't sense anything." I moved over to one of the chairs and sat.

He shook his head. "Do not fear. It is a gift that takes time to master. The thoughts are quiet and subtle. That is actually something of a blessing. Could you imagine how terrible it would be to be deluged by the thoughts of others all the time?"

"I can." I frowned, seeing how terrible that could be.

"However, we are not mere readers of thought. We can also manipulate thought and we can use that to our advantage when hunting." He held out his hand. "Come, let me show you." Theron led me out into the courtyard. It was empty and all was quiet aside from the sound of the wind rustling through the leaves of the trees. Thankfully Kallius had left and we found the master's rooms and the courtyard deserted.

Theron led me through the gate and down a nearly deserted street to the waterfront. Once there, I was amazed how many sounds I could make out. I could hear wood creaking as anchored ships moved up and down in the waves. I heard seabirds calling to one another as they hunted. I could hear the distant sounds of drunken sailors continuing their revels late into the night.

"Do you hear the sailors?" he asked.

I nodded.

"Good. They are our prey."

He led me to a shadowed doorway and we waited. Soon, two sailors made their way down the street, singing happily. Theron stepped out from our hiding place and gazed into their eyes. They stopped and stared at him, transfixed. He beckoned me to come out from my hiding place and indicated the sailor closest to me. "This man is for you. Subdue him and drink, but only a little."

I looked at his muscular frame. His legs were like tree trunks and his arms like mighty limbs. Strong as I was from years of hard work on the farm, I didn't think I could move such a man. "How can I force him to move? He is much larger than me."

"You have strengths you do not realize. Listen with your mind, see his hopes and dreams. Use that to bend him to your will."

I quieted my mind and, sure enough, I could see that the sailor dreamed of home. I could see a picture of his wife. She was a good, stout woman who loved and missed her sailor husband. Muddled as his thoughts were with alcohol, it was a relatively easy matter to get him to look toward me and see her. I found I didn't have to force him to his knees, he was willing to descend of his own accord. I nuzzled his neck as his wife would, then bit down and let the warm, invigorating blood wash into my mouth. Some time later, Theron pulled me back. He shook his finger at me. "Not too much or he will die and you will be sick."

I nodded, having no desire to kill the sailor. I wanted him to go home to his wife.

He lowered the other sailor to his knees, then bit into his neck. He drank for a moment, then released him. "There is more at work here than morality," he explained as he pulled the sailor into the shadows. "Killing too many will arouse suspicion. They would hunt us down and kill us."

"I thought you said we are immortal."

He nodded and indicated that I should pull my sailor into the shadows as well. I found the large man was far easier to move than I would have guessed. "Our lives are very long," he said. "I was born in a land called Sumer centuries ago. I traveled to Egypt during the time of the Pharaohs. However, as with men, our lives can be cut short."

Satisfied with the placement of the sailors, Theron turned and walked uphill toward his house. I followed close behind. "I see we are very strong," I noted.

"Indeed. It is necessary when you are a hunter, as we have become."

"Your strength is so great you should have bested me when I tripped you the day before yesterday." My tongue played over my fangs for a moment. "How could I have defeated you so easily?"

He caught his breath momentarily, then inclined his head. "I wanted you to defeat me." Perhaps there was some truth in that, but I sensed it was not a complete truth.

"Yesterday, you said we could not be awake during the day," I pressed.

"I said we could not walk in sunlight," he corrected. "However, you will find that for a time, you will not be awake during the day."

"Then, how were you awake during the day?"

He pursed his lips. "As you grow older, you will occasionally rise before sunset. It allows you to protect yourself. Even then, you will not be able to go outside."

"What would happen?" I asked.

"Sunlight burns us greatly." He held his hand up by his cheek, indicating his pale skin. "We will die."

I nodded and sighed. The prospect of never feeling the sunlight on my skin again was, indeed, a curse. We walked for a time in silence and I began to understand how I defeated Theron. I was a strong human because of my years on the farm and he was weakened because the sun had not yet set. I looked at his lithe movements, then down at my own arms. Now that I had been transformed into a lamia or a gorgon, I wondered if I was actually stronger than him.

Another question came to my mind. "If we can survive in the manner you just showed me, why do you feed on your slaves?"

"Feeding on the streets is dangerous. There is always a chance you may be caught." Again, I felt like Theron was telling me only a partial truth.

We walked in silence for several steps while I formed my next question carefully, hoping I would neither anger him nor give him room to evade the question. "Why is it necessary to punish your slaves when you feed on them?"

He smiled. "It is not necessary," he admitted after a moment. We walked for several more steps and I sensed he was considering his words as carefully as I had considered mine. "The appearance of punishment is prudent. It camouflages the bite marks, which would be suspicious alone."

"Because bite marks alone would appear to be abuse." Bile rose to the back of my throat even as I said the words.

"Abuse or vermin in the household." He nodded. "Either would prompt authorities to ask questions."

I remained uneasy, as though he still held something back. "There is more to it, isn't there?"

"Did you feel it with the sailors, the thrill of the hunt?" He turned toward me and even though it was dark, I saw a gleam in his eyes. "That thrill diminishes if hunting is too easy. I have found a way to put the thrill back in the hunt."

I shivered, even though the night air was not really cold. "You find whipping your slaves ... entertaining?" I lifted my eyebrows.

"Are you familiar with cats?" I shook my head and he continued. "Some of the nobility kept cats in Egypt. They would play with their food before they ate it. It was instinct for them. I'm afraid it is instinct for us as well."

I frowned. I spent enough time on the farm to know that slaughtering an animal was sometimes necessary for survival. Perhaps it was occasionally necessary for our kind to slaughter humans in much the same way. However, I never felt the need to toy with an animal before I slaughtered it for food.

At last, we reached Theron's house. He held the gate open for me and we entered. "May I draw a bath for you?" he offered.

"Thank you. That would be lovely." Though troubled by Theron's words, I was touched by the gesture and I could use some time alone with my thoughts. "May I stay out here while you draw the bath and look at the stars?"

He nodded. "Absolutely."

I watched as he strode back toward his rooms. After he was out of sight, I made my way into the slaves' rooms and entered the men's sleeping quarters. Finding Kallius, I pulled back his blanket slightly and brushed his hair from his forehead. I had not lied when I told Theron that I did not love him. However, he was human and I cared for him a great deal. I kissed him lightly and silently vowed that I would not allow him to be used as an "entertainment."

In spite of the tension that came between us the night we hunted the sailors, the following weeks were pleasant enough. Theron instructed me in the way of the gorgons, as he referred to us, and when I hungered, we would go out into the streets to hunt. My ability to sense the thoughts of others and bend them to my will improved. I also sensed that I grew stronger. I could climb up walls using finger- and toeholds that would have been too small for me to use before I was transformed. I could blend into the shadows and become virtually invisible. With no need to breathe, I didn't give myself away.

Theron had slowly built up his wealth over the centuries and was a banker because he enjoyed his luxuries. However, I was growing restless and found myself desiring to move on. As my abilities grew, I sensed a path that would allow me to support myself. Also, much as I was loath to admit it to myself, I did find myself reveling in the hunt. Unfortunately, Theron sensed this and two months after he turned me into a gorgon, he instructed Democritus to bring a slave to attend us for the night.

When I awoke, I entered the central room to find a fire going. Kallius was bound with leather straps to the iron rings on the great wooden table. Theron stood beside him, stroking his hair, calming him as a farmer might calm an animal before the slaughter. He looked up after a moment and smiled. "I have brought you a gift. You have been doing so well in our evening forays, that I thought you would enjoy dining in tonight."

I shook my head. "Please, don't do this."

"I know you well enough to know that once you get the scent of blood, you will be delighted to join in." He uncoiled the whip and struck Kallius, then struck him again.

"Please stop," I implored.

Theron's eyes went wide. He was already caught up in the blood lust and delighted in watching Kallius squirm. I quickly cast about for some way to stop the unnecessary savagery. I may have enjoyed the thrill of the hunt, but I could not condone the beating of a helpless man. I lashed out and grabbed the arm with the whip.

"What do you think you're doing, girl!" Enraged, Theron spun around and shoved me. It was clear that I had underestimated his strength. I fell in a heap next to the fireplace. Theron struck me with the whip, ripping my peplos and causing blood to rise on my naked breast. "How dare you attack your master?" he called. "I'll teach you manners!" He struck me again.

No longer under Theron's control, Kallius cried out and began to struggle against the leather straps that secured him in place. Theron lashed out with the whip again. However, this time he missed, and he knocked over the stokers next to the fireplace. One of them fell near my hand. I grabbed the stoker and stood. As he reared back to strike me with the whip again, I lunged forward and drove the stoker through his heart. The whip fell out of his hand and he dropped to the floor. He looked up at me with wide eyes.

I couldn't believe what I had done. "Master, forgive me," I said. "I only meant to stop you."

A rasping, rattling chuckle came forth. "After all these centuries, a new experience. The fates have cut my thread of life and I will see Anubis at last."

I knelt down beside him. "Theron, I'm sorry."

"Don't be, Alexandra," he said. He reached out and wiped a tear from my cheek. "Life has gone on long enough. It will be interesting to see what comes after."

His hand fell to his side and he closed his eyes.

"Alexandra," called Kallius. "What happened?"

I stood, untied Kallius and helped him to stand. "It's over," I said. "The master is dead."

He looked frightened as he moved around the table. Several emotions played across his face. I led him out of the room and through the secret door. We embraced and finally, he looked down into my eyes. We kissed and as his tongue sought mine, he recoiled, his eyes wide. "You're like the master, aren't you?"

I nodded. "In some ways, but not in others."

Kallius continued to hold me and I held on even tighter. "Does this mean you're our master, now?"

I looked around at Theron's house and thought about the responsibilities that go with tending slaves and property. It occurred to me that Theron was as much a slave as we were. That was the last thing I wanted. Even if I did want it, Greek law would not be kind to a concubine who murdered her master. "I am a criminal," I said. "I would be killed if I admitted to my crime. Seek out Democritus and tell him what happened. He will believe you. He knows you could not have escaped on your own."

"What will you do?" There was genuine concern in Kallius's eyes.

"I must flee and find my own way." I pulled Kallius close and the two of us kissed long and deep. I could taste the blood as he nicked his tongue on my fang and I knew it was time to go before I hurt my dear Kallius. Gently, I released myself from his grip and stepped out of the courtyard. I took one last look over my shoulder, then crept quietly past Democritus's quarters and out into the streets of Athens.

Interlude 1
Joseph of Arimathea

The year 32, in Saxony:

A group of carts wound their way along a Roman road – really more of a trail – that cut a swath through dense forest in the barbarous lands of Germania. One man huddled in the back of a cart, pulling a wrap around him to stem the encroaching evening chill. Already he missed the sunshine of Judea, his homeland. With a sigh, he looked down at a chest that contained two precious items he had been charged with keeping safe. He thought of the man those items had belonged to, who died so cruelly at the hands of the Romans. Joseph of Arimathea had not known the rabbi Jesus of Nazareth very well before the crucifixion, but he had known the teacher well enough to know that he had been a special man who did not deserve the death sentence imposed upon him. As such, he had offered his tomb to the rabbi's body so it could be laid to rest before Passover. Since that time, he had been caught up in a series of events that now propelled him toward the farthest corner of Roman influence – the island of Albion.

Looking skyward, Joseph caught sight of an eagle flying above them. The eagle started flying overhead soon after he joined the caravan in the north of Rome. It scanned the forest, apparently hunting for mice and other small prey. At first, Joseph thought it had tagged along to scavenge from the tiny caravan, but it never seemed to prey on the trash the humans left behind. At some point, Joseph assumed that the eagle would turn southward, to return to warmer climes as he wanted to. However, the eagle continued to follow the caravan.

As the shadows grew long, the caravan came to a halt. Joseph covered the chest with a canvas tarp and hopped from the cart to help gather firewood. The eagle lit on the cart's side, seemed to examine the tarp-covered chest, then closed its eyes.

The caravan's guide was a retired Roman centurion named Gaius who had served in Albion and claimed to know the route from Rome to the island well. Joseph had been delighted that the ancient warrior was more interested in Joseph's money than the politics of Judea. "I don't blame you for wanting to get away," the centurion had said. "Albion is sure to be a lot quieter than Judea, what with the Jewish uprisings. I've heard they have a new … what do they call it? … a new Messiah practically every day."

Joseph had pursed his lips at the time and remained silent, even though he began to believe what many whispered before he left – that his rabbi, Jesus of Nazareth, was in fact the one true Messiah. Even many of Jesus's closest followers had been afraid to admit their belief in the days and weeks following the crucifixion. Joseph himself was not a close follower, though he admired the man very much.

At last, Gaius had the fire started. Two women set up cooking pots and began assembling a pottage and flavored it with meat and cheese. The men gathered around the fire and started rubbing their hands and holding them toward the heat as fog began to descend.

"What miserable weather," grumbled Joseph.

"It don't get much better where you're goin'," laughed Gaius. "You'd better get used to it."

"I thought you said that Albion was a pleasant land," said Joseph, raising an eyebrow.

"Oh, it's temperate enough, sir," said the retired centurion. "And the people are nice – as long as you don't wander too far west or north."

"Is it true what they say about the Picts in the North?" asked a man who was traveling to Gaul. "Do they paint themselves blue and fight like demons?"

"Aye, they do," said Gaius. "I was in a few fights near the Caledonian border and I never want to go back."

The group fell into silence as the women finished the pottage. They ladled it into bowls and passed it around. Before scooping the pottage into his mouth, Joseph simply sat and held the bowl, letting the warmth permeate his fingers. Finally, he delved into his meal and let it warm him from the inside out.

As they ate, the fire grew dim. One of the men stood to retrieve more wood, but stopped short, when something moved in the forest. Joseph looked up and noticed that the eagle had opened its eyes and followed the man's gaze.

"What is it?" asked Joseph but the other men quickly shushed him into silence.

Gaius stood slowly and crept toward his own cart where he retrieved a bow. He nocked an arrow and aimed at something moving in the forest. Joseph thought he caught sight of gray fur – possibly a wolf circling around the campsite. After a moment, the figure emerged from the trees and Joseph breathed a sigh of relief when he realized that it was not a wolf, but a pale man wearing a wolf's skin. Gaius kept his arrow aimed at the stranger.

The stranger spoke in a language that Joseph didn't recognize – presumably one of the Germanic languages. Gaius spoke a few tentative, halting phrases at the man and the man replied. At which point, Gaius lowered the bow and arrow and put his head back and laughed. "We do find ourselves joined by a wolf," explained the centurion. "For that is this man's name: Wolf." He stepped closer to the fire. "He wishes to warm himself He says he is alone."

The people around the campfire nodded assent and men beckoned for the man Wolf to join them.

"What say you, Master Joseph?" asked Gaius, returning to the fire.

Joseph opened his mouth to answer, then looked up to see the eagle staring at him. Something in the bird's gaze told him that he should object to the man called Wolf's company. Joseph shuddered, then shook away the feeling, thinking he was beginning to hallucinate. He forced a smile. "Please, join us," invited Joseph.

The man said something and for just a moment, Joseph thought he heard the phrase, "Thank you very much," in perfect Aramaic. The circle opened next to Joseph and the stranger sat. Joseph of Arimathea shuddered in spite of himself, feeling waves of cold from the man called Wolf.

A woman offered pottage to the stranger. He waved her offer away, simply preferring to warm his hands by the fire, although he did take a goblet of wine when it was offered.

"So, Master Joseph, what is it you carry in that chest you guard so closely?" asked Gaius as he sipped his own goblet of wine. "Is it gold or jewels? Perhaps that is why you are reluctant to let a lone stranger share our fire."

Joseph's cheeks warmed, partly from embarrassment and partly from the wine he, himself, consumed. "No," he said, shaking his head. "It is nothing more than a cup, much like this one," he said holding up the goblet, "and a scroll written by a teacher from the village of Nazareth."

"That must be some scroll for you to guard it so closely," said the man traveling to Gaul. "What is it, a map to buried treasure?"

"Or perhaps the secret to life eternal," joked Gaius.

Wolf looked up suddenly at the caravan leader and said something in his native language.

Gaius shook his head rapidly, smiled and then said something in response. "He says that life eternal is not a blessing, but a curse. I told him that it depends on who you spend it with." Gaius put down his goblet and patted the rump of a passing woman. She rolled her eyes and continued on.

"You may be closer to the truth of what's in that box than you think," muttered Joseph under his breath. He took a sip of the wine, then looked up. "My teacher brought good news about our God – that he is a God of Love and forgives us our trespasses." All but one of the men around the fire laughed. Joseph looked up and found Wolf staring at him intently with ice-blue eyes. For a few moments, Joseph felt the campfire fall away. His feet pounded the ground as he ran through the woods, alone, looking for prey. Through strange eyes, he saw himself falling upon a woman, then an old man. He sank his teeth into their necks and drew the blood from them. He found a question floating in his mind as a dead child fell from his arms: *Would your god forgive me that?*

Joseph swallowed hard as he blinked and realized he had not moved from his seat by the fire. Gaius said something about Jews and their God that couldn't keep them from slavery at the hands of Romans, Egyptians and others. Joseph remembered that horrible moment when he pulled the broken and bloody body of Jesus from a Roman crucifix then placed it in the tomb. He remembered the moment three days later when Mary of Magdala told him that the body was no longer in the tomb. He was certain that grave robbers had stolen the body, but in the following days, he grew far less certain. *Yes,* thought Joseph, *my God has the power to forgive, if you have the power to believe.*

When Joseph looked up at the fire again, he realized the men and women were pulling out their bedrolls. Wolf still stared at Joseph. Forcing his eyes away, Joseph drained the rest of his wine, stood shakily and went to his cart to retrieve his own bedroll.

Joseph awoke a few hours later. The fog had lifted and wan moonlight filtered through the trees. He rolled over to go back to sleep when a branch snapped. Sitting upright, Joseph saw Wolf standing near his cart. He pushed the blankets aside, prepared to stop the stranger when the eagle spread its wings. At first, Joseph thought the eagle would fly away, startled by the stranger's approach. Instead it leapt forward and began to glow. The eagle transformed into the figure of a man with feathers on its head instead of hair and landed between Wolf and the cart. "The contents of that chest are not for you, Blutsauger. Be gone!"

"What are you?" asked Wolf, squinting his eyes against the golden light emanating from the man that had been an eagle.

"I am an angel of the Lord, sent to see this chest safely to its home in Albion." Without further warning, the angel drew a sword and swung it in a perfect arc sending a spray of blood from Wolf's chest. The stranger howled much like a real wolf, then turned and ran toward the forest. As he did, he seemed to fold and crumple, falling onto all fours. Joseph of Arimathea was convinced that he saw a real wolf loping away amongst the trees. When he looked back at the cart, the angel had vanished. The eagle sat perched on the cart's wheel. Joseph of Arimathea fainted.

Part II
The Dragon's Quest

Chapter 7

May of the year 480, on the River Bassus:

A tall, thin man stood atop a grassy knoll and surveyed the surrounding countryside. His hair was cut uncharacteristically short – more like the hair of the few remaining Romans in the land than the long plaits of his fellow Britons. In his experience, Roman soldiers were wise to crop their hair. It gave enemies less to grab onto in close fighting. At birth, the man had been named Aonghas Deas-Mhumhan. The name Deas-Mhumhan came from his father, an Irishman from Munster. Aonghas came from his mother who named him for the Celtic god of choice because she, herself, had faced a choice early in life. Though she was betrothed to a minor, but wealthy, Roman land holder, she chose to marry the man she loved – the wild Irishman who had left his homeland to settle in Western Britain for reasons he rarely discussed.

The man on the knoll turned and studied a nearby encampment. Cooking fires were starting and the men and women quietly went about the business of settling in for the evening. The people of the encampment had come to know the man – who at that time was just short of forty years old – as Deas-Mhumhan Dragwn or Desmond the Dragon. The British title, Dragwn, was reserved for warriors who had earned respect from the people and power in the court of Duke Ambrosius Aurelianus, the Roman administrator of the Isle of Britain. Rome, however, was so distant and its power in such decline that Ambrosius was virtually a king. Ambrosius was an effective leader and had done his best to maintain order in Britain, in turn earning the respect of the Dragons.

The sound of drums heralded another group's approach. Shielding his eyes against the light of the setting sun, Desmond saw men on horseback and soldiers marching along the River Bassus. He shook his head at the disorderly line.

A man with long, raven hair and a shaggy black beard streaked with gray ran up the knoll toward Desmond. "I see you've heard the approach of Arthur's party," said Bran, Desmond's friend and closest advisor.

"How could anyone miss the roar of the mighty bear?" said Desmond. His lip curled up with just a hint of amusement and sarcasm. The name Arthur literally meant 'bear' in old Welsh.

"That 'mighty bear' – Arthur Dragwn – has led his men to five major victories in our Duke's name." Bran turned to look at the approaching men. "He inspires loyalty in his people and they fight fiercely by his side."

"The way he throws people at his enemies it's a wonder there are enough left to carry the dead and wounded away from the battle," said Desmond bitterly. "Still he manages to find more men to replace those who've died under his command."

"He's popular." Bran shrugged. "He's also your friend."

"Perhaps it's because he's my friend that I'm so critical. I do not want to see him hurt." Desmond faced the ground. "He tends to indulge his excesses unwisely. His sister, Morgana, is his lover, after all."

Bran shook his head. "You know as well as I do that Morgana is not really Arthur's sister. They only say they're brother and sister to bypass the Duke's decree that warriors should not marry."

Desmond snorted. "There is wisdom in the old Roman laws. A war leader cannot be distracted by the pleasures of the flesh."

"I'm glad to hear that," said Bran with a smirk, "especially since I share a tent with you."

"I would have no company but yours, my friend."

Bran's smile fell for a moment as Desmond's gaze remained a little too fixed for comfort. Suddenly Bran threw his head back and laughed. "You had me going there for a moment. I was beginning to think that maybe you really did favor men over women folk."

Desmond's smirk returned for just a moment. He reached out and tugged Bran's shaggy beard. "I'm afraid you have too much hair in the wrong places for my pleasure, my friend." Briefly, the face of a beautiful woman – the Duke's eldest daughter Guinevere – came to his mind. The war leader patted his advisor on the arm and started down the knoll toward the encampment. "Come, we need to prepare for the war council. Arthur and his 'sister' will be here before long and we have much to plan."

Ambrosius had sent Desmond and Arthur up the River Bassus to quell an uprising by a Pictish war leader called Caw. The Picts had long resisted Roman rule of Britain and it was apparent that Roman power was in decline as Saxon settlements began springing up on the island. Ambrosius had made a vow to rid the island of Saxon invaders and Caw saw the opportunity to lead a successful insurgency. He had already led demoralizing raids south of Hadrian's Wall into the villages of Luguvalium and Corstopitum. Desmond and Arthur were ordered to end the insurgency as quickly as possible.

Within Desmond's pavilion, hay bales had been set out in a crude semi-circle, like the Roman 'omega' couches, and covered with blankets. Desmond sat with his hands on his knees, waiting. On one side of him was Bran. On the other side was his seneschal, Cynddylig. Desmond watched as three people clad in chest plates, ring mail and plaid trousers, approached the pavilion. Arthur, with hair cut short like Desmond's, was unmistakable even from a distance. The man radiated charisma. He carried a shield on his arm with the image of a god-like woman: Mary, mother of the Christian god, Jesus. Desmond knew little of the Christian faith, which was just making itself known in Britain, but he knew many of Arthur's people were followers. Next to Arthur was a powerful woman with long, black hair. She was his constant companion, Morgana. The red-headed giant of a man who followed behind them was Kai, Arthur's own seneschal and mentor. As Arthur ducked into the pavilion and set his shield down, Desmond stood. The two clasped arms. "It is good to see you again," said Arthur with a genuinely charming smile.

"And you, as well," replied Desmond, businesslike. He indicated the hay bales and the group sat. Desmond's seneschal retrieved goblets and poured water into them.

"Nothing better for your guests?" chided Arthur. "It has been a long journey. Wine would be welcome right now."

"You know I don't drink wine while discussing strategy. There will be enough time for celebration after the battle." Desmond raised his goblet and then drank.

Arthur grinned and followed suit. Lowering the goblet, he smacked his lips. "So, where is the villain Caw holed up?"

"According to my scouts—" Desmond gave a brief nod to Cynddylig, also known as 'the guide' "—he's assembling his forces just outside the village of Cambuslang. He does not yet have great numbers." Desmond picked up a stick and began drawing in the mud at the center of the circle. He showed the River Bassus and the location of the town, then he drew the location of Caw's camp and indicated a nearby forest and several nearby hills. "I believe with a small force we can sneak through the forest and get close enough that I can put an arrow right through Caw's heart. Without a leader, the Pictish rebellion will fail."

"You would make a martyr of him?" Morgana's voice seemed far away. Though Desmond knew her, he looked at her as though for the first time. Her arms were well muscled and there was a scar on her chin. She had seen many battles but still, somehow, seemed quite fay as she looked off into the distance and contemplated Desmond's plan of action.

"I'm afraid she may be right," said Bran. "Lord Desmond, I agree we must assure Caw's death, but his army must be dealt a firm defeat or his generals will regroup and attack again."

As Desmond turned to face Bran, Arthur took the stick and pointed to the map. "I must agree with Morgana and Bran. I think it would be better if we treat this as a two-pronged attack. Your men should come through the forest as you suggest and focus your attack on Caw himself." Arthur pointed to the nearby hills. "My men will come in by this route. Doing so, we will cut off the Picts' escape and we will have them surrounded."

"Except by the river." Kai stroked his thick, red beard. "They can still escape down the valley."

Desmond pursed his lips and studied the map. "I can't bring most of my men through the forest with me. They'll be bogged down and make too much noise. The Picts will know we're coming." He took the stick back from Arthur. "But, I can place most of my men here." He indicated a position south of Cambuslang. "That will block their escape down the valley."

Arthur reached for his goblet. "In spite of your lack of hospitality and good wine," he said, "this is why I enjoy fighting by your side. You are a good planner." His pleasant smile returned and he lifted his goblet and took a long draught. Sitting the goblet down, he looked first to Morgana, then to Kai. "I believe we should return to camp. We have a big day tomorrow."

"I will set out when twilight first brightens the sky," said Desmond.

"And we shall position ourselves as the sun is coming up over the horizon. That should give you enough time to strike," affirmed Arthur as he stood. With that, Morgana stood and moved to Arthur's side. Kai stepped from the pavilion first, followed by Arthur who paused to retrieve his shield, and then Morgana.

Desmond retrieved his own goblet and drank greedily. Sitting the goblet down, he looked to Bran. "Spread the word among the men. Let them know where to position themselves in the morning. Then, it will be time to turn in for the night."

"It does seem a sound plan, my lord," said Bran with a confident smile.

"A good plan … as long as Arthur does as he says, when he says."

"You sound as though you don't trust him." Bran looked at Desmond with eyebrows raised.

Desmond shook his head. "No, it's not that. Arthur is fiercely loyal to Ambrosius…. It's just that he's like his namesake – a bear, big and clumsy. I only worry that there will be more bloodshed than necessary tomorrow."

Bran smiled reassuringly. "I think all warlords fear that the night before a battle."

"Perhaps." Desmond sighed, then moved over to the bedroll, laid out by Cynddylig. The guide had already left for his own tent, so he would be ready to lead Desmond through the dark forest before the sun rose.

Desmond tossed and turned that night as he thought about the next day's battle. Cynddylig had given him a careful and thorough description of Caw from the times he'd scouted the Pictish camp. Not only that, the guide would accompany him into the enemy's territory. Still, Desmond feared killing the wrong person. Even that wasn't the warlord's worst fear. There was always the chance that Caw's men would sense trouble long before Desmond attacked and put a barrier around their leader. In addition to his concerns about the battle itself, he continued to see Guinevere's face in his mind. More than anything, he did not want to fail and disappoint her. These worries plagued Desmond until he fell into a fitful slumber.

It felt as though he'd only just fallen asleep when Bran nudged him awake. Desmond rubbed his eyes and, still dressed in his trousers and jerkin, crawled out from between his blankets. He yelped slightly as his feet touched the nearly frozen ground. He felt around in the dark for his boots and pulled them on. Cynddylig brought his armor and helped the warlord fasten it on. As Desmond donned his helm, Bran handed him a loaf of bread and some cheese. "Our men are standing by," explained Bran. "Three of our best warriors will accompany you, me, and Cynddylig. The rest will block the Picts from escaping down the river."

"Very good." Desmond bit off a chunk of bread. He reached over and found a goblet. He shivered as he took a drink of the icy water, then bit into a small block of cheese. Still holding the cheese and the goblet, he stepped out from under the pavilion and examined the sky. The cloud cover kept him from seeing any stars, and it was still quite dark. They would be setting out with torches – which would be fine – the trees of the forest would obscure their approach from the Picts. He took another bite of the cheese and swallowed some more water. His nervous stomach rumbled a slight protest, so he took the remains to the pavilion and left them behind. "It is time," said Desmond to Bran and Cynddylig.

They joined three other men, then set out from the encampment. There was just enough light that, out in the open, they could walk along the riverbank, parallel to the tree line without torches. After marching for approximately two miles, Cynddylig made a silent gesture and they ducked within the trees. The men brought out torches and lit them with flints from their satchels. Desmond looked up through the trees. The sky was already lightening. His stomach rumbled as he worried that the cloudy skies kept the nightwatch from rousing them early enough.

Setting his nervousness aside, Desmond followed Cynddylig as he led them through the forest. He did his best not to step on twigs that might cause Caw's lookouts to raise an alarm. At last, Desmond and his men came to a place where they could look down on Caw's encampment. Cynddylig pointed out Caw's pavilion and showed him several routes to it. The guide also pointed out the guards that stood around the perimeter of Caw's camp. Desmond studied their placement, then pointed to one that stood near the forest. "He's visible to the others, but I think we can pull him into the forest before anyone sees and makes a run for the camp."

"Agreed," said Bran studying the situation.

Desmond looked out at the sky and frowned. The gray clouds brightened, but he guessed they still had time before the sun actually rose. Desmond ordered the torches extinguished and the men moved toward their target's position.

Bran and the three soldiers quickly darted out of the forest, grabbed the Pictish guard and pulled him into the woods where they quietly slit his throat. Desmond looked around a tree and saw no sign that an alarm had yet been raised. "Cynddylig, you come with me. The rest of you stay here," he whispered. "Don't follow unless those guards start pursuing us. I want to catch Caw as he break's fast...or even better while he still slumbers."

Cynddylig and Desmond broke from the trees and sprinted for Caw's camp. Just as they passed the first tent, Desmond's ears caught the sound of drums. "Damn," he growled. "Arthur's early."

The perimeter guards began shouting. Cynddylig grabbed Desmond's arm and led him through the camp. Pictish warriors emerged from their tents, bleary-eyed, but neither the guide nor the warlord stopped. As the Picts realized they were under attack, they darted back into their tents to retrieve their weapons and armor, clearing the path for Desmond.

They came to the central pavilion. Desmond retrieved his bow and nocked an arrow. Within, several men donned armor. Others smeared blue paint onto their faces. The Dragon pursed his lips and tried to decide which bearded warrior was his target. "Caw!" he yelled. Several of the men looked up at him. Desmond rolled his eyes, but then realized that one particularly large man stood bare-chested with a stick in his hand. He had been drawing in the mud of the pavilion. He was the leader. The Dragon took aim and let the arrow fly. The big man went down with the arrow in his heart. Some in the tent rushed to their leader's side. Others went for their own bows. Desmond smiled, dropped the bow, then turned and ran, drawing his short sword as he did.

Cynddylig followed as soon as Desmond passed him. Arrows began raining down on the camp. Desmond looked to his left. The arrows weren't coming from behind. Rather, they were raining down from outside the camp. Again, the Dragon swore as he realized that Arthur's men were already attacking. Several Pictish soldiers rushed by Desmond and Cynddylig, not paying them any mind as they ran past. "We've got to get back to the forest as quickly as possible," said Desmond.

"Toward the river would be best," said Cynddylig looking around and assessing how the Picts were forming up against the Britons. "It'll put us out of the line of fire. Once we're out of the camp, we can make for the tree line and meet up with Bran and the others."

Without further comment, Desmond nodded. They ran

toward the river. One man that Desmond thought he recognized from Caw's pavilion reached out and tried to grab the warlord's arm. Desmond swung the sword and smacked the man in the head with the flat of the blade. The man, though not mortally wounded, went down. Cynddylig and Desmond kept running.

They emerged from among the tents of Caw's encampment and saw Arthur's battle line. Caw's generals struggled to form their own men into lines. Desmond picked out several cries in Pictish, the general sense of which were confusion over Caw's location. Some men openly broke ranks. Absorbed as he was by the action, Desmond nearly ran headlong into a woman carrying a crying boy and leading a stunned girl by the hand. The warlord noticed they were attempting to make their escape down the river toward his own men.

"Woman," he called in Pictish. "Flee the other direction. Go to Cambuslang. You will be safe there." He wasn't fluent, but he thought he made himself understood.

She looked at him with wide eyes. "You are Briton. Why should I trust you?"

"You are a woman and you have children. I mean you no harm," said Desmond.

She nodded and turned. "Come along Cwyllog," she said to the girl. "Hush, Gildas," she said to the boy. "You will have to walk. Mommy can't carry you anymore." Desmond watched as they retreated back through the camp. Briefly, he thought of Guinevere and hoped she was well.

Cynddylig took Desmond's elbow and led him toward the forest. "You realize that was Caw's woman. Those were his whelps."

"What would you have me do?" asked Desmond, his eyes ablaze. "Cut them down in cold blood?"

"Didn't you kill Caw in cold blood?" asked the guide.

"That was different," muttered Desmond as he turned and sprinted toward the woods.

That night, Arthur, Morgana and Kai once again sat in Desmond's pavilion. This time, Desmond brought out his wine. Arthur raised a toast, "To the man who brought us a swift victory. You will be known as the hero of the River Bassus."

Bran and Cynddylig raised their goblets as well. Desmond looked to the ground, his cheeks flushed. At last, he looked up, nodded, and all drank. Kai refilled their glasses and the smells from the cooking fires wafted into the tent. Desmond's stomach flipped again as he contemplated the battles that lay ahead. How long would it be before he could settle down and claim his destiny and the woman he loved?

Chapter 8

September of the year 480.
In the Great Hall of Ambrosius:

The Great Hall of Ambrosius resembled few known structures in the Celtic world. It was a massive building made from timbers, similar to the tent-pavilions of field commanders but more permanent. Admittedly it lacked the splendor of buildings back in Rome, but it was the biggest structure that could be built with the materials, artisans, and craftsmen available in Britain. Although Ambrosius was a Roman, he had been born in Britain and had never seen the land of his forefathers. To him, the hall was just as splendid as it was to the Britons who followed him.

The sounds of raucous laughter and shouting voices along with the aromas of roasted pig, freshly baked bread and luscious honey mead filled the hall. Duke Ambrosius sat at the head table, joined by Arthur whose company he enjoyed, and the druid Myrdden whose advice he valued. The Duke smiled fondly at the sight of all his loyal friends and warriors filling the hall. He held the feast to celebrate the fall harvest and the recent victories of his Dragons. The Duke nodded to Desmond, who sat at a nearby table, scratching the ear of a dog. His goblet of mead sat virtually untouched. Ambrosius frowned and leaned over to Arthur. "Is Desmond well?" he asked with a note of genuine concern.

Arthur looked to where his friend sat in silence. Turning to Ambrosius, he smiled. "He is well as ever, my lord. He is often quiet like that. I suspect he is making plans and strategies, even now."

"Ah, yes," said Ambrosius, amicably. "I gather he was of great assistance to you in your defeat of Caw in the spring."

Arthur shifted nervously in his chair. "I could not have won that battle without him, my lord."

"It is of battles that I wish to speak," said Ambrosius, stroking his long, graying beard. "Several villages have been plagued by Saxon pirate raids. My most trusted scouts believe they have located their harbor – in Caledonia." The Duke cast a meaningful glance at two soldiers standing near the door wearing Roman helms and armor, but draped with Celtic plaid.

Arthur frowned deeply. "That's far to the north, in lands controlled by the Picts. I don't think any of us could march all the way there."

"No," agreed Ambrosius. "I need someone who has seafaring skills to sail up there and deal with that settlement."

Arthur the Dragon reached out, grabbed his goblet, and then took a sip of mead. "I can have *Prydwen* ready to sail in a week's time my lord."

"Winter is coming on," cautioned Ambrosius. "The seas will be getting rough."

Arthur nodded slowly and set the goblet down. "The pirates will be returning to port. It will be easier to destroy all of their ships in a single raid." He reached down and hefted a pork shank. "I'd better eat," he said, his jovial smile returning. "I'll need my strength if I have a sea voyage ahead."

Myrddin cleared his throat. "The pirates are supported by a base farther inland at Cat Coit Celidon. Desmond has shown great prowess in such fighting. Perhaps it would be wise for Arthur to bring Desmond's men along and deposit them south of the pirate's port so they can march inward and cut off the supplies at the source."

Ambrosius smiled and clasped his friend on the arm. "You are wise. We will make it so."

A tall woman with golden hair and a thin, aquiline nose moved through the bustle of the great hall and sat down on the bench next to Desmond. She was draped in fine linen, imported from Rome. No one could miss Ambrosius's daughter, Guinevere. Desmond smiled at her, then slipped a scrap from his plate to the dog under the table and patted it on the side. He turned to face her. "I was hoping I would get to see you," he said.

She set her hand upon his wrist – as much as she dare do in the crowded hall – and looked at the Dragon's plate and his goblet. She frowned. "You've hardly touched your food. Are you well?"

"Well enough," said Desmond with a ghost of a smile. "You know me, I'm happier with the quiet of the meadow than the boisterousness of the feast hall."

"And happier still in the heat of battle than in times of peace."

Desmond snorted. "No, it's not that." He looked around. Two young men wrestled in the front of the hall, each trying to win favor in the eyes of Ambrosius and Arthur. In a corner, a bard strummed a harp, preparing to tell a story to those gathered. "No, I almost envy the bards and their ability to collect and retell stories."

Guinevere squeezed Desmond's wrist. "You would grow bored doing nothing but collecting tales of battles won and lost."

"They also tell of how the gods created the earth and man." He turned and looked her in the eye. "Have you never wondered if there was more to those legends? Have you never wondered about the world beyond Britain?"

Guinevere laughed lightly. "You worry about things beyond your control, Desmond." She looked up at the head table. "You should worry why it is that Arthur sits next to Ambrosius and not you. You're the one that brought about the victory at Bassus, not Arthur. You are the one that preserves the Roman ways, not Arthur. You're the one who possesses knowledge, not..."

"Yes," said Desmond dismissively, "but Arthur is a genial man, as is Ambrosius. Myrddin is the power behind the Duke."

"That may be true, but I fear my father may choose a husband for me and he may choose Arthur and not you."

Desmond frowned. "What do you suppose Arthur and your

father are speaking about?" He reached out and took his goblet. "Do you know?"

"That doesn't matter. What matters is where I'm going." Guinevere stood from the table and casually stepped toward the door of the great hall. A few minutes later, Desmond looked around and then followed her outside.

With the celebration going on inside, the tents surrounding the great hall were nearly deserted. Desmond strode to his own tent, unobserved. Opening the flap, he found Guinevere reclining on his blankets. The Dragon Lord retrieved a bottle of wine and two goblets. Sitting down next to Guinevere, he filled the goblets and handed one to her. She drank while gazing into his eyes.

Without a word, Desmond sat the goblet down and took Guinevere into his arms. His hand found its way inside the linen of her dress and sought out the supple curve of her breast. She arched her back, welcoming his caress. They kissed, their tongues intertwining.

She undid the leather belt holding his pants and helped him remove them. He groaned as she took his cock in her hands and stroked it lovingly. With a look that was almost one of regret he moved back and lifted her fine, linen peplos. She wore no undergarments and he bent down and tasted her moisture-laden folds, then moved up and kissed her belly. She opened the top of her dress and he suckled her breast as she took his manhood and guided him inside her. She matched his thrusts and moaned with unrestrained pleasure as she reached climax. He kissed her as his seed spilled into her.

Spent and breathing heavily, they lay next to each other. Finally, Desmond looked into Guinevere's eyes and brushed a hair from her forehead. "What would we do if a child came from one of these unions?"

She smiled at him. "I am always careful with the time of the month," she said. "Also, I have brought Myrddin into my confidence. He agrees that you are most fitting to be my husband and my father's successor."

"How can I thank you?"

"With your tongue," said Guinevere slyly. "But please, do not use words this time."

Desmond reached down and stroked the golden triangle of hair between her legs, then set out to properly thank the woman he intended to marry.

A week later, Desmond stood in the bow of a wooden sailing boat, rocked and pitched by the rough coastal waters. Looking to starboard, he could just see the green trees of the British coastline. Ahead, astern and to port, he counted eleven other vessels of similar size. His boat was packed full with sixteen men and their supplies. The ships were bound for Solway Firth. From there, Desmond would march his men farther north to the forest of Cat Coit Celidon. He looked up at darkening skies and worried about the chill air. Once the battle was over, he would march the troops to Luguvalium, just south of Hadrian's Wall for the winter. After stopping the Pictish raids and removing the Saxons, Desmond hoped the people of Luguvalium would be happy to house his people. Though his eighty men would consume supplies, they would also help tend the animals and hunt for game that would extend the village's supplies.

A tall wave struck the boat's side causing it to pitch to starboard. Desmond grabbed onto the boat's rail to keep himself from falling over the side. His stomach lurched and he nearly lost his hastily consumed breakfast of biscuits and salted meat. Normally he had no problems with sea travel, but these rough autumnal waters were making him reconsider. Looking over to the flagship, *Prydwen,* with its red dragon banner streaming in the wind, he could just make out the silhouettes of Arthur and Morgana. He found himself at once missing Guinevere and realizing that she would not be happy on this voyage.

Bran held onto the deck rail with white knuckles as he moved forward along the heaving deck. He stopped next to Desmond and followed his gaze toward *Prydwen*. "So, Arthur is traveling to Caledonia and he is taking us to Cat Coit Celidon. What do you want to bet that the bards merge both of our victories into one and credit it all to Arthur."

"I am not a betting man," said Desmond dryly. He turned and looked at Bran. "You sound confident in our victory."

"I am absolutely confident in *your* victory, my lord. First off, it would not be proper for an advisor to express anything less than confidence in his Dragon. Secondly, we are going to battle in conditions that are perfect for your skills. Cynddylig the Guide can lead you right to our enemies and *you* will lead us to victory."

Desmond chewed his lower lip and looked toward Arthur's ship again. "Then why is it you feel so confident that the bards will remember Arthur over me?"

"Because sea battles always sound more glorious than pitched battles in deep dark forests." Bran then inclined his head and smiled mischievously. "And Arthur has a prettier smile than you."

Desmond snorted and looked back toward the coastline, resuming his thoughts about the approaching battle as Bran laughed aloud and moved back to the boat's stern.

Late that afternoon, the British fleet came to the point where the river Annan emptied into Solway Firth. Two men from each boat hopped out into the shallow, but frigid water and pulled the boats ashore. The waters were sufficiently rough that one boat tipped over sideways spilling men and supplies into the icy waters. Desmond, Bran, and several others launched themselves over the side of the boat to retrieve the precious supplies and help the men ashore.

Fires were started at once and the men changed out of their wet clothes. Rations of smoked fish and dried fruit were passed around. After the harrowing episode in the water, and the morning meal of salted meat and tough biscuits, the afternoon meal was like a fine repast. Desmond found himself sitting under the cover of his pavilion, sharing his meal with Arthur. As he took a bite of dried fruit, Desmond caught sight of Arthur's shield with the image of the Virgin Mary painted on its face. "I thought you were instructed by the druids," he said.

"I was," said Arthur around a bite of smoked fish. "I won the shield in a game of chance." Arthur laughed lightly as though remembering a private joke.

"Then why carry it?" pressed Desmond.

"More and more people on the island follow the teachings of Jesus," said Arthur with a shrug. "Those that don't follow Jesus see Brigiantia, who brought light and knowledge to the Britons. Such a symbol can be very important for a Dragon. Perhaps you should find one of your own." Arthur sat upright, his eyes narrowed. "Why the sudden interest in my shield?"

"My father used to talk about the Christians of Ireland...."

"Did your father follow St. Patrick, then?"

Desmond snorted and shook his head. "I don't think my father followed anyone's religion – the Christians or the Druids. He sought adventure – and women."

"There are those in our ranks as well ... and Mary is a talisman for them as well."

Desmond sighed. His eyelids began to sag and he remembered a summer several years before. He was chosen to serve under a Dragon named Cador, the cousin of Ambrosius Aurelianus himself. While serving and training under Cador, Desmond first met Guinevere. She was the most beautiful girl he had ever seen. The two were little more than teenagers at the time, but still Desmond took her horseback riding and brought her flowers. At a tournament, she gave him a favor – a scented handkerchief that he wore as he fought other warriors. He could remember none of the actual fights, only Guinevere's sweet kiss when he won the tournament and the other favors she gave him years later.

Arthur nudged Desmond. "It looks like you're falling asleep on me." He laughed. "I'd better turn in. You've got a long march the next few days."

Desmond yawned and waved as Arthur retrieved his sword and

shield. He trudged off into the darkness of the camp. Cynddylig spread out Desmond's blankets and the Dragon Lord fell into a sound sleep.

Chapter 9

October of the year 480:

Desmond and his men marched inland for three days until they came to a place where the terrain became rougher and woods were thickened with more evergreens. Marching a little farther, they found a point where a stone bridge crossed the river and a Roman road turned into the forest. They had reached Cat Coit Celidon. The scouts dispersed and found level terrain to set up camp. That night, Desmond conferred with Bran and Cynddylig the Guide. They agreed that Cynddylig and the other scouts should enter the forest to find out where the Saxons were located and determine their numbers.

The next day, Cynddylig and five other scouts set off down the Roman road. At several points, they found spoor indicating people had left the road to go into the forest. Cynddylig sent the scouts to follow several of these trails, then report what they found. The guide himself discovered a footpath so worn that it was virtually a trail leading into the woods. He moved somewhat farther along the Roman road, observing that it continued through a pass between two mountains. He turned off the Roman road and went into the forest, paralleling the trail he'd discovered earlier.

As he moved through the forest, he heard the sound of flowing water and realized he must have come back to the River Annan. He turned and followed the river's course away from Desmond's camp. As he walked, the sound of the water grew louder. Cautiously, he moved closer to the river and saw a magnificent waterfall pouring down the mountainside. Downriver from the waterfall, he caught sight of several wattle and daub huts. He crept back into the forest and continued downriver. Finding a suitable tree, he climbed to a point where he could get a good view of the huts. He counted them and nodded to himself, satisfied. Numerous women and children wandered among the huts. The men must be out hunting. Cautiously, he climbed back down. As his feet touched the soil an arrow caught him in the shoulder and sent him spinning to the ground.

An hour later, one of Cynddylig's scouts saw what appeared to be an unusual log drifting down the river, then become entangled in some reeds. Looking closer, the scout realized the "log" was a man's body. He splashed into the river and looked at the face of the man and realized it was Cynddylig himself. His face was growing blue and an arrow's shaft protruded from his shoulder. The guide still breathed, so the scout quickly pulled him ashore and into the forest, where he covered him with leaves and branches so only his nose and mouth showed, then ran for help.

Within the hour, Bran and Desmond, together with a healer were brought to the spot. Out of the water, Cynddylig's color had improved, but he was pale from blood loss. The healer examined him, then looked at Desmond. "We need to get him back to camp so we can warm him up. Then I can cut the arrow from him."

Desmond and Bran hefted Cynddylig and carried him back to the camp. They set him beside the fire and covered him with furs. The healer felt his forehead and noted that a slight fever had set in. Cynddylig began mumbling. Bran brought him mead and helped him to drink, which in turn caused the guide to fall into a deep slumber.

Later that afternoon, the remaining scouts converged on the camp and reported what they had learned to Desmond. Another scout had fallen, shot through the heart. "The forest is crawling with Saxon hunters," reported one.

"And they know we're here," grumbled Desmond. "I feel their eyes upon us." He asked Bran and the scouts to join him in the pavilion after they had their evening meal. Desmond himself ate only lightly, then stood outside and watched the stars appear. Catching sight of the moon he smiled.

Once Bran and the scouts joined him, Desmond looked at them with his hands behind his back. "We have little choice but to withdraw. Otherwise the Saxons will descend upon us before we are ready to attack."

"Withdraw?" Bran jumped to his feet. "We can't admit defeat now."

"We're not admitting defeat," said Desmond calmly. "We will only withdraw half a day's march down the river. Far enough that the Saxons will think we have retreated. In six days' time, the moon will be at its peak. If the weather holds, we will be able to attack their encampment at night without the aid of torches."

Bran smiled and sat down. Desmond also sat and asked the scouts to relay details about the Saxon encampment. A scream interrupted the reports. It was Cynddylig. The healer had taken the knife to his shoulder to remove the arrow point. Later that night, Desmond stood by his seneschal's side and held his hand for a moment while he slept fitfully with the aid of more mead. Finally, the Dragon Lord retreated to his own pavilion where he laid out his bedroll confident that his friend would recover and they would be victorious. Guinevere would be proud of him.

The next morning, Desmond's men packed up the camp and marched back down the Annan in the direction they'd come. After a half day's march, the Dragon Lord called a halt and they set up camp. The following days were like a holiday for the men. They fished in the river and relaxed. Desmond even allowed the men to have rations of mead and wine in the evenings. He watched the skies with concern. The first night they arrived at the new camp, it was cloudy and it looked as though it would remain so.

As the days progressed, Cynddylig regained his strength. Finally, he was able to report to Desmond and Bran what he had seen of the camp. "I will lead you to them personally, my lord," he declared.

The healer shook his head. "He will not be well enough," he said somberly. "He will be able to march without assistance, but he should not go into battle."

Cynddylig opened his mouth to protest, but Desmond held up his hand. "There are still three more days," he said. "We will see how you are then."

The night before the full moon, the clouds broke partially and it looked as though the weather might clear. Bran asked if they should begin the northward march. Desmond studied the skies. "I think we should hold for one more day," he said.

Indeed that night, fog rolled across the land, but the next day, the fog burned off by noon. The Dragon Lord ordered them to march north along the river again. When they came to the site of the original camp, he told the men to cook a meal, but not to pitch their tents. "We will leave most of our gear here," he told Bran, "but we will not make it obvious that we're setting up camp."

Night fell and the moon rose in the clear sky, casting a wan light over the landscape. Bran had the men form ranks and Desmond walked down the line, inspecting them. "We will go into the forest in groups of six. Each group will have a scout that knows the location of the camp from Cynddylig." Desmond caught sight of the guide standing in the line, doing his best not to slump. "If my guess is correct, the Saxons rise early and go to sleep late, hunting at twilight and guarding the forest by day. However, I suspect they only leave a small watch by night. I hope that watch has been reduced now that they think we have retreated." There were some muffled "ah's" of understanding and laughter as the men began to comprehend their leader's plan.

Desmond stopped, and looked each of the men in the eye. "Just because the watch will be reduced doesn't mean there won't be a watch at all. They will have men out in the forest. In each six-man group, one man will look high, one man will look low. Each man will be attentive and silent as you make your way through the forest. Am I understood?" There were murmurs of ascent.

"Very good," said Desmond at last. "I will start out halfway through primus vigilia with Cynddylig and four men of his choosing." Desmond referred to the Roman system of keeping time. "Bran will follow when the timekeeper signals it's three-quarters through primus vigilia, then the next group will start at secundus vigilia and so on until only those assigned to watch the camp remain." Again, there were murmurs of ascent from the assembled men. Desmond smiled openly. "May Lugh and Teutates be with us." He invoked the names of the Celtic gods of light and war respectively. Though he didn't believe in them, he knew many of his men did and took strength from the invocation. Even though some of the men, like Arthur, were beginning to believe in the new Christian religion, most still clung to the gods of their youth in times of trial.

When the timekeeper gave the signal, Cynddylig led Desmond and four other men down the Roman road and then darted into the forest. Desmond held up his hand, silently indicating that the men should stop and allow their eyes to adjust to the moonlight-dappled gloom of the woods. Once their eyes had adjusted, they proceeded. Cynddylig was the first to spot a Saxon squatting in the branches of a tree, eyes ranging about the forest. Quickly and quietly, Desmond nocked an arrow and let it fly. The Saxon fell to the ground with a whump. One of the men rushed over and cut the man's throat to assure he was dead. They waited and listened to the silent forest before proceeding.

The next lookout they found was relieving himself by a tree. Just as he hiked up his trousers, one of Desmond's men grabbed him from behind and another leapt in front and drove a sword through his heart. They reached the Saxon encampment without meeting further resistance and waited silently until Bran and his party joined them. A while later more men arrived. Desmond had them spread out along the tree line, looking for new Saxon guards.

The creature called Wolf sat in a small cave, partially obscured by a waterfall. He pulled a wolf skin around himself as he warmed his hands by a small fire. The moon was high in the sky and it would soon be time to seek blood from the village nearby. He had been following a small band of Saxons as they moved from the European continent to the island of Britain. He sighed to himself as he realized it would soon be time to leave this idyllic place and look for fresh prey elsewhere. During the summer, the Saxons were content to blame the bite marks he inflicted on sleeping men and women on the insects that laid their eggs in the calm places along the river's banks. As the air turned cold, they would begin to realize they were not being bothered by such things as fleas and mosquitoes, but something more sinister.

Listening to snippets of conversation, Wolf knew there were Briton towns and villages not far away. He would be able to spend the winter near one of them without danger of being hunted. Besides, he needed to move on if he was to continue his quest. He stood and stretched, thinking it was time to get on with the night's hunting when he heard someone cry out in the night. A few moments later, he heard terrified screams and excited yells.

The Blutsauger, as the people of his native land knew him, crept forward and carefully stepped out onto the stones that led from the cave, across the river and onto the bank. Crouching down, he looked toward the village. Smoke billowed from flaming huts. Someone was attacking. Wolf found himself running through a mix of emotions. On one hand, this meant that it was unlikely that any surviving Saxons were going to come hunt him down. It also meant that he might be able to have quite a feast this night on the dead and wounded. The problem was that if the attackers succeeded in destroying the village, his food supply would be gone, forcing him to move on several days sooner than he would like.

With a sigh, Wolf dropped from his crouch onto his hands and knees, which transformed into paws. Now literally a wolf, he decided to investigate the attack and see what might be left for him.

Bran was astounded by how quickly the Saxon men had leapt into action once they realized they were under attack. He swung his sword and gutted one man, then turned and drove his sword into the throat of another. He caught one of his men preparing to run through a young boy. "Stop right there," he called.

"What?" The warrior turned and blinked.

Seeing an opportunity, the boy ran off.

"Now he's escaped," complained the British warrior. "Do we want that nit to grow up to be a Saxon louse?"

"Desmond's orders are that no women and children are to be harmed. Without their men, they will pack up and go home. We aren't murderers."

The man nodded and looked to the ground just as an arrow caught him in the chest and he went down. Bran cursed himself for distracting a man during the course of battle. Looking up, he followed the arrow's direction and ran for the man who had loosed it. Before the Saxon could nock another arrow, Bran's sword entered his chest. As the man fell to his knees, dropping the bow, Bran put his boot on the man's chest and pushed, freeing his sword.

The fighting diminished. It was clear that the Saxon village was destroyed. Desmond's men set fire to the huts. Some women and children had fallen victim to sword and arrow. Bran shook his head, sorry that it could not be helped. Taking a deep breath, he gathered what remained of his men and they made their way back toward the camp. Adrenaline coursed through his veins. He smiled and looked forward to raising a goblet of mead to their victory with Desmond.

The Dragon Lord had taken an arrow to the thigh and had gone down. Distracted by the battle going on around them, his men hadn't noticed and they pressed the battle away from his location. Desmond watched helplessly as two of his men went down with fatal arrow wounds. Another was cut down by a Saxon's sword. He reached up and grabbed Guinevere's handkerchief that he still wore into battle, summoning his resolve. He tried to stand, but the pain in his leg was too intense.

Soon after, men lit the village's huts on fire. Desmond tried to call out, but found he had little strength. Looking down, he saw the blood pooling by his leg. The arrow had punctured his femoral artery. If no one found him, he knew he would be dead before morning. If the flames from the huts lit the nearby trees on fire, he wasn't sure whether he would die first from blood loss or from the forest fire. He tried to rise again, but an overwhelming urge to lie down and sleep hit him. He fought to keep his eyes open. It was then that he noticed a wolf standing beside a nearby tree.

The wolf approached slowly and tentatively. Desmond made an effort to look it in the eye, to let him know he was not afraid of the creature. However, his eyes went wide as he watched the creature assume the form of a man wearing a wolf's skin. At that point, Desmond began to wonder if he was hallucinating.

Without word or prelude the man who was a wolf reached out and grabbed the arrow's shaft and ripped it from Desmond's leg. The Dragon Lord's scream was lost among the screams of those dying in the nearby village. The man lapped up blood that spurted from the wound. Summoning an inner resolve, Desmond lunged forward, pushing the creature with all of his remaining strength. His nose plowed into the creature's shoulder. Without thinking, Desmond clamped down with his teeth and blood flowed into his mouth. Too determined – or perhaps too weak – to let go, he held on and kept pushing until he lay atop the creature. As he swallowed the blood, he sensed that he was gaining strength, but he also grew dizzy from his own blood loss. At last everything went black.

Chapter 10

From the writings of Aonghas Deas-Mhumhan:

I awoke some time after the wolf creature attacked me. My head swam as though I'd consumed far too much mead and at first, that's what I thought had happened. I closed my eyes for a few minutes and let my body get its bearings. I was flat on my back on cold, hard ground. Last thing I remembered, I was in the forest. Moving my fingers around, I felt no leaves, no twigs, no mud – only solid rock. My eyes flew open as a hunger pang struck. At first, all I saw was darkness, but then my eyes began to adjust and I was able to make out some details – a craggy ceiling and flickering light.

I tried to sit up, but couldn't quite summon the strength. I think I must have moaned as I lay there, because a shadow fell across me. Turning my head, I realized it was the wolf creature. He knelt down beside me. His head was completely bald and even in the wan, flickering light I could tell he was unnaturally pale. The creature's ears seemed unusually large to me, though that could have been because he was bald and they stuck out slightly from his head. The tunic he wore had a wide neck, and it was ragged, threadbare and dirty. I noticed a nasty looking wound on his neck and that's when I remembered biting him. I looked down and saw a ragged hole in my plaid pants. Tentatively I touched the wound, and though it still hurt and my fingers came away bloody, it seemed amazingly well healed for a place where an arrow had pierced the major artery in my leg.

The wolf creature looked longingly at my bloody fingers, but didn't move. Instead, he spoke to me in a language I didn't completely recognize, but the intonation reminded me of the Saxon tongue. As he spoke, I saw two large wolf-like fangs in his mouth. He rolled his eyes as I narrowed mine to examine him. He spoke again and somehow I began to understand. The meaning of his words was, "You need food." The actual words were incomprehensible, though if I didn't listen too closely, I found that the meaning was clear in my mind nevertheless.

"Do you have food?" I asked in my native language.

He shook his head. "I can show you." Again, even though he spoke in the Saxon-like tongue, I found I could understand his meaning. Water roared in the distance, as though we were near a waterfall. He stood, took my hand, and helped me to my feet. I put my arm around his shoulder and he helped me hobble toward the cave's entrance. As we moved awkwardly together, I managed to bite my tongue. At first I was tempted to spit the blood out, but the taste seemed to awaken something within me. I realized what I was craving. "Do you have rare meat?" I lisped. My mouth felt strange.

"It is not the meat you crave," he answered.

As we continued forward, I felt around my mouth with my tongue. The lisp made me think that I must have lost teeth in the fighting. Though I had been lucky before, I knew it was certainly a possibility. However, I found not missing teeth, but rather that two of my teeth seemed unusually large. "What do you mean it's not meat that I crave?" I asked. "I know what my stomach is telling me."

"Not yet," he said. We arrived at the cave's entrance and I realized we were behind a waterfall. Moonlight glinted through a curtain of water. From the moonlight's direction, I realized that a night or two must have passed since I'd fallen in battle.

The wolf creature helped me find footing on stones that led from the cave to the riverbank. He then led me downriver a short distance until we came to the remnants of the Saxon village. The smell of decay hung heavy in the air. Despite the cold, flies swarmed in a thick cloud. Few bodies actually remained. Not far away, I saw fresh burial mounds.

"Those that were able buried what dead they could in the short time they had available," explained the wolf creature. "Most have fled."

"Most?" I asked.

"The wounded and those too sick to travel are still here." He led me into the burned-out remains of a hut. An old woman lay on the ground. Her skin hung on her bones like the wrinkled flesh of an overripe fruit that had sat on the ground too long. Unable to move, the woman lay in her own filth. I tried to turn away but the wolf creature put his hand on my elbow. "You have the power to end her suffering," he said.

I shook my head, not understanding what he meant.

He knelt down next to the woman and raised her head into his lap. Her watery eyes opened and she looked up at me. The mind behind the eyes was so far gone that I could not read the emotions. I would like to imagine that she pled for help, but what I probably saw was fear – if not of me, then fear of having been left alone.

The wolf creature gestured that I should kneel next to him and the woman. A new instinct began to dawn and I suddenly realized what I truly craved. I shook my head violently even as the hunger pangs compelled me to kneel down. The old woman's eyes followed me as I leaned in and bit down on her jugular vein. Her blood flowed into my mouth and I swallowed greedily. She made a noise and, at first, I thought she would scream. However, it soon became apparent that she was moaning – as though remembering some long lost lover. The woman had little blood left and she soon fell silent. The wolf creature reached down and gently closed her eyes as I sat back, horrified at what I'd become and even more horrified by the fact that I still suffered hunger pangs.

He looked at me with sympathetic eyes. "You still hunger?" He was becoming easier to understand. I nodded fiercely. "All right," he said, laying the old woman's head down. "One more and then it will be time to rest, whether you are hungry or not. We Blutsauger do not require much blood. Too much and we become sick."

The word Blutsauger caused me to blink. I heard the word

in the wolf-creature's language, but for some reason I didn't understand what it meant. "Bloot-zow-ger?" I asked, pronouncing the word slowly.

"I will explain later," he said. He helped me to my feet and took me around behind another hut. There was a young child lying on the ground. Gangrene was already setting into an arm twisted at an impossible angle. The child's breathing was shallow. She was unconscious, near death.

Again I shook my head and outside of the hut's confines, I backed several steps away. My leg was already getting stronger and I found I could walk without the wolf creature's assistance. "I cannot take the life of this child," I cried.

The wolf creature looked at me with fire in his eyes. "She was abandoned for dead." He moved closer to me. "You ordered the attack on her village. Very possibly you killed her father and mother. You are the one that left her to suffer."

I turned away and hid my face in my hands.

The wolf creature spun me around, grabbed me by both shoulders and stared into my eyes. "You are the one responsible for this child's condition. You will end her suffering now!" I could feel his spittle on my face with each word.

The hunger in my stomach warred with my revulsion at the idea of drinking blood from the child. The wolf creature pushed me down into the mud next to the child's body. She stirred, as though having a nightmare, but did not wake. With tears in my eyes, I bit into the child's neck and drank her blood. When she was dead, the wolf creature helped me stand. "She is in a far better place now than the place you left her, rotting and suffering in a mud hollow." The creature turned his back on me and made his way back toward the cave. Looking around, I found a shovel abandoned by the Saxons. I dug two holes near the other burial mounds and placed the body of the little girl next to the body of the old woman. As I covered them over, I wondered if the woman was the girl's grandmother. When I finished, I threw the shovel deep into the forest, then found my way back to the wolf creature's cave.

I had many questions I wanted answered.

I found the wolf creature in the cave, warming his hands by the fire. His back was toward me and he didn't look up, but he tensed, as though he heard me. "I still hunger," I said. "But, I can't bring myself to eat any more."

"That is for the best," he said softly. "The hunger is worst when you are newly reborn. It is better not to attempt to satisfy it. Those who do, become very sick."

I moved around and sat opposite the fire from the creature. "I have so many questions…."

"My name is Wolf," he said as though plucking one of the questions directly from my mind. He said the name like "Voalff" but I understood him to mean the animal whose skin he wore. I smiled slightly and he nodded. "I chose the name because of what the animal means to me," he explained.

"My name is Aonghas," I said. "I was named for the god of choice. Will I need to choose a new name?"

Wolf shook his head. "The name I was born with has no meaning in the modern world. I barely remember it, I have been alone so long. I simply chose a name that I would not forget."

I narrowed my eyes and studied the creature carefully. "How old are you?"

"I have lost count of the years," he said. "Although I remember a time before the Caesars, when the Greeks had an empire of their own. I was created by a vampire that called himself Theron, which means 'hunter.' I was a slave in his house and this was his way of setting me free."

My mouth fell open as I tried to count the years: five hundred or even a thousand? My mind began to reel. Once again, I let my tongue play over the new sharp teeth that had grown in my mouth. More questions came into my mind.

"You are now like me – Blutsauger – an undead blood drinker." When I shook my head he continued. "I fed on you like you fed on those poor creatures in the village. I drained you of most of your blood, but then you attacked me." He pointed to the wound on his shoulder. "You drank your own blood that had passed through my body. Doing so, you became Blutsauger."

I looked down at the ground, my mouth working helplessly. I wasn't sure what to say. From his tone, it seemed as though he sought an apology. "I'm sorry for your wound," I said. "But, I'm not sorry that I'm still alive."

He looked up at me with moist eyes. "That's the problem. You are not alive. You did die, but yet you exist still and the only way you will continue to exist is by drinking the blood of the innocent."

"I could starve myself to death."

He shook his head. "I have tried. You will become a mindless husk. Eventually that husk will seek and kill for blood. It will keep killing until you become like a living being again. It is better as we are. We only need a little blood. We do not need to kill."

I jumped to my feet. "You made me kill that woman and that girl!" I shouted and stomped away to the far wall.

"They were already dead," he said in the same level tone. "When you first become Blutsauger, it is hard to control the hunger. You ended their suffering. It is better than what happened to me."

I turned and looked at him. A tear slowly made its way down his pallid cheek.

"My daughter was only three years old…" he said before his mouth slammed shut over the words, as though afraid of the torrent that might follow.

"You brought me into this life that's not life?" My words were clipped and I took several short steps toward him.

Again, he shook his head. "No, I merely fed off you. My only intention was to slake my thirst. You chose to attack me."

Slowly, I sat down on the rocky ground. Even more questions churned and roiled in my mind. Finally, I practically screamed the one that kept coming to the forefront. "Am I doomed to live this way forever?"

For the first time, something like a smile spread across Wolf's features. "Perhaps not and perhaps fortune has led you to me."

He bade me come closer to the fire and he told me the story of an encounter he had had almost four hundred years before. He met a man traveling to Britain called Joseph of Arimathea. "Are you familiar with the one they call Christ?"

I nodded, remembering what my father told me about the Christians of his youth and about the teacher called St. Patrick. I recalled my conversation with Arthur about his shield and the image of Christ's mother emblazoned on its front. "Those who follow him consider him a god, do they not?"

"Those that follow him say he is an incarnation of the one and only God," corrected Wolf. "They say he has the power to forgive even the most heinous sins." He went on to tell me about a cup and a scroll that Joseph of Arimathea carried. "The cup was used during Jesus's last Passover feast. Some say it holds the blood of Christ himself, even to this day. Others say that you pour wine into it and it transforms into His blood. You are but a fledgling, but could you imagine what it would mean for one such as us to drink of that cup? If that is the blood of a god – of *the* God – and it contained forgiveness of the magnitude claimed."

"You said there was also a scroll?" I asked. My mother had taught me to read Latin and that knowledge served me well. No doubt it helped bring me to the attention of Ambrosius, his daughter, and the first Dragons who instructed me. I loved to read but there was little of value to read.

"Joseph said that it contained the writings of Jesus himself."

I let out a breath. Through my father, Arthur, and others, I knew a little of the writings about Jesus. However, I'd never once heard that Jesus himself had left behind any writings. That would, indeed, be a treasure. "Why didn't you simply take the cup when you had the chance?"

"It was guarded," he said bitterly. He went on to describe the eagle-like creature that attacked him, preventing him from taking the chest that contained the scroll and the cup. "Over the centuries, I have encountered and heard many stories of creatures like that. Many take elemental forms, such as flames or water. Others take animal forms like this creature. Some people worship them as gods.

I believe the Christians call these creatures, angels."

"What can one do against such a creature?" I asked.

"They say these angels are immortal," said Wolf, barring his fangs, "but I believe they can be wounded or even killed. I have been studying them over the centuries and I think I know a way. That's why your becoming a Blutsauger may be particularly fortuitous."

"So, where do we find this cup? This scroll?"

"All I know is that it's on one of the islands of Britain. I don't know where to begin the search."

"I may know someone that can help," I said. Even as I thought of enlisting Bran and Arthur's aid and seeing Guinevere again, I worried what she would think of my new sharp-toothed countenance along with my need to drink blood in order to survive.

Chapter 11

From the writings of Aonghas Deas-Mhumhan.
October of the year 480 through May of the year 481:

A few days later, Wolf and I made our way south. At first, I suggested rejoining my men in Luguvalium where they planned to spend the winter, but Wolf rejected the idea. "What will you tell them?" asked the ancient Blutsauger. "How will you explain that you are only awake at night and must feed on human blood? They will see you as a demon. They will turn on you."

"At some point I must enlist Bran's aid if we are to find the cup and scroll of Joseph of Arimathea," I reasoned.

"Learn to live as a Blutsauger first," argued Wolf. "Only then can you hope to find a way of explaining what you have become."

I took a deep breath and though I didn't like Wolf's advice, I accepted that it was the best course of action. As a Dragon Lord, I could order Bran to accept me as I was. However, I would have to win over both Arthur and Guinevere. The thought that she might turn away from me in horror caused a knot to form in my stomach.

With the Saxon village gone, there were no humans around to sustain Wolf and me. So, we moved on and followed the River Annan for a time. Wolf showed me how a Blutsauger could attack animals and use their blood for survival. I was actually proud when I managed to catch a rabbit barehanded. My new, faster reflexes were a delight, but I nearly gagged when I drank the creature's blood.

"Human blood is far more satisfying to us, I know," said Wolf in sympathy.

As dawn approached, we looked for a cave. Finding none, Wolf showed me how a Blutsauger could dig into the earth and cover up to keep from being burned by the sun's rays.

"Won't we suffocate?" I asked.

"It is why we are called 'undead,'" explained Wolf. "We don't actually need to breathe. Our blood does not flow during the day. We are truly like dead bodies when we sleep. There is no need to fear, young one."

I balked at being called 'young one' but did not speak my objections aloud. I had some sense of how old Wolf must be to have seen the things he talked about. With a sigh, I set to work digging a hole in the ground, creating a burrow in which to spend the day.

After two weeks with Wolf, my clothes were dirty and ragged. I looked with despair at my fingernails, which were short – not from trimming but from digging in the earth. I felt my shaggy and mud-encrusted beard. "Just because we are Blutsauger, must we live like burrowing animals?" I asked. "Surely there must be a better way."

Wolf rubbed his bald head and his naked chin. "There are reasons I keep myself shorn. You would be well advised to do the same. It would avoid the need for grooming."

I snorted. Though I kept my hair short for practical reasons, I didn't like the idea of completely removing my hair. We continued to walk and I examined the terrain in the dark. "If I'm not mistaken, I believe we must be coming near Dumfriesshire. It is big enough that we should be able to find an inn. At least we could wash up and get our bearings."

"The advantage to towns and villages is the human prey. That would be good for us. The problem—" Wolf held up a finger "—is that inns require money and we have not come upon any travelers to steal from."

I reached into a pouch that hung from my belt and retrieved a gold coin emblazoned with the image of Caesar. "Fortunately,

I have a little money. It should be enough to get us a room for a month or two." Looking up at the starless, black sky, I nodded. "I think we will need it if we don't want to spend a winter digging into frozen ground."

"I have spent many winters digging into frozen ground," said Wolf with an odd air of longing. I looked at him, an unspoken question in my mind. "Still, I think a month or two in a warm inn would suit me well."

As I hoped, we were able to secure lodgings in Dumfriesshire. Arriving early in the evening, the landlord showed us to a room. After most of the other lodgers had gone to sleep, and I had taken a much-needed bath, we struck out and soon found a singing, happy drunk wandering the streets alone. Wolf showed me how to look into a victim's eyes and quiet his mind. Then Wolf bit down on the drunk's neck. With no little regret, he withdrew long before the drunk was in danger, looked him in the eyes again and set him on his way, no wiser about the encounter.

Wolf looked at me a little bleary-eyed. "Easy, isn't it?"

"The alcohol he consumed affected you, didn't it?" I asked.

"What makes you say that?" asked Wolf as he walked an uneven line down the road.

A short time later, we came to a small wattle and daub hut near the outskirts of town. "I believe there are only one or two within," said Wolf, concentrating on the small sounds from within the hut.

Carefully, I let myself in. A lone, young man lay on a straw mat. Slowly, I lowered myself down and bit his jugular. After the rabbits and squirrels I'd been forced to subsist on, the young man's blood was like nectar. I couldn't get enough and no matter how hard I tried, I couldn't stop drinking. Finally, Wolf pulled me to my feet.

"The young man is dead," said Wolf. "Come. It is time for us to return to our room."

We spent the following day in our room covered by several

layers of woolen blankets. The walls of the inn were poorly constructed and sunlight poured through freely. When we awoke the next evening, I found myself covered with fleabites. "I almost wonder if it would have been better to have remained on the road," I sighed.

Wolf and I decided to remain in Dumfriesshire through the winter. Though our first day at the inn had proven less than ideal, a small hut became available and no one argued with a Dragon Lord and his advisor about the right to claim such a hovel. In fact, there was a certain sense of relief that we did not try to move in with someone else.

Since I wasn't required to spend all of my budget on lodging, I set out within the week to find a weaver who would make us new clothes. I was quickly finding that the worst part of my existence was attempting to transact all business after nightfall when people were reluctant to open their doors for any reason. However, I did find one weaver who was willing to do business with us.

I explained that I was one of the Dragon Lords who had defeated Caw and put an end to Pictish raids on her village. She looked at our torn and dirty clothes askance, and then shook her head. "It was Arthur and Desmond what ended those raids. You don't look like either of them to me."

When I showed her a gold coin, I suddenly looked much more like the descriptions she remembered hearing. While the weaver worked on our new garments, Wolf and I started making modifications to our new home. We sealed up as many gaps as we could and repaired the thatch roof. I soon discovered another problem with becoming a creature that lives only during the night. People frequently yelled at us to stop making so much noise.

I originally became a soldier because I liked a life on the road. In a world where no one traveled more than a few miles from their home, a soldier's life was a way to see as much of the world as possible. I suppose I'm also what one might call a loner. Though there is camaraderie among soldiers, there is also discipline. When the general, Dragon, or Duke gives an order, there is no thought about how it inconveniences anyone. In a town, you must worry about your neighbors and what they observe of your habits. If I had been anyone but Desmond the Dragon Lord – the man who defeated Caw – I'm sure we would have had many more instances of people prying into our affairs. As it was, my companion and I were merely viewed as eccentrics.

Still, even with its troubles and inconvenience, there were advantages to living in a town. Hunting became much easier. Since our kind don't need to kill to survive, it was easy to hunt and not be discovered. Both Wolf and I grew healthy and pink-faced. Also, in this environment, it was easy for Wolf to teach me about the ways of the Blutsauger. I came to understand the word literally meant "bloodsucker" but it held additional meanings for Wolf, including "undead" and "immortal." I guessed that explained why I still heard the word in his native tongue.

One night, while wandering the streets of Dumfriesshire, I turned to Wolf. "I have been meaning to ask. When we first met, you were in the form of a wolf. However, as time passes, I begin to question my memory. Were you a wolf or was I merely delusional?"

Wolf looked into the distance, but didn't stop walking. "You were not delusional. I can assume the form of a wolf."

"Can you teach me how to assume the form of an animal?" I asked. The advantages in stealth, tracking and hunting seemed great and I wondered why I had never seen Wolf transform since that first time.

"It is not a skill that can be taught," he said simply. "The first time, it just happens and it was rather painful for me. It felt as though I fell down through a hole and suddenly I was looking out through the eyes of a wolf. It happened to me three times before I could control it. Now I can transform when I want." In unusual candor he looked me in the eye. "I still find it a frightening experience. The mind of the beast is not entirely your own."

I pondered that last comment for several minutes, not knowing what Wolf meant. I supposed he meant that wolves are not reasoning creatures like men and that our reason diminished. "Can you transform into any other beasts?"

"No, only wolf," he said.

"So, that means I will be a wolf?"

He shook his head. "It is different for each. You will know when it happens to you the first time."

I ran my tongue over my fang and turned my gaze forward. Wolf's explanation of transformation felt a bit too much like what fathers said to sons concerning the mysteries of women and love.

As that first winter wore on, I began to sense that Wolf didn't view time in quite the same way as ordinary humans. One night, I pressed him for details about when and how we would start our quest for the Grail and Scroll of Jesus. His eyes went vacant and he said, "It has taken me four centuries to travel from Saxony to Britain. Do you think time is of consequence to those such as us?"

"But the paper and skins that scrolls are made of deteriorate," I retorted, being primarily concerned with the writings of Christ.

He blinked at me a few times as though that thought had simply not occurred to him. "Time is in our favor," he finally replied. "I have seen many religions born. I have seen many die. If this Christianity is like the rest, it will pass into the realm of mere curiosity like so many other beliefs."

Part of me agreed with Wolf's assessment. Part of me wasn't so certain. Though I'd never met them, I knew about the fervor of Patrick and Germanus from my father. I saw the way Christianity struck a chord with Arthur – a man raised in the Druidic tradition. "If that is what you think," I retorted, "why do we even seek this cup? Why do you believe that it holds any more power than any other religious symbol?"

That caused Wolf to frown. "Two things," he said at last. "The fact that a creature as powerful as an angel would take an interest and, perhaps even more importantly, the fact that Joseph so believed this Jesus had the power to forgive."

"Compelling arguments," I said. "So, I would think we should pursue the quest with that much more fervor…."

His lip curled upward. "Ah … but like all living creatures, there is one problem."

"What is that?"

"I am afraid that if I find this cup, that if I am forgiven, I will also find true death." He sighed, then looked up into my eyes. "Like all living creatures, I am afraid to die."

Wolf's lack of urgency was contagious as was the relative comfort of our situation in Dumfriesshire. We loitered there a good deal longer than we originally intended. In winter we stalked people in their homes. However, as spring came, the nights grew shorter, and more people wandered the streets after sunset. It gave a new kind of thrill to the hunt. The blood I drank seemed to warm with the air.

In early summer, when the nights are shortest of all, we received word that Ambrosius and Arthur had kept up their campaign against the Saxons through the winter. With the onset of spring, Ambrosius had dispersed his Dragons throughout the land to keep the peace. I knew the Saxons were only temporarily gone, and I gathered Ambrosius believed that as well. Of perhaps greater interest to me was the news that all of the Dragons were now under the command of one Pen-Dragon – none other than my old friend, Arthur. However that news paled in comparison to what I heard next.

We sat in an inn, sipping wine slowly – for both Wolf and I found it went to our heads very quickly – when a traveling bard mentioned that Arthur was named Ambrosius's heir and he had married Guinevere. I spit out the wine I had consumed and sat bolt upright and bared my teeth, incautiously revealing my fangs to those assembled. My hand crushed the wooden goblet I held.

Wolf put his hand on my forearm, but I swept it away. I flew from the inn. Though it was summer, the night air was still cool and a breeze blew. I fell against the wall and put my face in my hands and let tears flow.

Just then, a hand fell upon my shoulder. From the phantom-like lightness of the touch, I thought it was Wolf. However, when I looked up, I was surprised to find a prostitute at my side. She knew me as a man with money. I had taken her blood before and left without paying anything. Still, I always managed to leave her with the memory that I had paid her generously for services well rendered.

"What's the matter?" she asked, with serious concern, her deep brown eyes wide.

"I have just learned that Arthur has married the Duke's daughter," I said bitterly.

Unfazed by my tone, she smiled. "Isn't it wonderful? The Duke finally has named an heir."

I narrowed my eyes and frowned, evaluating her coldly. "I love Guinevere."

"I can make you forget about the Duke's daughter," she said, gently, soothingly.

I started to turn away, but she reached out and took my arm. I turned back and flashed a silver coin at her. She led me to her room where she removed her dress. She lay back on the mat, her legs opened provocatively. I smelled her scent – not just her womanly musk – but her blood. I pulled off my boots and my trousers and I fell upon her, thrusting into her. My teeth found her throat and I bit in and drank greedily, not stopping when I was merely full, but continuing until I was both spent and bloated. Sluggishly, I stood up and looked at her dead body lying on the mat and licked the blood from my lips. "Women," I spat. "The world would be better off without their distraction."

Casually, I pulled on my trousers and my boots, confident in the contempt that the world showed women who sold their bodies. Few would question her death. Even those that did would not even conceive that I – a Dragon Lord – would be responsible. No one would be able to imagine that I would have need of her services nor that I would be capable of killing one such as her. Still, as I stood there, looking down at her, I couldn't help but remember the sympathy she expressed in my earlier tears. A new tear fell. I turned on my heel and left the room before I could question whether I was mourning the prostitute or my own lost soul.

Chapter 12

From the writings of Aonghas Deas-Mhumhan:

Amonth later, we heard that a Dragon and his men approached Dumfriesshire. Wolf and I decided that was a good point to depart the town and continue our journey to Ambrosius's hall. We thought it would be awkward should we encounter another Dragon Lord. We were lucky that more questions weren't raised about why we had lingered so late into the summer without rejoining my men.

"Also, you are growing bloodthirsty," cautioned Wolf. "I have seen it in some of our kind. Your strength and your nobility make you cock-sure. However, your nobility will fade as those who know you grow old and die. If a death sentence is passed against us, all it requires is a man with a sickle to come upon us in our quarters. He can behead us and that will be that." I began to turn away, but he grabbed me by the shoulders and forced me to look into his eyes. "In many ways, it is easier for a human to kill a Blutsauger than it is for a Blutsauger to kill a human. Remember that."

I nodded somberly. Within a week, we had packed our few belongings and continued down the road. Traveling through the short nights of summer on foot proved slow going. We had to stop periodically to hunt and find shelter. Sometimes, we could find no human prey and we were forced to subsist on rabbits and squirrels. I believe Wolf was trying to teach me humility, and it seemed to be working.

As we traveled, the nights grew longer and the leaves began to change color. We saw more people on the roads the further south we traveled. Stopping at an inn to rest, we learned that Ambrosius had died in his sleep. Arthur was Duke of Britain.

We arrived at the timber hall less than a week later. It was shortly before dawn and, in the moonlight, the hall looked just as I remembered it – perhaps even better, as though portions had been repaired.

Though the timber hall sat upon a low hill in the midst of a grassy field, the terrain around was rocky and there were tombs for honored British and Roman heroes nearby. I led Wolf to these. Together, we were able to roll away the stone in front of one of the tombs, then roll it back once we were inside. Though I shivered when I lay down on the cold ground of the cave and small stones poked me here and there, I soon fell into my death-like slumber and did not awaken until after twilight.

Wolf and I, once again, rolled away the stone barring entrance to the tomb and made our way to Arthur's hold. The previous night, I had noted pavilions and tents set up nearby. Apparently the Dragons were returning to the hall for autumn. This did not surprise me at all. However, I was surprised to see my own gold dragon banner flying over one of the tents. Someone had claimed my title.

As we approached the timber hall, two guards crossed spears in front of our path. "Who approaches Camelot?"

Wolf and I looked at each other and I shook my head. Arthur had a penchant for naming his weapons: his sword was Caliburn, his shield was Wyneb-Gurthucher. I could only assume that he had taken it into his head to name his hold as well. "We are two weary travelers," I said after a moment. "We seek shelter from the wind and a morsel to fill our bellies."

Wolf looked at me with a wrinkled brow. I assume it was because we Blutsaugers don't eat, but I quickly waved him aside. I knew Ambrosius never refused admission to a weary traveler. I hoped Arthur still maintained that tradition. The guards looked at each other. "The King is conferring with several of his knights," said one at last. "We will give you food and a place to rest in the antechamber. You must not disturb the council."

"Very good." I nodded.

They led us through the big doors into the timber hall's first room. Voices filtered through the door at the other end of the room. We were taken to a small table and told in hushed voices to sit.

Once we were seated, one of the guards quietly stepped through the door into the hall's great room. He emerged a few moments later and, without acknowledging us, returned to his post outside.

A short time later, a girl – perhaps no older than twelve – entered the room, bearing a platter of bread and cheese. She poured us two tankards of weak ale, then with a brief curtsey, skittered back into the main room.

I sipped the ale then broke the bread and toyed with it for a few minutes. At last, curiosity got the better of me and I stepped to the door leading to the great hall. The sight that greeted me caused my mouth to fall open. The multitude of tables that had occupied the hall had been replaced by a large bench, which curved around in the form of an omega. In the center was a great, round table. There was no "head" of the table or front of the hall. Arthur sat among his Dragons as an equal.

I felt Wolf creep up beside me. After a few moments he pointed to one of the Dragons. "Who is that? He is magnificent."

I looked where Wolf pointed. There sat a man with a neat mustache and impeccable, long golden hair. Instead of rough plaid, he wore fine, dyed linen – finer clothes than Ambrosius himself used to wear. I rolled my eyes and pulled Wolf back from the door so no one inside would hear us speaking. "He is Prince Galahad Anguselus," I explained. "He likes to be called The Ancelot."

"Ah, L'Ancelot," said Wolf, mimicking a Gaulish accent badly. We both laughed. A silence descended in the other room. Wolf and I soon followed suit. We listened for a time until the conversation resumed. "Still," whispered Wolf, stepping back toward the door and looking in again. "Wouldn't he make a fine Blutsauger?"

"I was created by accident. Would you really think of making a Blutsauger deliberately?" Somehow, I felt a strange hollowness thinking that Wolf would be looking at a human like that.

"I only think of preserving such a face for eternity," whispered Wolf.

"Then take up sculpting," I retorted.

Just then, one of the Dragons whose back was toward us excused himself and stood from the table. I hustled Wolf back to our own table and we sat. The Dragon Lord tugged at the top of his plaid trousers and I knew he was going outside to relieve himself. Just then, I looked up and saw his face – it was Bran. He continued toward the door. Just as he reached it, he turned around suddenly and looked at me. His mouth fell open.

"By the gods," he said. "Is it … is it … you?" he asked.

I stood and led him outside. "I believe you were on an errand and I do not wish to detain you," I said. Wolf stood and followed us outside.

"Can you leave the meeting for a time?" I asked. "I have something very important to ask you."

"For a short time," he affirmed. He then retreated into the bushes. A little while later he re-emerged. He led us toward his pavilion, asking questions the entire time. "We thought you were dead. What happened? Why haven't you appeared before now?"

I held up my hand. "I was wounded." I introduced Bran to Wolf and explained that he had found me and stopped the flow of blood. By the time he had nursed me back to health, Bran had already led the men to Luguvalium.

We found our way to a roaring campfire beside the pavilion. Bran bade us sit and he called a young seneschal who brought us mugs of spiced cider. The warm liquid was welcome, though my stomach growled. I needed blood. "Where is Cynddylig?" I asked.

"Arthur was in need of a guide."

"Alas," I said. "I'm sorry you had to lose his services."

"Aye," he said, taking a sip of his own cider. He took a deep breath and let it out slowly. "Last year, Bedhwr brought back strange news from Dumfriesshire. He'd said the people there told of a man claiming to be Lord Desmond. Was that you?"

"It was," I admitted.

"But why?" asked Bran looking hurt and confused. "Why

haven't you made yourself known before now?" Suddenly, his look turned sharp and he glared at me. "You haven't fallen prey to cowardice have you?"

I frowned, wounded by the accusation. "No," I said simply. "I am on a quest and I want to enlist the Pen-dragon's aid."

"Years ago," said Wolf, "I met a man who told me of holy relics here in the islands of Britain. They were brought here when the Romans still called the islands Albion."

"And what were these relics?" Bran's eyebrows came together.

"The cup of Christ," explained Wolf. "There was also a scroll that was said to be penned by Jesus."

Bran fell silent again and stared into the flames. "It is said that Arthur's shield – the one with the image of Mary – saved his life at sea. The shield saved his life again at the battle of Badon. It saved him from an arrow fired by Octha himself. I saw it." Bran called for more cider. "Since then, he has converted fully to Christian teachings and is obsessed with anything to do with Jesus. He would not leave any stone unturned if he thought this Grail or this book really existed."

I sat forward on the edge of the rock. "You'll help us then? You'll take us to Arthur so we can make our case to him?"

Bran shook his head, then looked up at me with a gaze as hard as flint. "I know you well enough to know that you tell me the truth. But Arthur … Arthur would see you as a deserter and a coward." He turned his attention to Wolf. "You are clearly a Saxon, sir. I presume you must have been from the village at Cat Coit Celidon. I am thankful that you saved my friend. However, Arthur's fame and his reputation ride on the fact that he rid the islands of the Saxons. You are not safe here."

"Then, what shall we do?" I asked.

"I will tell Arthur that this information about the Grail and the book has come to me. I will meet you tomorrow and let you know what has been decided," he said.

"Tomorrow night," I said, meaningfully.

He arched an eyebrow, but nodded. "Very well." He took another drink of his cider then smiled more amiably. "You may avail yourself of my camp's hospitality." He set the tankard down, stood up, and put his hand on my shoulder. "It is good to see you again, old friend."

"Thank you for your kind offer." I clasped his forearm. "Wolf and I have our own accommodations."

Later that night, after all but the guards were asleep, Wolf and I made our way through the encamped soldiers. "Do not feed on the men that sleep under the golden dragon banner. They are mine." I think he understood what I said to mean that the men were mine to feed upon. However, I meant that they were mine to protect.

After we parted, I made my way up to the great timber hall. Reaching into the minds of the guards, I blinded them to my presence and slipped inside. I passed through the antechamber into the main hall with the great round table. Off the great hall was the sleeping chamber of Arthur and Guinevere. A fire burned in a pit in the center of the room. Arthur slept on a mat on one side of the fire, Guinevere on the other. It was, perhaps, not the most romantic of sleeping arrangements, but it was practical. I knelt down next to Guinevere and brushed an errant strand of hair from her face. I kissed her lips, then her cheek, and her jaw.

She shifted slightly in her sleep. I bit into her neck and her blood and thoughts rushed into me. I blinked several times and withdrew, then looked at her. Her mind was filled with images of the pompous L'Ancelot. I sighed and looked at my one-time friend, Arthur. I sensed his mind was full of images of a golden goblet and I knew then that Bran had succeeded. I also understood why Guinevere would look elsewhere for affection.

Again, I leaned over and drank from Guinevere's throat, this time taking a chance and probing past the images of L'Ancelot. There I found an image of myself as seen through her eyes. I saw myself on the day she gave her favor to me at the tournament. I felt the flush in her cheeks and the warmth in her belly as she looked upon me.

I followed the thread of her memory to a day two years later when I first took her in my arms and kissed her. We separated, breathless, and she led me away from her father's timber hall and into the woods. She took me to a grassy meadow and we lay down together on the soft grass with sunlight streaming in upon us. I remembered feeling clumsy and awkward that day as I fumbled with the laces on her dress. As I peered into Guinevere's mind, I was surprised to find out that she had similar feelings. She hoped I wouldn't find her a poor lover. However, neither of us had known another. I only remembered how good it felt when I first eased myself into her delicious folds. She took my hips in her hands and encouraged me to go deeper. I did and she yelped, but then I moved back and forth with no more resistance. I remembered being surprised how quickly my seed spilled that first time and I sensed that she was disappointed. Still, I was hard enough that she was able to ride me until she also climaxed.

I rode the wave of memory to another year. It was late at night and we sneaked into the great timber hall. She had me sit in her father's great chair as though I were the king. I looked out upon the hall illuminated by moonlight shining between the timbers and felt the power that Ambrosius must have felt when sitting there. My cock stood at attention at the sense of power. Guinevere unlaced my trousers and slid them down to my ankles. She lifted her skirt and slid onto me. As we moved together on her father's throne, I knew I was destined to be her father's successor.

Next, I experienced Guinevere's pain upon learning that I had not returned from Cat Coit Celidon. She had wept for days. Her father and Myrddin worked hard to convince her that she should marry Arthur. It was a loveless, passionless marriage. She knew that Arthur really loved Morgana and suspected that their relationship still continued. She saw L'Ancelot's beauty, and found him attractive. He could give her a fulfillment that Arthur could not, but she did not love him any more than she loved the man she married.

Just then, Guinevere's eyes fluttered open and her breath caught. I delved into her thoughts again and told her she was dreaming. Her eyes fluttered closed and I lifted her bedclothes and turned her dream into a most pleasant one.

Covering her, I kissed her on the forehead and then looked over at Arthur. "You betrayed Morgana by marrying her, my friend. Guinevere will betray you in return."

I left quietly and returned to the tomb. I found Wolf waiting. Normally Wolf was very good at concealing his thoughts from me, but not that time. "You are thinking of the Ancelot, aren't you?"

"He was as delicious as I imagined," he said as he helped me roll back the stone from the tomb.

"You didn't…"

"He lusts after your Guinevere, you know."

"I know. What do you think will become of them?"

He shook his head. "Love and lust are such complicated things. Theirs could fizzle quickly or it could burn so furiously it will destroy Britain itself."

"Could Guinevere and I rekindle our love for one another?"

He smiled sadly. "You would have to make her one of us. That would change her. I suspect your love for one another has reached the end of its journey." With that, he helped me roll the stone closed and we found our places and lay down.

The following evening, we met Bran at his pavilion. He told us that Arthur had been excited at the prospect of this Holy Grail. He left immediately to consult with Myrddin. Later that afternoon, Arthur returned and announced that he would dispatch Gawain to search for clues. "We should meet in a year's time," said Bran. "At that point, I can tell you what Gawain has found."

"And if Gawain fails?" asked Wolf, arching an eyebrow.

"If Gawain fails, Arthur will likely send another." Bran put his hands on his knees. "You should have seen him last night when I told him about the Grail. His eyes widened and his cheeks flushed as though he had been drinking." Bran called over his seneschal and asked for mulled wine.

"Those of us who seek the Grail, seek forgiveness," said Wolf.

I thought of Arthur. He left the woman he loved – Morgana – in a quest for power. Some said he had killed thousands of Saxons. I thought if anyone had reason to seek forgiveness, it was him. "Where shall we meet you?" I asked.

"You have a home?"

I considered that. I didn't want to return to Dumfriesshire. I remembered where Bran and the men spent the winter. "We will call Luguvalium our home," I said.

"I will seek you out."

Chapter 13

From the writings of Aonghas Deas-Mhumhan:

Wolf and I traveled to Luguvalium. Though the prospect of waiting a year to hear from Bran was daunting, I had persuaded him to give me some more of my gold. It was enough for me to buy land in the area. Under the Roman system, Dragons were encouraged to be landless. This way a soldier felt no more loyalty to one section of the territory than another.

Setting up my lands, encouraging people to move onto them, work the fields, and raise their livestock proved a new and interesting challenge. It preoccupied my mind for much of the year. It also became the foundation for more income in the future.

One day in the fall as my first profits were coming in, I looked at Wolf. "Have you never thought about investing some gold? Over your lifetime so far, I would imagine you could have grown quite wealthy."

"I have been wealthy," he admitted. "There was once a time when I possessed more gold than you do now."

"What happened?"

"Just because one owns gold does not mean one gets to keep it. There are many types of thieves. Highwaymen are easy to dispatch for those such as us. Kings, soldiers and governments are much harder thieves to deal with. A Blutsauger may kill one tax collector or a soldier, but kings always seem to have more at their disposal. Ah yes, I once owned land." He sighed, then looked me in the eye. "Enjoy your holdings while you can. Blutsaugers must fight just as hard as other people to hold onto what they have earned."

Wolf's words did little to deter me from my enterprise. Because he and I had no need of the crops raised on our land, we were able to sell everything to continue raising funds – though we had to do so carefully so that no one became suspicious of our true natures.

The following year, as the spring planting began anew, Bran found our house as promised. He told us that Gawain had not learned anything on his quest, but that Arthur was preparing to send the Ancelot. I doubted the pompous self-styled prince would have any better luck, and suspected Arthur's reasons for selecting him had more to do with Guinevere than his competence for the mission.

When Bran next returned to our land, I found out my assumptions were correct.

The years passed and my holdings and wealth grew. No matter what else one might say about him, Arthur proved to be a good leader. I had never heard of such an extended time of peace and prosperity. Any attempts by the Saxons to invade were quickly repulsed. Arthur sent emissaries to the Picts and the Scots and soon they were within the British realm's fold.

My only complaint was that as each year came and went, it became easier to predict that Bran would arrive only to tell me once again that there was no news of the Grail. Also, I began to grow restless. I was born and raised a warrior. Sitting on my land as a gentleman farmer wore thin and old urges made me wish to travel again. I found myself plotting strategies whereby I might reintroduce myself to Arthur and offer my services to him as a soldier. After ten years, Bran had aged considerably, though I hadn't aged a day. I began to doubt that Arthur would even see me as the same person he had known so many years ago.

The primary thing that kept me away from Arthur's court was the prospect of seeing Guinevere again. I still loved her and thought of her often, but I knew she aged while I did not. I had toyed with the idea of turning Guinevere into a Blutsauger, but I could not bear the thought of her beautiful mouth drinking blood to survive. As Wolf had cautioned years before, the very act would certainly change her.

"Peredur thinks he's stumbled on the location of the Grail," announced Bran on one of his visits.

"Where?" Wolf and I asked anxiously.

"There is an ancient Roman fortress near the Island of Manau," explained Bran. "It seems to be guarded by many strange enchantments."

"Yes, and there are Christian sites out there. I've heard that Patrick visited the island."

"Indeed," affirmed Bran. "The fortification is on a tiny island just off Manau's coast. The people call it St. Patrick's Island because he visited the site so often."

"What would Patrick want with a Roman fortress on a tiny island?" asked Wolf shaking his head. Even as he said it, his eyes lit up. "Is there any way we can get there and check it out for ourselves?"

"The waters are rough this time of year," said Bran. "But I can have a ship ready and we can sail within the month."

"Excellent," I said. "That will give us time to make preparations for the voyage."

A month later, Bran appeared again. Luguvalium sat on a small inlet on the eastern edge of Solway Firth and his ship stood ready. We agreed to set sail in the predawn hours. I showed him two boxes. "Wolf and I will sleep in these during the day," I explained. "You must keep them covered with canvas. We will awaken at twilight."

"You have kept odd habits since you fell at Cat Coit Celidon." Bran's eyes narrowed. "Is this some part of a sacred vow that you cannot be out during the sunlight? The spring weather is so beautiful, I wish you could enjoy it."

I had to look away at that point. "Yes," I said gloomily. "It's part of our 'vows' that we can't be out in the sunlight."

He accepted our explanation and met us in the predawn hours. Without question, his crew loaded our boxes onto the ship. Wolf and I slipped inside. It grew dark as canvas tarpaulins were thrown over our resting places. I heard the crew speculate about the reasons we slept while they toiled. Loyal Bran silenced them. "It's none of your business," he said. "The lords have their ways..." The sleep took me at that point and I heard no more.

Apparently we had fair winds since when I awoke, the ship was not moving. I opened the lid of my resting place and discovered we were on St. Patrick's Island. There stood a grand old Roman fortress just as I had been told. Wolf lifted the lid from his box, then looked at me and nodded.

The ship's crew was ashore, enjoying a meal. Bran invited us over to break bread with them. I shook my head and declined. "We are anxious to begin our quest. Will you wait for us?"

"We will," said Bran.

"I would like to accompany you," said one of the men.

I looked him up and down. He seemed familiar. "Do I know you?"

"I am called Galahad," said the man.

Indeed, he resembled Galahad Anguselus – L'Ancelot – so much, that I thought it must be him, except he had not aged. I cast a suspicious glance at Wolf, remembering his desire to preserve the man's beautiful visage for eternity.

"I presume you are L'Ancelot's son," said Wolf.

The man nodded. "I am."

"He is trusted," said Bran, "and I believe Arthur would like a knight to accompany you."

I sensed no deception from this Galahad, so I nodded. "You may come with us."

The island was rather small. Wolf, Galahad, and I made our way up the hillside to the fortress's door. We stepped through the portcullis and into the courtyard. "Where do we begin?" I asked.

Wolf pointed to a tall tower near the fortress's center. "My instincts tell me that we will find it there."

"Very well," I said.

He set out toward the tower, each of us carrying torches to light the way. Galahad and I followed close on his heels.

As we entered the building, there was a palpable sense of dread. Wolf paused for a moment, seeming to feel something as well. Galahad pushed past us and beckoned us forward. Wolf squared his shoulders and continued forward until he came to a set of stone steps. I took a deep breath and stayed right behind him. Galahad rushed upstairs ahead of us.

I had grown used to a certain lack of physical challenge due to my Blutsauger strength. However, with each step I took as I climbed the stairs, my heart pounded harder and harder until I felt a distinct, dull ache in my chest and my arms. I stopped and panted. Wolf looked back at me. "Don't stop. Whatever you do, don't stop."

"I'll die if I continue."

"That's what it wants you to think," growled Wolf.

"What who wants me to think?"

"Whatever we will find at the top of the stairs." With that, he continued around the next bend. I took a deep breath and forced myself to continue.

I heard the creaking of hinges before I saw the door. The last few steps required all my will. At last I made it into the tower room. As I stepped across the threshold, the weight was finally lifted from my legs and I could breathe again. Galahad and Wolf stood in front of a stone casket. "Help me push off the lid," he cried.

I placed my torch in a sconce and ran to their side. The three of us pushed. Just as the stone lid crashed to the floor, an eagle landed in the tower's lone window. I spared the bird hardly a thought as I retrieved my torch and looked inside the casket. There I saw a simple metal bowl – presumably the Holy Grail. Next to it lay a brown scroll.

The eagle shrieked and its cry transformed into one of "No!"

I looked up in time to see the eagle metamorphose into a golden giant of a man wielding a sword.

Wolf leapt forward and pushed the man backwards. "Grab the cup," he called. "Get out of here!"

Quickly, I reached into the stone casket. My hand hovered briefly over the cup, but I grabbed the scroll. I turned and bolted for the stairs.

At the door, I glanced back. Galahad held the Grail, his mouth agape. The golden man-like creature swung the sword in a wide arc, taking Wolf's head from his shoulders. The blood splattered Galahad. The man-like creature lunged at Bran's man.

Without hesitation, I dashed down the stairs. The oppressive weight that had made it so difficult to reach the top of the tower had vanished. I was able to escape without resistance. At the bottom of the stairs, I had the choice of running out into the courtyard or turning into a hallway. I took the hallway and ran. From behind me, I heard a pitiable cry.

I came to a room that was fitted out as a Christian chapel. There was an altar. Behind the altar, a giant cross hung on the wall. Some instinct told me to avoid the cross. I swallowed hard and listened. I heard no footsteps approaching. The temptation to view my prize was too great.

I found a candle and lit it, then set about carefully unrolling the brittle, leather scroll. I saw the words written in Aramaic – the words of Jesus Himself. Words that were transforming the world. The leather of the scroll cracked. I started to roll the precious book back up and realized flakes of dust wafted from the leather – odd for something that had been stored in a stone crypt.

Before I had time to react, two things happened. The golden man-like creature – the so-called angel – appeared in the doorway and the scroll I held crumbled to dust. The angel and I cried out simultaneously. A small gust of air blew through and carried the dust away.

I looked up in time to see the angel rushing toward me with his sword. I leapt backwards and expected to land on the floor.

Instead, I kept falling and falling until I was looking out at the world through hundreds of thousands of eyes. I didn't know what had happened to me, but somehow, I could see everywhere within the chapel at once. I could see the angel from the front and the back. He swung the sword wildly trying to connect. All at once there was pain, as though a finger or toe had been broken. I didn't know what had happened, but I knew I must depart.

I moved toward the small window. In no time at all, I was outside. Somehow I was flying and I set my course for the beach. I saw Bran and his campfire. I rushed for him and tried to cry out. I tried to tell him that he needed to launch the boat. Somehow my words never came. With a force of will, I calmed my mind and centered myself. My corporeal body dropped to the ground. When I caught my breath, I noticed Bran and his men were swatting at themselves as though trying to ward off something.

"Quick, we must launch the boat!" I cried.

"Where did you come from?" asked Bran. "We were suddenly assaulted by a swarm of flies and now you appear as if out of nowhere."

"Never mind that," I said. "Launch the boat. We've got to get out of here."

Bran was too good a soldier to question my orders further. He and his men pushed the boat out into the water, then helped me aboard. Before long, they had hoisted the sail and we made for open water. I chanced a look back toward the island and I thought I could hear the cry of an eagle mourning the loss of a treasure.

"What's become of Master Wolf and Galahad? Did you find the Holy Grail?" asked Bran.

"I didn't find anything I could hold onto. I fear Galahad perished at the hands of our pursuer." I turned and looked in the direction of Britain. A single tear escaped my eye. I wiped it away furiously. Surely there had to be other writings by this man called Jesus. Such an important figure couldn't have left but one scroll. I couldn't possibly be responsible for destroying the only work written by his hand.

"And Master Wolf?" pressed Bran.

"He found what he was seeking," I said, shivering in the cold sea breeze.

It may seem obvious, but the day the scroll of Jesus fell apart in my hands, the world changed. I returned to my home and let the tenants work the land. My coffers kept me comfortable and I paid scant attention to the world outside my home. Sometimes I would hear an eagle's cry when I went outside to hunt for blood. I would search the skies. Yet, in those years after the quest, I never again saw the creature that had guarded the scroll and the cup. I often wondered what became of him. Did he remain at the castle to guard the one remaining artifact? Was his mission over when the scroll of Jesus had been destroyed? For years, I thought I would be the focus of the creature's vengeance. However, the creature either chose not to seek me out or was unable to find me. I couldn't help but think that it must be the former. It seemed inconceivable to me that such a creature couldn't find me if it so desired.

Bards sang songs of Arthur, Guinevere and the Ancelot. They were becoming legend and as time progressed, I was glad not to be part of the story. Over time, their story grew more complex. Spurned Morgana had a son named Medraut. Arthur's "nephew" raised an army, hoping to usurp the throne from Arthur. As they marched on Luguvalium, I sold my lands and sailed across the channel to Gaul.

Soon after I reached Gaul, I heard that Medraut killed Arthur at a place called Camlan. Guinevere was sent to a convent and heartbroken L'Ancelot soon vanished from the bardic tales. I wondered what became of Bran.

As the years progressed, I thought less of my mortal life and I found myself pulled by curiosity toward the homeland of Jesus. Surely I could not have destroyed the one and only copy of the book he wrote. I began moving eastward. The world itself seemed to be descending into darkness as Roman civilization whithered and vanished. However, I found I could still communicate with some learned men in Latin. The further east I traveled, the more my Celtic identity fell away. I was no longer Aonghas Deas-Mhumhan, the Dragon. I had become Desmond, Lord Draco.

Interlude 2
Guinevere and the Stranger

The Benedictine Convent at Almesbury.
The years 524-534:

Twenty years after King Arthur's death, Guinevere lived in a convent of stone and mortar a scant two miles from the timber hall they once called a palace. The sun was low in the sky and the scent of pine wafted in on the light breeze from the nearby woods. She closed her eyes and smiled, remembering a day years ago when she led Aonghas Deas-Mhumhan to a meadow of soft grass, ringed by trees. Her smile wavered as she recalled the day Bran brought news of his demise. So many years had passed since that carefree time and Aonghas – Desmond – still haunted her dreams.

Her marriage to Arthur had simply been one of political expedience. He was kind enough, but when they made love, she sensed his mind was elsewhere – whether it was a problem with one of the farms, the quest for the Holy Grail, or even memories of his own first love, Morgana, she could never tell. Whenever Arthur came to her, it felt like he was performing another duty, and not necessarily one he enjoyed much.

Was it any wonder that Prince Anguselus – L'Ancelot – was able to seduce her? Or did she seduce him? It was all such a blur. She remembered that he paid attention to her and was genuinely interested. Unlike Arthur, who always reminded her of a big hairy bear, L'Ancelot was strikingly handsome. She never could decide if he was more handsome than Desmond, but he was better groomed.

No matter what, L'Ancelot's love was tender much like Desmond's had been. Like Arthur, though, Guinevere always suspected L'Ancelot loved another more than her. He was a man in love with himself.

A bell rang within the stone walls. Guinevere closed her eyes. Now she was a nun – a bride of Christ. Christ seemed hardly more attentive than Arthur, who championed his religion. Nevertheless, Christ – or his worshipers – kept her safe in the dark and uncertain days after her husband's death – at least until a few nights ago.

Guinevere scanned the nearby tree line, looking for any sign of movement. Seeing none, she turned and stepped back within the walls, helping a nun close and bar the heavy wooden gate. The wood seemed solid enough. Nevertheless, something had made it inside on two separate nights of the previous week. Each time, a nun was found dead in the morning, her throat virtually ripped out. Despite the grievous wounds, little blood surrounded each body, as though the creature responsible had consumed it all.

Thoughts of the killings fresh in her mind, Guinevere hardly touched her supper. She went through evening prayers methodically, not really feeling any emotion, just wanting to understand what kind of creature found its way into the convent and killed the women she had come to think of as sisters. After prayers, she went to her chamber and lay down for a while, feigning sleep.

Once she heard the soft snoring of her fellow nuns, Guinevere crept out from under her covers, slipped on her boots, and retrieved a bow and arrow from under the simple wood-and-rope bed. Of all the men in her life, it was her father who had insisted that she learn archery, and though she rarely needed to hunt on her own, she had kept in practice over the years.

Guinevere stepped out into the chill evening. Clouds diffused the moonlight, washing the courtyard in pale light. The former queen nocked an arrow and made her way around the grounds, peering into the shadows as she went. The convent was not large, but she began to yawn during her second patrol of the grounds. As she reached the vegetable garden, she convinced herself that whatever was killing the nuns must have moved along to find better hunting grounds. She decided to go back to her quarters and get some sleep. Approaching the front gate, she noticed movement from the wall above. Looking more closely, she saw a figure silhouetted in the moonlight.

A man stood atop the wall.

He leapt into the courtyard. Heart pounding furiously, Guinevere raised the bow. She took aim and launched the arrow. It stuck square in the man's breast. Instead of going down, he howled with pain. He grabbed the arrow and wrenched it from his chest. Raising his head, he looked around. Guinevere's breath caught. The face was a memory – but a memory out of a nightmare. The stranger looked like Prince Anguselus, as though he had not aged a day, but his mouth was contorted in pain, revealing horrible fangs.

The stranger caught sight of her and rushed forward. With a yelp, Guinevere dropped the bow and ran. A teeth-chattering blow landed on her back and Guinevere dropped to the ground, grass and dirt filling her mouth. She sucked in air as she was turned over onto her back. The stranger reared back as though about to strike with his mouth, but he stopped short. He peered into Guinevere's eyes and for a moment, there was a quizzical expression on his face – a mixture of recognition and confusion.

The man stood and backed away.

"L'Ancelot, is that you?" asked Guinevere once she found her voice.

The man shook his head and ran for the wall.

"Galahad," she called, using L'Ancelot's birth name.

He stopped, as though that name might mean something. She took a step forward. Without turning, he climbed to the top and jumped off the other side.

Guinevere wasn't sure who the stranger was. Her rational mind said it could not have been L'Ancelot. The creature was much too young. In fact, the more she thought about it, the more she thought he seemed younger than L'Ancelot had been when she had known him. A son or grandson, perhaps? Guinevere knew L'Ancelot well enough that she would not be surprised if he had left offspring among the nearby villagers or farmers. Perhaps the illegitimate child had been left in the woods to starve, but had somehow survived and gone feral. Could that explain the fangs? Perhaps they were God's way of helping a poor hapless creature survive in the world when no man would help.

Guinevere couldn't help but feel a twinge of responsibility for a creature that could be a son or grandson of L'Ancelot. Moreover, she was a nun and it was her duty to help those who had been abandoned to the world. She realized there might be a way she could help the creature and prevent more deaths. That evening, she went to the kitchen and retrieved a rare steak and left it just inside the gate before going to supper and prayers. Inside the gate, most creatures couldn't get at the meat, but she guessed the stranger could.

Later that night, she armed herself with the bow and arrow and waited. Stars dotted the clear sky and a breeze chilled the air. Guinevere brought a blanket to keep warm. As the night wore on, she began to doze. Some time later, a noise startled Guinevere awake. She looked up. The stranger stood in the courtyard. His nose worked like that of a dog. Finally, he spotted the steak and lunged at it. Instead of eating the meat, he simply lapped up the congealed blood and juices from the wooden plank that contained the steak.

Guinevere stood and approached him. She nocked the arrow, but kept it pointed toward the ground. The stranger looked up. Seeing the nun with the bow, he reached up to his chest. With a snarl he began to back away.

"There's no need to fear me," she said. "I'm the one who brought you the food."

The creature inclined his head as though trying to comprehend the words. She pointed to the wood plank, then to her chest. "I brought the meat," she repeated.

The stranger blinked a couple of times, then gave a sharp nod.

"Thank you," he lisped, as though unaccustomed to words.

"If you promise not to attack the nuns here, I'll bring more food tomorrow."

The stranger's brow furrowed, as though concentrating on something long forgotten. Finally, he looked up into Guinevere's eyes. "No food, just blood."

"Very well then, I'll bring blood."

The creature gave a sharp nod, then leapt to the top of the wall and down the other side. Guinevere took a deep breath and let it out slowly.

Ten years later, Guinevere died peacefully in her sleep and was buried outside the walls of the convent. A cloaked figure approached her grave and left a simple bouquet of woodland flowers. Over the years, Guinevere had taught the stranger to write and encouraged him to help in the garden. Of course, he only came by night. He never could tell her his name. Because of his Gaulish accent and resemblance to L'Ancelot, she gave him a Gaulish name. Because he liked to keep his face hidden under the hood of a cloak and he'd come so far since his days as a savage, she called him Roquelaure, a word that referred to a place cloaked by laurels. Now that she was gone, it was time for Roquelaure to move on. He would miss Guinevere. He couldn't help but love her. He couldn't remember his life before he first scaled the convent's walls to attack the nuns within. She had been like a mother to him, nursing him back to health. Now the woman that was like a mother to him was gone and he would have to find his own way in the world. Hidden under the cloak's hood, a single tear fell as Roquelaure looked at Guinevere's grave one last time, then he stalked off into the night.

Part III
The Dragon's Love

Chapter 14

From the writings of Desmond, Lord Draco.
The years 558-560:

My trek across Europe was a slow one. Partly, that was a deliberate choice because I had never been away from Britain and I wanted to see more of the world. Partly, my journey was slow because chaos reigned in the wake of the Roman Empire's collapse. Even though Rome had pulled out of Britain and we were not directly under the Empire's rule, we still clung to the Empire's traditions. I had assumed it was much the same in continental Europe as well.

Instead, I was surprised to discover that continental Europe had disintegrated into numerous tiny principalities. Some were benign but most were extremely tyrannical. The tenants living in these principalities were treated no better than slaves.

The result of this chaos was multifaceted. In the worst lands, I actually found hunting rather easy. The peasants were overworked and already so weak from hunger that no one sought any particular cause when I drained one of blood, killing him. However, living in these lands was not particularly pleasant. There was no way to occupy a dwelling without attracting the prince's attention – so I could only survive by living in caves or burrowing underground.

In the better principalities, I could often find shelter, but hunting proved more difficult. I was a stranger, and thus closely watched.

I was hunting in one such land, known as Lucilinburhuc, and had just captured my prey when I looked up and found myself surrounded by soldiers. Each one pointed a spear at me.

They took me to their prince in an ancient Roman fortress. At one time, it had been an outpost guarding a Roman road. However, the small fortress had fallen into a horrible state of disrepair and the road was overgrown with weeds.

"The captain of the guard tells me you have been attacking my tenants," said the prince, whose own garb was little better than those of the peasants. I started to answer but he held up his hand. "I don't care about the reasons. I would have you executed except the captain also tells me that you demonstrate great stealth – that you are nearly impossible to track and that you hunt only at night."

I nodded my head, warily.

"I think you could be quite useful to me." The prince then told me about his neighbor, the Baron of Trier, whose men often raided cattle and sheep from the prince's lands. "I would invade his territory and take back what is rightfully mine, except that his men outnumber my own."

"I don't understand."

"They are all organized by the force of his will. My agents tell me his men would prefer to be under my rule, but they are afraid to rebel against him."

"And you think I could kill this baron."

"If you killed him, you would be welcome to an eighth's part of his treasure."

I looked around at the decaying Roman fortress and nodded my satisfaction. It was clear this prince had little to offer me. However, an eighth share of a wealthy baron's coffers would nicely replenish my dwindling funds. I quickly agreed.

The next night, I slipped across the border and onto the baron's lands, sneaking through densely wooded country. I found my way to the Moselle River that ran near the baron's castle and followed it for several miles as instructed. When daylight approached, I was grateful to find a cave where I could spend the day, so I didn't have to dig into the ground.

That night, I emerged from my hiding place and made for the castle. In fact, the baron's "castle" was little better than the Prince of Lucilinburhuc's crumbling Roman fortress. Few guards patroled the perimeter. I was able to approach the castle's wall unobserved.

As a Blutsauger, I was considerably stronger than I had been as a human, and my eyesight had improved. I saw a myriad of finger- and toeholds that no human would be able to grab onto. I shifted my pack into a comfortable position, then grabbed on and scaled the wall.

When I reached the first window, I tried to wriggle through, but quickly realized I'd made a mistake. The window was built so that arrows could be fired out, but little, including myself, could come inside. I found myself stuck fast. Taking a deep breath, I closed my eyes and disintegrated into a hundred component parts. I could see all directions at once.

At first, I was rather disconcerted that the entity I transformed into was a swarm of flies. I remember thinking of Wolf and his pelt, and I couldn't help but wonder if my human form would take on the physical characteristics of an insect over time.

As a swarm of flies, I flew down the length of the hall. The prince's agents had given me instructions about where to find the baron's sleeping chambers. It took a while, but I finally located the rooms near the fortification's heart. With a force of will, I brought my component parts under control and assumed human form again.

I shivered in the room's cold, damp air. For several years it didn't occur to me to ask how it was possible that I could transform into a swarm of flies and back again yet still have my clothes – even my pack. I dismissed it as magic – and I suppose I still do to some degree, since I have no better explanation.

I slipped over to the baron. He was a fat man and snored loudly. Tiny, wiry hairs covered his neck. I knelt down beside him and grimaced as I smelled the stale sweat that clung to his body. With a quick exhale, I bit through the hairs, into his neck, and his blood gushed into my mouth.

His eyes flew open and he began to flail about with his arms. I put the image of a young, well-endowed woman into his mind and he quieted somewhat as he grew less surprised and more aroused.

He had thrown back the blankets in his wild thrashing and I could see his cock standing at attention. At least his last thoughts would be happy ones.

Once I had my fill of his blood, I withdrew my teeth, grabbed his head and gave it a swift jerk. Standing, I made my way to a door next to the baron's sleeping chamber. I threw it open, delighted to discover his treasury. I loaded my satchel with as much gold as I could carry – which was quite a lot, but still not a full eighth of the treasury – and left the chambers. I found a dark corner near the portcullis to await the changing of the guards.

When the gate opened an hour later, I watched one guard go out and another come in. As the gate closed, I quickly slipped through. I heard a shout from behind me, but by the time any arrows flew in my direction I already approached the Moselle's banks.

I disappeared into the cave I found the night before. The prince had indicated he wanted to give me my share of the treasure personally, but I preferred simply taking it for myself. I had a feeling the prince might betray me, and that would leave me without any treasure at all.

It was in this way that I learned how to make a living in this savage landscape and gained passage through hostile territories. The next night, I purchased a wagon and a pair of horses and continued on my way.

As I continued through the Germanic lands, I began to hear legends that people told of dead friends and relatives that would die, and then come back to life – to drink the blood of those left behind. I heard the word Blutsauger a few times, but I also heard new names: Nosferatu, Neuntoter, and Vampyr.

After leaving Lucilinburhuc, I continued along the Moselle until I came to the Rhine. There I turned south until I came to a land called Mainz.

Winter rapidly approached, so I decided to stay there for a time.

I learned that the Graf of Mainz, like the Prince of Lucilinburhuc, was a rather benign ruler.

Soon I found and occupied a small wattle and daub hut not too far from the fortress, but deep enough in the woods that no one took a strong interest in my presence.

During my first nights in the region, I heard tales of a Nosferatu that hunted in the region. In the years since Wolf's death, I began to despair of ever meeting another of my kind. I was still new enough to the region and careful enough on my hunts that I doubted any of the rumors I heard were of myself.

I discovered a small tavern near the fortress of Mainz and I began to frequent it so I could hear what stories I could of this Nosferatu. As it turned out, the tavern's ale was quite good and I found that if not for the debilitating effects of the alcohol itself, the rich malty liquid came close to sustaining me.

As I listened to stories, it became clear to me that there was a pattern to the Nosferatu's attacks. They occurred most frequently near an old burial ground adjoining the fortress itself. As such, most people tried to avoid the fortress in general – and that burial ground in particular. I decided to investigate the burial ground.

I found the place easily enough. It occupied a plot of soft earth alongside the fortress. Crude stone markers had been erected to mark the places where the departed lay. I found a place near a tree and waited. As the moon began to rise – well after midnight – my keen ears detected shuffling footsteps on the grass.

Turning toward the sound, I saw a creature who, at first glance, reminded me of Wolf. He was bald and his skin was gray. I tried to hail him, but the figure ignored me.

Standing, I ran to him.

As I approached, I discovered he had an earthy smell and his clothes were a shambles, much as mine became when I dug down in the earth for shelter from the sun's rays.

"Hallo," I tried calling in the strange Germanic tongue that people of the region spoke.

The creature turned and, as though seeing me for the first

time, bared its teeth and hissed like an enraged cat. His bloodshot eyes opened wide.

I revealed my own fangs to the creature.

Becoming agitated, he ran at me and knocked me to the ground. "Halt, halt!" I cried. "Ich bin Nosferatu."

The creature lunged at my neck, but I put my hand up under his chin and slammed his jaw shut. A terrible growl-like noise came from somewhere down deep in his throat. He reached out to grab the wrist that I had on his jaw, and that movement, in turn, caused him to unbalance himself.

With my free arm, I pushed him off me. I stood and brushed dirt from my clothes. "I am like you," I tried to say, but the creature pushed himself to his feet and rushed at me again.

This time, prepared for his attack, I dodged to the side, then ran for a nearby tree. It was clear to me that this creature – though a Blutsauger or Nosferatu like me – was quite mad. The cause – living alone or whatever else – I did not know.

I grabbed a tree branch and pulled with all my might until it snapped off. As the creature ran at me, I swung the branch and knocked him to the ground. Before he could get up again, I forced the branch through the creature's chest, pinning him to the ground.

I dropped down beside him and sat there panting. Tears came to my eyes as I looked at that poor, mad creature who I truly believed had simply been defending himself.

The sound of running footsteps came from the fortress. I looked up to see a pair of guards. They looked at the body on the ground and then they looked at me. "You've killed the Nosferatu," one said.

"I think the graf would like to see you," said the other.

I sighed, but pushed myself to my feet. "Very well."

The Graf of Mainz proved to be quite impressed with the story of my Nosferatu slaying. He offered to let me remain on his lands, rent-free as long as I defended his realm from such creatures. I kept my composure as best I could and accepted the graf's offer. I was already prepared to stay in Mainz. However, I did find irony in the idea of being a Nosferatu that slayed other Nosferatu.

Although no other Nosferatu appeared in Mainz to dispatch, the graf soon found he could make use of me as an agent to keep watch on his neighbors' activities. I found myself making frequent excursions to the surrounding principalities and climbing walls at night to listen in on conversations and bring the information back to the graf.

The graf also found I was invaluable at ferreting out spies in his own court, as I could hear conversations that people thought were hidden and I could see comings and goings at night that the guards missed. Though I have a certain limited ability to see and hear the thoughts of others, sometimes my most valuable gift is that I can literally become the proverbial 'fly on the wall.'

After a year and a half in Mainz, I grew restless. Working for the graf kept me near enough to people that I remained well fed and could live in warm, comfortable housing. Unfortunately, I was no closer to learning about any copies of the book penned by Jesus, aside from the one that had crumbled to dust in my hands. I wanted to continue my journey eastward toward the Holy Land. Also, I wanted to learn if there were others like me. I began to worry that most Blutsaugers might go mad as the fellow I had slain in the burial ground. If true, was that my destiny as well?

I bade farewell to the graf in the spring and continued my journey with my faithful horses and wagon. The graf had paid me generously and I sensed that he was genuinely sorry to see me go.

I followed the Main River over mountains and into flatlands. Though I came across settlements here and there, I found little of interest until I crossed through the Bohemian Forest and encountered the Czech tribes.

These people were surprisingly friendly to a night traveler making his way across their country. I suspect they recognized me as a kindred spirit, always on the move.

From them, I continued to hear stories of other night creatures such as the vilkodlak and the muro. I spent one pleasant night in the company of Bohemian tribesmen that told me they had recently dispatched a muro by burying him at a crossroads.

"Why would that do any good?" I asked, curiosity getting the better of me.

"The muro gets lost and can't find its way back to our houses," said a tribesman, his hands placed proudly on his hips.

"Where did you bury this muro?" I asked.

The tribesman looked at me suspiciously for several minutes, as though I had just proposed marriage to his youngest daughter, but with a little encouragement, and some silver, I convinced him to tell me. I waited until the people of the tribe had gone to sleep, then I quietly loaded my wagon and made my way to the place he described.

I found the site shortly before dawn. I saw evidence of a burial, but no sign that the muro had dug his way out as I thought he would have.

I looked at the sky and decided to wait before figuring out what happened. I led my horses into the woods and hid my wagon. I tied my horses up so they could graze, and I found soft earth to dig down into. The thing I most hated about this familiar routine was the time before I fell asleep, those long minutes of feeling dirt drift into my nostrils as I lay there, trying not to open my eyes, lest the soil get into them as well. Fortunately, unlike ordinary humans, we Blutsauger are not plagued with sleeping problems.

I awoke the next night and burst free from the soil. The horses shook the soft dirt and peat from their skins and then looked at me as though seriously put out. I apologized and led them back to the crossroads. Again, I found no indication that a creature had tried to dig its way out.

Curiosity got the better of me. I dug down until I came to a dead body. The skin was the pale white of my kind, but when I pushed back the lips, there were no fangs. Instead, the gums were coated in dried blood.

His fingers were scratched and bloody, as though he had tried to dig his way to the surface, failed, then suffocated to death. I surmised the poor creature had not been one such as Wolf or I. Instead, he had been a plague victim, probably seeking help from the tribesmen. Because he was sick, they grew fearful of him and simply buried him alive. I swallowed back bile, climbed out of the hole I was in, and reburied the man.

Night creatures – whether they are called Blutsauger, Nosferatu, vampyr, or muro could, indeed be frightening. However, at that moment, what frightened me more than any tangible thing, was human superstition.

I continued onward to a village called Prague. It was one of the largest and most organized settlements I'd come upon since leaving Gaul and I sensed that I had returned to 'civilization' as I knew it to be. In many respects, the village reminded me of Luguvalium and other towns I'd left behind in Britain. Of course, I also closed in on Constantinople, the heart of the Eastern Roman Empire.

As I traveled, I learned that my ability to sense the thoughts of others was invaluable. I could sense images in a person's mind as they spoke – making it easy to pick up languages as I moved. As a result, even though the Czech and Bohemian languages were quite alien to me, I found I could speak them within a week or two of arriving in the land.

It was only early autumn when I arrived in Prague, but I decided to settle in for the winter anyway. The city seemed a comfortable enough place to get my bearings while I learned news of points farther south and east.

I still had to travel through a number of wild lands such as Hungary and Transylvania before I reached Constantinople.

As a young man, I'd heard stories of a vicious leader called Attila the Hun who had presided over many of the Eastern lands. He had finally been defeated, much as we had defeated such barbarians as Octha and Caw back in Britain, but I wasn't sure what state the lands were in.

I learned few people inhabited Transylvania, but a man called Fastida ruled the land. I vowed to learn more about him.

In the meantime, I discovered a Christian monastery in Prague. I decided to pay a visit early one winter's evening. A rather imposing man in brown robes greeted me at the gate.

He looked me up and down. "Who are you and what do you want?"

"I am Desmond, Lord Draco." I bowed low and then met his eyes. "I am a stranger to these lands and though I know a little about your Christian faith, I would like to know more."

He frowned deeply. "Draco…. Are you from Western Rome?"

"In a manner of speaking." I shifted from one foot to the other. During my father's life, Britain had, indeed, been part of the Western Roman Empire, with its capital in Rome.

"Why do you come here seeking to learn more? There is more to be learned in your own land," he said.

I sighed. Clearly this fellow manned the door because he was big and intimidating, not because he possessed a particularly acute intellect. "Actually, I'm making my way to Constantinople and Jerusalem," I explained as patiently as I could. "I am passing through Prague, but I would like a chance to understand more of what I might find further down the road."

The monk scratched his head, but finally stood aside and let me inside. "I will take you to the abbot. Perhaps he can help you."

The monk closed the gate behind me and then led me to an inner building. The place was frighteningly quiet and as we entered the stone structure, gooseflesh appeared on my arms. I was reminded of the fortress on St. Patrick's Island. I swallowed and continued to follow the monk.

He rapped on a wooden door. There was a muffled response from within. We entered and found another monk sitting up in a short type of bed. Soon after this encounter, I would learn that these types of beds were becoming popular with certain churchmen and nobles that feared lying down when they slept. Wisps of white hair framed the elderly monk's bald pate.

"What do we have here?" asked the senior monk.

The monk from the gate relayed the information I'd given him. His accuracy surprised me, given my low opinion of his intellect.

"Very well, Mikhail. You may leave us." The elder monk climbed from his bed and donned a black robe as Mikhail turned and left. "I am Father Vladimir. It would have been better if you'd arrived at a more hospitable hour."

"I apologize." I bowed my head. "I'm afraid that I have vowed not to appear during the daylight until I find a certain artifact." I then went on to tell him about my quest for the Holy Grail and the book of Jesus – omitting the fact that I'd actually seen the Grail with my own eyes and that the book disintegrated in my very grasp.

He smiled warily, but not unkindly. "Be careful who you confide in about your quest, my son," said the father. "There are many within the Church who would consider the only true words of Jesus to be those recorded by His apostles. You could find yourself charged with heresy."

I shook my head, not certain what he meant by words recorded by apostles. "I am from the land of Britannia and we have few books. Word of Christ has mostly been taught by such men as Patrick and Germanus."

Father Vladimir smiled and nodded. "I have heard of those men. They are great missionaries. I have even heard of your King Arthur and his quest for the Holy Grail." He appraised me carefully. "You are younger than I would expect for one of his knights, but still...." He patted me on the back and led me out into the corridor. "Yours is a quest I respect and—" at that point he triumphantly threw open a door, "—we have numerous books that may help you in your quest, Lord Draco."

I looked into the cavernous, dark room and gasped. Even before the father lit a torch that would reveal, to ordinary human eyes, what was contained within, I could see there were shelves upon shelves lined with scrolls.

Once the torch was lit, he looked at me and smiled. "Can you read Latin, Lord Draco?"

My mouth hung open and I merely nodded.

He stepped over to a table at the room's center and opened a leather-bound book. I approached and discovered a book filled with sheets of parchment and the parchment was filled with precisely formed, hand-written words.

"Within this book you will find the gospels of Matthew, Mark, Luke, John, Thomas, and Mary Magdaline. You are welcome to read. If you have questions, please feel free to see me before you leave. I arise for morning prayers before sunrise."

I reached out and lovingly touched the volume before me, then I looked around at the shelves lined with scrolls. Never in my wildest dreams had I imagined such a place – such a repository of knowledge. Why hadn't the book of Jesus been preserved in such a place? "Do you suppose there are any other copies of the Gospel according to Jesus?" I asked, my voice barely more than a whisper.

"If there are," he said, "you are heading in the right direction." With that, he patted my shoulder and bade me good night.

I spent as many nights as I could afford within the library at the monastery in Prague. Brother Mikhail and Father Vladimir came to know me quite well. Every now and again, I would look up and see other monks staring at me from the library's doorway. I would invite them in and sometimes hold extended discussions with them about what I found within the pages of the Bible and the other books.

Though tempted to spend more time in Prague and explore the library even further, I decided I should continue on my way come spring. My quest was for the actual words of Jesus. Although many of his students had recorded his words, I noted many variations and discrepancies – many of which were easily explained, given the span of a man's life and the different people that came and went from it.

However, Father Vladimir was correct. The only way I would learn more would be to continue on – to Constantinople and beyond.

Father Vladimir introduced me to a businessman called Janos

Kazar who would lead a caravan through Transylvania and onward to Constantinople. I regretfully told Kazar that I could not join his caravan, but I paid him handsomely to take several parcels – including a rather large, man-sized box – with him to the capital of the Eastern Roman Empire.

Chapter 15

From the writings of Desmond, Lord Draco.
The years 560-567:

Traveling as part of a caravan, I had to adapt to a new routine. In many ways, it was easier than traveling by myself. I did not have to tend horses nor do upkeep on the wagon. However, I didn't dare show myself until most of the people within the caravan had gone to sleep for the night. The result was that I'd often spend many hours in the early evening lying awake within my wooden crate, listening to stories being told and songs sung around the campfire. On one hand, those tales told by the Czech tribesmen fascinated me. On the other hand, it was rather lonely.

More than once, I wished I could simply emerge and join in the revelry. Unfortunately, that would lead to a situation where I would have to explain the reasons for my sleeping during the day and for not pulling my weight the rest of the time. My self-given title of Lord Draco gave me freedom for eccentric behavior in some circles, but not in all.

Once the men and women of the caravan had dropped off to sleep, I could finally emerge from my hiding place. I drank just a small amount of blood, usually from two or three people in the caravan. Often while I lay in the crate in the early evening, I would hear complaints about the size of the mosquitoes that populated Moravia and Slovakia.

Late in the second week of our travels, I gathered that we had entered Transylvania. When I emerged from my hiding place that night, the moon shone brightly, illuminating the rugged mountains and trees that surrounded us. Though my travels had taken me through much new terrain, this was the most exciting.

Before feeding, I took a walk and wandered out into the forest some distance. Away from the river and the road we followed, I stood quietly and listened to thousands of small noises, ranging from the chirpings of crickets and night birds to the soft shuffling of burrowing animals, to the squeakings of bats and the buzzing of insects.

Standing there, letting the breeze blow through my hair and rustle my clothes, it was possible to imagine that I was alone, except for the animals. I looked up to the sky.

In my youth, I remembered looking up at the moon and other objects that occupied the sky. As I grew older, I lost interest in those objects. Instead, the business of war and running my land occupied me. I'd never really looked closely at the moon again.

That night, I noticed details that I never remembered. I saw mountains and small dimple-like impressions on the moon. Before, the moon had always seemed ethereal. Now, it looked like a real place. I reached upwards, as though to touch it. I wondered what it would be like to walk there.

I looked around at the evergreens and listened to the sound of the water running in the distance and fell in love with this wild land. In Prague, I had learned that few people inhabited this place. That could be a problem for a creature that needed human blood to survive. However, Wolf had shown me that I could live on the blood of other creatures.

Listening to the sounds in the forest around me, I realized I could live comfortably here and never have to take a human life. The fantasy tempted me, but then I thought of my quest.

I returned to the camp, took blood from two people in the caravan, then returned to the woods for a time. Before sunrise, I shut myself in my crate and wished – not for the first time since becoming a Blutsauger – that I could dream.

Two nights later, I awoke and was surprised not to hear the laughter and myriad voices that I had become accustomed to. I listened more closely and discovered that I didn't hear anything I thought I should – such as the river we followed and the animals that lived among the trees near the river. There wasn't even the sound of wind rustling through vegetation.

Something was distinctly wrong.

Cautiously, I pushed up on the lid of my crate and discovered I was in a dark room. My crate had been unloaded from the wagon and was stacked atop several other crates that were in the caravan along with mine. My heart sprang to life and pounded rapidly. One of those small crates contained my gold. I made a quick search around the storage room, only to discover that the gold had vanished.

Growling deep in my throat, I vowed to discover what had happened. I stepped to the room's door and opened it a crack. Outside was a darkened hallway. From the length of the hallway, I surmised that I was in a fortification of some sort. I crept down the passage until I came to a set of stairs that descended a level.

At the bottom of the stairs, I found I was in a dungeon. Small cells lined the room. I looked in the first and saw Janos Kazar. After a brief examination of the cell, I pulled the pins from the hinges and lifted the door away from the wall. I stepped inside and pushed on the businessman's shoulder.

His eyes fluttered open and he tried to see who I was, in the darkness. "Shh," I said, "I've come to rescue you."

It was clear that he could not see me, even though I could see him. "Lord Draco?" he asked, apparently recognizing my voice. "What are you doing here?"

"I'm not sure I know where we are," I admitted.

"How can you be here without knowing where we are?" he asked, more puzzled than before. "We're in the fortress of the Khagan Kandik. His soldiers fell upon us and when they discovered your gold and some of our other treasures, they decided to take them for themselves."

"Indeed," I said. Even though he could not see me in the

darkness, I looked him in the eye. "I'm sorry to have brought this trouble on you, but I think I have a way to get you out."

"I hope so," said Janos. "It's only a matter of time before Kandik decides that it's more trouble to feed us than bury us."

While in Prague, I had heard a little of the Khagan Kandik. His people, the Avars, were closely related to the Huns, much as the Scots were related to the Picts, and there were rumors that Kandik wanted Transylvania for his own people.

I slipped back out of the cell and replaced the door, then found my way back up the stairs to the first hallway I had been in. I walked along the hallway until I came to another stairway that led upwards to a torch-lit corridor. I looked both ways, then crept down the hallway until I found a guard wandering down the corridor, yawning.

I pressed myself against a wall, pulled a dirk from a scabbard at my leg, and waited until he came alongside. At that point, I leapt out and held the knife to the guard's throat. "Take me to Khagan Kandik," I commanded.

The guard let out a small noise, and I pressed the knife more firmly against his throat.

"Very well," he croaked.

He led me along the corridor until we came to a door with a guard on either side. The guards quickly drew their swords.

"Let me pass," I commanded.

When they began to advance toward me, I growled deep in my throat, ran the knife along the throat of the guard I held and pushed his slouching body into the closest of the advancing guards. I then leapt backwards which forced the second guard to lunge his sword. As he did, I grabbed his forearm, pulled him toward me, and bit into his neck, drinking enough of his blood to give me more energy.

Just then, the door opened and a man appeared with a long, thick mustache and skin that looked almost jaundiced. He wore a long nightshirt.

"Hold!" he cried. "What is the meaning of this?"

I let the man I had subdued drop to the floor and wiped his

blood from my chin. "I am called Lord Draco," I said. "I wish to offer my services as an assassin in exchange for the freedom of the men you hold in your dungeon."

"Indeed," said the man, who I gathered to be the Khagan Kandik. He looked down at the bodies of the men. "Come inside my chambers," he invited. "I believe we might be able to arrange a deal."

Kandik told me that Constantinople's Emperor Justinian had granted his people, the Avars, title to Transylvania – the land known as Dacia to the Romans. The problem was that the Gepidae, who currently possessed Transylvania, were unwilling to withdraw. "Their emperor is a man called Fastida," said Kandik.

"I've heard of him." I shrugged. "Though, I must admit, I know little about him."

"He is a formidable opponent," said Kandik. "He is named after one of the Gepidae's first and greatest rulers. To them, he represents a time gone by, a time when the Gepidae were a force to be reckoned with."

"If he were gone, would it be easier for you to take possession of Dacia?" I asked.

"It would be much easier," said Kandik.

"I believe I can eliminate Fastida."

"How many men would you need?"

"Only a scout to show me the way to his fortress."

The Khagan Kandik threw back his head and laughed at me. He stopped after a moment, merely grinning at me. "I don't believe you."

"All I ask, in return for undertaking this mission, is that Janos Kazar and his caravan be allowed to continue on their way. Their possessions returned to them."

Kandik stood and stepped over to the window of his chambers and put his hands behind his back. He stood silently for several minutes, then finally turned around and looked at me. He reached up and twisted the end of his mustache between his thumb and middle finger. "Their cargo represents several months of provisions for my men. Coming upon them was a windfall that I cannot afford to lose."

"I believe you found a chest of gold, silver, and jewels," I said, cautiously.

He gave a brief nod.

"That chest is mine," I said. "Send them with everything but those things that belong to me and I will eliminate Fastida for you."

He stood there and evaluated me for a moment. Then, he stepped to the door and looked out at the guards I had dispatched single-handedly. Finally, he smiled.

"Very well, I will release Kazar in the morning, and I will retain your possessions. If you fail, your treasure will be mine and it will minimize my losses. However, if you succeed, I will return your treasure and request that you remain in my service."

"For how long?" I asked.

"For as long as I say." The corners of his lips turned upward under the long, thin mustache. I swallowed hard and he laughed again. "Don't look so worried. If you do as you say, you will be duly rewarded."

"I will want a fortress of my own," I blurted out.

"Very well." He held out his hands. "If you succeed, you can have this one."

The next night, I awoke to find that Kazar and the caravan had departed without me. I climbed to the fortress's outer wall and studied the surrounding landscape. I noted that the fortress we occupied was cut from stone similar to the surrounding rock and was in the middle of a dense forest. However, there was a good view into the valley.

A river ran off into the distance. A figure joined me on the ramparts. I turned around and discovered it was Kandik, along with a young man.

"It is a good view, is it not?" asked Kandik. He followed my gaze to the river. "The natives call it Bistritza," he explained.

I nodded.

"I wished to introduce you to the scout who will lead you." He pointed to the young man at his side. "This is my son, Bayan."

I turned and bowed to the son. He merely nodded his head in acknowledgment.

"When shall we depart for Fastida's stronghold?" I asked.

"As soon as you are ready." Bayan eyed me warily.

"I am ready now."

His eyes widened and I could sense his pulse quicken. He had not anticipated my response. Still, he quieted his breathing and nodded his head. "Then I shall order the horses saddled and our gear made ready."

"I will need a horse," I acknowledged, "but I do not require food or other supplies." I looked around at the rugged terrain. "Is Fastida's stronghold more than a day's ride from here?"

"Three days," affirmed Bayan.

"We shall need to ride by night. We will sleep by day," I said.

Bayan swallowed hard and gooseflesh rose on his skin. "Surely we could ride by day until we are close to Fastida's stronghold."

I thought about challenging the boy's strength and courage, but thought better of it with his father standing right there. "We do not know where Fastida's scouts might be. They might be watching this very fortification. Speed is our ally. Delay could cause your enemy to be on guard."

"Very well." Bayan nodded, then turned on his heel and left.

Kandik chuckled once the boy was out of earshot. "He is a good boy – a good scout and tracker." The khagan turned and faced me, narrowing his eyes. "The fact that I am sending him should indicate to you how important this mission is to me."

"The fact that you let Kazar go without keeping the goods he is taking to market tells me how important this mission is to you. I will not disappoint you."

"No," said the khagan, "you will not."

Later that night, Bayan and I rode out from the khagan's fortress. We followed a trail that led away from the Bistritza and through mountain passes. As we rode, I discovered that Bayan was, indeed, a font of information. He explained that the mountains we rode through were called the Carpathians and that we approached the western lowlands. Fastida ruled the country from a village with the distinctly Germanic name of Klausenburg.

As morning dawned, we found a shaded spot to camp. After the boy had gone to sleep, I found a hidden spot and burrowed into the earth. The next night, we rode forth again.

I was surprised by how few people inhabited the land, and said as much to Bayan. "It seems this territory has a long history of foreigners who wish to occupy it. Yet, there are few people, and it seems that the terrain is not the best for farming. What is the value of this land to you, to the Gepidae, to the Huns and Romans?"

"Trade," explained Bayan, simply. "The people that control Dacia control trade between the Holy Land and the western reaches of the Roman Empire. They control trade between the Empire and Asia to the east and Africa to the south."

"This is true." I thought of Arthur, his ships, and all of the other ships that sailed from my homeland. "But why can't people simply bypass this land by sailing through the Mediterranean to the south?"

"Some do. Not everyone does," said Bayan. "For instance, why didn't you go south to a Roman city and sail past this land?"

I did not answer, but in truth, I remembered the rough waters when Arthur and I sailed against the pirates. What if a boat went down? Would I survive under water, the way I did in the earth? I determined to conduct an experiment in a safe place in the future, but for the time being, we moved on to other subjects. The more I spoke with Bayan, the more I began to like this young man, and, I believe, the more he began to trust me.

The following night, we arrived in the village of Klausenburg. We found an inn and left our belongings. Then he showed me around the village and explained the comings and goings of Fastida and his guards. Rather than occupying a great fortress, Fastida held court in a hall made from the land's abundant timbers. When Bayan showed me the hall, I was struck by its resemblance to the hall first occupied by Ambrosius then by Arthur.

I waited until late the following night to carry out my plans. I encouraged Bayan to stay in the inn and get some sleep. We would be riding hard and fast later in the night and I wanted him well rested.

I left the inn and crept toward Fastida's timber hall. Much as I hated transforming into a swarm of flies, I realized the easiest way to gain entrance would be to do so. With a force of will, I broke into my component parts and quickly covered the distance to the hall. I landed on the wooden structure, where each part of me found and climbed between gaps in the wood of the walls and the thatch of the roof.

Early on, I'd discovered that I was strongest as a swarm when I was close together. However in this instance, if I spread out, I could observe almost the entire inside of the structure – especially such a relatively small one as Fastida's timber hall.

I soon found Fastida's sleeping chamber, but it took some time for me to gather all of the flies together into one place so I could resume my human form.

Once I did, I crept to the emperor's side and quickly cut his throat, then left the knife in the hands of the woman that slept by his side. I did not know whether the woman was his wife or mistress, loyal or not. Still, the time it took to investigate her involvement in the assassination would be time that would allow Bayan and I to get farther away.

I crept from Fastida's chamber and slowly closed the door behind me and turned around to see two guards. Each held one of

Bayan's arms. "Who are you? What are you doing here?" asked one of the guards.

"I had business with the emperor," I said. Then, faster than he could react, I took a step forward while reaching down to retrieve the dirk in my boot.

I planted the knife in the guard's foot, then swung around and planted the heel of my hand into the jaw of the second guard. As I did that, Bayan drew a sword and ran it into the first guard's abdomen.

"I thought I told you to wait," I complained.

"I followed you," he said. "But I didn't see how you got inside. You disappeared."

"That's probably just as well." I looked around. "Were there guards at the door?"

He nodded, looking sheepish. Without further word, I hefted Bayan over my shoulder as though he were a frail woman or a child, and barreled through the timbers of the wall.

The guards shouted an alarm, but we reached our horses before they could give chase. We rode as fast as we could back toward the khagan's mountain fortress.

The khagan led his men in an assault of Klausenburg in the wake of the emperor's death.

The war went on for nearly five years. I stayed on as promised, and helped lead campaigns here and there when I could. During the war, Kandik was mortally wounded and my young friend, Bayan, became the new khagan.

He finally prevailed against the Gepidae and drove them from Klausenburg.

Bayan set up residence and ordered the emperor's timber hall burned to the ground. In its place, he began construction of a stone fortress. Ultimately, Khagan Bayan kept his father's promise to me and gave me the ancient Roman fortress in the mountains, along with a healthy sum of gold and supplies.

In the spring of 567, I moved into the first home I ever knew outside my native Britain. I dubbed the fortress, Castle Draco. I turned the deep, lightless dungeons into my sleeping quarters and I found a large room upstairs that let in plenty of star and moonlight and vowed that I would make it a library as great as the one I had seen in Prague. With a sigh, I realized that the only things missing were books.

Chapter 16

From the writings of Desmond, Lord Draco.
The year 569:

Though I yearned to continue my quest, I had grown weary of both travel and warfare after I helped the Avars take Transylvania. I decided to spend time resting and refurbishing my new home in the Carpathian Mountains. Ultimately, though, the desire to travel and seek out more information about the book of Jesus finally drove me to continue my travels. With the blessing of my patron, the Khagan Bayan, I set out for the world's largest city, Constantinople.

I built a new wagon that appeared to have two rows of solid benches over the wheel wells. Under one of the benches was a hidden, light-tight compartment where I could spend the day sleeping and, even if my wagon were found in its hiding place during the day, I hoped that it would be so innocuous as not to invite further inspection.

I did leave a small satchel of gold on the seat at night just in case the wagon were discovered by thieves, with the hope that they would take it and leave me and the rest of my money alone.

Bayan warned me that the inns of Constantinople would be expensive.

In all of my years, I had never seen one of the true cities of the Empire. In my experience, the largest towns I had seen were places such as Luguvalium, Mainz, and Klausenburg. I was completely unprepared for a city on the scale of Constantinople.

I approached the city along the Lykos River. From some distance away, the rounded and spired tops of buildings that sat atop hills grew visible. At first, these buildings reminded me of abandoned Roman fortresses, such as the one on St. Patrick's Island, or the one I occupied. However, as I grew closer, I realized that I was not seeing a single building surrounded by a few outbuildings, but rather I saw numerous buildings surrounded by a great wall and occupying an entire peninsula jutting out into the Sea of Marmara. When I arrived at the Wall of Theodosius, I climbed off the wagon and stared in awe at the structure that ran in either direction as far as I could see.

I turned north and rode until I found a gate that led into the city. The guard seemed nonplused at the idea of a merchant arriving at the city at such a late hour. Looking through the gates, my mouth fell open again at the sight of building upon building. I realized that anyone looking could see my fangs and I quickly shut my mouth again. I faced the guard.

"Good sir," I said, "can you tell me where I might find a respectable inn at this hour?"

The guard looked at me, somewhat askance. "You've never been here before?" he asked.

I shook my head.

"Continue down this road and don't stop until you're through the old Wall of Constantine. Go about half a mile beyond that until you come to the Aqueduct of Valens, then turn south. About another half mile on you'll come to the Forum Bovis. There are a number of respectable inns in that area with stables that will put your wagon and horses up for the night."

I thanked the guard and urged my horses forward, though my mind reeled at the idea of a city that extended for miles. As I rode, I had the presence of mind to examine the city carefully. The outer reaches of Constantinople seemed to consist mostly of poor dwellings and this area struck me as a good place to hunt once I secured an inn for myself. Once I passed through the Wall of Constantine, the buildings became much grander.

Even late as it was, I was struck by how many people walked the streets. It occurred to me that the streets must be literally alive with people during the daylight hours.

My heart thrilled at the prospect of so much human life. On one hand, it seemed a literal feast for one such as me. On the other hand, it terrified me. With so many people, how could I ever hope to move around undetected?

I approached a great bridge-like structure covered in beautiful mosaic tile that reflected the starlight. I could hear the sound of running water and I realized that I must have reached the Aqueduct of Valens. As soon as I found a street that turned south, I followed it until I came to the Forum Bovis. I had heard of the Roman forums, but again, it astounded me to think of a structure so large, built for no other purpose than to entertain the masses. In my experience, the business of agriculture and warfare took so much time that it was hard to imagine that people could do anything else.

I searched the neighborhood and soon found an inn. I pounded on a door and a man in a nightshirt peeked out at me. He started to send me away until I held up a gold coin. He looked at the horses and my wagon, then indicated that I could put them in a stable across the street.

"I will need to stay for several days and my room must remain undisturbed."

He quickly tucked the gold coin I had handed him into a satchel that hung from his belt, then held out his hand for more. I gave him two more and he finally said, "It's a pleasure doing business with you, sir."

I attended to my horses, then went into the inn where the man showed me to my room. I sat in the silent room and listened until his footsteps faded down the hall and a door closed. I took a moment to examine the buildings outside my room. I hung one blanket over the window to keep light from coming in, then placed another under the bed so I would have a comfortable place to sleep. Finally, I patted my stomach, and went out in search of food.

The problem with hunting for anything in a city the size of Constantinople is determining where to begin. I spent my second night in the city walking through the streets, trying to understand the city's layout and slipping into taverns where I might make discreet inquiries.

Unfortunately, taverns are not the best places to learn about obscure religious artifacts. However, they are good places to meet construction workers and artisans, and I soon met some men who were proud of work they had done in their youth on a church called the Holy Wisdom of the Logos. That church overlooked the Sea of Marmara from atop a hill. "It's near the Imperial Palace," bragged the worker I spoke to. "I don't know anything about holy books, but I'm guessing anything of value would be there."

The following night, I crossed the city and found the Holy Wisdom of the Logos. Smaller than Forum Bovis, the building still impressed me.

I would describe the central building as a great, tiered block, but that would do it no justice at all. Enormous, sweeping arches comprised each face of the block's upper tier. At four corners sat structures resembling fortress towers, except they didn't jut above the building's roof. Rather, they were integrated into the structure itself. Topping the structure was a tremendous, spired dome.

Away from the building on the lower tier stood four spires, taller than the building itself that pointed heavenward.

As a Dragon in Britain, I had seen many of the stone circles the ancient druids had built and the work required to place the great stones awed me. To my mind, the structure that stood before me that night dwarfed any of the stone circles the druids had built.

I crept through the courtyard in front of the structure, toward the main door, hoping that I would find someone who would be willing to let me in and talk with me. I reached up to knock, but the merest brush of my hand pushed the door open. My brow knitted as I examined the door. It did not take long to discover that someone had crudely jammed the latch mechanism so the door would not lock.

Only faint moonlight coming in through two rows of windows illuminated the building's interior. The building's lower tier seemed as though it housed offices or rooms. Possibly there was a library, but I had no clue which direction to turn first.

I decided to go forward, into the main sanctuary. There, the domed ceiling created a vast expanse and even inside, in the dark, I experienced the illusion that I was looking up into the heavens themselves. I walked toward the altar and discovered two doors.

Both were locked, but considering the building's configuration, I doubted those doors led to anything more than antechambers.

I turned around and studied the inside. One level above me, balconies overlooked the room. All had doors at the back and I gathered those doors led to a staircase. One of the balconies was notable due to the presence of two particularly grandiose chairs. I gathered that must be where Emperor Justinian II and his wife would sit during services.

Returning to the entranceway, I found a set of stairs that led upwards. Ascending the stairs, I found hallways that led to the balconies.

Out of curiosity, I followed the hallway toward the Emperor's balcony. When I came to the last door, I opened it. There, I discovered not the Emperor's balcony, but the one adjacent to it. There was a door at the back of the Emperor's balcony, but there was no obvious way to get to it. It struck me that there could be important secrets behind that door.

I transformed into the swarm of flies and quickly crossed the distance to the Emperor's balcony, reformed, and examined the door. I reached for the handle and discovered that the latch had been rigged, much as the church's front door. I pursed my lips and just as I was about to proceed, the door flew open in my face.

Stunned by the abrupt movement, I fell back against the balcony's railing and opened my eyes to see a figure in black turn around, remove a metal bar that held the latch open, carefully secure the door, and then step to the balcony's edge.

The person in black had a bag slung over their shoulder and made as if to leap from the balcony. I couldn't imagine an ordinary human making the jump without, at the very least, breaking a limb.

"Wait a moment," I cried.

The person turned around and I caught sight of dark brown eyes and smooth olive skin. This wasn't a man as I'd assumed, but was, rather, a woman. She lunged forward with surprising speed and pushed me over the balcony's side. She leapt down next to me and hissed, revealing fangs. However, she gasped and backed into one of the pews when I sat up, rubbing my head. "You are a Blutsauger, are you not?" I asked.

"I prefer the word vampyr," she said in an accent that seemed odd to me. "What are you?"

"I am Desmond, Lord Draco," I responded. I then opened my mouth, revealing my own fangs. "I've heard several names for our kind and I don't think I like any of them."

"We need to leave before the palace guards discover what I've taken," she said. She helped me to my feet and together we made for the door.

There, she undid her sabotage, and the door locked behind us. We ducked into a nearby alley and crouched down together as she took a peek into her bag. She held up several jewels and examined them in the moonlight.

"You're a thief," I said, beginning to understand.

"My name is Alexandra."

"What was behind that door in the Emperor's balcony?"

"Stairs," she said. "They lead underground to a passageway." She pointed to the Imperial Palace, not far away. "Through it, the Emperor can come to his most precious church without having to set foot on the same streets as the peasants."

"Ah..." I said, understanding. "You were stealing from the Emperor himself."

"What were you doing there?" Her eyes narrowed in suspicion.

"I am on a quest.... I'm looking for an ancient book," I explained.

"Not many books there," said Alexandra. "That building is the Emperor's showpiece. Oh, there are a few reliquaries with some bones they say belonged to the saints, but that's about it." She stood up and threw her bag over her shoulder. "Say, you look like something of a noble. Do you have someplace to stay?"

"I do."

"Let's get inside and you can tell me more about yourself and this book you're looking for. I only know a few vampyrs and it would be nice to know another."

I nodded. "The only other Blutsauger I know was the one who made me – and he's dead."

"Did you kill him?" She eyed me suspiciously.

"No."

"Good," she said. "Lead the way."

As we walked back to the inn, I realized this thief was nearly as tall as me. I hadn't recognized her as a woman since she wore loose-fitting black pants and a black tunic that helped her blend into the shadows and conceal her form. Her hair was braided and tied up in a bun at the back of her head.

When we reached my room, and I lit the lamp, she undid the bun and let her hair fall about her shoulders. I caught my breath as she removed her tunic to reveal a low-cut, white blouse with puffed sleeves and delicate flowers embroidered around the décolletage.

I swallowed, thinking that the women of Britain and the northern territories did not show their endowments so readily.

"Now, I challenge anyone who might have glimpsed me within the palace to identify me to the guards." She smiled as she caught me staring. "When I wore black, your attention was drawn to my face. Now, I guess, you could not even begin to describe it."

I cleared my throat and looked into her eyes with a deliberate force of will. She laughed at me.

"I am not accustomed to being laughed at."

"That's apparent enough," she said with a smirk. "Who are you, noble? I don't recognize your accent, though you remind me of some I've met from Northern Gaul."

"Close." I told her a little of myself, my service to Duke Ambrosius of Britannia, and how the Blutsauger, Wolf, had turned me into a night creature like himself.

"I am Greek," she said with a certain bluntness. She explained that she had been born a slave outside of Athens. "There was a noble, such as yourself, that bought slaves. He was a vampyr and he used us as food and ... amusement. From time to time, he would bring one of us to his chambers and put us under his spell. He would not only take our blood for his nourishment, but he would have his way with us as well. When he tried to take me, I resisted and fought back using the only weapons I had."

"Your nails and teeth," I said knowingly.

"Close." She inclined her head. "My legs were free and I was able to kick his legs out from under him. I think the idea of having a vampyr mistress amused him. He gave me his blood and turned me into a vampyr.

"I found freedom and it was good to have a mentor. However, one night he went too far." Alexandra looked out the window and was silent for a long time. "That's when I left," she said at last. "I've been making my way the best I can ever since."

"How long ago did you first become a ... a vampyr?" I asked.

"Alexander the Great was on the throne when I was born as a human. I had been a vampyr for almost 225 years by the time Julius Caesar conquered your home." She stood and stepped over to the window. "So, tell me, what did you seek at the Holy Wisdom of Logos?"

I told her about my quest for the cup and book of Jesus and then explained about what we had found at St. Patrick's Island. She continued to stare out into the night.

"Forgiveness is a dream that serves no purpose," she said. "The vampyr that created me used to speak of gods and beings both great and terrible. In all the centuries I've been alive, I've seen evidence of no such creatures. If I had to guess, I would say this Jesus was just another man claiming to be a god. It's said that Tiberius even offered to induct Jesus into the Roman Pantheon if it would quiet the Jews."

"I don't know if Jesus is anything more or less than the Christians claim," I said, rising from the bed and joining Alexandra at the window. "All I know is that the creature who guarded the cup and book was extremely frightening and that the teachings of Jesus hold a great power over those who hear them."

"Do they hold great power over you?" She looked up into my eyes.

"They held power over one of the greatest men I knew." I thought of Arthur.

She smirked, and her eyes sparkled. "Do you really seek forgiveness, Lord Draco, or do you seek something else?"

I hesitated and looked away. "I seek knowledge."

She reached up and touched my face, causing me to look back into her eyes. "Knowledge is power." It was as if she caressed the words with her lips.

"We are immortal," I said. "What do we need of power?" Even as I asked the question, I thought of my early days with Wolf, seeking shelter in caves and the burrows we dug.

Alexandra's smirk melted into a frown and she stormed away from me, and I thought of the story she had told me of being a slave.

"Power is everything," she said.

I considered the powerful men I had known. "No, but it is helpful."

She turned and looked at me again, then looked over at the bag of jewels and gold on the floor of the room. "Tomorrow I will meet the man who will buy these items from me and take them far away. Once I've done that, I'll take you to the place where you're much more likely to find information about the book you seek." She took a step closer to me. "There is a church older than the Holy Wisdom of Logos. It is the Church of the Holy Apostles. Constantine himself is buried there. They say the site was founded by Jesus's apostles."

The next night, I awoke during the twilight and discovered that Alexandra was already awake. Her back was toward me and her blouse was off. She poured water into a basin, then splashed it onto her face.

Without regard for me, she turned around, reached into her bag, retrieved a golden comb, and worked the snarls from her hair. I felt my cheeks warm as I watched her. She looked up at me and grinned. "I'm surprised a vampyr that's nearly a century old can still blush at the sight of a bare-breasted woman," she said.

"I'm sorry," I stammered, quickly trying to busy myself with getting ready.

"Actually, it's a bit flattering," she said as she returned the comb to the bag and retrieved her blouse. "I mean, seeing as you're a noble and seem to find me genuinely attractive."

"That's not the way of a Roman commander," I said, incensed.

"Apparently you haven't known the Roman commanders I have." She knelt down and planted a kiss on my nose. "Now, we should get going. My contact is waiting at a tavern near the Forum Tauri and that's a little ways from here. We can feed afterward, then go see about your church."

I quickly dressed and pulled on my boots, then followed Alexandra out into the streets. We walked around the Forum Bovis, then found a road that cut through a part of town that I imagined must have been a bustling marketplace during the day. That explained why the innkeeper was not surprised to see me and my wagon.

About twenty minutes later, we entered a tavern. People occupied tables, drinking wine and ale. Alexandra stepped boldly up to a big man and handed him her bag.

He looked in, examined what she handed him, then handed her another bag in exchange. She opened the top and I could tell it was filled with a considerable sum of gold and silver.

Without ordering drinks or anything else, we quickly left the tavern. "Joachim there, is one of the best fences in Constantinople. He always pays fairly for what I bring him."

I lifted an eyebrow. "I'm not sure I know what a 'fence' is."

"He takes what I bring him and sells it to merchants around town. He pays me so I won't get caught with all of that stolen merchandise from the palace." She led me back the way we had come.

"What happens if *he* gets caught with the things you took?" I asked.

"Probably nothing." Alexandra brushed a strand of black hair from her shoulder. "Thing is, that was such a small fraction of the Emperor's wealth that I doubt even he would recognize it as his … and I know I was not observed."

We took her gold back to my room at the inn, then she led me out through the Wall of Constantine to the poorer part of the city. The Lycos River flowed through this part of the city. Near its banks, we easily found two people huddled under blankets. We took our fill of blood, then returned to the inner city along the river.

Alexandra led me up a hill and we found ourselves facing the Church of the Holy Apostles. Somehow, this building wasn't as grand as the Holy Wisdom of the Logos. However, it was still quite impressive.

It consisted of four wings, two ran north and south and two ran east and west. A blue dome topped each wing. In the center, where the four wings intersected, there was a great dome similar to that of the Holy Wisdom of the Logos – though not quite as grand.

"They say there are a number of relics from the apostles in this church," explained Alexandra. "I have never been in here – I never felt the need. The types of relics most churches hold have little appeal to me." She stepped up to the front door, reached into a pocket in her pants and pulled out some tools.

The door was open in a matter of seconds.

We entered and she closed the door behind us. As we approached the building's midpoint, I realized that something was wrong.

My footsteps grew heavier as I progressed. I found it hard to breathe. It was like an unseen force tried to hold me in place. I looked over at Alexandra. Her eyes had grown wide. She struggled to walk as though weight had suddenly been added to her pack. "What's going on?" she asked.

"This reminds me of something I felt once before," I said. "When Wolf and I entered the fortress on St. Patrick's Isle, we encountered such a force. I assumed it was somehow caused by the angel guarding the relics of Jesus."

"Do you suppose there's an angel guarding the relics of this place?" she asked.

I shook my head. "I don't know." I thought for a moment. "Can you transform into a beast?"

"Well...." It was her turn to look embarrassed. "I don't exactly transform into an animal. When I transform, I sense I'm alive, but I'm not exactly corporeal."

"Do you fly?" I pressed for an answer.

"I rise above the ground." She shrugged.

I looked at her, confused, then waved it aside. "Let me try something. You head back toward the door. I'll meet you outside in a few minutes."

She nodded, turned around, and seemed to gain strength with every step she took back toward the entrance. I felt my skin writhe and separate as I transformed into the swarm of flies. Once the last of my myriad tiny feet left the ground, I gained strength. I flew toward the center of the church. There I saw an altar and a cross-shaped crypt. I spread out through the building, looking for any sign of books that might be of interest. The only books I could see were similar to those in the library in Prague – copied by hand in the last century or so.

I had a growing sense that there was little to be found in that place. I gathered myself and flew back to the church's entrance. There I pulled myself back into human form and found Alexandra staring at the building as though seeing it for the first time. I felt a certain relief seeing her stronger, a sardonic grin on her face.

"Did you find any angels?" she asked.

I shook my head. "Nor did I find any books more ancient than perhaps a century or so."

"I just realized," she said, "this building is in the shape of a cross."

"So?" I asked. "What does a cross have to do with anything?"

"There are legends among the Christians of my homeland that a cross can harm a vampyr. Though I've been through the Holy Wisdom of Logos a number of times, I've never felt a need to approach any of the crosses before."

"What's special about crosses?" I asked.

"Jesus was crucified on one."

"Why would that have any effect on vampyrs?" I held out my hand to her. "After all, you were a vampyr before Christ was born."

She reached out and took my hand. "I have no idea," she said. "Let's go back to your room and discuss it there. I suddenly feel quite tired."

Hand-in-hand we left the Church of the Holy Apostles.

Chapter 17

From the memoirs of Alexandra the Greek:

There was something compelling about this man who called himself Desmond, Lord Draco. Certainly he was physically attractive – tall, with lithe movements reminiscent of a great cat, and blue-green eyes that seemed to look right into me. However, there was more to him than his physical beauty.

Something about his quest for knowledge intrigued me. I realized, early on, that he did not seek mere forgiveness as he said, and as so many humans claim to seek. After the night he searched the Church of the Holy Apostles, we returned to his room, and we spoke late into the night.

He told me more about himself. I realized that he was too good a warrior, too good an assassin, and too ready to sell his services as a mercenary, to worry over much about the occasional life we vampyrs took in the course of our feeding, much less the blood we took without bringing a life to its end.

I began to realize Draco sought the answers to larger questions. Why did humans exist? How was it that certain humans were transformed into vampyrs, like us, to prey on humans?

"There have been certain great teachers in my homeland who say that the knowledge you seek cannot be found through the teachings of holy men. They say the answers you seek lie in understanding nature itself, and that the only way you can understand nature is through honest, dispassionate inquiry."

He sat back in a wicker chair and put his hands behind his head. "I think, perhaps, there's truth in what you say." He remained silent for a long moment and I watched, entranced, as thoughts played across his face. Finally, he sat forward. "The thing I keep coming back to is the angel. If something as powerful as an angel guarded the book of Jesus, there must have been something there that was close to the truth I seek."

I sighed, unable to think of any argument against that point. "Then where do we go next?" I considered that question. "There is a rather old monastery here in Constantinople called St. John the Baptist of Studios."

Draco shook his head. "No, my sense is that, wealthy as Constantinople is, it's too new to contain the books I seek. If what I'm seeking exists, we'll find it where this all began, in Jerusalem … or possibly in Nazareth where Jesus lived for so long." He sighed, then looked up at me with a sparkle in his eye. "Did you say, 'we?'"

I stood and stepped over to him, then knelt down and put my arm around his shoulder. "Lord Draco, I'm beginning to think my luck as a thief in Constantinople is coming to an end. Perhaps I should scout some new territories. I've never been to the Holy Land. I would like to see what's there."

He turned thoughtful. "I don't relish the idea of traveling overland to Asia Minor. How are the waters of the Aegean Sea and the Mediterranean this time of year?"

"I hear they are calm."

"Perhaps we should book passage on a ship."

"A sea voyage sounds delightful." I leaned in and brushed his lips with a kiss. He blinked at me in surprise.

I smiled at him, then stood and looked out the window. Twilight began to lighten the sky. I hung one of Draco's blankets over the window, then laid out two more, side by side in the corner of the room where sunlight would never reach. In Draco, I saw the strength of the vampyr, Theron, tempered by the sensitivity of my friend, Kallius. The more I learned about this Draco, the more I wanted to remain at his side.

The next evening, Draco arranged passage for us as cargo aboard a ship bound for the seaport at Joppa. I have to admit, I found it somewhat less than flattering that we would be traveling as cargo. Still, I understood the practicality of the arrangement and I met with my friend, Joachim, afterwards and asked him to introduce us to workmen who would build us boxes to Draco's specifications in short order.

Draco gave them instructions to build light-tight boxes with latches on the inside. "What you want are coffins," said one of the workmen. "But why do you want handles on the inside? Afraid that you might bury someone alive?"

"Something like that," answered Draco sardonically.

The workmen set about their task and were done by the next evening. That night Draco made arrangements for his horse and wagon to be taken care of, then we loaded the possessions we would need into the boxes, and carried them down to the seaport. With a brief kiss, we each closed ourselves into our coffins and waited for the journey to begin.

The sea voyage from Constantinople to Joppa only lasted four days, but it felt like an eternity. Draco suggested that we should only emerge briefly each night to feed, so that we didn't startle the crew and cause them to hunt us down.

This meant long hours lying within our coffins, listening to nothing but the creaking of the ship's wood and the scuttling of tiny rodent feet. Several times, I caught myself trying to listen for Draco's breathing and heartbeat during our waking hours and was surprised how glad I was to hear them. Those things, along with the brief nightly conversations and hunting with Draco, kept me from drifting into a kind of permanent sleep.

I was relieved, on the fifth night, to find our ship docked at Joppa. Draco and I crept off the ship to find an inn.

In the morning as twilight was just lightening the skies, we appeared at the ship, claimed our "cargo," and returned to the inn. The coffins actually made it much more convenient to sleep through the day, though I have to admit that I missed falling asleep next to Draco.

The next night, we arranged to have our boxes carried overland to Jerusalem.

I'm not quite sure what I expected of Jerusalem. I suppose I expected it to be much like Constantinople and, in many ways, it was. It was a large city, but somehow it felt much older. The buildings were in worse repair than those in Constantinople, or worse even than in my own homeland. It was a city that looked as though it had faced many wars, and it sat perched on its mountain as though cringing in anticipation of many wars to come.

Draco secured us an inn and we began to scour the city for information about where we might find books of the antiquity that he sought. I was used to finding information in taverns. However, the city seemed strangely devoid of drinking establishments – at least ones that were open into the late hours.

Draco sought out a number of monasteries around the city. Most did not admit women, so I let him scour through these books alone. Each morning before dawn, he returned to our room at the inn with an armload of scrolls and books.

"It would seem that you're having luck in your search," I said.

He shook his head. "Not as much as it would seem." Draco rubbed eyes that had grown bloodshot from staring at too many books, for too long. "Even the Christians debate about which books are 'true knowledge' and which aren't. It seems that very little actually survives from the time of Christ."

"It has been five hundred years," I reasoned aloud.

"You would think that if the teachings of Christ were so important to these people, they would have tried to preserve his writings. They would have tried to preserve the writings of those who followed him."

"They did," I said. "They sent the writings of Jesus to Britain with Joseph of Arimathea."

He looked as though I had just placed a knife in his side. "Surely there must be more." He shook his head and sighed.

"Do you think we should try Nazareth?" I asked. "That's where Jesus lived for most of his life."

He gave the briefest of nods. "Perhaps, but there is one place I'd like to see first. A few years after Jesus died, Herrod Agrippa extended the borders of the city and included the hill they call Gethsemene. The Christians have built a church over the place. It is supposed to include the tomb where Joseph of Arimathea buried Jesus after the Crucifixion." He stood, clasped his hands together, and turned his back to me.

"That's where Joseph of Arimathea's journey began. Without that event, I would not be on this quest." He looked over his shoulder at me. "Do you care to join me?"

"You couldn't stop me," I said.

Autumn had arrived and the nights lengthened. This allowed us to set out for the Church of the Holy Sepulcher early the following evening. The building was surprisingly small, especially when compared to structures such as the Holy Wisdom of Logos and the Church of the Holy Apostles.

I was also surprised to note that the building did not look much older than the Church of the Holy Apostles, in Constantinople.

"It isn't," said Draco, when I asked him about it. "I gather this building was constructed during Constantine's reign."

We stepped into an atrium that was open to the outside, and came to a large set of double doors. Draco pounded on the entryway.

Just as I was about to give up on receiving an answer, and began reaching for my lock picks, an elderly priest opened the door. He frowned disapprovingly at us. "What do you want?" he asked. "The hour is late."

"I am Lord Draco of Britain, and this is Alexandra of Athens." Desmond gave a slight bow. "We are on a pilgrimage to the Holy Sepulcher."

"All who come here are," said the priest. "Come back in the morning."

"I wish we could." Desmond stared into the priest's eyes. "We have come a long way and it is urgent that we see the site tonight."

At first, I thought the priest would resist Draco. After all, our ability to control minds is rather limited. However, after a moment, the priest finally heaved a deep sigh and stepped aside from the doorway.

"My name is Father Justin," he said. "Allow me to show you to the sacred site."

I'm not sure whether he succumbed to Draco's will or simply decided it was easier to show us what we wanted than send us on our way.

The priest led us through a grand basilica, not unlike those churches in Constantinople. At the other end, he opened a door into an enclosed courtyard. The stars shone overhead. "This was the site of Calvary," explained the priest.

"Was this the site where Joseph of Arimathea took the body of Jesus from the cross and carried him to the tomb?" asked Draco.

"It was." The priest projected an air of confidence.

"It was here that he caught Christ's blood in a chalice, was it not?"

Father Justin simply nodded, then led us across the courtyard into another room. In there was a great domed rotunda. At the center of the rotunda was an ancient-looking structure made of stone.

Draco reached up and touched the structure's door. "This was the tomb of Christ?" asked Draco.

"It was," said Father Justin.

I walked around the tomb-like structure and examined it carefully. Then I looked through the open door into the courtyard. "This is all wrong," I said. "I could believe that the site out there was Calvary, but this structure is not the tomb of Christ."

Both Father Justin and Draco looked at me with open mouths.

"Look," I said, walking up to the structure. "This is the kind of tomb they started building during Constantine's time. It's only about two hundred years old, not five hundred. The Jews of Jesus's time buried people in hillsides, not Christian crypts."

Draco closed his mouth and nodded, as though recognizing my knowledge of the period, and understanding what I spoke about. If anything, Father Justin's mouth opened even wider and his eyes went round. "You speak heresy," said the priest. "This tomb has been guarded through the ages as a sacred site."

"Then open the door," I demanded, folding my arms across my stomach. "Let me see."

"I will not open the door," said the priest.

Draco looked from the priest to me, then back again. "You have urgent business in the basilica," he said.

The priest sighed. "I have urgent business to attend to. I'll be back soon." With that, he shuffled off, leaving us alone with the tomb.

"Let's see what's down there," said Draco.

I pulled out my lock picks and opened the tomb. Draco retrieved a torch from the wall of the rotunda and together we entered.

It wasn't what I expected. Instead of a Roman tomb, there were stairs carved into the earth. We descended into an old cave. There were shelves roughly carved into the walls.

"Well, what do you think?" asked Draco.

I whistled long and low. "I take back my words. This could be a Jewish tomb of Christ's time."

"But no one has been buried here." Draco's voice held a hint of regret. "At least not for a long time." He stepped over to the walls of the cave and touched them, then sat down on one of the shelves. "There is no smell of death. If this was once a tomb, where did the bodies go?"

"Perhaps they've been removed," I said.

"Perhaps," he conceded. After a moment, he stood up and climbed the stairs. I followed him up to the top and we closed the door. The priest shuffled into the room just as I retrieved my lock picks and placed them back into the satchel on my belt.

"Is there anything else you would like to see?" asked the priest. "The hour is late and I must go to bed."

"Do you have any scrolls, any books?" asked Draco.

"We have one of the most ancient copies of the Bible on this site." The priest straightened himself up with apparent pride.

Draco smiled so broadly he almost revealed his fangs. "Would it be possible to see it?"

"Briefly," said Father Justin. He led us out of the rotunda and back into the basilica. There, we followed him up to the altar. Behind the altar, a mosaic depicting Christ hanging from the cross hung on the wall. I found myself shying away from it. The memory of the cross-shaped church in Constantinople was still fresh in my mind.

Father Justin opened a concealed door and retrieved a leather-bound book.

Draco's face rapidly fell. "Wouldn't the oldest copies of the Bible be scrolls?" he asked.

The priest shrugged. "The earliest scrolls have been lost to antiquity. It is said that this book was copied from books that were copied from those scrolls."

"A copy of a copy," said Draco sadly as the priest kissed the volume and laid it on the altar. The priest stepped back and allowed Draco to examine the book.

Almost lovingly, Draco reached out and flipped through the old paper pages, at first being very careful not to damage any of them as he examined the Latin script. However, the more he looked, the more his hands began to shake, and the more quickly he turned the pages. At last Father Justin came up and put his hands on the top of Draco's.

"What's the matter, my son?" asked the priest with genuine concern.

"There are books missing," said Draco. "Where is the Gospel of Thomas … the Gospel of Mary?"

"Those books are apocryphal," said Father Justin. "They are not part of the true Bible."

Draco threw the priest's leathery hands off his own. The old man nearly tumbled to the ground, but I quickly ran to his side and supported the priest. I looked up in time to see Draco storming toward the entrance. I helped Father Justin to a chair, then ran after Draco.

"They are not interested in preserving their own writings!" shouted Draco when we were once again in our room at the inn. "They are only saving those parts that say what they want to hear."

"Knowledge is power, but keeping the masses ignorant is almost just as good." I took a deep breath and let it out slowly. "You didn't have to toss the old priest aside like that. In a way, he's just as much a victim as anyone."

He turned sharply and looked at me. "We are hunters," he growled. "What do we care for mere human lives?"

"If that were completely true," I said softly, "why do we avoid killing when we take blood? Why do we feel for those humans we attack? Why do we have feelings at all?"

He turned on his heel and stared at the wall. Even through his shirt, I could see the muscles in his back tense. The hairs on the back of his neck practically stood on end.

"Those are the very answers I seek. How can I find them if humans, in their petty quests for power, secret the answers away? How can I find them if humans destroy the answers they do have, for their own gain?"

I stepped up to Draco, put my arms around him, and rested my head on his shoulder. "You can't find all the answers to understanding feelings in a book." He relaxed somewhat as I held him.

"I know." His tone softened. "I'm just angry that those answers that might have been preserved, seem to have been destroyed. They are lost for all time – not just to me, but to all humans."

"The key phrase there is 'might have been.' Do you know for a fact that the book of Jesus contained any information not preserved in the other books that do exist?"

"No, I suppose I don't." He turned around in my arms and I found myself looking up into his eyes — blue-green like the ocean in daylight, which I hadn't seen in centuries. I untucked his jerkin from his pants and ran my fingers along his bare back.

He tried to push my arms away, but I resisted and held them in place. "I can't allow myself to be distracted," he said.

"Why not?" I asked. "What are you afraid of?"

A shadow seemed to cloud his eyes for a moment. He looked away, but I reached up and pulled his chin toward me. "I'm afraid I'll lose you," he said at last.

"I'm not yours to keep ... or lose." I pulled him close and kissed him deeply, letting my tongue play over his fangs. Pulling away, I looked into his eyes again. "I lost the daylight, but gained my freedom when I became a vampyr. I want you to love me, but you can never possess me."

He looked at me as though I had just revealed a truth to him, one he had never considered. He untucked my blouse from my pants and his hand explored my spine, then found my breast.

I kissed his neck and teased it gently with my fangs, then I moved away and pulled my blouse over my head. "So what is it with those pants you wear?" I stepped close and rubbed my hand down the plaid fabric.

"They remind me of my homeland." He undid the clasp and lowered them to the floor.

"The time has come to forget about your homeland." I sat down on a blanket that covered a straw mat and pulled off my boots followed by my trousers. He knelt in front of me and caressed my hips, then teased the soft flesh of my inner thighs with his fangs. I gasped when I felt his tongue play over my labia.

A fire began to smolder in my belly as he explored me with his tongue and his lips. I looked at him and he seemed as enthralled with my sex as he had been with his books. I finally took him by the shoulders and brought his mouth to mine. I felt him enter me as I tasted myself on his lips. I wrapped my legs around him and pulled him in as deeply as possible.

"Some mysteries cannot be learned in books." I scarcely

breathed the words.

He responded by nibbling on my ear and thrusting into me, slowly and deliberately. However, his need soon increased and his thrusts grew more forceful until I moaned in ecstasy. I lifted my head and bit into his jugular.

Just as his blood entered my mouth, his seed exploded within me. I withdrew my fangs and he was panting. He started to withdraw, but I grabbed his hips. "You're still hard, my love. Satisfy me."

He nodded and continued to thrust. Then he bit my jugular. My body rode wave after wave of sensation, and I did not want him to stop. Finally, I realized he no longer bit me. He just kissed the wound on my neck as it healed. His member was limp within me and he finally rolled off to the side.

"I feel you," he said. "I feel your emotions, your sensations."

"And I feel you. We're bound now, like you were with Wolf before he died."

"This is not possession?" he asked.

"No," I said as I snuggled up beside him, "this is sharing."

The next night, we packed up and made arrangements to return to Constantinople. We packed the gold and the books he'd acquired into one of the coffins and we shared the other one. Somehow the return sea voyage seemed far less lonely as we spoke in soft whispers to one another.

"Why don't you return with me to Castle Draco?" he asked one night, shortly before the time came to hunt. "It would give you a home and we make a brilliant team. You wouldn't have to live as a thief."

"Thing is, I like being a thief," I said, and kissed him on the nose. "I promise, I will visit you often."

"Why not come with me now? I'll be leaving for home once we return."

I gazed into his eyes. "I think you should take time to sort through your new library. Besides I have business to attend to in Constantinople. Maybe, though, I'll spend this winter with you at the castle. The prospect of snuggling in front of a fire sounds rather nice."

Both satisfied, we hunted that night.

Two nights later, we arrived in Constantinople and I helped him load his books onto his wagon. He did end up visiting the Monastery of St. John the Baptist of Studios and persuaded them to part with some of their books. Afterward, I stood on the wall of Theodosius and watched his wagon as it rattled along the Lykos River.

I waved, torn between wanting to run after him and wanting to flee the other way. A chill wind suddenly blew, and all at once winter seemed both very near and all too far away. I climbed down from the wall and wondered if books would be too difficult to steal. I knew a good book would be the perfect Christmas present for a dragon hoarding a treasure of knowledge.

Interlude 3
Freedom

Zanzibar.
The year 712:

Earning an income as a thief, Alexandra kept a watchful eye open for new places she could fence the goods she had stolen – places where those goods could not be traced back to her. During her days in Constantinople she had heard of a Persian trading post called Zanzibar, far to the south, off the coast of Africa. In the year 712, Alexandra packed numerous items she'd been unable to sell in Europe and hired an Arabian ship to take her cargo south. She shipped herself with the cargo so she could transact business – and she looked forward to seeing a new place.

Alexandra awoke soon after sunset. Cautiously, she pushed the lid of the crate open and peered into a darkened room. The ground was steady, so she gathered she was no longer aboard a ship. She stepped out onto a sandy rock floor. Her eyes quickly adjusted to the gathering gloom as waning twilight came through cracks in a door. Several crates surrounded her and it soon became clear she was in a storeroom.

She crept toward the door and peered outside. Stone buildings lined a cobbled street. Vendors were hastily closing up shop. The scent of exotic cooking spices hung on the air, a delicate reminder of foods that Alexandra could no longer enjoy. She left the storeroom and decided to look for an inn or perhaps a tavern where she might find a buyer for her merchandise. Of course, Zanzibar being a Persian port meant that many in the town would be Mohammedans. That might make finding a tavern difficult – but it was a port city, so she doubted such a task would prove insurmountable.

As she walked down the street, a whip cracked nearby accompanied by a bone-weary moan. She caught the metallic scent of blood, which drew her more strongly than the smell of exotic spices. A short distance from the storeroom, she came to a gap between two of the stone buildings. Concealed by night's encroaching shadows, she followed the path until she came to a courtyard, lit by torches. A few men were gathered around the perimeter. In the center, a woman was tied to a post. She had skin the richest shade of brown Alexandra had ever seen. A man flicked his whip across her back.

Alexandra's brow furrowed as she remembered her time with Theron. Was this some kind of sadistic game for people's amusement? She listened more closely. Her sparse knowledge of Persian along with her ability to read thoughts helped her understand. The men around the outside were bidding on the woman being whipped. It became clear, this was a slave market.

Alexandra peered around the corner again. The woman slumped against the post, panting. A man in a turban and fine robes stepped forward and paid the man with the whip. The woman looked over her shoulder and narrowed her gaze, evaluating the man who paid. Others from the courtyard's perimeter began to grumble and turned toward the alleyway where Alexandra was concealed. With a force of will, she transformed herself into a cloud of mist and wafted overhead. As a cloud, her senses were dull and she wanted to know what transpired in the courtyard. She continued to rise until she was over the nearest building, then transformed back into her natural form and dropped onto the roof.

She watched as the man who paid led the dark-skinned woman from the courtyard. The woman held her head up, defiant and proud, but it was clear from the way she limped that she suffered great pain from the whipping she had endured. Alexandra recognized a kindred spirit. Although she had traveled to Zanzibar on a specific mission, she vowed to help this proud woman.

Keeping to the rooftops, Alexandra followed the slave and her owner to a dwelling a few streets away. They entered and within half an hour, the lights from within were extinguished. Alexandra waited another half hour, then transformed herself into mist once again and drifted down to the now-quiet street. Twilight had nearly ended and darkness enveloped the town.

Alexandra opened the dwelling's wooden door. Although the outside was simple stone, lavish Persian rugs and tapestries adorned the inside. Gold ornaments sat on pedestals around the room. It seemed likely this was the home of a wealthy trader. Alexandra chewed her lip, considering the value of the items in the room. She wondered if she could take just a few and get them back to Europe.

She sighed and focused on the task at hand. The soft sound of snoring could be heard from an adjoining room. Alexandra could make out sounds from two people – very likely the trader and his wife. In addition to the snoring was a low voice, singing softly so as not to wake anyone. It was a language Alexandra had never heard before, but she sensed sadness in the words. The woman sang a dirge.

Alexandra followed the soft voice and found herself at a door with a padlock. She retrieved a lock pick from a pouch she wore on her belt and released the lock, then opened the door. She peered into the gloom until she caught the deep brown eyes of the woman. "You are free to go," said Alexandra, both aloud and in the woman's mind.

The woman gasped, then shook her head. She said something in her native language, but Alexandra heard the meaning in her mind. "Free to go? Go where? Great waters separate me from my homeland. I don't blend in here."

"I don't care where you go," said Alexandra, "but I need to go before I'm caught. You should as well."

The woman stood slowly and regally. "Then take me with you. Perhaps I can help you."

"I prefer to travel alone." Alexandra turned to leave.

The slave moved up beside her so fast and so silently that even Alexandra didn't hear her. Despite the speed and the stealth, she still maintained her regal bearing. "I cannot be free here. Even if I escape this house, I will be retaken and made a slave in someone else's house. I sense you can take me someplace where I can be free."

Alexandra heard a catch in the snoring from the other room. She shushed the woman. They could continue their conversation at another time. She motioned the woman to follow. On her way out through the house's main room, Alexandra grabbed a golden urn. In light of the way the woman was whipped, Alexandra guessed the trader would miss the urn more than the slave. His search for it would prove a distraction. Alexandra walked out to the street followed by the woman and closed the door behind her.

They went around the corner and down a few doors. From the sign over the door, Alexandra gathered this stone building was a shop of some kind. She opened the padlocked door and placed the golden urn inside.

"Why did you do that?" asked the woman.

"The trader who bought you will stay busy looking for that urn. If he finds it, his argument with this shop keeper will distract him, keeping him from looking too hard for you." Alexandra folded her arms. "Now, you should be on your way."

"I already told you," said the woman, "I have no place to go here. No ship will take me back to my homeland. If you cannot help me, I am better off returning myself to the slave quarters and having you lock me in."

Alexandra closed her eyes and ground her teeth. Finally, she looked up into the woman's eyes. "What is your name?"

"I am called Nabila," she said.

"Nabila, if you come with me, you will leave the world of light and enter a world of darkness."

"I entered a world of darkness when I became a slave," growled Nabila. "If I must live in darkness, I would rather be free like you. If you won't help me, then take me back and lock me up. Please."

Alexandra took a deep breath and let it out slowly. "Very well. It might be useful to have a partner ... at least now and then." Alexandra turned and stepped into the shadows. Nabila followed close behind.

Part IV
The Dragon's Mercenaries

Chapter 18

From the writings of Desmond, Lord Draco.
The year 1067:

I was out for a walk along the ramparts of my castle in February 1067. A cold, brisk wind blew, making me feel alive. More stars than I could count dotted the clear sky above. I treasured these long nights of winter because I had time to take a leisurely walk, hunt when I needed to, and yet could settle in my library for long periods.

As I strolled along the ramparts, I heard the sound of hooves clopping against rocks and wood creaking. Someone drove a wagon to my door. Every now and again, a traveler would stop by, seeking shelter. I would oblige them. Little did they know I often took some blood in exchange. It saved me the trouble of going out to hunt. The next day, they would go away, complaining of a sore neck or thigh, but generally, grateful for a night's rest that did not require precautions against bandits.

When the wagon cleared the tree line, I was surprised to see a woman driving the horses. She drove the wagon with an air of confidence, and I took note of her long, black hair, pale-olive skin, and full figure. I smiled and nodded, glad to see Alexandra again.

I met her at the castle's gate. "Few manage to get a wagon up this road."

"Few is not the same as none." Alexandra wore a sly grin. "If the occasional human can manage it, I certainly can."

"It is a delight to see you again." I took her in my arms. We kissed and my tongue delighted in the taste of her. We parted after a delicious moment. "What prompted you to drive all the way up here?"

She stepped over to the wagon and threw back the canvas tarp that covered a cargo of scrolls and books.

"You've been busy." I picked one of them up and scanned it, then looked up at the two horses hitched to the wagon. "Those are strong horses to bring this much paper up the steep trail to the castle."

"They're expensive, and I stole them just so I could bring these books to you."

"Alexandra, I do believe I love you," I declared.

She simply smiled and let her hand rove over my back and then downward.

We led the horses into the courtyard and closed the gate. She unhitched the horses from the wagon and led them to the water trough. She then retrieved a bottle of wine and we took it inside to the great hall, where I set out two goblets.

"I have been hearing tales of your homeland. Last October, there was a rather fierce battle," said Alexandra.

"Saxons again?"

"No, this time it was the Normans, from France." She went on to describe the battle between King Harold Godwinson and William of Normandy, at a place called Senlac Hill. As she spoke, I sipped my wine and allowed my thoughts to wander over the last five centuries. After all, Transylvania had been my home longer than Britain, and I had been rather busy.

I returned to Transylvania in 568, after my travels to the Holy Land with Alexandra. My friend, the Khagan Bayan, paid me a visit and told me that he had formed an alliance with the Persians. He believed the Avars and the Persians together might be able to capture Constantinople itself.

Having been to that city, and having seen its fortifications and population, I advised against the attack. After all, the population of Constantinople alone, nearly equaled the entire population of Transylvania. Bayan went against my advice and attacked anyway. I went with them as one of his generals. As I suspected, the siege was driven back. However, I did feast well during that time.

Bayan eventually passed away and the Slavs began a series of revolts against the Avars. I helped to repress several of them. The Avars were my benefactors, and I owed them my home, which I found more and more comfortable as the years went by. Even so, I watched the Avars go into decline.

Their khagans, living in the plains, forgot about me living in my ancient mountain fortress. As time went by, the pendulum of Roman power swung back toward the west and ultimately, I offered my services to Charlemagne in 796. He ordered me to assassinate the last khagan.

Even though the khagans were no longer loyal to me, nor did they have any knowledge of the pact their ancestors had made with me, I still shed a tear as I bit into the last khagan's neck. I felt as though I killed an era. However there was a feeling of rebirth when Charlemagne gave me a new title to my land in the Carpathians.

Less than a century later, the Magyars came into the region. They were little more than terrorists, attacking sites on the Holy Roman Empire's eastern frontier. It was my pleasure to help King Otto break their hold of the region in 955. The ownership of my land was confirmed and I was paid handsomely by Duke Vajk, who owed fealty to Otto, and ultimately came to control Transylvania for the Empire. With the money, I refurbished much of my fortress and bought a new bed. My thoughts turned to that bed as Alexandra concluded her tale of William the Conqueror.

"Have you even been listening to me?" Alexandra's gaze narrowed.

"You were telling me how William fired over the English shield wall and managed to kill many of the ranks clustered at the rear." I nodded. "Sound strategy, especially since they managed to kill King Harold."

Her lips pursed, and I hid my smirk by raising the goblet to my mouth. A moment later, I stood, retrieved one of the candles from the table, and offered my hand to her. She accepted it and I led her to my bedchamber. The room had no windows. It could be absolutely dark, even to a vampyr's eyes. Using the candle, I moved around the room, lighting other candles from the one I carried.

"Some say it is more romantic with no light." Alexandra came up behind me and put her arms around my waist.

"The light allows me to appreciate your beauty." I turned within her arms and kissed her neck, then let my teeth play over her earlobe.

She unlaced my shirt. One hand explored my chest and another moved along my thigh. "Sometimes sensation is more pure in the dark." She blew out one of the candles, then another. She led me to the bed and told me to sit. She moved around the room blowing out the candles I had just lit. "Close your eyes," she said.

I did as she instructed. Fabric rustled. A moment later, there was a tugging at the drawstring around my waist. I opened my eyes as she began pushing the pants below my hips. Just enough light came in from the open doorway that I could still see. Her blouse was gone, but she still wore her skirt.

"No peeking," she admonished.

I closed my eyes again. She pulled off my boots and then removed my pants. Soft flesh pressed against my thighs, and fabric rustled against my shins and feet. She moved, and soft, dry flesh rubbed against my cock. I was tempted to open my eyes, but decided to play along with Alexandra. It felt as though she were allowing my manhood to rub against her naked breasts. The sensation was lovely. She kissed my belly and then proceeded upward. She took my nipple into her mouth and I squirmed.

"Vampyrs should not be ticklish," she said.

"I can't help it."

As her kisses continued toward my neck, the fabric of her skirt enveloped my hips and loins. The fabric was coarse, but that only served to stimulate me further. She began to nibble at my neck. Just when I didn't feel I could take any more of this stimulation, she lifted herself up slightly and adjusted the skirt. A moment later, she settled down, and my cock was enveloped in the moist folds of her sex. I sighed.

Just then, she bit into my neck. As our blood mingled, I felt not only my manhood, but the sensations she felt within her sex as well. As she rose and descended, I felt almost ready to explode within her. However, I could feel that she still built to a climax.

I tried to quiet my mind, to feel her sensations rather than mine. It was all too much, and I fear that I came before she was ready. Still, as a vampyr, I found I not only could control the beating of my heart, but how much blood remained in my member. I was able to stay hard for her. She continued to rise and descend until I felt a second orgasm. However, this one was deep within her body.

A short time later, she lay down beside me. "You can open your eyes now."

"I'm almost afraid to," I said. "I don't want the sensation to go away."

"Sometimes the dark is good."

I opened my eyes and rolled onto my side. "How long will you be able to stay this time?"

"I'm afraid I must leave tomorrow evening."

"So soon?" I frowned.

She rubbed her shoulder and shimmied into a different position. "I would stay longer if you had a better bed."

"What's wrong with my bed? I earned this bed fighting for Duke Vajk."

"And just how long ago was that?" She squirmed again. "The bed's too hard and the straw pokes me in places I'd rather not talk about."

"You haven't complained about it before," I said.

She simply smiled, kissed me on the nose, then rolled over and went to sleep.

As the hour of sunrise approached, I patted the straw mattress and looked at the headboard's dry wood. The bed *was* over a century old. Perhaps it really was time for a change.

Chapter 19

From the writings of Desmond, Lord Draco.
The year 1067:

lexandra and I went hunting early the next evening. A small Pecheneg Turk encampment had been established on the Bistritza River not too far from my fortress. Several huts huddled together as though keeping each other warm. Smoke from cooking fires rose through holes in the roofs.

We lingered in the shadows near the village until a young man went out to gather firewood. I admired Alexandra's skill as she lured the Turk near. She gazed into his eyes and he gave himself over to her. She nuzzled his neck and bit in, but drank just a little. Afterwards, she led him to the woodpile, loaded up his arms, and sent him back to the hut.

No one else seemed interested in leaving the warmth of the structures. I made my way around the village's perimeter, listening with my ears and my mind to the sounds within the ramshackle huts.

I heard singing and storytelling from most. However, quiet sobbing came from one hut. Very little smoke came through the roof's hole. I entered and found a young woman huddled by the fire, her face in her hands. Two older people slept under skins nearby – I gathered they were her parents. She opened her mouth to scream, but I covered it with my hand before a sound could emerge. I quieted her mind, and bit into her neck. She moaned in ecstasy and I saw ger thoughts.

She imagined one of the young men from the village caressing and loving her. I gathered that young man's family had just spurned her. After taking my fill, I kissed her neck and laid her down beside her parents.

"You have a full life ahead of you," I whispered. "Don't give up on it because that family foolishly decided their son could marry someone better." I wasn't certain whether or not my words would leave an impression in her mind, but I hoped they would. I rekindled the fire. Once it had warmed a little, I left the hut and joined Alexandra.

We returned to my fortress and briefly retired to my chambers before she went to the courtyard and began tending her horses.

I helped her pack some fresh supplies. She hitched the horses to the wagon. We embraced one last time before she climbed aboard. As I watched her ride out of sight, I wished she would stay a little longer.

The next evening, I carried an axe into the forest that surrounds my castle and sought out a good, solid tree. In the distance, I could hear strains of music coming from the Pecheneg camp. I began chopping in time with the music. It took me a little more than an hour, but the tree finally creaked and groaned, then fell to the forest floor with a crash.

The music stopped and I could sense the Turks listening. I waited until the music resumed before I grabbed hold of the top branches, and began dragging the tree back to my fortress. The tree would have been too big for a human to move, but my vampyr strength allowed me to accomplish the task.

Once the tree was in my courtyard, I began the long, slow process of carving boards and making slats.

During quiet times in the mountains, I found projects of such magnitude helped to stave off boredom. The new bed was completed in the spring. I entered my chambers, dismantled the old bed, and replaced it with the new one.

The first evening I awoke in the new bed, I simply lay in my chambers and stared into the inky blackness. My first thoughts were of Alexandra and how delighted I hoped she would be with the new bed. I knew she was restless and never remained in one place long, but I hoped she would be inspired to linger a while longer during her next visit. My thoughts then turned to her most recent visit, and as they did, I remembered what she told me about the Battle of Senlac Hill.

It suddenly occurred to me that I had been living in my fortress for exactly five centuries. I began to think about Britain – the green fields I played in as a child, the revels in the halls of Ambrosius Aurelianus, and even the time I had spent with Wolf on the estate outside of Luguvalium. I thought of my first love, Guinevere, and how she ultimately betrayed both Arthur and me.

I began to wonder what Britain had become.

At first I dismissed my thoughts as a simple bout of homesickness; they happened every now and then. However, as the days and weeks wore on, I couldn't get Britain out of my mind. I realized it was time to return home, to find out how different William of Normandy's "England" was from my Britain.

A week later, I loaded my own wagon – which had been sitting, forgotten in a corner of the courtyard for many years. Then, I sealed up my fortress and rode to Varna.

Before leaving, I wrote a letter to Alexandra and left it on the table of my library. If she came calling, she would know where I had gone.

In Varna, I arranged passage on a ship bound for Venice.

In the eleventh century, Venice was already a flourishing trade center. I remained a few days and hunted the streets of the populous city. I took time to visit two of the monasteries and their libraries. Unfortunately, one of them had suffered a recent theft.

Still, I smiled. It was likely those books were among the ones Alexandra recently brought me. Because Venice flourished, it was easy to find a shipping office open late enough to arrange passage to Granada for myself.

Granada was fascinating for different reasons than Venice. The city had fallen firmly under the influence of the Mohammedans. Unlike the simple nomadic Turks that had made their way into

Transylvania, these were a sophisticated people with highly developed art and science.

The architecture there was beautiful. Although smaller than Constantinople, I felt the city had potential to reach a similar grandeur. Unfortunately, the Mohammedans had a tendency to close their shipping offices before sunset. I was forced to seek out pirates.

"England is a war-torn and primitive country," complained the pirate captain. "There is no profit to be made by going there."

He changed his mind when I held out a pouch of gold coins. The next day, my boxes were loaded aboard a pirate ship and we sailed around the Spanish peninsula and landed at a Cornish port that held the name of Plymouth.

Even though I had watched cities grow up in Eastern Europe, I was surprised to find one of such magnitude in my homeland. When I left, there had only been small villages in Britain. However, what surprised me even more than the size of this Plymouth was that no one spoke the British tongue.

When I went to the port agent to collect my boxes – including the one I had slept in on the journey – he looked at me oddly. "I don't speak Welsh," he said. "Only English."

"Angle-ish," I said, trying to understand the pictures in his mind. I shook my head and we exchanged a few more words. Slowly, I began to understand this strange new language.

"People still speak my mother tongue?" I asked.

He nodded. "In Wales." He stepped over to a map that hung on the wall, and pointed at the western counties, called Cymru in my time. I thanked him, then left to find an inn.

My stay in Plymouth was brief. I really wanted to travel northward and see if my estate still existed in Luguvalium. I only stayed long enough to buy a new wagon and some horses. Within a few nights I was on the road. Along the way, I stayed in a number of small inns and my English began to improve. I eventually learned that Luguvalium had been renamed Carlisle.

As I continued northward, I was saddened to learn that many places I knew in my youth no longer existed, as though they were simply wiped off the face of the Earth. Cadbury, which had been a favorite gathering place, was merely a serene, green hill. Only a few foundations existed at Viroconium. Deva had been renamed Chester. When I ultimately reached Carlisle, I discovered I could not even find the place where my land had been.

Small, wooden houses stood everywhere.

I secured a room at an inn.

Hunting in Carlisle proved easier than it had back in the days of Luguvalium, simply because there were more people. I went to a tavern, found a drunk and lured him into a dark alley, drank what I needed, and let him go.

I considered leaving right away, but decided I would go speak to the lord of Carlisle Castle.

As usual, the gateman was reluctant to allow me entry after dark. However, I was surprised to hear him speak French instead of English. I suppose that was to be expected in light of William's recent conquest. Although I spoke French moderately well, the gateman seemed to understand my desire to meet his lord much better after I handed him a few silver coins. He let me in and introduced me to a servant. The servant was not impressed by the silver, but a gold coin found me a seat in the lord's parlor with a goblet of wine at my side.

The lord arrived a few minutes later. "May I help you?"

I stood and bowed low. "I am Lord Draco of Transylvania," I said in French. "I had ... ancestors from this region. I was curious what became of their land."

The lord poured himself a goblet of wine. He waved at the chair, indicating I should return to my seat. He remained standing. "How long ago did they live here?"

"They were subjects of the Dux Bellorum." I sat down and picked up my wine goblet, though I did not drink. "That was nearly five centuries ago."

"During the Roman occupation." The lord wrinkled his nose. "Those people are long gone, I'm afraid." He sipped his wine. "Many were driven north into Scotland. Others went into Wales."

I took a sip of my wine and avoided looking up into the lord's eyes. "It was a little cottage with several acres of land around it."

"You know," said the lord with a faint snort. "There are stories still told, of a knight called Desmond. He lived here with a Saxon knight. It seems unusual enough that a British Knight and a Saxon would share land.... I suppose that's why the stories are still told."

"Do you know where the land was?" I looked up, hopefully.

He nodded, then set his goblet down. He led me to one of the castle's towers and pointed toward the coast. Even though new buildings had been constructed, I thought I could make out the lay of the land as it once had been. Waves of invaders had obscured the countryside and in a similar way I found the memories of that time fading.

The weight of five hundred years descended upon my shoulders all at once. I looked into my host's face and I saw an invader – no different than the Saxons who had tried to conquer my land all those years before. I continued staring into his eyes and I could feel him fall under my spell.

I grabbed him and bit into his neck. His blood coated my tongue and I savored the flavor. I drank until I was well beyond sated.

I didn't take enough to actually kill the lord, but enough that he would be sick for days. I left him on the floor and returned to the inn.

The next day I started south. The Normans, the Saxons, and the Angles – they had taken my land from me. They had given new names to all the places of my youth. I was told my people still existed in Wales.

If I couldn't reclaim my land, I could at least see what had become of my people.

I was born in a place called Gwynedd, in Western Cymru. I'd left when I was ten years old, and had never returned. Several days' travel brought me to a town in Gwynedd called Caernarfon. The castle there was occupied by a prince named Bleddyn ap Cynfyn.

He was a tall, broadly built man with long hair, tamed by a leather strap. In that way, I was reminded of Arthur and Bran. However, his long hair was sandy blond, which reminded me of Guinevere. I wondered, if I'd had children, would they have looked like Bleddyn?

The hour was late and the prince eyed me warily. "Why do you disturb me at this hour? Why not arrive during the day?"

I closed my eyes and drank in those Welsh words, harsh as they were. They were so similar to my native British tongue that I knew I was home.

"I am sorry to intrude. I am a Transylvanian Lord descended from the British. I am a seasoned warrior and am willing to trade my services for lodging in this city of Caernarfon."

The prince scowled at me. After a moment, he snapped his fingers and summoned a servant. He ordered the servant to bring us two tankards of his best ale. "Tell me of your experience," he said.

I recounted a number of my battles in the East. I gave him enough details that I hoped he would recognize my skill. However, I also left out enough names that I hoped he wouldn't recognize that I was describing battles that happened over a century in the past.

He sipped his ale slowly and when I was finished, he set his tankard aside and wiped his lips on his sleeve. "I am glad to find a kinsman such as you, even though you speak Welsh like my grandfather."

He stood and stepped over to a nearby window and looked out at a moonlit landscape. "The Normans are a scourge. They won't be content until they have control of the entire Island of Britain. I intend to stop them before they get that far. Will you help me?"

I felt my heart come alive in my chest. The blood of countless victims coursed through my veins. I stood and held up my tankard of ale. "I pledge myself to you, Prince Bleddyn."

He stepped back to the table and clapped his hand on my shoulder. "Then you are welcome in the kingdom of Gwynedd. We shall find you lodging. On the morrow, we will discuss strategy."

I cleared my throat and bowed my head. "Begging your pardon, my prince. I have taken a vow and only appear at night."

He stepped back and scowled at me again.

"In my experience," I continued, "much can be done at night to drive out invaders. It is when the enemy least expects an attack."

He nodded slowly, considering my words. "I think your arrival may have been quite fortuitous, Draco. I look forward to hearing more of your thoughts, even if they are not presented at the most civilized of hours."

Chapter 20

From the memoirs of Alexandra the Greek.
The year 1067:

In my experience, most vampyrs are completely hideous creatures. They live in the graves and tombs where they were mistakenly buried, emerge each night to feed, then return to the graves and tombs. They become dirty, loathsome, and lonely creatures, confused by their need for blood. A few weeks of that kind of existence would be enough to drive most people mad.

Every now and then, though, a vampyr comes along that rises above that level of existence. Either they were nurtured by the vampyr that made them or they had a strong force of will – or some combination of both.

In my case, it was definitely a combination. The vampyr that made me was intelligent, but he was also perverse. He had a secret chamber where he would torture slaves with whips and red-hot pokers. I stayed with him so I could learn about my new existence. However, he crossed a line when he brought a dear friend to his chamber of horrors.

When I tried to stop Theron, he lashed out at me with his whip. I grabbed the only weapon available, a stoker that was near at hand. I lunged at Theron, meaning only to stop him from hurting my friend and me. Instead, the stoker pierced the vampyr's heart and killed him.

I left my friend behind. Although Kallius was lovely to look at, he was a simple man who only desired to be a slave in a better household. He did not desire freedom and, if it had been granted to him, he would not have known what to do with it. Having grown up as a slave my entire life, I really didn't know what freedom meant either. I had enough to do understanding freedom and being a vampyr without trying to teach someone else at the same time.

When I encountered the slave named Nabila, I sensed things were different. Her bearing told me she understood freedom. She is one of the few I have made a vampyr. Like any parent with a child, I hope I nurtured her well. She remains a friend. I enjoy seeing her when our paths cross.

While Theron still lived, I realized that vampyrs, with their speed, strength, and agility had the skills to become first-rate thieves. After all, it seemed we were made for stealing blood from victims who we confronted directly. How much easier, then, to steal gold and silver from victims who were asleep in other parts of their houses? However, becoming a thief was not as easy as I first thought.

When I started, I was clumsy when I broke into homes, making loud noises as a door or window gave way. As a result, I sometimes confronted not a *single* victim, but numerous members of a family, or even armed guards. My only recourse was to flee into the night.

With time, and a little practice, I finally developed finesse and could break into houses and palaces quietly.

The next challenge was learning to steal the right things. If I stole jewels or amulets that were easily recognized, fences would often refuse them, lest they found themselves captured by palace guards when trying to resell those items. I found it best to stay in a place long enough to learn which items princes and lords would show off in public and what things people knew about, as distinct from those secret treasures that were hoarded away, out of sight.

Desmond, Lord Draco – who I love dearly – is one of the few vampyrs I've met who was actually nurtured as a vampyr should be.

Even though his mentor, Wolf, seemed to possess an overdeveloped desire for forgiveness, he stayed with Desmond and taught him skills that would serve him well in his vampyric existence. Of course, in Draco's case, it helps that he was a trained soldier. Those skills have certainly served him well over the years.

However, there is one vampyr that has long remained a

mystery to me. He calls himself Roquelaure. Like Lord Draco and me, Roquelaure often finds himself in the employ of humans.

He typically works as an assassin.

Unlike Draco who works for kings, lords, and emperors, Roquelaure tends to work for criminal gangs in cities. Because I am a thief, I tend to run in the same circles as Roquelaure. So, perhaps it's not too surprising that Roquelaure and I found one another and began to work together from time to time.

I don't know anything at all about Roquelaure's history. All I know is that I met him in the city of Köln, about three hundred years after I met Draco. I don't know if he was newly created, as old as Draco, or as old as me. He simply never talks about his past.

What I do know is that Roquelaure is perhaps the most stunningly beautiful vampyr I have ever met. Most vampyrs are pale, simply because they can't go out into the sunlight and the amount of blood they consume does little to color their features. Because of that, most vampyrs look like unhealthy humans who have remained indoors all of their lives. However, Roquelaure's pallor is more like pure Egyptian alabaster. Though Draco is ruggedly handsome and strong, Roquelaure has smooth, chiseled features like the most pleasing Grecian busts after the centuries have stripped them of paint.

Unlike most men who wear bushy beards and mustaches, Roquelaure keeps his mustache trimmed to precision.

I may have loved Draco, but I lusted after Roquelaure. Sharing Roquelaure's bed was very different than sharing Draco's. Both were satisfying but in different ways. Roquelaure was the kind of man who had many lovers, while Draco had few. Roquelaure was a skilled lover while Draco was a considerate one. It was even said that Roquelaure had spent time in Lady Godiva's bed. To my knowledge, Lord Draco shared his bed with no one but me.

You may wonder why I was not more faithful to Lord Draco. The simple answer is that I loved my freedom more than I loved either of these two men.

I regretted only spending a couple of nights with Draco in the winter of 1067, but Roquelaure had sent me a letter telling me

that he had a potentially lucrative opportunity for us. I traveled
to the city of Arles, on the Mediterranean, and found Roquelaure
working for a rather unsavory group of men that owned property
in the city.

In addition to owning the property, they charged a tax to
assure that any businesses in their buildings remained safe. If the
tax was missed, burglars visited the property. If the tax was missed
too often, or if the business owners complained to the Arlate, that's
where Roquelaure came in.

"You should join us," said Roquelaure one night as we sat at a
table outside an inn, under the stars. "This kind of work would be
perfect for you."

I scowled at him. Roquelaure may have been a good lover, but
he was not a very good judge of character. "I'm a skilled thief, not
a petty burglar."

"I don't mean to insult you." He leaned over the table and
took my hand. "I know how proud you are of your skills ... but,
the work is easy and the profits are high."

I looked into his sky-blue eyes and sighed. "I'll think about
it."

Against my better judgment, I allowed him to take me to the
landlords a few days later. He led me to a dank basement room
that seemed more befitting a crypt than a center of commerce.

Seven men in fine robes sat at a long table. Their skin was sickly
and pale, like that of many vampyrs I have known. In Greece, a
thousand years before, it was fashionable for the nobles to compete
with one another in games of physical prowess. In Europe of the
eleventh century, the fashion was for nobles to stay inside, showing
their contempt for work.

Roquelaure bowed low to the men at the table. "I wish to
present my friend, Alexandra." He stood upright. "She is perhaps
the finest thief I know."

The noble at the center of the table scowled at me. "I find it difficult to believe that a woman would have the skills necessary to be a thief."

A tapestry hung behind the table. It did not lie entirely flat against the wall. Instead, almost imperceptible ripples moved through it from time to time, as though a slight draft pushed it.

I stepped around the table and shoved the tapestry aside. There, in a small alcove, was a chest. I took the chest and set it upon the table. Grabbing the lock in my hand, I twisted and broke it. I threw the top open, revealing the gold coins within.

Another of the nobles grinned, and this time he reminded me more of a shark than a vampyr. "A lady thief could be good."

The landlord sitting next to me nodded agreement. "If she's caught, she won't be associated with us."

"Trust me," I said. "I will not get caught."

The landlord at the center of the table continued to scowl as he addressed Roquelaure. "You may take her on your next assignment. If she continues to demonstrate her skills, we will pay her the same as you."

Roquelaure bowed low and motioned for me to join him. "You are very generous, my lord."

That morning, before the sun rose, I sat beside Roquelaure in a forgotten chamber underneath Saint Honorat Church, at Les Alyscamps Cemetery, in Arles. He had made a rather cozy nest within the chamber. We sat upon a large feather mattress, illuminated by flickering candles. We sipped wine and gazed into one another's eyes.

"You were magnificent," he said.

"I don't know if I like these men." I set the wine goblet down on the floor.

"You don't have to like them," said Roquelaure. "Just accept their money. You will find the work easy."

I frowned as he set his goblet upon the floor. He moved closer and I shied away. He reached up and took my chin with his smooth, beautiful hand, and turned my face toward him. Before I could protest or pull away, he kissed me with a confidence that Draco never seemed to possess.

Roquelaure's sure hand found my breast and caressed it. His touch was firm, yet loving. His free hand made its way under my skirt and moved along my thigh.

I unlaced his trousers and moved my hand inside to find his aroused manhood. Reaching further down, I gently massaged his balls and felt them retract slightly.

He took the hint and his fingers moved up to my sex and rubbed me. I felt delicious, warm and wet desire. His fingers moved inside me, then he lifted them to his lips and licked them, as though savoring a grand feast. "It's better even than blood," he said.

He stood and pushed his trousers off, slowly, letting me have a good view of his lovely manhood, standing at attention. He knelt down beside me, lifted my skirt and with skill and care, eased himself into my slick folds. His thrusts were practiced and rhythmic. He sped up slightly as though he was about to come, then he withdrew and we changed positions. I was on my knees and he plunged into me from behind. He was deep within me and I moved to keep up with his thrusts. This time, we both climaxed together.

He lay down beside me and I allowed my teeth to play along his neck. His hand moved to my breastbone and he gently pushed me back. "Sharing blood would be dangerous."

"What are you afraid of?"

"I have my secrets and you have your freedom. I think it's best if things stay that way."

His hand moved along my neck to a place where Draco had once taken blood from me. I nodded, finding that I agreed with Roquelaure.

Chapter 21

From the memoirs of Alexandra the Greek.
The year 1067:

The landlords did not have a mission for us until two weeks later. At that point, they ordered me to break into a store that sold rugs imported from Persia. With our vampyr strength, Roquelaure and I were able to carry every rug out of the store between the hours of dusk and dawn. Using contacts from previous visits to Arles, I was able to fence the rugs. It proved far easier to sell this merchandise than crown jewels and I took a healthy sum of gold to the landlords. They smiled and paid Roquelaure and me twenty percent.

"Not bad, eh?" he said the next night as we sat together in a tavern.

"Not bad! They only gave us twenty percent! Tell me, why didn't we just take all of the rugs for ourselves and leave?"

"Because these men have connections," said Roquelaure.

I frowned wondering if these men could possibly have any more dangerous "connections" than a vampyr that was a little over a thousand years old.

With his share of the money, Roquelaure bought a rather nice house near the old Roman Coliseum in the town. We shared the house for several weeks and continued to do jobs together. Nice as the house was, I almost missed the damp smell of stone from the underground chamber at Saint Honorat. However, the more I thought about that, the more I wondered if I was missing Saint Honorat, or Draco's castle in the Carpathians.

One night, I accompanied Roquelaure on one of his

assassinations. It was fascinating to watch him work. He did not view his victims as food. Instead, he took time to hunt before he undertook the job. He found a young man, making his way through the streets after dark. He waylaid the boy and quickly bit into his neck, taking just enough blood to satisfy his hunger. When Roquelaure was finished, the young man blinked in confusion. Roquelaure handed him a silver coin and sent him on his way.

"I prefer not to feed on my victims," explained Roquelaure. "Bites on dead bodies arouse suspicion."

We continued on to the house of the business owner who refused to pay the "tax" to the landlords. Roquelaure waited outside the man's room and cleared his throat. When the man stepped out of the room to investigate the noise, Roquelaure leapt at him and slammed him into a wall.

The dazed man recoiled and looked around, confused. Roquelaure reached out and grabbed the man's head. He twisted quickly and there was a horrible snapping sound.

I turned away and put my hand to my mouth. I remembered my brother killing rabbits and chickens with the same cold efficiency. Even though I had been a vampyr for several centuries, such killing still shocked me.

"People recognize arrows and knives." Roquelaure stepped close, apparently sensing my unease. "They are completely confused when they see a head virtually wrenched from the body. The officials assume the killer must be large, not someone small of frame such as I am."

I nodded. With his clothes off, it was clear that Roquelaure had well defined muscles. Obviously he had been strong even before he became a vampyr, but he certainly had not been strong enough to break a human's neck, barehanded.

After the assassination was complete, I looked around the business owner's house. I found a small satchel of gold and a few other small trinkets of value. The next evening, I fenced the trinkets and took the money back to the landlords, save for a few gold coins I kept from the merchant's purse.

Again, they gave me twenty percent of what I brought them. I was pleased that I had not given them everything.

Late that summer, Roquelaure received a letter from none other than Lady Godiva. I knew that the Lady of Coventry must be rather elderly and I wondered if she and Roquelaure were still lovers.

Without any sign of embarrassment, Roquelaure showed me the letter he had received. Lady Godiva wrote to Roquelaure on behalf of William the First of England. Apparently there was an uprising on the Welsh border and William was looking for an assassin to take care of the uprising's leader.

"It is a job much more worthy of your skill," I said to him.

"Unfortunately, I don't think it is a job that requires a thief." He looked at the letter and held it up to his nose as though trying to catch the faint scent of a time gone by. The only scent I had caught was the musty one that comes from old women's boudoirs.

"What will you do? Will you stay here and continue your work for the landlords? I suspect this job will not take long."

I thought about it. The nature of the work didn't agree with my sensibilities and the landlords didn't really pay enough. I preferred breaking into places that were more challenging than homes and businesses.

"I'm thinking I might go east. Maybe I'll go to Rome – or back home to Greece."

He eyed me suspiciously. "If I didn't know better, I would think you had a lover that you weren't telling me about."

"If I did tell you, would you care?"

His only response was to smile.

I did return to Greece for a short time. In 1067, the Byzantine Empire was at its height, and Greek was once again the language of civilization. Athens was a center of commerce, much as it had been in my youth.

I walked the streets of the city and even found my way back to Theron's house. I was surprised to find it still stood. Even the fierce gorgon bust was still there, albeit weathered. I shuddered, wondering who now occupied the house.

I made my way down to the sea and hunted near the taverns. I found a lone sailor and fed from him. There was a shout and I looked up, cursing myself. Lost as I was in memories, I had not been careful about bringing my victim into the shadows.

I pulled the sailor into an alcove and climbed a steep wall. From my perch, I saw several sailors run through the streets past me. I climbed down and made my way back to the inn where I had a room.

When I awoke the next evening, an old Orthodox priest in ornate robes came to see me. "The innkeeper tells me you sometimes go out at night."

I nodded cautiously. "Sometimes I do, yes."

"You must be careful. There is a vrykolakas in this neighborhood." Vrykolakas was the word the Greeks had adopted for our kind.

"Thank you for the warning," I said.

"Do not worry. The creature will not haunt this area for long."

"Why is that?" I leaned forward, peering at the old man.

The priest smiled and retrieved several items from his robes, including a long metal stake much like the stoker I had used to kill Theron. "I have been to the island of Santorini and have learned to hunt vrykolakas. The foul demon will not hide from me for long." It seemed like the priest was gazing at me meaningfully.

I swallowed hard. "Thank you for the warning. I assure you, I will stay close to the inn."

Apparently satisfied, the priest gathered up his items and left. That night, I went to my rooms, packed my belongings and waited until there were only two hours left before morning. At that point, I rode as far away from Athens as I could.

I decided to continue east, without any particular thought

as to where exactly I was going. However, after working for the landlords in Arles and spending much of the summer with Roquelaure, I knew I needed to spend some time in the fresh air of the mountains. Draco's fortress seemed the perfect place to revive myself.

When I arrived, I was disappointed, but not entirely surprised that Draco did not greet me at the gate. He often left on extended trips. I was certain he would be back within a few days. I climbed the walls of the castle and dropped down into the courtyard. I opened the gate and led my horse and wagon inside and cared for them. With the gate secured behind me, I crept down into Draco's sleeping chamber.

As I opened the door, I smiled and my eyes grew moist, in spite of myself. Draco had made a new bed. On the frame was a soft, feather mattress, covered by linen sheets and a quilted blanket from Asia. No more straw and wool. I slipped underneath the blankets and snuggled up, feeling secure for the first time since I left Draco's castle earlier that year. I dropped into a deep sleep and didn't awake until late the next evening.

When I awoke, I felt around to see if Draco had slipped in beside me. I sighed when I found he wasn't there, then decided to make my way upstairs. On a hunch, I entered the library and there I found a parchment in the center of the table. It was a letter, addressed to me. It told me he was going to England.

Then, I looked at the date on the letter. He had left in the spring and it was now late into the summer. I thought about Roquelaure's letter from Lady Godiva telling of an uprising in the western territories. Tired as I was, I knew I needed to find the fastest possible route to England.

Chapter 22

An account of the battle of Hereford.
August of the year 1067:

P rince Bleddyn ap Cynfyn spent a day conferring with his
generals and composing letters to his brother Rhiwallon and
to Edric Silvaticus of Hereford. Tired, he yawned and rubbed
his eyes. He opened the door to his study and gasped when he saw
the lamp lit and the man called Desmond sitting in a chair reading
one of the five books he had in his collection. It was a prized copy
of *De Excidio et Conquestu Britanniae* by St. Gildas.

Shaking his head, Draco closed the book and looked up at the
prince as he entered. "Gildas only skims the surface of the events.
He doesn't even mention Arthur. At least he mentions Ambrosius."
He sighed. "I suppose that's what they mean when they say history
is written by the victors."

Bleddyn shook his head. "I don't know what you're talking
about."

"Surely you know the Battle of Camlan where Medraut
defeated Arthur? Gildas was Medraut's brother-in-law," explained
Draco as he replaced the book on the shelf. Bleddyn turned and
looked out the window, not seeming to pay attention to the strange
Transylvanian lord. Draco ceased his explanation and asked a
question. "So, have you reached a decision?"

Edric of Hereford's castle had recently been seized by a
Norman Earl named William FitzOsbern. Edric had written to
Bleddyn and his brother asking for help in reclaiming the castle.
Draco pointed out to Bleddyn that this might be the perfect
opportunity to test the strengths and weaknesses of the Normans

– to find out if they really could be driven off the island.

At first Bleddyn had been hesitant, but he finally conceded that he might be able to accomplish the task with the help of his brother's forces, as well as Edric's. "We march on the morrow," said Bleddyn.

"Very good," said Draco. "I will ride out ahead of you – tonight. I will meet you at your camp outside of Hereford."

The muscles relaxed in Bleddyn's back. "Why not ride with us?" The prince posed his question more from courtesy than a genuine desire to be joined by Draco.

"Given the nature of my work, it is best if the men know as little about me as possible." Draco put his hands to his chest.

"Very well," said Bleddyn. "Godspeed."

Draco turned and left the room.

Draco rode hard through the following nights. He stopped at villages along the way to rest and feed. He knew that Bleddyn and Rhiwallon had barely enough men for the assault. He didn't dare weaken the force by feeding on them as they traveled. He also wanted to get a better idea of Hereford's armaments and learn a little more about the generals and lords commanding the forces. He was sure Bleddyn's scouts were quite competent, but he wanted to form his own opinion.

A week after leaving Bleddyn's stronghold, just after sunset, Draco stepped into an innocuous looking inn in Herefordshire. The innkeeper stood behind a wooden bar and eyed him warily.

"Can I get you something to drink?"

Draco waved the question aside and continued through to a back room. Nine bleary-eyed men had gathered around a table and examined maps of the surrounding countryside. Without a word, Draco sat at the table and brought the maps toward him and studied them. "You intend to attack the castle?" he asked.

"It is my home," said Edric Silvaticus. Several days' growth of beard sprouted from his chin. His hair literally stood on end from running his hands through it numerous times.

Draco indicated a point on the map. "That is William's strongest point." He referred to the Earl who occupied the castle. "You'd have better luck taking Herefordshire itself. Roger of Hereford holds the city and his manor is easily attacked."

"Roger flows in and out with the tide," sneered Edric with contempt. "He was with me until William arrived. The only reason Roger is not here at this table is because he's afraid of forces from the Norman garrison outside of town."

"You have no hope against the castle unless you rally the people of Herefordshire and get them to join your side," argued Draco.

"That's what I've been trying to tell him." Bleddyn shook his head, apparently exasperated.

Draco looked over at him and noticed his goatee was in bad need of a trim; hairs jutted out all over. Still, he looked far less wild and harried than Edric.

"What about a two-pronged attack?" asked Bleddyn's younger brother, Rhiwallon, the Prince of Powys. "One group can attack the castle and the other can take the city from Roger."

"I would agree to that," said Bleddyn.

"Two-pronged attacks rarely work unless your army is very large," cautioned Draco. "Your forces are limited. There is danger in splitting them up."

Edric grabbed a blade from his boot and pointed it at Draco. "I thought you said you could do something to weaken the garrison and the castle. So far, all you've done is show up in the late hours and tell us why our plans won't work."

"I plan to take action against the garrison tonight," said Draco.

"How many men do you need?" Rhiwallon put his hand on Edric's forearm and nodded, indicating he should put the knife away.

"I'll do this alone." Draco held up his hand at the collective gasp from around the table. "I will weaken the forces at the castle, if I can. But, that's necessary even if you direct your attack at the city. I don't know if I can do enough to guarantee a successful attack against the castle."

"Do your best, or I'll cut your throat myself." Edric wrenched his arm from beneath Rhiwallon's and waved the knife at Draco.

Draco bared his teeth. Catching sight of the Dragon lord's fangs, Edric dropped the knife and made the sign of the cross. Draco shook his head and stood. "Do what you will. I will do what I can to weaken the forces at the castle." With that, he turned and strode from the room.

Draco left the inn and rode overland in the direction of the garrison. Before he came in sight of the guards he'd seen positioned there the previous few nights, he dismounted and made his way on foot through the lightly wooded terrain. There was no moon, which made it difficult for the scouts to see, but his eyes worked well in the near darkness.

When he reached the garrison, he scaled the outer wall and dropped within. One guard above him turned at the sound of his feet hitting the ground, but Draco quickly withdrew into the shadows. He edged around the buildings until he came to the storehouse. There he found a stockpile of tallow. He dipped a bucket in and carried it to the armory.

Draco moved through the armory and coated as many of the large weapons as he could with the tallow. It would make the swords and spears slick and hard to handle. Also, if they lit fires, there was a chance the weapons themselves would ignite.

He next turned his attention to the bows and arrows. He broke as many of the arrows as he could, but it was a slow process. With his strength he could have broken large bunches as easily as kindling. However, the sound of the snapping would have quickly brought the entire garrison down on him.

Draco looked out the window, noting the positions of the stars. The hour grew late and he knew he had other work to attend to. Sabotaging the weapons was only of limited value. The Normans had a strong force and more weapons at the castle. He would have to get there before dawn, to complete his mission.

Leaving the armory, he climbed atop the garrison's outer wall, and jumped down again. Stepping a short distance into the woods, he found where his horse was grazing.

He rode across country toward the castle. Again, he dismounted before the guards could see him. The trees around the castle were smaller than those around the garrison, so Draco took his time approaching, stopping periodically to listen and make sure the guards hadn't noticed his presence.

Once he was close enough to the castle to cover the distance as a swarm of flies, he concentrated and shattered into his component parts. He crossed the distance more slowly than he would have liked. Fortunately, it was late summer and the air relatively warm. In cold air, he found that when he dissolved into flies, he could become torpid and it was difficult to move at all.

Inside the castle, Draco made his way along the corridors until he found the chambers belonging to William FitzOsbern. One guard stood outside the door.

Draco pounced, grabbed the sword from the guard's hand, and bit his neck, taking enough blood to give him strength for the final part of his assault. Finally Draco took the guard's head and twisted … dropping him quietly to the floor.

Just as Draco reached for the doorknob of William's chambers, a cloaked figure emerged from the shadows. "Rather crudely done," said a velvety voice. "From what I'd heard of Lord Draco, I expected a bit more subtlety."

Without word, Draco lunged at the cloaked figure, who stepped aside, easily evading the lord's attack. The cloaked figure threw back his hood as Draco turned.

"You," he gasped. "How can that be possible?" He looked more carefully and saw the figure before him was a vampyr. He stood upright and shook his head. "Wolf couldn't have…. There wasn't time … unless…."

"I don't know what you're jabbering about," said the vampyr. "I am called Roquelaure. I thought you would prove to be far more of a challenge."

"Oh, I will be a challenge indeed," said Draco. Without

another word, he leaped at the cloaked figure.

Roquelaure stood his ground and grabbed the Dragon lord's arm. Using his attacker's momentum, he hurled Draco toward the wall. The Dragon lord grinned as he spun and allowed himself to rebound into Roquelaure. The two vampyrs tumbled to the ground.

Roquelaure managed to throw Draco off and then scuttled into a corner. Draco looked over to the guard on the floor. Lunging, he grabbed a sword and advanced on Roquelaure, who threw his cloak open and drew his own sword. The two vampyrs met in the middle of the hall.

As the swords clanked together, shouts came from the lower level. An alarm had been raised and men gathered. William appeared at his own door and watched the two men fighting. "Is this the assassin you spoke of, Roquelaure?" he asked.

"Please, my lord, don't distract me," said the cloaked vampyr as he parried a blow from Draco. "Seek safety with your men. I'll attend to the intruder."

William darted down the hall, away from the sword fight.

As Draco and Roquelaure continued to battle, they both became aware of a mist drifting between them. The mist coalesced and they found themselves staring slack-jawed at Alexandra. She held her hands up and looked from one man to the other. "Don't do this," she said.

"My love, what are you doing here?" asked Roquelaure.

Draco looked around Alexandra at the other vampyr. "Wasn't Guinevere enough for you?" he howled. In a rage he tried to push past Alexandra, his sword raised high.

Roquelaure leapt backward, and Alexandra pushed him into the wall.

"Shut up and listen!" shouted Alexandra. All three could hear guards running up the stairs at the end of the hall. "We'll work this out later, but for now it's time to get out of here." She looked back at Roquelaure.

"I am charged with keeping William FitzOsbern safe. I must kill Draco," said Roquelaure.

Alexandra glared at him. "I will not allow you to kill him."

The guards appeared at the top of the stairs only to find a dissipating mist and a swarm of flies that breezed past them. Only one of the guards saw the rat scuttle into a hole in the baseboard.

The next day, Edric lay siege to William's castle while Bleddyn and Rhiwallon joined forces to attack the city. The two brothers captured a bridge over the River Ludd and left men to hold their position while they joined Edric at the castle.

As Draco had predicted, the castle did not fall, and ultimately the attack was repulsed. That night at the camp, Bleddyn and Rhiwallon sat drinking ale. "Draco has failed us," growled Bleddyn.

"Are you really surprised?" said Edric.

The brothers looked up and saw Edric standing at the edge of the pavilion. Without invitation, he entered the tent and sat down at the table. "Draco is a coward," he continued. "It's obvious he took no men because he did not want them to witness his flight. He never intended to help our cause."

Bleddyn shook his head sadly. "He was so knowledgeable about tactics. He seemed sure of our victory."

Edric nodded his head. "Exactly what you'd expect from a spy sent to lure us into a lost cause to weaken our forces."

Rhiwallon shook his head. "But Edric, you're the one who wanted us to help you retake your castle.

Edric sneered. "Aye, but you listened to his plans and not mine. Who knows this country best? Me or some Transylvanian."

Bleddyn nodded sadly. "I fear you are correct, Edric. If I see this Draco again, I shall execute him as a spy."

Chapter 23

From the memoirs of Alexandra the Greek.
The year 1067:

After our encounter in Herefordshire, I had to decide whether to track down Draco or Roquelaure. Truly, Roquelaure was one of the most important people in my life. I enjoyed working with him, I could share my existence as a vampyr with him, and I cherished the way he made me feel when we made love. However, I always felt I shared something just a little deeper with Draco.

We had traveled together to the Middle East in search of one of the world's greatest mysteries. Also, Draco never held knowledge back from me – he shared it freely. My only fear with Draco was that he didn't respect my freedom as much as Roquelaure did. In spite of that, there was one thing above all other considerations that helped me decide to look for Draco first.

Draco seemed to recognize Roquelaure as they battled in front of FitzOsbern's door. Perhaps Draco could tell me who the mysterious vampyr really was.

Although Draco could transform into a swarm of flies, he could not travel far in that form. I searched the woods near Hereford Castle and found a place where a horse had apparently been left to graze near the road. From the tracks in the ground, it looked like someone climbed on the horse and took off in a hurry. I followed the tracks to a fork in the road and saw that they continued south, toward Monmouth.

I returned to Hereford, retrieved my own horse, and rode as fast as I could to the south.

I arrived in Monmouth the next night. I went to two inns and asked about a lord who was not seen during the day. Neither of the innkeepers knew anything about Lord Draco. When I stepped into the third inn, I caught sight of Draco walking down the stairs. He saw me at about the same time. "What are you doing here?"

"I'm trying to find you," I said.

He sneered and turned away.

"Draco, I would like to speak with you."

He took a step up the stairs, but stopped. His head drooped. Finally, he turned and came down. Sitting at one of the tables, he summoned the innkeeper and ordered two goblets of wine.

"What were you doing at FitzOsbern's castle?" Draco leaned forward on the table. "What do you know of the vampyr guard that was there?"

"I was going to ask you the same thing." I folded my arms. "It sounded as though you knew him."

Draco took a deep breath and let it out slowly. "It has been many years – so many years, that I'm not entirely sure I'm correct. However, the vampyr guard looked like a prince that used to serve my friend Arthur?"

"A prince?" My eyes widened.

"His name was Anguselus," explained Draco. "He was called the Ancelot and he had an affair with Guinevere."

The landlord brought the wine just then and I brought the goblet to my lips to hide my shock and disbelief. He continued his tale. Draco had been a rival of Arthur's and had expected to be named Pen-Dragon and married to Guinevere. Whenever Draco spoke of Guinevere, I sensed a pain of loss. There was something more to their relationship than merely friends who expected to be paired off in an arranged marriage.

While sitting in taverns, as I often do, I have heard tales from many bards. One of those tales told about the knight, Sir Lancelot, who had an affair with Queen Guinevere, in Britain. Somehow I had always assumed that "Lancelot" must be Draco. However, that didn't fit with the story Draco just told me. Had Roquelaure betrayed both Arthur and Draco?

I took a drink and placed the goblet back on the table. "Do you think it's possible that Roquelaure – the vampyr guard – is really this Anguselus?"

It was Draco's turn to eye me carefully. "Roquelaure? You do know him."

"I do," I admitted. "He's an assassin who lives in France. I've worked with him on occasion." I leaned forward and asked my question again. "Is he Anguselus?"

Draco shifted uncomfortably in his chair. "I never knew Anguselus well, but the vampyr that made me – Wolf – once saw him and thought him beautiful. He spoke of preserving his beauty for all time."

My breath caught at that.

He nodded, then seemed to lose himself in thought. "There was another. The day Wolf and I found the Holy Grail and the book of Jesus, we were accompanied by a young man called Galahad. That was also L'Ancelot's given name. At the time, I thought he must have been L'Ancelot's son. I never saw him eat. It's possible it was L'Ancelot and he was already a vampire…"

I narrowed my gaze. "You seem uncertain."

Draco sighed. "When the angel killed Wolf, blood sprayed everywhere. What if the young man really was L'Ancelot's son? Is there a chance he could have consumed enough blood to have become a vampyr?"

I shook my head. "I have no way of knowing that. L'Ancelot, Galahad, or someone else who resembles a faded memory. It would seem Roquelaure is still a mystery." I took another drink of wine. "What are your plans?"

"I failed to kill William FitzOsbern." Draco shrugged. "Bleddyn ap Cynfyn will not take that lightly. I was just coming down to pay my bill when you walked in the door. I plan to continue south."

"Where will you go from there?"

Draco pursed his lips and shook his head. "Perhaps back to Transylvania. It saddens me to think of it, but I think William of Normandy is too well entrenched in this country. I think there is little more I can do." He looked up at me hopefully. "Come back with me. I built a new bed. I think you will find it more comfortable than the old one."

I smiled at that. "I saw … and I like it." Then I looked away. "There is someone I must find before I join you."

"The Ancelot…." The look on Draco's face nearly broke my heart.

"Roquelaure," I corrected. "Even you're not certain he's Lancelot."

Draco nodded and sighed. "When will I see you?"

I reached across and took his hand. "As soon as I can, my love."

I feared Roquelaure would be more difficult to locate. He was quite skilled at staying in his rat form as long as he needed to elude search. However, since Draco indicated William FitzOsbern employed Roquelaure, I assumed he would not travel far from Herefordshire. I returned to Hereford Castle the next night.

Scaling the wall, I dropped down into the courtyard.

"I gather you're looking for me," said a voice from the shadows.

I turned and faced the familiar, velvety sound. "I thought you came to England at the summons of Lady Godiva." I narrowed my gaze. "As I recall, she's a Saxon. What are you doing working for a Norman Lord?"

Roquelaure shrugged. "Godiva has always wanted what's best for the people. She does not entirely like William of Normandy, but she and her husband Leofric have allied themselves to him and don't feel it's in the people's best interests for him to be deposed. I am here protecting William FitzOsbern on their behalf."

"How long do you plan to stay?"

"As long as necessary." He stepped closer and peered into my eyes. "That might be some time, given your vampyr friend who seems intent on assassinating FitzOsbern."

I inclined my head. "You might be interested to know, then, that he is retreating. Possibly away from England itself."

Roquelaure pursed his lips and nodded, seemingly satisfied.

"Do you know him?"

Roquelaure's eyes narrowed. "Know him? Why should I know him?"

"He thinks he knows you." I stepped over to a tree. The moonlight played through the branches and cast shadows on the ground, reminding me of Master Theron's fascination with Gorgons. All at once, it seemed I played a dangerous game. "Do you know the name Anguselus?" I turned around. Roquelaure's expression was unreadable.

"That is a very old name," he said.

"What about Lancelot?" I pressed.

"*That* name is merely legend." He smiled and stepped over to me.

"Why won't you tell me who you are?"

"Because whoever I might have been, no longer exists." He frowned briefly. "What would it matter if I was a prince or a legend?"

I shook my head. "I'm not entirely sure." Reaching out, I took Roquelaure's hand. "However, it does matter to a friend of mine."

"The other vampyr asssassin?"

I nodded.

"I have never met him before today." Somehow, I sensed Roquelaure told the truth, but I wondered if it was the complete truth.

Footsteps approached. A guard soon appeared. "Roquelaure, our scouts have brought us news. Bleddyn ap Cynfyn and Edric Silvaticus are retreating toward the south – toward Monmouth."

Roquelaure nodded. "Very good news. Perhaps my services will not be required much longer."

"There is more," continued the guard. "Apparently their advance scouts captured a prisoner in Monmouth. They've been given orders to hold him until Bleddyn's arrival. Perhaps it's the very assassin you drove off."

I looked from the guard to Roquelaure. "Do you suppose that's possible?"

Roquelaure looked to the guard. "How did they capture this prisoner?"

"I gather he was sleeping during the day at an inn," said the guard.

I shook my head. "Why didn't he leave?"

Roquelaure took my chin and lifted my face so I looked into his eyes. "Very likely, he decided to await your return."

I closed my eyes for a moment. The guard walked away, very probably dismissed with a nod from Roquelaure. Finally, I opened my eyes again. "We have to help him."

Roquelaure's grin was sardonic. "No, we don't."

"All right, then," I growled. "I have to help him. Will you come with me?"

He was silent for a moment. The vampyr assassin looked toward the castle's main building, then toward the wall. "I am not the only one with secrets. This could prove interesting."

Chapter 24

From the writings of Desmond, Lord Draco.
The year 1067:

When I awoke at sunset, I found myself chained to a wall. From the stars I could see through the room's tiny window, I gathered the room faced the east. If I couldn't find a way out before morning, the sun would come in. I had never seen firsthand what the sun did to our kind, but Wolf had told me that direct exposure to sunlight would kill us as surely as a stake through the heart.

I yanked on the chain holding my wrist, but found the chains stronger than I could break. The mortar holding the chain in place was sound, and I could not pull the chain from the wall. I sighed and closed my eyes. All was not lost. I could simply transform into a swarm of flies and be free of the chains and fly out the window. However, I had transformed several times in the last week. I was tired and I needed to gather my strength, and my resolve. It also would have helped if I had fed in the last day.

The chamber door opened and Bleddyn ap Cynfyn strode into the room along with two guards and a man adorned in robes. "Ah, you are finally awake," said Bleddyn. "I'm amazed you slept so well. Very convenient that you slept in a crate. It made it easy for my guards to bring you here."

I took a deep breath and let it out slowly. "Bleddyn, I demand to be released. I have done you no wrong."

Bleddyn pursed his lips in disgust. "We were defeated at Herefordshire. None of my men saw you during the fighting. You did not appear afterwards. There is no evidence you did anything at all.

"When my men arrived here in Monmouth, they simply found you asleep in a room. As far as I can tell, you just ran away from the fight." The prince stepped over to the window and looked out to the night sky. "What do you have to say for yourself?"

"I sabotaged the weapons at the armory," I said. "I broke many of the arrows...."

"Not enough," said Bleddyn.

"I dipped their weapons in tallow."

"They still handled them well." The prince turned and faced me. "And many of them were flaming when they came toward us. It was very demoralizing to my troops and contributed to our loss." He shook his head. "Draco, I trusted you, but at best, you are an incompetent coward. At worst, you are a traitor. I have no choice but to sentence you to death."

I scowled. "I am no traitor!"

The prince nodded. "Perhaps, but you are a mercenary. I don't believe you are loyal to anyone either. Your death will not be a loss – it might even help me regain trust with my men."

As Bleddyn turned and strode from the room, the man in robes began chanting. I recognized the words as Latin and concentrated, curious about what the old man was doing. I caught the words, "Through this holy anointing may the Lord in his love and mercy help you with the grace of the Holy Spirit." With that, the man reached into a small pouch on his belt and retrieved a vial. Taking out the cork, he put some of the contents on his finger and made a cross on my forehead.

My brow creased as I realized the substance from the vial was oil. The man must be a priest of some kind and I was being anointed. The priest then reached out and made a cross of oil on each of my outstretched palms.

"May the Lord who frees you from sin, save you and raise you up." He returned the vial to his pouch then brought out a small wafer of bread and a flask with a red substance that I realized must be wine. "I offer you one last Eucharist."

"I don't eat bread, and I'm not a Christian," I said. "I have never had a first Eucharist."

The priest frowned. "Then may the Lord have mercy on your soul." He placed the bread and wine back in his pouch, turned, and stormed from the room. The guards whirled around, left the room, and closed the door behind them.

Thankful to be alone again, I closed my eyes and tried to quiet my mind. A short time later, I was ready and willed myself to transform into the swarm. I made an effort, but something was wrong. My body refused to change. Again, I tried and nothing happened. I wracked my brain, frantically trying to think what could be wrong.

Growing desperate, I yanked on the chains again. They refused to budge. Once more, I tried to quiet my mind and transform. Still, nothing happened. I looked toward the window and wondered if I had finally been defeated. Would Bleddyn behead me the next day, and that would be the end of Lord Draco?

I sighed and tried to think what I could do. If the chains would not budge and I could not transform, my best chance would be to overpower the guards when they came to retrieve me the next morning. If the execution was scheduled to happen at sunrise, I had a slim chance.

I held onto that chance as I waited out the night. Periodically, I tried to break the chains again or transform, but I had no success.

Finally, I noticed the sky was beginning to lighten. I only had a short time left. There was a squeaking near my heel. Looking down, I saw a rat. "Such lovely accommodations Prince Bleddyn has for his guests," I said.

Looking up, I noticed that a fog must be rising with the dawn. Mist drifted in through the window. Just then, I thought of the battle at William FitzOsbern's.

The rat transformed into the mysterious vampyr who looked so much like the Ancelot. The mist coalesced into Alexandra.

"What are you doing chained up here?" she asked. "I would have thought you could have transformed and gotten out of this."

"Something's preventing me from transforming and the chains are too difficult to break," I said.

The vampyr mercenary that Alexandra called Roquelaure,

examined me carefully. "What is this? Oil?"

He reached up and wiped the oil from my forehead. I felt myself grow stronger. "There's more oil in the palms of my hands."

Roquelaure cleaned one hand and Alexandra cleaned the other.

There was a sound from the corridor. "It's the guards," said Alexandra. "They must be coming for you."

Again, I closed my eyes. With a force of will, I found I was able to transform this time. Without hesitation, I darted for the window. One of my flies lingered and sat on the windowsill, watching as the guards entered the chamber. They didn't understand what happened to their prisoner. All they saw was mist rolling out of the room.

My last remaining fly lifted off and followed the rest of me. I needed to find a place to dig into the ground, a place hidden well enough that Bleddyn ap Cynfyn would not find me again.

Two weeks after escaping Monmouth, I found myself sitting at an outdoor café in the south of France, in a town called Arles. At the table with me were Alexandra and Roquelaure.

It was a clear night and the stars shone brightly above. A few birds still chirped in the trees around us. Despite the idyllic atmosphere, I glared at Alexandra. "Am I to understand that you have shared Roquelaure's bed, even as you have shared mine?"

Alexandra raised her chin. "Do not presume to lecture me about morals, young one."

I was over five hundred years old. Being referred to as "young one" pricked my nerves and she knew it. Standing, I strode a few steps from the table. "Why would you betray me like this?"

Her chair scraped against flagstones. A moment later, she stood at my side. "Why do humans – ordinary humans – mate for life?"

I blinked at the question. It was something I had simply not thought to ask before. "I suppose they do it so they can provide a stable household for their children."

She stepped around me and looked up into my face. Her

grin was sardonic. "As far as I have been able to learn, our kind is incapable of having children. If that's your only argument, I don't see why you are angry."

I looked at my feet and then back into her eyes. "A man and a woman should choose to be loyal to one another. It's natural."

"Exactly what about our kind is, in any way, natural? In what way does my relationship with Roquelaure betray you?" She turned and took a few steps back toward the table.

I refused to turn and look in her direction. "He was working for my enemy."

"I'm a mercenary," came Roquelaure's voice from the table. "Lady Godiva paid me to do a job."

I turned around and glared at him.

Alexandra pointed at the seated vampyr. "You keep out of this." She then turned her attention back to me. "He's right though. He's a mercenary and you're a mercenary. Exactly how are you any different?"

I sighed and looked at Roquelaure. His face was unreadable. I tried to decide if he was Prince Anguselus, his son, or someone else altogether. "Why won't you tell us where you came from? Why do you hide your identity?"

He looked down at the table. "I do not know the vampyr that made me. I spent many years trying to understand what I had become." Roquelaure looked back up into my eyes. "If I was this Prince Anguselus, what would it matter?"

"It matters because Anguselus stole the woman I loved," I said simply.

"Did he, or did you abandon her?"

"Then you do know Guinevere!" I slammed my fist on the table.

"I don't have to know her," growled Roquelaure. "All I know is that you stand here alone. If you were truly loyal to the woman you loved, why didn't you make her one of our kind? At the very least, you abandoned her to death."

His voice was quiet, almost a whisper. However, the words were like a knife twisting in my gut. I dropped into my chair and looked at my hands. Another chair moved and Alexandra sat down next to me. She put her hand on mine. I looked up into her eyes and found her expression hard.

"I value my freedom more than anything else." Her voice was firm. "I do not give my loyalty to any country or any man. I have never left you for Roquelaure, nor have I left Roquelaure for you. I have simply gone where I desired and followed my heart. I have been fortunate enough to find two men I love. To leave either of you would diminish me and deny me my freedom. Is that what you want?"

I sighed and fell silent for a time. I reached out and touched her long, dark hair. "I love you because of who you are. I would not change you."

She took my hand and kissed it. "I love you, Draco." She looked over and put her hand on Roquelaure's. "I also love you, Roquelaure." She chewed her lower lip for a moment and brought her hands together. "You each have strengths that I value. I begin to wonder if those strengths could be united in some way."

I sat back and folded my arms. "You mean like an alliance?"

She nodded. "Could you imagine the money we could make if we all offered our services to one lord or country?" She looked to Roquelaure. "Look at what we were able to accomplish together for the Arlate. Imagine what three of our kind could do."

From her gaze, I could see the trust Alexandra had for Roquelaure. I didn't trust him that much, and my trust in Alexandra had been shaken. However, both of them had just given me reasons to question some of my oldest and deepest beliefs. I nodded slowly. "I would be willing to consider such an alliance – at least, try it out."

"Like you, Alexandra, I value my freedom." Roquelaure pushed his chair back from the table and met her gaze. "I asked for your help for one particular job. I am hesitant to commit to any future jobs." He turned and looked at me. "The fact that you have doubts about me only increases my hesitation. If you cannot trust me, how can I trust you?" He stood and walked away from the table, into the night.

Alexandra's body tensed and I believed she wanted to run after him, but that was not in her nature. Instead she turned to me. "Where are you going now?"

"I thought to return to the Carpathians. Now that England is in the hands of William of Normandy, my castle is the only home I have left."

"Do you mind if I come with you?"

"You are always welcome," I said. We stood and I took her into my arms.

Waking up one evening, a few weeks later, I turned over and snuggled up to Alexandra's back. We were in my castle, and it was good to be home. I stroked her long, luxuriant hair. Her eyelids fluttered open and she reached down and began stroking my manhood. I moved my attentions from her hair to her breasts. She rolled onto her back and opened her legs. Although I was still sleepy, I gladly obliged her desires and plunged into her sex.

I allowed my teeth to play over her neck, but did not bite. She nibbled on my ear and then drew me deep within her. Her muscles contracted tightly about me and my seed spilled into her. After a few minutes, we parted and lay side by side, out of breath.

"I grow hungry," I said after a time. "Would you care to hunt with me?"

"I would be delighted," said Alexandra, "but, I would like to bathe first."

I rose and went to the great hall. After retrieving wood, I started a fire so I could heat some bath water. Just as I started the fire, there was a banging at the door. Alexandra emerged wearing a dressing gown and looked at me with a puzzled expression.

Together we went to the door. Roquelaure stood on the other side. Draped over his arm were three red cloaks. "May I come in?" he asked.

I stood aside and indicated that he could enter. He entered the great hall and deposited the cloaks on the table. He looked at Alexandra. "I have been thinking, and I believe you are right. There are circumstances under which the three of us could be of assistance to one another."

"I'm glad to hear it," said Alexandra.

"Does this mean that you've decided to trust me?" I asked.

He shook his head. "I don't trust you any more than I believe you trust me." He put his hands behind his back. "However, I have been contacted about a little matter in Cappadocia. Do you think we could work together, despite our mutual distrust?"

I pursed my lips and nodded. "We were about to hunt. Perhaps you would like to accompany us. Then we can discuss this matter."

"Most gracious," said Roquelaure.

Alexandra picked up one of the red cloaks. "This is nice material," she said. "What is the purpose of the cloaks?"

Roquelaure nodded. "I thought that it might be useful if we had a uniform – something that symbolized our alliance. Since we are bonded in blood, and cloaked in shadow, I thought the scarlet robes would be appropriate."

"We would be like a special order of mercenaries." Alexandra looked to me. "It seems fitting."

"Indeed. We could call ourselves the Scarlet Order." I looked to Roquelaure. "Let us endeavor to prove ourselves to one another."

With that, I went out to fetch water for Alexandra's bath.

Interlude 4
Cloaks and Thorns

Munich. The year 1168:

Roquelaure's travels often took him along the "Salt Road," a route traders used when carrying salt from the mines near Bad Reichenhal on the Austrian border to the city of Augsburg in the Dutchy of Bavaria. Along the route were fine inns that Roquelaure found much to his taste. As he traveled the Salt Road in the year 1168, he discovered the path diverged and there were now two roads. The older path went by the familiar northwesterly route that led to Freising and the other went more directly west. A sign on the northwesterly road indicated that the bridge was out, so Roquelaure decided to try the newer road.

When he came to the River Isar, he found a bridge with no tollbooth that led to a small cluster of buildings, which for the most part seemed rather new. The one exception was an old monastery situated on the river's bank. Roquelaure nodded as he looked at the monastery and realized that he must have arrived at the place called Munich. He guessed the salt miners had either grown weary of the taxes and tolls imposed by the Burgermeister of Freising or simply wanted a more direct route to Augsburg and implored the Duke of Bavaria to move the road further south. For his own part, Roquelaure was pleased to avoid a toll when crossing the bridge.

Entering the village in the early morning hours, just as twilight began brightening the sky, Roquelaure quickly found an inn and stepped inside. He was surprised when the innkeeper immediately accosted him. "Who are you?" he demanded.

"I'm a weary traveler, seeking lodgings for this day and evening," said Roquelaure.

"At this hour of the morning?" The innkeeper narrowed his gaze suspiciously.

"I often travel by night. It is a requirement of my … order." He indicated the cloak he wore.

"Only cutthroats and thieves travel these roads by night," grumbled the innkeeper.

A moment later, Roquelaure heard people shuffling around upstairs. A man and a woman appeared at the top of the stairs carrying something wrapped in a blanket. Familiar as he was with death, Roquelaure was certain the item was a corpse.

The vampyr swallowed. "I presume one of these cutthroats has recently visited your inn."

"Not just my establishment," said the innkeeper, "travelers have been killed at an inn in Munich each night for the last week. I had hoped I'd be spared, but apparently not." The two people carrying the body, shuffled past the innkeeper and out through the front door. "As you can imagine, fewer travelers are stopping. Either they pass right through, or they go north on the old road to Freising."

"I thought the sign on the road said the bridge was out."

"Aye, the Duke ordered the bridge destroyed, but the Burgermeister of Freising has started a ferry service across the river – for a price."

"I am not easily frightened by cutthroats," said Roquelaure, "and because my order requires that I remain awake at night, perhaps I can be of assistance tracking down the killer."

The innkeeper considered Roquelaure's words and finally nodded. "It would be a great help to us if you could end these murders."

"I must retire soon," said Roquelaure, noticing the sky's brightness through the window, "but what can you tell me of this most recent murder?"

"It was horrible. It looked like the man had been attacked by a vicious animal. There were jagged puncture wounds in the man's throat – as though he had been stabbed by a fork." The innkeeper produced a two-pronged fork from a nearby table and thrust it through the air for emphasis. "The strange part was how little blood surrounded the wound – and the victim was deathly pale."

Roquelaure pursed his lips and nodded thoughtfully. "I've … heard of this method of execution. I definitely think I can help you."

"If so, I'll give you your room for free," said the innkeeper.

"Most kind."

The innkeeper directed Roquelaure to a room upstairs. Just as the vampyr turned to leave, the innkeeper stopped him. "There's one more thing, every time the killer strikes, he leaves a calling card. It's a blood red rose. The only place I can imagine such a flower coming from is the garden of a wealthy man."

"Thank you. That may be helpful." With that, Roquelaure made his way upstairs. He found a dark corner of the room just before sleep took him for the day.

Roquelaure awoke before sunset. Keeping to the shadows, he made his way downstairs and found the landlord. The man seemed in better spirits than when Roquelaure left him. The vampyr suspected he was pleased at the prospect that someone might solve the mystery of the murders happening in the town. The innkeeper offered Roquelaure food. He declined, but accepted a glass of wine.

"What can you tell me of the men who've died?" asked Roquelaure once he was seated at a table.

"They are typically men who have made a lot of money at the mines. They are generally quite free with their gold."

"Popular men," Roquelaure mused. "The kind of men who influence decisions." He looked around at his fellow patrons, sitting at other tables. There weren't many, but perhaps there were enough for his objective. The vampyr withdrew two gold coins from his pouch. "Would that be sufficient to buy food and drink for each man in this room?"

"More than enough." The innkeeper beamed. "You are very generous, Herr…" He paused, apparently realizing that he did not know the stranger's name.

"You may call me Herr Mantel," said Roquelaure, using the Germanic word for cloak.

"Very well, Herr Mantel, but you realize such generosity is dangerous."

"I'm counting on it," said Roquelaure. "Please let it be known to these men that I have paid for their drinks and meals." He lifted the goblet of wine and took a drink. "I will be in my room, hopefully awaiting a visitor."

"As you wish, Herr Mantel."

From the innkeeper's description, Roquelaure had deduced that the killer was a vampyr – most likely hired by the Burgermeister of Freising to convince people how dangerous it was to stay at Munich's inns. Roquelaure didn't feel strongly one way or the other about helping the citizens of Munich, but he was interested in this vampyr. Such a creature could be a useful addition to the Scarlet Order of vampyr mercenaries he was helping Draco to build. Alexandra had already brought the lovely Nabila into the order. Since then, they had recruited two others. The problem was there were so few vampyrs and most of the ones they found were creatures who had lost their minds after becoming creatures of the night. However, a vampyr that was already working as a killer … such a creature had a lot of potential.

As the night wore on, Roquelaure grew restless. He wondered if his strategy was sound. Was the vampyr assassin really hunting rich and popular people, or was there another method? Perhaps there was no method at all. Shortly after midnight, Roquelaure's stomach began to rumble. He realized he needed to hunt. The problem was that he might be mistaken for the killer in a town already on the lookout for someone stalking the streets at night. He decided he would wait just a little while longer.

A short time later, Roquelaure's patience was rewarded. His sensitive hearing detected footsteps on the stairs. He lay down on the bed and closed his eyes. A moment later, the door creaked open. Roquelaure sat up. "A rose for me? How kind."

The creature that entered the room yelped, dropped the rose and turned. Roquelaure was faster. He sprang from the bed and pushed the door shut, barring the creature's escape. Turning around, he took a good look at the creature for the first time. Roquelaure's breath caught. The creature was bald, with ears that stuck out slightly from the side of his head. He'd seen such a creature before, but had buried the image deep in his memory.

"What are you called?" asked Roquelaure.

The bald vampyr glanced toward the window. He turned ever so slightly, but Roquelaure leaped forward and pushed him into a wall, pinning him. "Tell me what you are called."

"I had a name once," said the vampyr. "I barely remember now."

Roquelaure looked down at the rose, discarded on the floor. "Perhaps I should call you Rosen."

"A name is a name," said the vampyr. "What manner of creature are you?"

Roquelaure opened his mouth, revealing his fangs. "The same as you." He led Rosen over to the bed and both sat. "Am I correct in assuming that you are paid to murder men in Munich by the Burgermeister of Freising? The rose is from his garden?"

Rosen nodded.

"How much does he pay you?"

"A silver piece for each victim."

Roquelaure shook his head. "What if I told you there were lords and kings who would pay much more for your services? What if I told you that you could live in comfort?"

"I think I would be very interested," said Rosen.

"Then come with me and let me tell you about the Scarlet Order."

Part V
The Dragon's
Reflection

Chapter 25

From the writings of Desmond, Lord Draco.
The year 1447:

Summer in Transylvania was something of a mixed blessing to me. On one hand, the warm air caused the borrowed blood in my veins to flow more freely. On the other hand, the brief nights forced me to move quickly to take advantage of the balmy weather. I felt more alive and energized in the summer, but I needed to.

Fortunately, I had discovered that just as human bodies change and mature over time, so do vampyr bodies. When I had been a newly made vampyr, my body's cycles were locked to the sun. I would rise just as the sun went below the horizon and, no matter where I was, I would drop into a heavy slumber the minute the sun appeared in the morning.

By 1447, I'd been a vampyr for almost a millenium, and I found I could now rise before sunset and stay up after sunrise. Even so, I was still deprived of sunlight itself. To go out during the daytime would cause intense, burning pain, and eventually death if I remained out long enough. However, as long as I remained in a darkened room, devoid of natural light, I could take advantage of a few extra hours, even during the summer.

I awoke early on one such July afternoon. I sat up in bed and I struck flint to fire-steel and lit a candle by the bedside. Looking to my left, I saw that Alexandra had thrown off her blankets. The sight of her nude form aroused me and I snuggled up to her back. My hands reached around and found one of her full breasts. Her nipple responded to my caress, and she sighed as my member throbbed against her thigh.

Older than me, she was no more constrained to the sun's cycle than I was. She moved her hips so that my cock slid into her. Although she didn't open her eyes, her face betrayed a certain enjoyment as she ground her hips into mine. Soon, I could stand it no longer and my barren seed shot into her equally barren womb.

In many ways, I was thankful that we could not produce children. I truly feared the kind of monstrous creature vampyrs might produce after mating.

Alexandra opened one eye and her lips turned up in a mischievous grin. "You're awake early."

"I'm looking forward to this night." I moved her long black hair away from her neck and kissed her gently. "The moon will be full and I look forward to strolling along the Bistritza River with you. It has been too long since you last visited alone."

Her grin faded. "It is difficult to travel in this part of the world, even for creatures such as us. On one side is Hungary. The Ottoman Turks are on the other side. In between are princes vying for favor from one side or the other."

She turned and looked into my eyes. "I wish you would come to the West with me. Italy and France are going through a rebirth. There are cities in those countries even grander than the ones that existed during the days of the Roman Empire."

I shook my head. "I'm a mercenary. All these princes fighting for power here in the East mean income for me. That's hard to ignore."

"And it's hard to come here alone when you summon Roquelaure and his friends."

It was my turn to frown. Roquelaure had indeed recruited a good group of vampyrs – or vampires, as our kind was increasingly being called. They fought well and had many useful skills – and they always came when I summoned them. They were all part of our Scarlet Order of vampire mercenaries, but there were times when I wondered whether they were more loyal to Roquelaure, or me.

Alexandra kissed my nose, startling me away from my thoughts. "You should definitely come west with me. You need to relax."

"I am relaxed." I stretched out on the bed and put my hands behind my head.

She struck me with a pillow and laughed as I jumped. "You're as tense as a lyre string." She stood up and retrieved a candle from the nightstand. Stepping around the bed, she lit it from my candle, then strode to the door. "Since I'm awake now, I think I'll take a bath. *I* know how to relax."

I sighed as she stepped through the door. Standing, I retrieved my clothes and dressed quickly.

I took up my candle and then followed the corridor past the bath chamber and up a set of stairs into my library. There, I retrieved a book Alexandra had brought me from Italy and sat down in a comfortable chair. Just as I opened the book, there came a loud banging from the castle's main entry.

Even though the sun no longer dictated my rising and retiring, the room's high windows let in enough light that I could tell it was not yet sunset. I decided to ignore the banging. It was probably a peasant seeking shelter for the night. They could wait the half hour until the sun had gone down.

As I read, the banging grew more persistent. I found I could not concentrate on the book any longer. I placed a ribbon in the pages to mark my place and rose from my chair. The sun would be well below the walls of my castle now, and I could open the door safely and send the interloper away.

The banging continued, even as I strode through the castle. When I arrived at the door, I threw it open and prepared to strike out at the person who dared to interrupt my reading. However, there was more than one man. Two heavily armored men stood before me, holding pikes.

In my courtyard was a gilded carriage. The door opened, and out stepped a man with a receding hairline and a thick, black mustache. My breath caught and I bowed low to the former Vovoide of Transylvania and current Governor of Hungary, Janos Hunyadi.

The governor strode toward me and indicated I should rise. "I've heard of your strange habits, Draco, but you took a damned long time to answer the door."

"I was not expecting you, Governor Hunyadi," I said. "I am honored by your visit and trust it must be a matter of some importance for you to visit me in person." I led the governor toward my sitting room. His guards kept their place by the door.

"It is." He dropped onto one of my chairs and crossed his legs. "Are you familiar with the Prince of Wallachia?"

I sat across from Hunyadi and nodded. "Vlad Dracul is his name."

"He has allied himself with the Turks. That brings the Ottoman Empire far too close for comfort."

I pursed my lips. "You would like the Scarlet Order to rid Wallachia of Prince Vlad."

"I would indeed."

Standing, I retrieved two goblets and a flask of wine from a nearby shelf. I poured the wine and handed one goblet to Hunyadi. "I will gather my men and await your signal."

Hunyadi smiled and raised the goblet to his lips. "This is very good wine," he said, appreciatively.

I inclined my head. As a vampire, I could not enjoy solid food. However, I did seek out the best liquid refreshment available. It was true that I could not garner nourishment from anything aside from blood, but I did enjoy a good red wine now and then.

Hunyadi drained his goblet and then stood. "Thank you for your hospitality, Draco. You will hear from me soon."

I followed the governor to the door and watched as he climbed into his carriage and rode off into the night, escorted by his men.

After Hunyadi left, I refilled my goblet and returned to the library. Just as I sat down to read again, Alexandra appeared in the doorway. Her brow creased as she scanned the room. "You're alone," she said. "I thought I heard voices."

I set the book on the table next to me and picked up the wine goblet. "You heard me speaking with Janos Hunyadi." I raised the goblet to my lips.

"The Governor of Hungary?" Alexandra glided from the doorway to a chair near my own. "What did he want?"

Instead of answering, I swirled the wine in the goblet and smirked. "I'm sure he would have desired you, had he seen you dressed in naught but your dressing gown."

She looked down at herself and leaned forward, giving me a rather delicious view of her breasts.

"He would only have seen me if I desired it." She sat back, but left the gown gaping just enough to tantalize. "I presume he wants to hire you, since he came here himself?"

I set the goblet aside and explained about Vlad Dracul of Wallachia. "He is a wretched man. He gave two of his own sons over to the Turks as slaves. I do not trust a man like that in a neighboring country."

Alexandra laughed lightly. "So, does this mean you will do the job for free?"

I scowled at her. "Of course not."

She shook her head. The bemused expression never left her face. "So, I suppose this means that you want me to summon Roquelaure and the Scarlet Order."

Instead of answering, I picked up the goblet and took another sip of wine. When I looked up, I realized that Alexandra studied me.

"You're worried," she observed.

I snorted and folded my arms across my chest. Alexandra stepped over and put her hand on mine.

"Roquelaure enjoys travel more than you. He has more opportunity to recruit members for the Scarlet Order," said Alexandra.

"He is more popular ... more likeable...." The words were out of my mouth almost before I realized I had spoken them.

A sudden look of realization came over Alexandra's face. "It's not worry about loyalty," she mused. "It's jealousy."

I stood and took two steps away, my back toward Alexandra. "I am not jealous of him." I turned slowly. "However, I am concerned that if there were a dispute of any sort, the members of the Scarlet Order would follow him rather than me."

Alexandra took a step toward me and nodded. "You're worried he'll be the next Pen-Dragon."

"What?" I shook my head. "That's ridiculous."

One more step and Alexandra put her hands on my hips. "It is. The Scarlet Order may follow Roquelaure, but Roquelaure follows you. He is not like your friend Arthur. He is more like your friend Bran."

"He is not at all like Bran," I said emphatically.

"From what you've told me, Bran would follow you anywhere. Roquelaure would as well."

"And how do you know that so well?"

Instead of answering, she leaned forward and I felt her lips – warmed from the recent bath – against my own. Her tongue caressed my fangs and her hands moved from my hips to my back and then continued their explorations lower. There would be time to continue our conversation during our walk – later that night.

Less than a month later, I found myself in the neighboring country of Moldavia, in marshes outside Bălteni. The land had no leader, and both Janos Hunyadi and Vlad Dracul were working to place a man loyal to their respective interests on the throne. The only thing Hunyadi and Dracul had in common was a dislike of the Poles to the North, who also extended their influence into Moldavia.

Alexandra went west to retrieve Roquelaure and the other members of the Scarlet Order, but Hunyadi had summoned me before they returned. Fortunately, Hunyadi did not require an army, just a simple assassination. He wanted to demonstrate Hungary's power so he could get his man on the throne.

Vlad Dracul met with a group of powerful Moldavians in Bălteni. I waited in the marshes, not far from Dracul's camp. The men were raucous and loud. It looked as though women from the village had come out to entertain the soldiers. Undoubtedly, they wanted to curry favor with Vlad and his men, just as Vlad wanted to curry favor with them.

Despite the warm, moist air, I wore a long-sleeved jerkin and heavy trousers to keep the mosquitoes off me. Even so, they had a tendency to land on any exposed part of my skin. I looked at one that had landed on my hand and considered it as it drank blood I had borrowed from another.

I had become a vampire by drinking blood that had passed through another of my kind. I wondered if the mosquitoes went through any kind of transformation. I frowned at the thought, and smashed the mosquito on my hand, leaving a tiny smear of blood – too little to worry about. I found some water and washed it off. Still, I hoped the men in Dracul's camp would finish their revels before too long, so I could be done with my assignment and escape my insect kindred.

I only knew a little about this Vlad Dracul. Also known as Vlad II, he had ascended to the Wallachian throne about four years before. His title, Dracul, was given because he belonged to the Order of the Dragon. It was hard not to feel a little bit of kinship and nostalgia for this Eastern Pen-Dragon. However, he was constantly afraid of losing his power. Dracul believed the best way to retain the throne was to ally himself with the Ottoman Turks to the south.

In 1444, Hunyadi met with Vlad Dracul to remind him that he'd sworn an oath to the Order of the Dragon to keep the Ottomans out of Wallachia. Dracul declined, which led to the fissure between Hunyadi and him and also precipitated a great battle at the port of Varna.

What I knew about Vlad Dracul, indicated that he was a man who betrayed his oaths. He was more interested in power than helping his own people. As I had told Alexandra, he gave two of his sons to the Turks as hostages, to show his loyalty to them. Moreover, he sent a tribute of Wallachian boys to the Turks to be used as slaves.

As a mercenary, I seldom concerned myself with the people I fought and killed. And, Vlad Dracul was the kind of man whose death I would not mourn under any circumstances.

Finally, as midnight approached, the camp settled down and

lights were extinguished. I willed myself to transform into a swarm of flies and drifted over to the camp. Mosquitoes and flies of all sorts flitted to and fro anyway. The guards who stood outside the largest tent in the encampment hardly noticed me.

Over the course of a half hour, my component parts, flew and crawled through the tent flaps and past the tent's foyer into Vlad Dracul's sleeping area.

The prince slept on top of blankets, in a simple shift. Silently, I brought my component parts together and stood over him.

His eyes flitted back and forth behind closed lids. He dreamed. I wondered if he dreamt of power, or if he had nightmares about the boys he sent into slavery. I didn't bother to look into his dreams as I bit into his neck and took my fill of nourishing blood. His dreams were finished by the time I raised my head.

I retrieved a dagger inscribed with Janos Hunyadi's seal and quickly slit Vlad Dracul's throat. I watched as his life poured out.

Mosquitoes swarmed to the blood. I dropped Hunyadi's dagger atop Dracul's corpse. His guards would find it in the morning and the rumor would be started that Hunyadi had crept into the camp and assassinated Dracul. Somehow, such rumors did not seem honorable to me, nor were they a way to curry favor with the populace, but Hunyadi felt sure the Moldavians would see it as a sign of Hungary's strength.

I looked down at Vlad Dracul's remains like I had looked at the smashed mosquito on my hand earlier that night. The world was rid of one more pest. However, like the mosquitoes, as they swarmed about his cooling body, I was all too aware there would be plenty more where he came from.

Chapter 26

From the writings of Desmond, Lord Draco.
The year 1447:

I took my time returning to my castle in the Carpathians. Alexandra proclaimed that I do not like to travel as much as Roquelaure does. I really don't know if that is correct or not. In fact, I do like to travel and meet new people. However, I had also been growing comfortable in my castle in the Carpathians. Meeting people and experiencing new ideas through the books Alexandra brought me was, admittedly, much easier than meeting people in person – especially since my travels are limited to the nighttime hours.

The first nights of my journey home, I traveled faster than the news of Vlad Dracul's assassination. I sat in Moldavian taverns and listened as people spoke of Vlad and Hunyadi.

As one might expect, there were heated discussions about who was the better leader. I also learned something interesting – and in retrospect, it should not have been that surprising. More than either of those men, the Moldavians hoped one of their own would rise up and challenge both men. Of course, the problem was that the ruling families of Wallachia, Transylvania, Moldavia, and Hungary were so intertwined, it was hard to say who was truly Moldavian. In fact, I gathered that Moldavia's Prince Bogdan was Vlad Dracul's brother-in-law.

Eventually, the news of Vlad Dracul's assassination caught up with me in my travels. The conversations in the taverns ranged from anger and outrage to fear and suspicion. Those who supported Vlad expressed hope that his eldest son, Mircea, would stand up to Hunyadi.

I merely nodded and sipped my wine, suspecting that's where Hunyadi would turn his attentions and order me next.

At first, my time on the road was fascinating, but the tavern conversations began to grow repetitious and I wanted to return home to my books, where the ideas were often more stimulating. I began to think Alexandra was right – that I should travel to Central and Western Europe where art and science were beginning to flourish again.

Still, the unrest in Transylvania could prove lucrative. I decided to remain – for a time at least.

I returned to my castle about a month after I left. As I approached, I heard faint sounds. On my guard, I approached quietly.

I was relieved when I saw Alexandra's wagon parked in my courtyard. No doubt, she had recently arrived with Roquelaure and the members of the Scarlet Order. Even though the invaders were friendly ones, it still piqued my ire that they had entered my home of their own accord while I was away.

I had to admit, I was also curious to know how the vampires of the Scarlet Order occupied themselves in my castle while I had been traveling. I decided to enter through a back way. There was a hidden entrance to my chambers that I had not even told Alexandra about.

I eased the door open and stepped down the stairs. My own bedroom appeared undisturbed. It seemed even Alexandra had not made use of the room since her return. At once I appreciated her respect for my privacy and was suspicious of where she had been spending her nights.

Stepping out of my chambers, I noticed a warm glow of light from upstairs and heard soft voices from different parts of the castle – vampires engaged in conversations. Keeping to the shadows, I found my way to the dining hall's door.

Roquelaure sat at the table engaged in conversation with two other vampires who wore the order's scarlet robes. One was a Saxon with a shaved head, who reminded me a little of Wolf. He called himself Rosen. The other was a stunningly beautiful, and startlingly swarthy vampire called Nabila. Beautiful as she was, it was Roquelaure who held my attention.

His face was both strong and smooth. His eyes were bright and thoughtful as he listened to Rosen speak. His conversation was light and casual, indicating no disloyalty to me at all. In spite of all my misgivings about him, in spite of the fact that I strongly suspected he was none other than the L'Ancelot, now a vampire, my balls contracted and my trousers seemed to have less room than before. No wonder Alexandra found him attractive.

I swallowed and stepped from the shadows.

Roquelaure stood and bowed low. The other two quickly followed suit.

"Glad to see you are at home, my lord," said Roquelaure.

"I trust you have made yourself comfortable." I indicated that the vampires should sit. I moved to a shelf and retrieved a goblet, then took my place at the head of the table.

"We have. Thank you." Roquelaure nodded. "However, we have only been here a day."

"A day?" I lifted my eyebrows. "Did you encounter difficulty in your travels?"

Roquelaure shook his head. "Not really. We did encounter Janos Hunyadi, and he sent us on an errand." He took a sip of his wine. "I gather you were sent to dispatch Vlad Dracul?"

"I was." I poured wine into my goblet.

"Hunyadi realized that once Vlad was gone, his eldest son was likely to step in and take his place."

"Indeed," I said. "I have heard such speculation in the taverns during my return journey."

"It's not going to happen now," said Roquelaure. "We have taken care of Mircea."

"I trust you encountered no difficulty." I lifted the goblet to my mouth.

"I had hoped to work quietly, but Hunyadi's forces had already encountered Mircea's." Roquelaure took a deep breath, then let it out slowly. "I found Mircea in his tent. We fought. I stabbed him with an iron stake, but that did not kill him."

I sat back and folded my arms. "You did finish him off, though, didn't you?"

Roquelaure shook his head. "I didn't have time. Hunyadi's men overran the tent. They captured Mircea and buried him alive."

I closed my eyes. "People fear us as monsters and yet they, themselves, do such monstrous things." I took another sip of wine, then looked up into Roquelaure's captivating eyes. "I saw Alexandra's wagon outside."

Roquelaure nodded and I could not read his expression. "I believe she's in the library. She has found new books for your collection."

I smiled inwardly, warmed by the wine and the fact that Alexandra had thought of me. I stood and excused myself.

Two months passed without incident. Roquelaure and the other vampires grew restless. They considered packing up and returning to the West. I freely admit, that unless one enjoyed reading, there was little to do in my remote mountain hideaway.

Intellectuals gathered in France and Italy, often meeting at taverns and cafés late at night to share their ideas. A little conversation and a little blood stimulated both the body and mind. Blood was plentiful in Transylvania, but meaningful conversation could be sparse.

Before Roquelaure began to pack his satchel for the journey home, there came a familiar, insistent knocking at the castle door. I was not surprised when I opened the door and I discovered a gilded carriage.

Hunyadi brushed past me and went directly to the sitting room. He nodded, satisfied as he glanced at the assembled vampires in scarlet robes seated and standing.

"The Ottoman Turks have invaded Wallachia," declared Hunyadi without prelude. "They have placed one of Vlad's sons on the throne."

"Was this one of the children that Dracul gave to the Turks as tribute?" asked Roquelaure, stepping forward.

Hunyadi nodded hastily. "Like his father, he is also named Vlad. He calls himself Dracula – son of the Dragon. The Turks are using him to rally the support of the Wallachians. Even the Moldavians are beginning to believe the Turks could help them put one of their own on the throne."

Alexandra stepped up and put her hand on Roquelaure's shoulder. Seeing that, I gritted my teeth, but did not say anything. This was not the time or the place. "The Moldavians and the Wallachians are fools if they think the Turks are better rulers for this region than the Hungarians," said Alexandra. "The Turks will simply use the people to defend their borders."

Alexandra looked toward me and I guessed her thoughts – at least the Hungarians were kindred, but she was smart enough not to say that in Hunyadi's presence. The bloodlines that divided the Hungarians, Moldavians, Wallachians, and Transylvanians might have been thin, but all were proud of their individual cultures.

I folded my arms. "The Turks are a force to be reckoned with, whether or not they have a figurehead on the throne. I doubt killing this Vlad Dracula will make much difference in the conflict."

Hunyadi nodded forcefully and pointed at me. "Indeed. I do not want him dead. I just want him removed from Turkish influence." He looked from me to Roquelaure. "I have a feeling we could use him for our own purposes later."

"His uncle is Prince Bogdan of Moldavia," I said. "We could take him there."

Hunyadi nodded slowly. "I believe that would suit my purposes. If you accomplish that, I will make sure you are handsomely rewarded." He strode toward the castle's door. "Now, if you'll excuse me, I have a war to fight."

The Scarlet Order traveled to Bucharest the next night. The city was virtually crawling with Ottoman Turks. Because of that, we split up into pairs so that our band would not attract too much attention. Alexandra and Nabila worked as a team. Roquelaure and I met with them in our rooms two nights after our arrival.

"I met one of Dracula's guards," said Nabila. "He was well disciplined and did not say much despite the wonderful night I promised him. Even so, his mind was an open book." She went on and told us where we could find Vlad Dracula's sleeping chamber and the number of guards we could expect. I breathed a sigh of relief when Nabila told us Vlad's room was only on the second floor.

Getting into Dracula's chambers would be easy. I would become a swarm of flies and Roquelaure would become a rat. The problem was getting the boy out.

We couldn't just walk outside with him. The Turks might call him the prince, but he was as much a prisoner as a poor wretch in the dungeons.

We formed a plan and made arrangements to carry it out two nights hence. That would allow Alexandra and Nabila to get word to other members of the order.

Two nights later, I transformed into a swarm of flies. Autumn was nigh and the air cooled. Insects still lingered, but they were not as numerous as they had been in the swamps when I killed Dracula's father.

I divided myself into several groups and entered through a half-dozen second-floor windows. The experience always disoriented me. I could see all those different places at once and it took all of my concentration just to get inside the castle. Once inside, my component parts kept to the shadows and crawled to Dracula's room. The experience of walking on small fly legs was slow and painstaking.

I was sure Roquelaure would get to the prince's room before I would. I hoped he would stick to the plan and do nothing to alert the prince to our presence before we were ready to act.

The swarm that I was gathered on the ceiling just outside Vlad Dracula's door. I had never counted how many flies comprised my swarm, but I knew it was over one hundred. We no longer had to remain in the shadows. We actually *were* a shadow on the ceiling.

Two guards stood outside the prince's room. I waited and hoped Roquelaure was already in position.

Someone shouted on the first floor and an alarm bell rang. If I had had a human mouth, I would have grinned. Rosen and his men raised a ruckus at the castle gate. One of Vlad's guards nodded to the other and ran away to see what was happening.

I pulled all my component parts together and dropped to the floor. The remaining guard was so astonished by the sight of a hundred flies morphing into the form of a human being that he didn't have a chance to raise his pike and challenge me before I fell on him and sunk my teeth into his neck. Fortunately, I was hungry, and I was able to drain the guard to unconsciousness. I lowered him to the floor, then dragged him into the prince's room by the ankle.

Looking around, I did not see Roquelaure at first. A moment later, a rat emerged from the shadows. The rat stood up on his hind legs and grew tall as he assumed the form of a cloaked man.

I quickly scanned the room. Against the far wall was one of the short beds that were still fashionable in those days. A half-asleep boy, about fifteen or sixteen years old, reclined against pillows, rubbing his eyes. As his vision adjusted to the darkness, his gaze fell on Roquelaure, just as he pushed back the cloak's red hood. The boy opened his mouth to scream. I dashed across the room and covered his mouth with my hand.

"Boy, we are here to rescue you from the Turks," I whispered.

He tried to bite my hand and smiled as I pulled it away before he drew blood. "I do not need to be rescued." His smile turned into the cocky sneer of a teenage boy who thinks he knows everything. "I am the prince. These disreputable Turks are my servants. They do my bidding."

"You are a puppet," I said. "The Turks pull your strings. If you want real power, then come with us. We'll take you to your uncle in Moldavia, and you can rally the people to your cause. You can rise up and defeat the Turks."

He looked at me, then looked at the body on the floor. His eyebrows creased as though from a memory of pain. He seemed to consider something he had never considered before. "The Turks tortured me and my brother...."

The way he said "Turks" reminded me of the way I once said "Saxons."

Roquelaure approached and knelt beside the bed. "Here you think you have power over those who brought you pain." He looked toward the door. Like me, he knew it wouldn't be long before Rosen retreated from the front gate and the other guard returned. "Go to your uncle and you can have revenge on the Turks."

The boy's eyes flashed from Roquelaure to me.

"How do I know I can trust you?"

I peered deeply into Vlad Dracula's eyes. For a moment, I felt like I gazed at a reflection of my younger self. I quieted his mind just as I would quiet the mind of my prey. "I can give you no reason to trust me."

Just as I said that, the image of Vlad's father – throat slit and bleeding out – came to my mind. I hoped the boy could not see into my mind as I could see into his. "I simply give you no choice."

I stood up and looked at the boy, who stared slack-jawed into the room's darkness. He would not remain that way long. He'd soon wake and we needed to act fast. I went to the window and threw it open.

Behind it were bars. I nodded, thinking how much the boy really was a prisoner.

Reaching out, I grabbed the bars and pulled them apart – wide enough for the boy to slip through – and looked to the ground. Alexandra and Nabila waited just as planned. Roquelaure scooped up the boy and brought him to the window, then unceremoniously pitched him out. Alexandra caught him deftly, just as the boy began to recover his senses. Fortunately, he seemed too shocked to scream.

A moment later, Alexandra and Nabila disappeared into the

shadows with their charge. "I wonder what this land will be like when Dracula comes seeking his revenge," I mused.

Roquelaure shook his head. "I can't imagine that it will be any more fragmented than it is today." He pulled his hood up as he shrunk and the fur bristled through his scarlet cloak's fabric.

I nodded and sighed. It was time to leave. There would be time to contemplate the future once we were safely back in Transylvania.

Chapter 27

From the Memoirs of Alexandra the Greek.
The year 1459:

Peace never lasted long in those forsaken countries that separated the Turks from Europe. Although I loved the stark beauty of the craggy and isolated Carpathian Mountains, I never quite understood Draco's almost tenacious desire to remain in that region. If he wanted isolation, he could find it in the Pyrennies, or the Alps – and he would be a lot closer to libraries that supplied the books he most desperately craved. Still, he hung on, and I really wasn't surprised when a dozen years after we delivered Vlad Dracula to his Uncle Bogdan II, the young prince was back in our lives.

Three years before, Janos Hunyadi gave Vlad Dracula an army, and together they threw the Turks out of Wallachia. Although Hunyadi died soon afterward, Vlad continued an alliance with Hunyadi's son, King Matthias Corvinus.

One of the things that long puzzled me about Draco's love of Transylvania had to do with the nobility. Many of the nobles were of Saxon descent – the very Saxons he fought against when he was a human. Those same Saxons had allied themselves with the Turks and aided them when they first captured Wallachia.

When Vlad began to consolidate power, he hired mercenaries to kill the Saxon nobles. Draco readily offered to aid the prince's cause as though he had been anxious for just such an opportunity. Fortunately, he did not ask the Scarlet Order to participate in this fight.

I'm not sure I would have accepted if he had.

Frankly, all the fighting in Moldavia, Wallachia, and Transylvania wore on my nerves. Alexander the Great in Greece and the Caesars in Rome were all about power. They rained death and destruction on countless areas. However, they also left civilization in their wake. Nothing like that happened in this conflict. All I saw were a bunch of men out to prove who had the biggest cock.

Even so, Draco seemed to enjoy this endless conflict, in a way. And it did cause his coffers to grow. Remembering the fact that Draco rescued him as a child, and grateful for his help disposing of the Transylvanian nobility, Vlad announced that he would renew Draco's title to his land and give him a position in his court. Draco invited Roquelaure and me to attend while he met with Vlad.

At first, Roquelaure was reluctant to travel to Transylvania again, but for some reason, he finally agreed to go.

"We are mercenaries," implored Roquelaure, practically leaning over the table in Draco's dining room while we awaited Vlad's arrival. "You have said, yourself, that we only should take jobs because they pay well. We cannot afford to become personally involved in a conflict."

Draco sat with his arms folded, glaring at Roquelaure. "I am not becoming personally involved." He growled. "Accepting a title within Vlad's court simply means more money than we would get as soldiers. I am no more loyal to Vlad than I am any other prince or king we have fought for. Besides, the lives of mere mortals are so short that a title in his court means nothing."

Roquelaure snorted. "Nothing! You tell that to the Turks when they decide to take Wallachia back from Vlad, and when they decide to keep moving up into Transylvania!"

Draco rolled his eyes. "The Turks will not make it back into Wallachia – not if the Scarlet Order sides with Vlad!"

I sighed as I watched the two of them. I realized that it wasn't just the princes and kings of the surrounding countries who felt they had something to prove. In point of fact, Roquelaure was loyal to Draco. If not, he wouldn't have bothered trying to talk him out of actions he thought foolhardy. He would simply have let Draco burn.

Still, Roquelaure was also loyal to his other friends and he didn't want to see them thrown into a conflict he considered never-ending and pointless – and, to be honest, I couldn't blame him.

Roquelaure drew in a deep breath and blew it out, clearly attempting to calm himself. "Draco, there are fissures developing throughout these lands. Sooner or later, the Ottomans are going to take advantage of that fact, and just sweep over the countryside. No human or vampire will be able to stop them."

I sighed and placed my hands flat on the table. "You know something," I interjected. "I think both of you make good points."

They both looked at me like I was stark raving mad. Still, I continued on. "The thing is, you both care about the vampires of the Scarlet Order." I looked at Roquelaure. "Draco sees a way to bring more money to the order's coffers than has ever come before."

I turned to Draco, reached out and took his hand. "Roquelaure is just concerned about getting into a fight that we cannot win." I squeezed Draco's hand and stood. "You both raise excellent points. However, there are literally centuries of uncertainty and distrust between you. You just don't *want* to see each other's points."

Draco narrowed his gaze. "What exactly are you getting at?"

"When we vampires share blood, we share a part of ourselves." I stepped back to the table and looked from Draco to Roquelaure. "The three of us should share blood with each other, open up the barriers between us. It would be like a ritual, letting us see into each other's hearts and souls."

Draco's eyes widened for a moment, then he turned and narrowed his gaze on Roquelaure. Draco had long held his suspicions about Roquelaure and it seemed I had just given him a way to find out if Roquelaure was really L'Ancelot.

Roquelaure stood and slammed his hands down on the table. "That would be outrageous. Why can't we just trust each other?" He whirled around and stormed from the dining chamber.

I looked to Draco for a moment and he simply shrugged. I shook my head and started after Roquelaure.

"Alexandra," called Draco. "I'd like you here when Vlad arrives. He'll be here soon."

I held up my hand. "I'll be back up as soon as I can." With that I followed Roquelaure down the hall.

I found Roquelaure in his chambers. Unlike Draco's they were above ground level, but the window had been bricked up and allowed no light to penetrate during the day.

I stood in the doorway, my hand against the doorframe. "I don't understand," I said.

"I just feel like we are fighting a losing battle here." Roquelaure shook his head. "I don't care how much money we make. Getting too caught up in the struggles between the Wallachians and the Ottomans is only going to end in disaster. I feel it in my bones."

"That's not what I mean." I took a step toward Roquelaure. "You and I have been intimate for over five hundred years. Even so, I barely know you. I don't even know your real name."

"Roquelaure *is* my real name." He looked at me with eyes so deep and blue that I thought I would lose myself in them.

I swallowed, then shook my head. "I know that's not true. You were given that name after you became a vampire. It's become a cloak – a cloak you have hidden behind ever since I first met you. I want to know who you really are."

He rolled his eyes and turned away. "You're beginning to sound like Draco. I have never hidden anything from you. All that you see is all that I am."

"The question is, who were you before you became a vampire?"

"What does that matter? That man died nearly a thousand years ago." His voice was quiet.

"It must matter." I took another step toward him. "If it really doesn't matter, open your mind to me. Open it to Draco. Let us see who you are."

He closed his eyes and was silent for a moment. Finally, he spoke again. "Even if I opened myself to you completely, are you sure you would understand who I really am? Are you sure you would know me better than you do now?"

I reached out and took his hands. "I can't really answer that unless you do open yourself to me."

He pulled me close and held me for a long time. "You and Draco both assume that I know what I was before," he said at last.

My brow creased. "Don't you know?"

He gave a short, sharp laugh. "Perhaps I'm afraid I'd find out."

I was about to ask another question, but he bent down and kissed me gently on the neck while his hands caressed my back. My breath caught and a fire ignited deep within. Feelings warred with one another as he continued his explorations of my body. My intellect had grown tired of the mystery of Roquelaure's identity long ago, and it had been a long time since I'd asked about it.

Despite my intellect, another part of me was excited by the mystery and actually didn't want to know who Roquelaure really was. Even as Roquelaure's roving hand found my breast, I wondered if he had been manipulating me, using the mystery of his existence to keep me near. I reached down and stroked his hardening manhood through his breeches. I knew his wonderful body so well. Was he really a mystery?

I kissed Roquelaure deeply, letting my tongue dance against his for a moment before I turned around and lifted my skirts. There was a rustling of fabric as he dropped his breeches. A moment later, I felt him enter me from behind. I closed my eyes and let out a long, low moan of pleasure as he inched his way further into my body. He stood there, not moving.

"Please, Roquelaure, don't stop." I opened my eyes. Draco stood in the doorway. My guts wrenched at his cold expression. At the same time, I wanted to crawl into a hole and hide, but I also wanted him to come closer so that I could pleasure him while Roquelaure pleasured me.

So many conflicting thoughts raced through my mind that I felt I was going to explode – whether from agony or from ecstasy, I do not know. Almost of their own volition, my hips started moving and Roquelaure thrusted in response.

"When you are quite finished," said Draco, "please come downstairs and meet our honored guest. There is a mission."

My heart felt like it would burst as I watched Draco turn and leave the room, his back ramrod-straight. The emotions inside of me were so intense that my body erupted in orgasm and tears simultaneously.

Soon after Draco left, Roquelaure and I hastily washed up, using a basin in his room, and then made our way downstairs. I remembered Vlad Dracula from our excursion to Bucharest a dozen years before.

Back then, he had wide and staring eyes, like a boy who had seen too much for his sixteen years. His lower lip seemed frozen in a perpetual pout. The man we found in the sitting room with Draco was still clearly Vlad. However, he had grown a thick, black mustache that obscured his pouting lip. His wide and staring eyes had taken on a hard edge, as though he was prepared to dish out all the cruelties he'd seen … and then some. Vlad had a distinctive face, but not a handsome one.

As we entered the room, Draco turned his face toward me. Normally, I found it almost irresistible to gaze upon. Normally his eyes held a wonder and a thoughtfulness that could hold me enraptured. However, his gaze had developed the same hard edge as Vlad's. Even though the two men did not look alike, Draco and Vlad seemed to be distorted reflections of one another.

"Prince Vlad has done me a great honor by coming to my home personally, so that he may bestow upon me the title of a knight in the Order of the Dragon," said Draco. "I wish to give him something in exchange."

Roquelaure and I quickly looked to one another, then turned our attention back to Draco.

"The Turks are an ever-present threat to Prince Vlad. He needs someone reliable, close at his side, to prevent assassination at night." Draco turned his gaze on Roquelaure. "I can think of no one more qualified than you, my friend." His lips were thin and he did nothing to disguise his fangs in front of the prince.

The words came out razor sharp.

Roquelaure bowed low. "As you wish, Lord Draco. I am your loyal servant."

Draco narrowed his gaze at those words, but remained silent.

It was Vlad who spoke. "Very good. I remember your service to me a dozen years ago. I would trust you with my life." The prince stood. "Let us leave tonight. I wish to be back in Bucharest as soon as possible."

"Very well, Your Highness," said Roquelaure. "If I may be permitted, I just need a moment to pack a few things. I will join you presently."

Vlad dismissed Roquelaure with a wave of his hand. I watched Roquelaure turn with a sweep of his cloak and leave the room. I looked back at Draco and his expression betrayed hurt as well as anger. I tried to convey an apology with a glance, but he simply turned his back on me. He took Vlad by the elbow and led him to the fireplace where he showed the prince a painting that Roquelaure had brought as a gift. A tear threatened to fall, but I wiped it angrily away.

Draco knew that Roquelaure and I were intimate. He'd known it for nearly five centuries. He had no right to act this way. I spun on my heel and went to Roquelaure's chambers. I found him quietly packing a few belongings into a satchel.

"You don't have to agree to this," I said. "He's known about us for a long time."

Roquelaure's expression was unreadable. "Knowing something and seeing it are often two very different things," he said. "I have often wondered how I would react if I saw you and Draco making love."

I shook my head. "I can't imagine that you would go into a childish rage. You're almost a thousand years old, after all!"

A smirk flashed across Roquelaure's face. "So is he. Could you have imagined his reaction before tonight?"

My shoulders slumped forward. "No, I suppose not."

Roquelaure stepped up to me and lifted my chin. He kissed me lightly on the lips. "Draco is hurt. He has not lived this long by letting wounds fester. He will be better by the time I return."

I chewed my lower lip for a moment, then looked up into Roquelaure's blue eyes. "I wish he could see how loyal you really are to him. That's why I want us to share blood. He needs to see into your heart."

"And that is exactly the reason I need to go," he said. "The time has come for me to look into my own heart because I do not know how loyal I really am. I will spend time with this Vlad Dracula and the people of Bucharest. Once I've done that, I'll know more about whether I should stay with the Scarlet Order or go my own way."

With that, Roquelaure grabbed his satchel, tossed it over his shoulder, and strode from the room.

Chapter 28

A series of letters written by Roquelaure to Alexandra the Greek. The year 1461:

My Dear Alexandra,

    I have lived a long time and worked as an assassin for many cold and violent men. However, I have never seen cruelty meted out as I did today.

Vlad occupies the very castle he did when he was a puppet of the Turks, fourteen years ago. As you no doubt recall, Bucharest is a fairly small, idyllic town. However, it is growing – prospering under Vlad's reign and with its freedom from the Turks. What it lacks in art and culture is often made up for by its pleasant green, rolling hills and trees. I enjoy strolling about the countryside on clear, moonlit nights, and wish you could be here by my side.

The people are friendly and I enjoy spending time in the public room of the inn where I stay, conversing with them late into the evening. There is a warmth to these people I often find lacking in the people of Western Europe. In a way, I begin to understand why Draco prefers to stay in the East.

However, the people's warmth is in sharp contrast to the coldness of their prince. He is a bitter and hard man who hates his father for giving him over to the Turks at a young age. Moreover, he despises the Turks for the tortures they heaped upon him as a child.

About a month ago, Vlad Dracula invited me to accompany him while he dined.

"Do you ever miss solid food?" he asked at one point during the meal.

"Sometimes," I admitted.

"I believe you know that my father sent my brother and me to Edirne when we were children, as a tribute to the Turks."

I nodded. The mention of Edirne sent a shiver down my spine. When Vlad was a child, the Ottoman Turks occupied a small corner of the world and Edirne was their capital. Less than a decade later, they would rise up and take Constantinople itself.

At that moment, I found myself wondering whether Draco was a hero for standing up with the Eastern Europeans against the Turks, or a fool for simply not getting out of their way.

Vlad's words brought me back from my reflections. "The Turks wanted to break us. They wanted to train us like good dogs. One night, my brother and I were taken out and flogged. We were just boys, yet our skin was left in tatters. They put us back in our cells to let the pain argue with us. There was nothing to eat or drink."

Vlad's eyes took on a faraway look. "Because of the pain, I really wasn't hungry, but I remember being terribly thirsty. My brother and I decided to drink each other's blood to sustain us. It was thin and salty – at once the worst thing I'd ever had, and the best because it kept me from being completely parched." He faced me and his gaze narrowed. "Is it like that for you?"

"I remember it being like that, when I was newly made a vampire," I said, inclining my head. "But I rather savor it now."

"If only I could be like you." He gazed off into the distance. "I would gladly drink the blood of every Turk."

"We vampires get sick if we drink too much blood," I observed.

He nodded. "Perhaps." He lifted his goblet and took a drink, then smiled as he set the glass down. "No, what I really want is for every Turk to know the experience of drinking their own brother's blood just to survive one more night. Just to survive in order to be tortured again."

I could see Vlad contemplating that thought, savoring it more than his wine. I was glad to leave the prince to his dark thoughts that night.

At the time, I believed those dark thoughts were mere fantasy driven by horrible memories. Now, I believe he would bring those dreams to fruition if he could.

Yesterday, Vlad summoned me to his castle. Sultan Mehmed II had sent envoys, urging Vlad to return to the Ottoman fold. The prince ordered the envoys to his dining room – the same room where he had related the incident that had happened to him as a child. The prince wanted me to wait outside, in case there was trouble.

I heard them exchange courtesies. Soon afterward, the Turkish ambassador began to speak. He told Vlad how much more powerful he could be as a governor for the Turks than as a Wallachian prince. "If you stand with us, you will be powerful and you will be comfortable. If you stand in our way, you shall die."

I heard Vlad take in a deep breath. "What would I need to do to assure your protection?" There was a razor edge to the prince's words.

"We only ask a small tribute – ten thousand ducats and five hundred boys to be trained as soldiers."

I couldn't see Vlad, but I could sense his rage through the closed door of the chamber. "Just five hundred boys in addition to some money." The words had a sibilant tone, as though spoken by an enraged serpent. "You dare ask for five hundred Wallachian boys and you do not even have the courtesy to remove your turbans?"

With those words, there came a cacophony of shuffling feet, crashing furniture, shouts, and wet, sickly thuds. Unable to restrain my curiosity any longer, I threw open the door and was nearly sick at the sight that lay before me. The Turkish envoys were dead, their turbans nailed onto their heads. Vlad's elite guard stood at attention, holding hammers, awaiting further orders.

"Ah, Roquelaure." Vlad smiled and stepped over to one of the recently murdered envoys, ran his fingers through blood and brain matter that oozed from his skull, and lifted it to his lips. "You know, I believe this is the sweetest thing I have ever tasted."

I turned around and left the room. No one stopped me as I left the castle. I just kept walking until I was outside of Bucharest – until the scent of death had left my nostrils and I could only smell pine and flowers on the night air.

I write this from a small village called Buftea. Part of me wants to leave this land and the monster called Vlad Dracula. Yet, I find myself thinking of the kind people in Bucharest and the fact that Prince Vlad stood up and refused to send five hundred innocent children into the hands of the Turks. I will have to think long and hard about what I will do.

Wishing I could be in your arms,

R

My Dearest Alexandra,

I remained in Buftea a few days after I posted my last letter to you. It is a pleasant village where everyone seems to know everyone else. I find hunting in villages like this rather difficult, but after witnessing Vlad's brutal murder of the Turkish envoys, I found I had little taste for blood.

Instead, I took in the sights of the family farms and the work of the artisans. Although not as urbane as the artists of Arles or Paris, there was a uniqueness to the villagers that I sensed would be lost if Wallachia simply became a territory within the Ottoman Empire. In the back of my mind, memories stirred of artisans I knew long ago – artisans whose work was already lost to time and destroyed by empires. Perhaps that is why I decided to return to Vlad's castle in Bucharest.

I also hoped that his rage had been spent in that one, horrible act.

When I returned, the prince seemed not to have noticed my absence. All trace of the repulsive acts committed in the dining room had been cleared away and Vlad had become his normal sullen self again. I returned to my quarters in Bucharest until summoned again to the castle. That summons came only a week after my return.

I am writing to you from Giurgiu, on the Danube River. Vlad has sent me to this village on the southern border of Wallachia to investigate reports that a small contingent of Turks has crossed the river and is camped near the village. Since my arrival, I have learned that the Turks have been attempting to recruit men into their army. Apparently the Turks felt that if Vlad could not be brought into the Ottoman fold, perhaps they could appeal their case directly to the people.

Last night, I made my way into the Ottoman camp after most of the Turks had fallen asleep. Transforming into a rat, I scurried past the guards and explored the encampment. Most of the tents held several men, asleep on simple, straw mats, but one tent stood apart. Inside, a lone man slept on a comfortable mound of pillows and blankets. I gathered this must be the leader of the expedition.

I allowed myself to resume my human form once again – always a rather strange experience. On one hand, I feel myself grow from rat into human form. On the other hand, I feel like I have stepped from some secret room where I control the rat, into the room where the rat was. Do you ever feel like that when transforming from one form to another?

At any rate, I found myself standing over the Turkish soldier. He was a muscular brute and his chin was covered with a thick, black beard. I would have been more comfortable simply assassinating such a man, but I knew that Vlad and his soldiers needed information. I knelt down and pushed the beard aside.

Apparently this soldier slept lightly, for he awoke and thrust a knife toward my belly. I knocked the knife aside and grabbed the Turk by the throat, gazing into his eyes and quieting his mind. Once he calmed, I leaned down and bit into his jugular.

As his blood flowed into me, I saw into the Turk's mind. The Ottomans had guessed that Vlad had allied himself with the Hungarian King, Matthias Corvinus. That information did not surprise me. What was interesting to learn was that the Ottomans were plotting to kidnap Vlad.

Soon, Hamza Pasha, the Bey of Nicropolis, would be on his way to Bucharest. The Turks would claim to be seeking a diplomatic meeting. However, they actually planned to ambush the prince and take him to Constantinople.

Having taken my fill of both blood and information, I released the Turk's throat and plucked a few stray hairs from my tongue. Looking down at his rough form, I felt a shiver of loneliness pass through me.

Although his blood filled my belly and sustained me physically, I longed for a smooth neck to press my lips against. I wished for your soft flesh against mine. I wanted a kindred spirit who knew what it was to steal through the darkness, to take blood and thoughts from one mortal and give them over to another – and for what? The artisans of Buftea and Bucharest who reminded me of some vague memory from long ago?

I grow weary of this land of schemes and plots. Perhaps soon we can return to Paris or Rome and I can read you the poetry of François Villon in the candlelight of some friendly café. After which I can make sweet love to you as we contemplate our human brothers and hope that God will absolve us all.

With all my love,

R

My Dearest Alexandra,

Two nights ago, I awoke to discover the fortress of Giurgiu deserted. It is winter, and snow covered the ground. With no fires going, it was bitterly cold. Lighting a candle, I warmed my fingers by its meager flame as best I could. The candle's flickering light fell upon a scrap of parchment – a brief letter from Doru, Count of Giurgiu, explaining that the Wallachian soldiers had marched north to Călugăreni under orders from Prince Vlad. I was to join them as soon as possible.

The note surprised me because I knew that Hamza Pasha had a thousand soldiers encamped across the Danube from Giurgiu. Their plan to kidnap Prince Vlad was underway. Although I thought Vlad would have the force at Giurgiu fight the Ottoman soldiers, it seemed Vlad planned to allow the Bey of Nicropolis and his men to enter Wallachia, and they would catch them at the narrow pass on the route to Bucharest.

I found a half-frozen horse waiting for me in the stables. Saddling it, I rode as hard and fast as I could to Călugăreni. There, Doru and Vlad were camped amongst the trees overlooking the narrow valley. Most of the men were asleep, huddled as close as possible to their campfires. Vlad and Doru were still awake, surveying the landscape and making plans.

"Ah, Roquelaure, it is good to see you again," said the prince. "I expect we will have quite a battle here tomorrow. Too bad you will not be awake to see it."

I considered his words, thinking that I far preferred assassination to battle. As an assassin, I set up the conditions of the engagement and control what happens. On a battlefield, an arrow or a bullet from an unknown quarter can kill, no matter how much you've plotted strategy or tactics. I was just as glad I slept through most battles.

"Since I will not be of use in the battle, I wonder why you have summoned me." I rubbed my hands together. The friction provided some modicum of warmth.

"There will be many bodies on the valley floor tomorrow." Vlad's wide eyes narrowed. "I thought you would appreciate the opportunity to feed." His tone suggested that I should be honored.

I was too cold to be agreeable. "With all due respect, my lord, I prefer the blood of the living to the dying. It helps warm me on nights like this."

The prince nodded and his meaty lips turned upward in a grim smile. "I intend to leave some alive – as a warning to any who should try to kidnap me. Their blood should warm you sufficiently. All I ask is that you don't completely end their suffering."

I did not like Vlad's tone, but I nodded just the same. I knew I had already risked enraging the prince as much as I dared.

He continued. "Also, I would like you to write to Draco. I suspect we will need all of your Scarlet Order in the coming months. This will surely not be the last we hear of the Ottomans."

Again, I nodded and the prince dismissed me with a wave of his hand. Glad to be away from Vlad, I scoured the area until I found a small cave – perhaps it was a bear's den at one time.

There, away from the dangers of sunlight, I pulled my cloak around myself, then awaited dawn – and sleep.

I awoke that night to the smells of blood and smoke and the sounds of moans and screams. Cautiously, I emerged from the small cave and crept to the place where Vlad and Doru had camped, overlooking the valley the night before. Bodies littered the pass.

Looking at the number of rotting corpses, it appeared that Vlad and his men had killed almost all of Hamza Pasha's force. It struck me as odd that no living people went through the carnage to loot the bodies of things that might still be useful.

I soon saw the reason for that. At one end of the battlefield, over a dozen great stakes had been thrust into the ground. On them were impaled Hamza Pasha's officers. Not all of them had succumbed to their wounds, the pain, or the cold. Perhaps half a dozen still writhed and cried out.

This was the "honor" Vlad had done me. The men were dying, but their blood was still warm. No doubt it was Vlad's way of thanking me for warning him about the kidnapping plot. If I had fed recently, I would have vomited blood over the white snow.

Instead, I swallowed the bile that had built up at the back of my throat, then marched down the hillside and snapped the necks of the miserable wretches that still lived. Afterwards, I rode back to Giurgiu.

Vlad is correct. The Ottomans will not stand for such carnage. An invasion will surely follow this spring, if not sooner. I believe we would be well suited just to leave before things escalate further. However, I will await word from Draco. I do not want to leave and find that I have missed seeing you again.

This place is so very cold. I long for the comfort of your arms. With love,

R

Chapter 29

From the Memoirs of Alexandra the Greek.
The year 1462:

Draco and I arrived in Giurgiu in the early spring. The other members of the Scarlet Order would meet us there in a few days. Even though night had fallen, the fortress was alive with activity. Men readied guns and ammunition. Provisions were being stocked. Strangest of all, men sharpened wooden poles. Roquelaure had written about how Vlad impaled his enemies, but I believed that to be an isolated act, not connected to the work the men were doing.

"What do you suppose those are for?" I asked Draco.

Draco shrugged. "Perhaps they're makeshift pikes – to repel the cavalry."

"They're for impaling Vlad's enemies."

We both turned abruptly, startled by Roquelaure's sudden appearance.

Draco looked toward the stakes, then looked back at Roquelaure. "But there are so many. How many people does Vlad plan to impale?"

"Every last Turk, if he can manage it." Roquelaure's voice was hollow.

I reached out and put my hand on his arm, heedless of Draco's gaze. Roquelaure simply put his hand on mine for a moment, then took a deep breath and released it. "I know you've just arrived, but I believe I should show you something before you get too comfortable." He turned and led us toward the fortress's gates.

Draco and I looked at each other, and then followed Roquelaure.

"We have been fighting all winter. The Turks keep sending men across the Danube and the Wallachian forces keep fending them off," explained Roquelaure.

"It sounds as though Vlad is doing quite well," said Draco. "Are you sure the Scarlet Order is needed here?"

Roquelaure shook his head. "I'm not sure whether or not there is anything the Scarlet Order can do at this point. Something is about to happen, something so big that I don't think we can prevent it." Roquelaure led us to the top of a hill that looked out over the Danube. The campfires' light revealed what appeared to be an entire city of people. "Sultan Mehmed has led his army here himself. By my estimate, there are over sixty thousand men across the river."

As Roquelaure spoke, I looked down to the near bank of the Danube. At first, I found myself puzzled that trees should grow so close to the river. Then I realized that the "trees" were not topped with leaves, but with human bodies.

Draco seemed to notice the sight at the same time as I did. His Adam's Apple bobbed up and down. Cautiously, he made his way down the hillside toward the "forest" of impaled bodies. I followed him as he walked through row after row of stakes. I watched as he looked up into the dead eyes of one Turk and then another.

"How many are there? How many has Vlad impaled?" Draco's voice was hoarse.

"I believe there are close to twenty thousand," said Roquelaure.

"Nearly a third of the force across the river." Draco dropped to his knees, put his face in his hands, and wept quietly.

I looked at Roquelaure. His face was expressionless, as though he had been numbed by so much violence and death. I knelt down beside Draco and pulled him toward my breast. He returned my embrace and I just held him for a time. Finally, he seemed to gain strength. He stood and faced Roquelaure. "I'm sorry, I didn't realize...."

Suddenly Roquelaure's face became a mask of rage. "Didn't

realize what? Didn't realize that you had allied us with a madman? Didn't feel that Vlad needed to avenge himself against every Turk for wrongs he thought they had committed against him?" Roquelaure took a step toward Draco. "You left me down here for three years while you've been sitting comfortably in your Transylvanian castle, with Alexandra all to yourself!"

Draco frowned, and for a moment I thought he was going to answer Roquelaure with equally heated words. Instead he sighed and looked again at the grizzly spectacle surrounding us, then looked back across the river at the army camped there. "I'm here now," was all he said.

"I'm afraid it may be too late," spat Roquelaure.

Draco nodded. "You're probably right." He turned back to Roquelaure. "I'm sorry."

Roquelaure looked as though he had been slapped. "Sorry?"

"I've treated you poorly." Draco put his hand on Roquelaure's shoulder. "I thought you were exaggerating when you wrote about Vlad. You are right. He is a monster."

I stood up from where I had been kneeling and took a step toward the two men. "So, what does this mean?" I asked. "Do we leave Vlad's service?"

Draco shook his head sadly. "No. We do not leave a contract that has been lawfully made because we disagree with the person who paid us. We will see this through until Vlad wins or is defeated."

"And what do you think will be the outcome?" asked Roquelaure, quietly. There seemed no more venom in his words.

"I fear we shall witness our employer's defeat." With that, we moved uphill, away from the forest of bodies.

"What do we do now?" I asked. "We will be asleep when the Turks cross the river. Even if we crossed and killed some, it would not be enough to stop the invasion."

Draco nodded. "There is nothing we can do. We must wait for the first wave of Ottoman Turks to crash upon Wallachia's shores. Tomorrow night we will make our way north. We'll need to intercept the other members of the Scarlet Order and then return to Bucharest as soon as we can. Then we can meet Vlad and see what we can do to aid him."

When we returned to the fortress, we found that most of the men were fast asleep, awaiting the coming battle. Draco, Roquelaure, and I retrieved our horses and rode northward to the pass at Călugăreni. There, Roquelaure led us to the cave he had described in his last letter. We huddled together in that cramped space and fell asleep as the sun rose.

While we slept, Sultan Mehmed II led his sixty thousand men across the Danube and took the fortress at Giurgiu. That night we rode close enough to see the city in flames. Knowing there was nothing we could do, we turned around and rode north, hoping to meet up with the rest of the Scarlet Order.

The members of the Scarlet Order regrouped over the next few days and we made our way back to Bucharest. There we learned that Vlad had retreated to his castle at Târgovişte. That made sense, since Târgovişte was further into the mountains and more easily defended than the Princely Court in Bucharest. I also found Dracula's home in the mountain village to be more charming than his urban dwelling.

The Princely Court in Bucharest was a cold, blocky structure with small windows. The castle at Târgovişte was topped with rounded towers and sloped, tile roofs. Larger windows let in more light, even after the sun had set.

The guards recognized Roquelaure and admitted us. A footman assigned us rooms in the sprawling castle, then took us to the study while he went to retrieve Prince Vlad.

The prince stormed into the study, his eyebrows close together. "You retreated like a coward in front of the Turkish invasion!" The prince jabbed his finger into Draco's chest, as though trying to impale him.

Draco sighed, but bowed at the waist. "My lord, the Scarlet Order is only a small band of mercenaries. There is little we can do by ourselves to stop an army of sixty thousand. However, there is, perhaps, a way we can help you retake Giurgiu with a minimum of losses."

Prince Vlad narrowed his gaze. "Go on."

Draco took the prince by the elbow and led him away. I looked toward Nabila, who stood nearby and quietly we decided to go to our quarters and unpack. Although more charming than the Princely Court in Bucharest, Vlad's castle in Târgoviște still had a certain coldness.

The rooms were sterile – with just enough furniture to be practical, but very little color or finery. These were military headquarters, not the living space of a prince who appreciated the finer things in life.

After unpacking, I returned to the study. There, Draco sat in an armchair, his fingers peaked under his nose. I sat down in a chair next to him. "How did it go?"

"We have a plan," he said. "In the coming days, Vlad will begin moving his troops into positions around Giurgiu. As they do, the Scarlet Order will infiltrate the town itself."

"Ah, just when I was looking forward to a couple of quiet months here in Târgoviște." I smiled at him, but he didn't smile back.

Instead, he just continued on with his explanation. "Over the course of a month, we should be able to obtain suitable clothes and become familiar enough to the guards that we can move about the fortress easily. We can take down their defenses and leave the castle open to invasion. Possibly we can kill Sultan Mehmed himself."

Draco fell silent, his gaze distant.

I reached out and took his hand in my own. "What are you thinking about?"

He blinked and looked into my eyes. "Just remembering the time Bran, Cynddylig, and I invaded Caw's camp back in old Britain. Alexandra, it seems so long ago...."

"You miss those days, don't you?" I asked.

He grinned. "Infiltrating enemies' camps seemed so much easier in the days before stone walls and guns."

"I've been dealing with stone walls my entire life, you young, primitive barbarian." I reached out and poked him on the nose with my finger.

He laughed outright. "All too true, that's why I want you to come with me. I could use the experience of an old woman."

"Watch it," I said, "or this 'old woman' will not grace you with her presence in your bed this morning."

"I thought you were sharing a room with Nabila," he said, suddenly coy.

"She snores, and she isn't as much fun as you."

Vlad and Draco's plans finally came to fruition in the late spring.

Draco, Roquelaure, and I, along with about a half dozen members of the Scarlet Order, entered the fortress by our usual means – much easier than trying to sneak past wary guards, even with disguises. However, our disguises would help once we were inside the fortress. We would easily be able to move around in human form without attracting attention.

Still, I found myself wondering if the guards would be curious about a small army of vermin approaching the castle – rats, bats, flies, and even a couple of wolves. We tried to be discreet, but I imagine at least some of us were seen as we entered through windows, sewers, and cracks in the walls.

Once inside, we gathered in a basement storage room. Roquelaure gave directions, sending the vampires to the armory and the guard towers. "I'm afraid you'll have to find your own way to the sultan's harem," he said to me. Draco and I each planned to assassinate the sultan. There would be little time before Vlad's invasion of the fortress began. If Draco couldn't get close enough before troops rushed in, perhaps I could later.

I smirked at Roquelaure. "I would have thought you'd know the way to the harem by heart."

"Alas, Vlad never kept a harem," said Roquelaure. His regret seemed almost too genuine for my taste. "The prince might have been in a better mood if he had."

"Or a far worse one, with all those wives," muttered Draco.

Roquelaure laughed at the joke. Although I had to admit
it was good to see Draco and Roquelaure getting along, I wasn't
entirely sure I appreciated the subject of their humor.

Draco looked from Roquelaure to me, then held out his arm.
"I'll be happy to help you find your way." Roquelaure's good humor
seemed to fall away from his features, but Draco interrupted before
he could say anything. "You'd better get to the front gate. We need
a little time to find the sultan."

Roquelaure nodded and went down the hall. We turned
and went in the other direction. Roquelaure had given us a good
description of the fortress and told us where the finest rooms were.
Once in the royal wing of the fortress, we found a room guarded
by two men.

Draco and I approached the men and gazed into their eyes. As
I felt my man fall under my spell, I asked, "Where would we find
the sultan's harem?"

"Inside this room, my lady," he replied. Looking into his
mind, I saw the members of the sultan's harem. There were only
three of his women with him at Giurgiu. I planted the image of
myself among the harem in the guard's mind.

Just then, a crash sounded from the front gate followed by a
scream. Guns barked an angry response.

"Damn," growled Draco. "Just like Arthur, that damned Vlad
is early." Leaving his man in a stupor, Draco charged off down the
hall, in search of the sultan.

The harem's door opened and two young women poked their
heads out. Although they didn't recognize me, the women ushered
me through the doorway and into the room's relative safety.

Soon there were shouts and the sounds of feet scuffling
down the hallways. More staccato gunfire erupted, followed by an
explosion, and screams.

The three women in the room huddled close together. All
three wore brightly colored dresses embroidered in gold and silver
thread. Translucent veils covered their hair and flowed down over

their shoulders, but didn't obscure their faces. All were under thirty and they trembled each time the cannons fired.

Despite their fear, they opened their arms to me. Although I wanted to listen to what was happening, I decided I should go to them, lest they think too hard about my presence and become suspicious. I huddled with them, doing my best to listen to the sounds of battle.

A few minutes later, a guard poked his head into the room. "The sultan has ordered us to retreat. Follow me."

We followed the guard through the hallways and into a secret tunnel that led toward the back of the fortress and the stables. We found horses saddled for us. I caught a movement in the corner of my eye. Looking closer, I recognized Nabila.

Discretely, I held up my hand, trying to indicate that she shouldn't intervene. If Draco succeeded in killing the sultan, so be it. If not, perhaps I would have a chance later on. Either way, I would learn more about the enemy's movements while among them.

Soon, I rode through the night behind the sultan's young wives, away from the fortress at Giurgiu. When I looked behind, smoke and flames rose from the fortress. It struck me that this was a battle that would likely go down in the annals of history. If so, it seemed a little sad that Vlad Dracula would likely receive all the credit for taking the fortress at Giurgiu, and Draco's role would be forgotten – much the same as what happened all those centuries ago at Cat Coit Celidon. However, this time, I thought Draco would prefer it that way.

That night, we rode, then forded the river to Razgrad. There, I saw the sultan himself, briefly. However, I never got a chance to be alone with him.

He immediately sent the harem south to his home in Edirne, whereas he rode east toward the Black Sea. I cursed the bad luck. It was clear Draco had failed to assassinate Mehmed II, and it seemed

I was unlikely to get the opportunity. Still, I continued with the harem to Edirne. I hoped I might, at least, get some information about Mehmed's plans that would be useful to the Scarlet Order.

As we traveled, and the urgency of our escape wore off, I looked into the minds of the harem's women and all of its guards. They began to accept that I'd always been a part of the harem and had no reason to question my presence with them.

Once at Edirne, I met the rest of the sultan's harem. They accepted me as a prize taken from the invasion in the North. I heard about battles raging, up and down the Danube, between the Wallachian forces and the Ottoman Turks.

About a week after we arrived, I sat next to the sultan's eldest wife, Raiza, at dinner.

"Mehmed must be very angry about losing the fortress at Giurgiu," I ventured.

She shrugged. "That is likely true, but Giurgiu was only meant as a distraction."

I narrowed my gaze. "What do you mean? Giurgiu is an important city on the Danube. Surely the sultan would want to hold it."

Raiza shrugged. "The only reason for holding it was to tie up Dracula's forces. Most of Mehmed's army is far up to the north across the river from Brăila. From there, they can come in behind Dracula's forces and attack them from the front and the rear. They can also enter Transylvania and attack the 'impaler's' allies."

I reached out, took a glass of juice, and drank it to cover my shock. Finally, I said, "I'm impressed that you should know so much about our husband's plans."

She smiled and took my hand. "He talks in his sleep. If you listen, you will soon be an expert in his machinations as well." Raiza then looked down at my plate. "You should eat more, you are awfully pale and cold."

Looking into Raiza's eyes, I planted the suggestion that she should forget about me. I gently extracted my hand from hers and left my place at the table. She blinked at me, but didn't say anything as I left the room.

I had one of the harem guards lead me to the stables and saddle a horse for me. Once done, I planted a similar thought in his mind and sent him back to the harem. Once he was out of sight, I rode north, out of Edirne.

Two nights of hard riding brought me back to Giurgiu. I found Draco at the fortress. He occupied a dark room in the cellar. A lone cot and chair had been placed in the room. He sat on the cot while I took the chair. Draco had sent Roquelaure and the other members of the Scarlet Order north to join the rest of Vlad's forces and assist them where they could.

"Then what are you doing here?" I asked.

"Waiting for you," he said with a smile, but his expression quickly turned serious. "I failed to kill Mehmed. Did you have better luck than me?"

"I'm afraid not." If I had fed recently, I would have blushed. "I only saw him once and there were too many people around. He sent the harem to Edirne while he rode to Brăila."

As I said the words, Draco gritted his teeth and snorted. "I've been a fool. Vlad has been concentrating his forces here at Giurgiu, but Brăila is far more vulnerable. He can get into the interior of Wallachia very easily."

"And he'll have access to the Carpathians," I said quietly.

Draco looked at me as though I had just struck him.

"Mehmed plans retribution not just against Vlad, but against all the lords in Transylvania and Wallachia who have helped him." I leaned forward and put my hands on Draco's shoulders. "I know you don't want to hear this, but I think it's possible that Roquelaure was right. Accepting a formal title from Vlad may have been a grave mistake."

"I'm beginning to think you're right, Alexandra." Draco stood and stepped to the door.

"Where are you going?" I asked.

"Home."

I stood and followed him through the doorway.

It took two more nights of hard riding to reach Draco's castle. When we arrived, we found the gates were smashed down and a thin stream of smoke trailed outside. Draco dismounted and rushed inside without bothering to attend to his horse. I shook my head at the sight, then dismounted and tended to both horses.

I followed Draco into the castle. The tapestries and paintings had been ripped from the walls, placed in the center of the main room, and lit afire.

A pile of ashes still smoldered in the great room. The wooden ceiling had burned and crashed down.

I made my way to the passage that led to Draco's private chamber. There were no candles to be found, and I did my best to feel my way to his room. The door to the room had been smashed in. Even in the low light, I could tell that the bed Draco had made for me was gone. No doubt it had become part of the bonfire above. I turned around and made my way to the library.

Draco was there, kneeling in front of another pile of ash. His hands covered his face and he wept quietly. All of the books and scrolls Draco had collected over the years were gone. Some were torn apart and scattered. Most had been burned.

Draco looked up at me. His hands were covered with ash, as though he had sifted through the pile, trying to recover something of his library. Tears cut a trail through the soot on his cheeks. "How could they do this?"

"They wanted to hurt you … and they have," I said gently. "If we stay here, they will kill you."

"I don't know if I have anything to live for now," said Draco. He turned and ran his hands through the hot ash again. His skin blistered and cracked, but he seemed oblivious.

"Alexandra is right," came a voice from the doorway.

We both turned and faced Roquelaure. He wore his scarlet cloak. The hood was pulled up – his face barely visible. He took a step into the room.

"I came as soon as I realized Mehmed's plans. Unfortunately, his Janissaries were already burning the castle. There was nothing I could do."

Draco stood and rushed at Roquelaure, knocking him back against the charred wall of the library. "Nothing you *could* do, or nothing you were *willing* to do?"

I rushed to Draco and pulled him from Roquelaure. "Stop it!" I shouted. "Look at this place. Even if the entire Scarlet Order had been here, they could not have stopped an entire Janissary force."

He looked at me and blinked.

"There are ten thousand men making their way through Transylvania, destroying every castle they come to, killing every lord they can find." Roquelaure pushed back the hood of his cloak. "The battle is lost. We owe no further allegiance to Vlad."

Draco shook his head, then turned and looked around at the ruins of his library. "I would drink the blood of every man who did this to me," he growled. "Men who treat knowledge like this are animals and deserve to die like animals."

I reached out and spun Draco toward me. "Now you're talking like Vlad," I said. "We need to get out of here. Vlad Dracula is doomed. This part of the world is doomed."

"Return to civilization with us," pleaded Roquelaure. "The Scarlet Order needs you. We can rebuild your library somewhere else."

"I don't want to leave my home." Draco hung his head.

"Your home is with the Scarlet Order. Your home is with books and knowledge," I said softly. "Neither of those exist anymore in this ruin of a castle. Come with us."

He continued to look down at the ground.

I lifted his chin and looked into his eyes. "Please, come with us."

Draco took several deep breaths, then closed his eyes. After a moment, he opened them again and finally nodded. "Take me where you will."

Roquelaure and I led Draco from the castle he'd called home for nearly five hundred years. Slowly, Draco climbed on his horse. Roquelaure went to the side of the castle where his horse had been grazing, unseen in the woods. The three of us rode down the trail away from the castle.

As we rode, Draco kept his eyes on the burned-out husk of a building until it was out of sight. Finally, he turned his eyes forward and spurred his horse into a run, racing headlong into the future.

Chapter 30

From the writings of Desmond, Lord Draco.
The year 1462:

My castle – my home – was gone. It had been destroyed by Ottomans. I rode with Alexandra and Roquelaure for days, perhaps weeks. I did not keep track of the time, didn't really pay attention when we stopped to sleep through the long days of early summer.

Although I had aged to a point that I could wake up before sunrise, I never did during that time. In fact, there were days I only awoke on Alexandra's prompting, an hour or two after dark. I would get on my horse and point it in the same direction as Roquelaure and Alexandra and simply follow along. It seemed as though my whole reason for existence had gone away, along with the destruction of my home.

Finally, we came to a city on a river. It seemed so much bigger than any city I had known in recent years – bigger than Giurgiu, Bucharest, or even Prague. "Where are we? Is this Paris?" I asked.

"No," said Alexandra, softly. "It's Arles. We thought it would be a good place for some quiet, where you could rest and recover for a while."

I didn't say anything. Alexandra and Roquelaure helped me down from my horse and led me to an ancient cathedral. Roquelaure pulled a large key from his robes and opened a door near the foundation. They led me into a crypt under the church.

Roquelaure lit a candle with a striker. There was a dust-covered couch with some pillows. It seemed strange to find such things in a crypt, among coffins. Alexandra swept some of the dust from the couch with her hand and helped me to sit.

Roquelaure sat down next to me. "Draco, you haven't eaten for days. You need blood."

"I do not feel like hunting," I said, shaking my head.

Alexandra sat down on the other side of me. "I have fed recently. Feed from me. I can hunt again tonight."

"I'm too tired," I protested. I leaned over sideways onto her shoulder.

She pushed me up and against Roquelaure. I was surprised how soft he felt. Perhaps it was just the softness of the scarlet robes he wore. Still, I felt a tenderness that surprised me. I closed my eyes, content to remain where I was. There was a rustling of fabric.

After a moment, Alexandra said, "Bring him down here."

Roquelaure lifted me gently and laid me down on the pillows. My head lay on Alexandra's bare thigh. I could smell the heady musk of her. There was the sweat from the hard ride along with her womanly scent. I heard blood rushing through her leg – someone else's blood that she had taken … but life-giving blood nonetheless.

My energy levels were so low that I gave no conscious thought to the act, but my head turned, seemingly of its own volition, and my teeth found the blood's source. Her blood flowed into my mouth and I felt a certain strength return.

After a moment, I opened my eyes and saw that Roquelaure had removed his cloak and breeches. He knelt next to Alexandra and kissed her.

Part of me wanted to be angry, but I could feel the thrill of his kiss through Alexandra's blood. I could feel an excitement creeping into my loins. Alexandra wanted Roquelaure. But, there was more. She wanted me as well.

She whispered softly to Roquelaure. I couldn't hear the words, but I heard Alexandra's thoughts on the blood. We would only stay, if he would give himself over to us.

I released Alexandra's thigh. Her desire was alive within me, manifest in my manhood, made erect by the blood that had passed through her. Without really thinking about it, I removed my boots and lowered my trousers.

Pillows were spread out. I bit into Alexandra's thigh again. Alexandra bit into Roquelaure's and Roquelaure bit into mine. Blood flowed from Alexandra to me to Roquelaure and back again. I had sensed Alexandra's thoughts before – of her growing up as a farm girl in Greece, being turned into a vampire by Theron, finding her freedom as a thief.

On top of those thoughts were new ones, but these were different and vague. It was like a black cloud, or a cloak. There were just flashes. I saw Wolf's face and I wanted to weep. However, the memory was disjointed from any time or place.

Roquelaure had met Wolf, but did not know who he was. He did not know where he'd met him. Was it England or France? Was it nine hundred fifty years ago ... or a thousand? I sensed a great loneliness from Roquelaure, a sense of unknowing.

I heard Alexandra's thoughts overlaying the images from Roquelaure's mind. *It is like this for some vampires. They do not know their life before. Most such vampires simply become monsters, given over entirely to their need for blood.*

I saw Roquelaure's earliest thoughts. A convent in Britain. The face of a woman he did not know – but I knew her. She was Guinevere, but much older than I had last seen her. Was that the first he had seen her?

That is Guinevere as I knew her. I heard Roquelaure's statement as his blood flowed into me. *I only knew her as a nun who took pity on a strange wild creature and taught him to read and write.*

I released Alexandra's thigh and Roquelaure released mine. "Are you L'Ancelot?" I asked.

Roquelaure looked into my eyes. "I tell you truly, my friend. I do not know." He shook his head. "From what I saw in your mind, I do not think so. I think I'm younger. Maybe I'm L'Ancelot's son, Galahad. Maybe I accompanied you to find the Grail. I do not know."

"Roquelaure was a mystery to Guinevere," said Alexandra. "Moreover, he's a mystery to himself. Even if he was Prince Anguselus, he stopped being him when he was born again as a vampire."

"He lost everything," I said. "As have I."

"No," said Alexandra, gently. "We have each other." With that, she reached out and took my cock that had begun to soften. She stroked it until it resumed its full length again. She took me into her mouth and cradled my balls almost lovingly.

Roquelaure moved behind her, took her hips in his hands and plunged into her. She moaned as her lips caressed my member.

I thought I ought to be jealous as I watched Roquelaure move in and out of Alexandra, but I found the sight only aroused me further, until my seed spilled into Alexandra. I guessed the same must be happening for Roquelaure as he pressed himself against Alexandra's luscious ass and closed his eyes. All three of us, spent, collapsed onto the pillows and did not wake until night fell again.

A week later, my brain was still swimming with thoughts of everything that happened in the crypt the night we arrived in Arles. There were so many impressions from both Alexandra and Roquelaure that I was still sorting them all out. I no longer thought of Roquelaure as an incarnation of Prince Anguselus, which in turn allowed me to release a certain amount of distrust. However, I had confirmed that Roquelaure was of my time, another vampire made by Wolf – and with that realization came many new questions. When had Wolf made him? Who exactly was he when he was alive? Did that matter?

Vexing as the questions about Roquelaure were, I found I had even more questions about Alexandra. I sensed she loved both of us, but she didn't want to be tied to either of us. In some ways she saw both Roquelaure and me as brothers. Because of that, she began to see our strange three-way relationship as almost incestuous.

She was thinking about moving on, exploring other parts of the world – perhaps the Russias, Africa, or the Far East.

How long would Alexandra be with us? Was the intimate phase of our relationship nearing an end? Or, was it about to evolve into something new and more spectacular?

Despite all of these questions running through my mind – or perhaps *because* of them – I felt more alive than I had in years. I was hunting, taking in the sights, and visiting the libraries in Arles. I began to see the destruction of my castle in the East, not as an ending, but as a new beginning. I longed to travel to Paris and London to begin collecting books anew.

Still, a part of me longed to return to Transylvania and rebuild my castle. There had been treasures in that castle – rare books – that probably could not be replaced. I wanted to make the Turks pay for what they had stripped from me.

All of these thoughts flitted through my mind as I sat outside, enjoying an early evening in late summer, sipping a glass of wine outside a café. A boy stepped up to me and bowed. "Lord Draco?" he asked.

I blinked back my surprise at being recognized and nodded. "Yes."

"I have a message from Bishop Lefèvre," said the boy. "He would like you to meet him at St-Trophime Cathedral."

"When?" I asked.

"As soon as you are ready."

I finished my glass of wine. Leaving a coin for the serving wench, I followed the boy into the night.

He led me to an imposing structure, bigger and newer than Saint Honorat Church where Roquelaure kept his furnished crypt. He led me through the great western doors, under a façade that depicted Christ as a majestic king. Together, we strode under the high, vaulted ceiling of the nave. This church was surprisingly austere on the inside compared to other churches I had been in.

An old man in white robes knelt at the altar. The boy knelt down beside him, which seemed to be a signal, since the old man stood, turned slowly, and faced me. "You are Desmond, Lord Draco of Transylvania?"

I bowed slightly at the waist in acknowledgement.

"His Holiness Pope Pius II has been following the news of you and your Scarlet Order with keen interest for the last two years," said the bishop.

I narrowed my gaze. "He has?"

"You see, in 1460, the Pope called for a crusade against the Ottomans. Vlad Dracula has been fighting in the pope's name and you have been among Dracula's most effective allies."

"I see." I narrowed my gaze at the bishop. "The Pope wants an explanation of why we left Wallachia."

A flicker of a smile lit up the bishop's face. "Not at all. Vlad's strategy and tactics were not well thought out. He has not made the best use of his ... resources."

I frowned, realizing that the Scarlet Order was one of the resources to which the bishop referred.

The bishop continued. "No, we have a more immediate problem here in the West. We are concerned about the Moors in Spain. We would like to know how much you would charge for your mercenary army to fight for the Western Church."

I took a deep breath and blew it out. "I just lost my castle – my home – I'm not sure if I'm ready to join another crusade."

"If Spain is won for Christendom, then the Pope can persuade the countries of the West to send forces to the East to join the crusade. They can free Transylvania and Wallachia. Perhaps Constantinople can be liberated again."

I let my tongue play over one of my fangs, heedless of the bishop's wide-eyed gaze. "I will consider it," I said at last. "How can I find you once I've reached a decision?"

"Send a message to me through this church." With that, the bishop turned, tapped the boy on the shoulder, and together they turned and left through a door at the north end of the nave. I stood there for several minutes, looking up at the starlit sky through the windows surrounding the altar.

New questions entered my mind. What did it mean for a creature such as me to come to the Church's attention? I was never a Christian. Crosses made me strangely uncomfortable and I avoided approaching too closely. Being an immortal creature with a fanged countenance, I was probably even seen as a demon by these people. However, if they could help me reclaim my home, who was I to argue? With a sigh, I turned around and left the church.

I found Alexandra and Roquelaure strolling among the tombstones at Les Alyscamps. I joined them and told them about my meeting with Bishop Lefèvre and his proposition.

"You're tempted, aren't you?" asked Alexandra.

I pursed my lips and nodded.

"If you decide to go, you can count on us," said Roquelaure.

I thought I detected a flicker of doubt flash in Alexandra's eyes, but she smiled and nodded enthusiastically. "Yes, you deserve to have your home back."

I looked up at the stars and then looked at my friends. I thought about all the things I'd seen in my long life, from Britain and searching for the cup and scroll of Jesus, to my quest in the Holy Lands, to Vlad Dracula. So much fighting … I wanted my home back, but I was a thousand years old. There was no reason to think I wouldn't live another thousand years. Spain and my home could wait … for a little while.

"I don't know whether I want to be a mercenary for the Church or not," I said after a moment. "However, I do know something I'd like to do."

They both looked at me, expectant.

"I'd like to see Paris. Will you come with me?"

Both agreed on the spot.

I held out my arms and they took them – Alexandra, on one side, Roquelaure, on the other – and we set out on a journey of discovery, together.

About the Author

David Lee Summers is the author of twelve novels and over eighty published short stories. His writing spans a wide range of the imaginative from science fiction to fantasy to horror. David's novels include *The Astronomer's Crypt*, a horror story set at an astronomical observatory, and *The Solar Sea*, which imagines humanity's first voyage to the outer planets aboard a solar sail spacecraft. His short stories and poems have appeared in such magazines and anthologies as *Cemetery Dance, Realms of Fantasy* and *Straight Outta Tombstone*. In 2010, he was nominated for the Science Fiction Poetry Association's Rhysling Award. In addition to writing, David has been a co-editor of the anthologies *A Kepler's Dozen, Kepler's Cowboys,* and *Maximum Velocity: The Best of the Full-Throttle Space Tales*. When not working with the written word, David operates telescopes at Kitt Peak National Observatory. Learn more about David at davidleesummers.com.